THE
KAIROS

ZIONICA - A THIRD GENERATION SECRET

Lesley Cashin

One - The Preparation

Bethelonia Publishing

All rights reserved; no part of this publication may be reproduced or transmitted by any means, electronic, mechanical, photocopying or otherwise, without the prior permission of the publisher.

First published in Great Britain in 2004
Bethelonia Publishing, B3 The Verdin Exchange, Winsford, Cheshire, CW7 2AN

Copyright © Text 2004 Lesley Cheyenne Cashin
Copyright © Jacket/Cover illustration 2003 Christine Bennett
Jacket/Cover illustration from original artwork by Christine Bennett

The moral right of the author has been asserted
A CIP catalogue record of this book is available from the British Library

ISBN 0-9546460-0-2
First Edition
Printed and bound in Great Britain by Biddles Ltd, King's Lynn, Norfolk

Co - edited by Lesley and John Cashin

Cover design by Lesley Cheyenne Cashin
Bethelonia logo design by Suzanne Scarlet Cashin

"Kairos" is a UK registered trademark of Lesley Cheyenne Cashin
"Magee" is a registered trademark of Lesley Cheyenne Cashin

Acknowledgments

Quotation from Sydney Carter's 'Lord of the Dance' reproduced by kind permission of Stainer & Bell Ltd, London, England

Sample text verses of Cecil Frances Alexander's 'There is a green hill far away' taken from: Mission Praise, published by Marshall Pickering

Selected Bible quotes taken from: New International Version and King James Version

Heartfelt thanks to all the kind people who have helped me bring this project to fruition, without whom I could not have succeeded, because no one does anything on their own. Without others we are lost. God bless you all.

This list is by no means exhaustive but these include:

Lynn Nixon
Cyd Williams
Christine Bennett
Anthony Lewis
Reverend Ken Burgall
Pamela E Ward
Keith M Wakefield
Suzy Scarlet Cashin
Fred McKay

Special thanks to my husband and Co editor John Cashin for his valuable love, support and dedication.

Finally, this book is humbly and prayerfully dedicated to:
The glory of
God the Father, God the Son and God the Holy Spirit.

Blessed is He who comes in the name of the Lord!

Chapters		Page
1	Miracle in a Storm	7
2	Losers in the Lane	35
3	Thieves in the Night	44
4	Storm's Passion	54
5	Fire and Brimstone	64
6	Two Dispatched Heavenwards	77
7	A Holy Reunion	91
8	Angelic Hosts	99
9	A Great C O - Mission	117
10	Arrival of the Magi	131
11	A Blessing and the Gauntlet	149
12	A Beautiful Spanish Mentor	156
13	The Garden of Lilies	172
14	A Snake in the Grass	187
15	A Bitter Appointment	209
16	Lambs to the Slaughter	228
17	I'll Lead You All in the Dance Said He	244

CHAPTER ONE

Miracle in a Storm

Wings could be heard gently fluttering, high above in the cavernous hall of archways. Droplets of glittery light coruscated around the pretty woman, Anna, as she glided along with some urgency. The droplets fell like tiny, golden snowflakes on Anna's wavy blonde hair and flowing pale gown, then they seemed to evaporate, blending into the aura of golden light which framed her. Despite the hint of an anxious frown, Anna's face radiated beauty - the kind of beauty that can only be a reflection of the soul.

Everywhere was a oneness of twinkling light and colour; it was bright - warm, golden, glowingly bright. Sparkles of colour gently swirled and flickered, like a prism-effect from thousands of crystals, almost as though the woman was right in the centre of a fantastic rainbow.

There were tall, golden archways down either side of the hall. Each archway had a different coloured light shining within it, which corresponded to the colour of a sparkling precious jewel at its pinnacle - jasper, sapphire, emerald, topaz, amethyst and every precious jewel that there ever was.

Anna came to an archway lit with turquoise-blue and without stopping, she glided straight through it, emerging into a small chamber which was bathed in the soft, turquoise-blue light. A man dressed in white, and enveloped in the same aura of golden light, stood in front of a large screen, watching what appeared to be images of a school rugby match. The Vista was not so much a specifically defined screen, but rather a 3D virtual viewing area, about eight-foot square.

'Nathan...' Anna breathed, a little hesitantly.

The man turned and a smile radiated from his handsome face.

'Anna,' he greeted her. 'Why such a hurry all at once?'

'It's Jean - she and the three little ones have just arrived through the Fugue in the Nursery,' Anna explained, a little anxiously.

Nathan's face dropped as he nodded, while Anna put a supportive hand on his arm.

'I'm sorry, Nathan,' she added softly.

'Well we saw it coming on the Vista, Anna,' Nathan said resignedly. 'The little ones will be all right. It's Jean I'm concerned about, she'll be devastated, she'll blame herself. I don't know what *"He's"* decision will be yet. Knowing He as we do though, I shouldn't be at all surprised if He makes an exception to the rules in this case.'

'I'm sure you're right.' Anna smiled, then continued hesitantly. 'I - I mean her mission was to comfort the little ones - and that's exactly what she did - totally without regard for her own safety.'

'And that will go in her favour, Anna, rest assured.'

Anna looked into the Vista. 'Is that your Son again, Nathan? Good-looking young boy...'

'Yes, that's my Joel - he's twelve now,' Nathan replied proudly. 'He's just been made captain of his school's junior rugby team.'

'He really is following in your footsteps then.' Anna smiled, then she became serious. 'It's nearly time, isn't it?'

'Yes, Anna, I think it will be this Easter holiday. I'm so looking forward to him joining the Kairos.'

'Well we certainly need him, Nathan, and now with Jean's untimely exit from the Kairos, we're going to need two recruits.'

'Don't worry, Anna,' Nathan smiled. 'I already have someone in mind for that second vacancy.'

'Oh?' Anna looked surprised. 'Anyone I know?'

'As it happens, Anna, it's someone you know very well...' Nathan looked at Anna with a twinkle in his eye.

'Not - my Peter?' Anna's eyes filled as she looked up excitedly at Nathan.

'I believe your Peter will be just perfect for the Kairos, Anna.'

MIRACLE IN A STORM

'Oh, Nathan!' Anna beamed. 'That's wonderful news!' A tear dropped onto her cheek, like a sparkling diamond.

'You know, Anna,' Nathan said, putting a golden arm round her and gently wiping the sparkling tear with a finger, 'when He said He wipes away every tear, He meant except for tears of joy. Now, run along to the Garden of Lilies and check on Jean, tell her I'll be along to see her - tell her not to worry, everything is going to be fine.' Nathan smiled. 'I just want a moment to watch my Son - I think he's about to score a try.'

'Right, I'll see you later - and thank you, Nathan, so much.' Anna beamed as she glided back through the archway. Even if there had been gravity, she would still have been floating on air.

Nathan turned back to the match on the Vista.

'Go, Joel! Yes!' Nathan punched the air.

+

It was early April and school had just broken up for Easter. Joel was cramming last-minute stuff into his travel bag.

'Come on, Joel!' Mum yelled from downstairs. 'We need to get on the road now to miss the traffic!'

'Coming!' Joel shouted back, carefully wrapping a large lantern inside a jumper and pushing it into an already bulging bag. Finally he managed to zip the bag shut; he dragged it out of his room, then it dragged him down the stairs.

'Are you sure you couldn't get anything else in that case, Joel?' Mum chortled.

'I wish I could fit my TV in,' Joel said, cheekily, as his case came to the bottom of the stairs with a resounding thump.

'It's only for two weeks, love, I'm sure you can manage without television for that long,' Mum said apologetically. 'I'm sorry to dump you on Grandad every holiday, Joel; you know I don't have a choice, don't you?'

'I know, Mum, I don't mind.' Joel shrugged. 'I like staying with Grandad and there's Peter, from the farm nearby, he's fun.'

'The crippled boy? Grandad told me you're kind to him and

stick up for him when he's teased about those callipers.'

'Oh yes. I like Peter, he's a very interesting person and he's one of the best friends anyone could have.' Joel frowned; 'He's not a cripple, Mum, he's just got a limp from having polio when he was young. Those callipers make it look worse than it is - it's just that they clatter when he walks. Most kids are nice to him; it's Tamara's brother, Presten, who bullies him and calls him Tin Legs.'

'See, you're doing it now - defending him.' Mum smiled.

Joel grimaced - he really liked Peter, he wasn't just nice to him out of pity.

'We'll have a good holiday together in the summer.' Mum smiled affectionately. 'Come on.' She struggled to drag Joel's case out to the car. 'You know, I always miss your Father, Joel,' she said, straining with the effort of lifting the bag. 'Times like this I realise how much I took for granted when he was alive.'

It had been the same routine every holiday since Joel's Dad had died four years ago. Joel was eight then; he remembered very little about the accident.

Nathan Asher, Joel's Dad, had been a brilliant Barrister for the prosecution, working closely with the Anti-drug Squad. He was constantly approached by headhunters, trying to poach him for private law firms as a defence Barrister, but he said there were enough Barristers earning shed loads of money defending people, some of whom were blatantly guilty. He said he couldn't put his hand on his heart and defend someone he knew deserved to be locked up. Whatever the pay, no amount of money could compensate for the sleepless nights, knowing violent criminals had escaped justice to carry on their crimes against young and vulnerable people. Dad's mission was to ensure these criminals were put where they belonged, behind bars.

Joel's Dad had been working on a big case which required him to work late at night and he would often arrive home well after Joel had gone to bed. Prior to that case, Dad was very often home early enough to read with him at bedtime. Joel had treasured those times and really missed them - and his Dad.

Miracle in a Storm

Then came the devastating news that Nathan had fallen asleep at the wheel of his car and crashed through a barrier, into a river. The car was fitted with all the latest technology - electric windows, sunroof, antitheft device. Everything designed for ease, comfort and to protect the vehicle. You almost had to be a computer boffin to get into it, or Hercules to get out - if it was at the bottom of a river. He couldn't even open a window to swim out.

Mum blamed it on his working too hard and too late at the office; she said he was so committed to his job, it killed him. The funeral was just a blur to Joel; he went through it like a robot, hardly able to take it all in.

Soon afterwards Mum got a job in the City and then *she* started working late. Joel got the bus home from school, then Naomi looked after him until Mum got home. Naomi was a young and pretty native American, studying English. She let Joel eat anything he wanted and had lots of time to go to the park, the cinema and to do fun stuff. Joel thought she was cool.

Mum got four weeks holiday a year, which she and Joel spent together. Joel had to spend the rest of the school holidays with Grandad, so Mum could keep on working when Naomi went to stay with her family.

The smallholding where Grandad lived was - well, Mum called it "the country" but Joel called it a *complete wilderness*! It was a stark contrast to their hi-tech, busy life in the City.

Grandad was the original country bumpkin: he kept a few sheep and hens and grew a few vegetables. He didn't own a T.V. Then there was his noisy, rickety old Jeep - thank goodness Joel's friends at home couldn't see him!

Grandad's place had been in Joel's family for three generations. It was Grandad's childhood home and also Mum's. There was a special secret part of his land, a hilly field where a shallow stream trickled down into a small pond. A few planks and logs provided a makeshift bridge. Several trees gave secluded shelter, but there was one huge old special tree, near the edge of the pond. This was where Joel had a really cool den.

Blocks of wood nailed onto its trunk made a sort of ladder up to the den. A rope-swing allowed for a faster descent to the ground. On the far side of the pond, a sandy bank edged up to a small grassy plateau, also fringed by trees.

It was child heaven - the perfect place to while away the school holidays, feast on good things to eat and share secrets. It was Grandad's den first; when he was a young boy he named it 'Zionica' because Zion is another name for Heaven. Then it was Mum's (she had been a real tomboy) and now it was Joel's - and the *secret* of Zionica was about to become his also.

Joel had made some good friends near Grandad's. His best friend was Peter, the boy with callipers. He was the adopted son of Mr and Mrs Jordan, local farmers who couldn't have children of their own. They found him at the age of two, abandoned in an orphanage in Hungary. They fell in love with him and battled humongous and expensive red tape to adopt him. That was ten years ago.

When he wasn't at school, Peter helped his father on the farm. He knew a lot about the land, animals and nature. He had a feel for things: it was a gift. He could even read cloud formations and predict the weather better than any radio forecast.

The two boys were quite different. Joel was the image of his Father. Captain of his school's junior rugby team, he was a good size for his age. He was fit and strong with dark wavy hair and eyes a warm amber colour, gregarious, quick-witted and popular, with a somewhat dry sense of humour.

Peter was slightly built, although quite tall despite his crooked legs. With his blonde hair, big blue eyes and long eye-lashes most girls would die for, he had an almost angelic look about him. He was not so much popular as idolised by the girls, who paid him lots of attention at school, which he found quite embarrassing. He looked forward to the holidays when Joel came to stay with his Grandad. To Peter, Joel was a link to the outside world, a glimpse that there was civilisation beyond this rural haven of tranquillity.

They spent many hours in Zionica, swapping stories about

Miracle in a Storm

their different lives, but just how special Zionica really was, Joel and Peter were very soon to find out. This holiday would be different, just about as different as it could possibly be. In fact after this holiday, their whole lives would be very different. They were about to discover the fantastic secret truth about Zionica and then they would have to keep the secret. For the next four years, Joel and Peter would both have to live a *double life*.

Peter was constantly tormented by Presten, whose Father was the Headmaster of the local High School. They lived in a large house near Grandad. Presten was in Peter's class at school and seized every opportunity to bully him. Though roughly the same height as Joel, Presten was not fit and athletic at all, in fact he was lazy, which could explain why he was a little on the chubby side. His favourite sport was causing some kind of havoc, or making someone's life a misery - usually Peter's. He had a mean, threatening, almost sinister manner. His brown hair was cropped very close to his head, which enhanced the whole bully/thug-like image he cut. Added to this, he almost lived in a patterned tracksuit that made him resemble a prison convict!

In the holidays it wasn't so bad for Peter because Presten was rather scared of Joel and hated him with a vengeance. His hatred had been further heightened recently, due to an incident in the previous holiday. Presten was being particularly bullyish to two young boys who were playing in the snow and he trashed a snowman they were building. Joel intervened and held Presten's arm behind his back and couldn't resist making him drop his trousers and bend over. Then Joel let the two young boys pelt Presten's jockey-shorted bottom with snowballs, in front of his posse of delinquent friends. Although it didn't physically hurt him but just made his shorts wet, the hurt was to his pride in the humiliation before his friends, who all found the incident immensely amusing - for which Presten had sworn revenge.

+

Grandad stood in his bedroom, staring at the small wooden box on his dressing table. He picked up the box and a vague, misty memory flashed through his head...

He was a young boy, about twelve years of age. The pond in Zionica had frozen over; there was snow everywhere. The sun was shining but there must have been moisture in the air, as a large bright rainbow dusted the snow with a hint of glowing colour, like a reflection of Heaven. He couldn't resist skating on the ice, although he knew he shouldn't. Then suddenly it cracked beneath him - he was too close to the edge where the ice must have been thinner. The freezing water caused him to catch his breath as he slipped helplessly under the ice, which then became a solid sheet above him. He felt himself drifting into blackness, when a bright stick was suddenly thrust in front of him; light exploded all around it, melting the ice as though it was a burning-hot poker. He reached for the stick and felt himself being hauled out of the water and dragged onto the snowy bank. He felt warm breath blowing on his face. Looking up he saw two incredible, flared, pink nostrils. The pure white horse lifted its head, a sparkling horn glowing between its ears. Then it galloped onto the plateau and vanished up into a powerful, blinding flash of light. He slowly opened his fingers and there in his hand was a small piece of pointed crystal, glowing brightly. Then right before his very eyes, it faded into a dull piece of plain horn...

Suddenly the sound of tyres on the yard brought him back to the present. Grandad placed the box back on the dressing table and looked out of the window. It was his Daughter, Elizabeth, arriving with his Grandson, Joel. Dusk was descending and the rustling trees and dark clouds threatened a mighty storm. He hurried down to help them in before the heavens opened.

+

'Goodbye civilisation and real life - hello wilderness and eccentricity!' Joel exclaimed, as he got out of the car in Grandad's yard. Much as he poked fun at Grandad's modest country life, Joel still felt that little spark of excitement; he

Miracle in a Storm

loved staying with Grandad really. He ran up to the cover of the porch, not only in his excitement to see Grandad, but also to get out of the fierce, chilly wind that was whipping up a frenzy.

Grandad came straight out to give Mum a lift with Joel's bag.

'Hi, Grandad,' Joel grinned, running straight inside, just as a massive flash of lightning lit up the sky and was swiftly followed by a loud peal of thunder.

'Hello, Joel,' Grandad grinned.

Inside, there was a welcome roaring fire blazing in the grate. Grandad's cottage was an Aladdin's cave of knick-knacks. Every corner and shelf was packed with all manner of paraphernalia he'd collected over the years, every item with its own tale to tell.

In a corner, in a very large dog basket, lay a very large dog. Grandad's ancient black Labrador, Rodney, at one time would have come bounding noisily outside to investigate the arrival of visitors. Now that he was happily retired, guarding was to Rodney, a dim and distant memory as he snoozed on regardless.

Grandma had passed away five years ago. She was found to have cancer, but diagnosed too late to be treated. Grandad missed her lots, and he kept the house going in much the same way as when she was alive. He was well able to look after himself: he was fit, looked younger than his sixty-five years and wasn't a bad cook. Elizabeth was their only child; he was proud of the way she had brought Joel up on her own these past four years. He looked forward to Joel coming to stay in the holidays; it gave him a chance to play substitute Dad.

Grandad put his large black kettle on the old-fashioned fire grate, while Mum flopped down in a rocking chair and sighed, exhausted.

'A nice cup of tea will perk you up, love, after that long drive,' Grandad said cheerily, as he settled on a little wooden stool by the fireplace.

'Thanks, Dad,' Mum sighed.

'I'm going up to my room, Grandad,' Joel said, dragging his bag up the uneven, twisty stairs.

'Don't forget to duck, Joel!' Grandad shouted after him. Grandad's tiny cottage was built a few hundred years ago, when the average adult height was less than five feet. So despite Joel's tender age, the tops of the doorways were actually level with his forehead. He ducked into his room and heaved the bag onto a trunk at the bottom of his bed. Opening his bag he took out the lantern, unwrapped it, placed it on the bedside table next to a picture of him with his Mum and Dad, and switched it on. A slightly wistful look came upon his face for a moment, as the yellow light lit up the room and he remembered his father. The lantern was the last thing Dad had given him before he died; he had said *"You'll always be safe, Joel, as long as you have light in your life."*

Joel crossed the uneven floor to the tiny window, which Grandad had left open to air the room. He knelt down to gaze outside as the sun was disappearing beyond the horizon (he had to kneel because the sill only came up to his knees).

The whole place was at the unrelenting mercy of an angry, howling wind. Joel watched the last fingers of light wave good bye, as the night fell like a final curtain on the day. He could just make out the silhouetted shapes of the barn and outbuildings, with the swirling trees and the wild, rustic landscape. It was going to be a very dark night indeed; thick cloud limited the chance of moonlight or starlight. He couldn't wait for morning, when he could go down to Zionica with Peter and open up the den for the holidays.

The window was rattling a little in the wind; Joel shivered and leaned out to grab its handle to pull it shut. Suddenly a fierce gust snatched it from his fingers. He gasped in fright as he lost his balance and began to fall headlong out of the window, towards the gravelly yard below. Then before he knew what was happening, he felt a force on his shoulders which stopped him and started to push him back up through the window! The next thing he knew, he was sitting on the floor in his room and the window was closed! He could just make out the shape of what looked like a Raven, perched on the window ledge. As he

Miracle in a Storm

stared at the bird, it cocked its head to one side and to Joel's surprise, he thought it raised an inquisitive eyebrow. Then, it spread its wings and flew off into the night. Joel shook his head and blinked, a little dazed. He rushed quickly back to the window, but there was nothing - or no one - there. It must have been his imagination - the fading light playing tricks on his eyes, he thought. Probably a strong gust of wind had blown him back inside and slammed the window shut.

'Joel!' Grandad called up the stairs. 'Come and have some supper, lad, and tell me all your news - I want to hear about this promotion in the rugby team.'

+

At first light, Joel was woken by Cedric, the cockerel. He sprang out of bed, put on his trainers and ran downstairs, almost tripping over Rodney at the bottom. Joel loved to go out to the coop first thing and collect fresh eggs for breakfast. Cedric had a harem of seven hens and considered it his role in life to protect them, a duty to which he was fiercely loyal. So venturing unarmed (a bucket of grain usually did the trick) into the coop was not advised, especially when Cedric was hungry.

The hens provided free-range eggs which Grandad sold along with other organic produce to the locals. This provided a lot of his own food and covered his modest living expenses. His one luxury was a good stock of brandy and benedictine which, mixed together was Grandad's favourite tipple and he swore, the best cure for any cold or flu. Also the occasional bottle of old malt whisky - one bottle lasted a long time because, much as he liked a drop of old malt, a few sips would surely guarantee to send him straight to sleep.

Picking up a small basket, Joel unlatched the back door and almost stepped on a present left by Martha. Grandad's old tabby cat was sitting proudly over the lifeless field mouse, waiting to be congratulated on her prize, hopeful the gesture would be returned in the shape of a bowl of fresh milk.

'Ugh, Martha! You murderer!' Joel shouted at the cat, before running off up the yard.

The gale-force wind of the previous night had been replaced by a steady breeze and though chilly, it promised a sunny day. Grandad was already out on the yard, feeding his small menagerie of sheep.

'Morning, Joel!' Grandad called. 'The hens are waiting for their breakfast!'

'O.K. Grandad!' Joel picked up the bucket of grain Grandad had left by the coop and let himself in.

Cedric immediately attacked the bucket, pecking at it furiously and trying to jump up onto it. Joel quickly flung a handful of grain on the ground. The mercenary Cedric abandoned the bucket (and his role of defender of the coop) swooping greedily onto the grain. The sound of the bucket and Cedric's squawks were all that was required to lure the hens away from their beds and they came over to join him, squawking their little heads off. This left the way clear for Joel to collect the newly laid eggs, still warm as he put them into the basket.

+

'These eggs are just how I like them, Grandad,' Joel said, stabbing another toast soldier into a boiled egg. The yellow yolk oozed gungily up over the toast and Joel stuffed the whole soggy mess into his mouth. 'Perfect.'

'You shouldn't talk with food in your mouth, Joel,' Mum said, delicately pushing scrambled egg onto her fork.

'Oh leave him be, Liz. The lad is on holiday, he's just enjoying his food.' Grandad winked at Joel.

'Don't you go spoiling him again over the next two weeks, Grandad,' Mum insisted. 'You only make it more difficult for me when he comes home and expects the same star treatment.'

'Well if I can't spoil my only Grandson occasionally it's a poor do - what do you say, Joel?' Grandad grinned.

'That's fine by me, Grandad, you can spoil me any time you

Miracle in a Storm

want,' he said. Returning the grin, he got up from the table. 'Can I phone Peter, Grandad?'

'Of course you can, lad.'

When Joel came racing back into the kitchen after phoning Peter, Mum was ready to leave to go back to the hustle and bustle of city-life.

'Thanks, Dad.' Mum said hugging Grandad.

'Not at all, I love having him. Don't you worry; we'll be fine, we'll look after each other - won't we, Joel?'

'Yeah, that's cool, Grandad,' Joel nodded.

'You just take care of you,' Grandad smiled.

'Well I'll see you two in a couple of weeks, then.' Mum gave Joel a kiss on the forehead.

'Bye, Mum.' Joel turned to Grandad. 'I'm just going to meet Peter, Grandad; he's on his way over.'

Joel ran behind Mum's car, down the yard to the gate, waving her off. The car disappeared round the bend. He waved to Grandad, then set off down the narrow country lane to Peter's farm. He was striding happily along, expecting to bump into Peter, but he didn't expect what he found.

Suddenly he stopped on hearing a muffled sort of moaning - it seemed to be coming from the ditch. As he walked over the grass verge he saw something moving and edged up slowly.

'Peter!' Joel jumped into the ditch and pulled his friend's head up. There was about three inches of water in the bottom of the ditch. Peter was all wet and covered in mud; he tried to open his eyes to look at Joel. His face was bruised, one of his eyes was swollen and his lip was bleeding. Joel hauled him out of the ditch onto the grass verge and tried to wipe some of the mud from his face with his sleeve.

'Peter - what happened?'

'Presten...' Peter coughed. 'He ambushed me in the lane - he's demented! He's torn my coat, my mum will go mad.' Peter looked down at his torn jacket.

'Never mind the jacket, Peter; are you all right? Can you get up?'

'Yeah, I don't think anything is broken, I'm just a bit sore.' Peter struggled to his feet.

'Come on, let's get you home and clean you up.'

'No! I can't let my Mum see me looking like this! You know how she'll fuss - can we go to your Grandad's?'

'Of course,' Joel nodded.

'Thanks, Joel.'

Joel put Peter's arm over his shoulder to hoist him up and they set off back in the direction of Grandad's place. Before they'd gone a few yards they heard the sound of hooves cantering up behind them along the grass verge. It was Tamara, on her small brown and white pony, Cherokee.

'It's Miss Bla de bla on her pony,' Joel said, joking fondly. He liked young Tamara really.

'Oh no! That's all we need,' Peter whined. 'Joel, don't tell her it was Presten - she'll go straight to her Dad. I know she means well but it'll just make Presten worse.'

Tamara came to an abrupt halt and leapt off the pony.

'Joel! You're back!' Tamara called excitedly.

At ten, she was a couple of years younger than Joel and Peter, but she had a smart head on her shoulders. She idolised Joel and secretly imagined being his girlfriend, although she'd have died if he ever found out. Suddenly Tamara saw Peter's face.

'Holy mush! What happened to you, Peter?' Tamara cried.

'I slipped and fell off the haystack,' Peter muttered unconvincingly.

'Yeah, right...' Tamara raised a suspicious eyebrow.

'I - I know what you're thinking, Tamara, but don't,' Peter said. 'Telling your Dad will just make things worse. Anyway, Presten will find out Joel is back for the holidays and I'll get two weeks of peace.'

'Oh you really think so, Peter - after last holiday? Presten has sworn revenge, you know.' Tamara sighed; 'come on, get on Cherokee - you look as if you can hardly walk.'

They helped Peter to mount the pony and Tamara led him along while Joel supported him at the side.

MIRACLE IN A STORM

Unfortunately for Tamara, she was Presten's younger sister, but she did her best to protect Peter from him. Tamara was a confirmed tomboy: she was one of those girls who are *one of the boys*. She'd always preferred boy-type activities and would more likely be found climbing trees than playing with dolls.

Although she dressed like a boy, Tamara couldn't have looked more like a girl. Long, silky, golden hair; cheeky, sparkly blue eyes; pale, English rose complexion; perfect rosebud lips. She was full of life and fun, though sometimes her impetuous nature caused her to speak first and think later! However, no one could have been kinder or more generous. In fact it was hard to believe that Tamara and Presten were even related - let alone had the same parents! Even their Father sometimes joked that when Presten was born, they must have brought the wrong baby home from the hospital. Tamara kept begging them to take him back. Mr Goodchild (yes, that was ironic - a fitting surname for Tamara - but Presten?) was constantly having to apologise for his Son's latest stupid prank.

+

Peter sat on a chair in Grandad's kitchen and winced as Grandad gently applied some cotton wool and antiseptic to his wounds, while Joel did his best to clean up Peter's muddy coat.

'It's just ripped a little under the arm, Peter,' Joel said.

'That's because Presten was swinging me round by the sleeve - until he suddenly let go and I went flying into the ditch,' Peter muttered.

'Boy, I'd like to have a go at Presten with my cricket bat!' Joel shook his head in fury.

'It wouldn't do any good, Joel. He'd just take it out on me again.' Peter said hopelessly.

'I'm afraid Peter is right, Joel,' Grandad agreed. 'You never stop violence with violence; it just makes bullies like Presten worse - they feed off it. You mustn't retaliate, you're only here for two weeks. Peter has to deal with Presten on a daily basis.'

'Can't the police do anything?' Joel asked in frustration.

'Huh - the police? They're as much use as a wheel on a walking stick in such matters,' Grandad said. 'They'd say it's a case of domestic fighting between two juveniles. It's a sad and ironic situation, but the police are handcuffed by the law. Besides, Presten's Father is well-respected in the community; a member of the Church Council - Head of the School. No one would risk upsetting him, despite his unruly Son.'

'Unruly? Demonic, if you ask me.' Joel frowned.

'Yeah, he knows there's nothing we can do,' Peter said weakly. 'It's best to just keep out of his way.'

The door opened and Tamara entered.

'Cherokee is quite happy in your barn, Mr Jacob; thanks for the hay,' Tamara smiled. 'How are you, Peter? Eoow.' She crinkled up her nose as she inspected Peter's swollen face.

'You're welcome, Tamara.' Grandad stood back. 'There you go, Peter. I'm afraid you'll have a black eye and fat lip tomorrow.'

'Look on the bright side, Peter,' Joel said attempting to cheer him up, 'it'll keep the girls off you!'

'You're joking, aren't you? This'll make them twenty times worse! They'll mother me to death!' Peter squirmed. 'It's just as well it's the school holidays.'

'Hey, I bet there's loads of frog spawn in the pond,' Tamara said, changing the subject. 'Let's go up to Zionica and see. Can we have some jam jars and string, Mr Jacob?'

+

It was barely chilly; a soft breeze carried the sound of their laughter, together with the dull clatter of Peter's callipers, as the three friends made their way over the field to Zionica. Patches of blue sky allowed the sun to shine intermittently through the trees making the gently rippling pond glisten.

They dangled their jam jars into the pond and scooped up masses of frog spawn. A coloured twist-tie round the string of each jar identified its owner: red for Joel's, white for Peter's and blue for Tamara's. This way they could monitor the hatching progress, to see who hatched the biggest and best tadpoles.

'I wish you'd let me tell my Dad what Presten has done to Peter,' Tamara said to Joel, as they retrieved the full jars from the water.

'Well you can't,' Joel replied firmly. 'You'll just make things worse for him.'

'You're not mad at me - are you, Joel?'

'No, sorry, Tamara - I'm mad at myself,' Joel muttered with a sigh. 'I should be able to protect Peter, but it seems I can't.'

'It's not your fault, Joel,' Tamara insisted. 'How can you protect him? Most of the time you're not even here.'

Peter carried his jar to the tree and began to climb up the nails and wood blocks to the den, an art he'd mastered despite his callipers.

'Hey - chill, guys, forget it - Presten is not worth getting upset about,' Peter insisted as he reached the den and began tying his jar to a branch. 'Honestly I don't think we'll get any trouble from him now you're here, Joel.'

'I don't know, Peter,' Tamara said, following him up to the den. 'Presten is mad as anything about, you know, the snowballing incident last holiday. He's determined to get Joel back this holiday.'

'Yeah, that was the funniest thing ever - I'm so glad I was there to see it,' Peter chuckled. 'Anyway, he got his revenge this morning, didn't he? Witness my face!' Peter pointed the first finger of each hand at either side of his face.

'No, Tamara is right, Peter,' Joel mused. 'That's just playtime for Presten. I suspect he's got some evil revenge planned for me too.'

After they'd secured their jam jars to a branch in the den, they restocked supplies. An important event at the start of each holiday was replenishing the various storage boxes and pots with essential items like sweets, pop, biscuits, books, comics, etc. They stayed in the den all day, catching up on each others news since the last holiday, only going back to the house to get some sandwiches and cake for lunch, which they took back to the den to eat.

By late afternoon, the chill wind suddenly seemed to get brisker. Peter looked up at the thickening cloud.

'I think we'd better head on back - there's going to be a corker of a storm,' he said. 'If you don't get Cherokee home soon, Tamara, you'll have to leave her overnight. It'll be too dangerous to ride back within an hour.'

'Hey, do you want to sleep over tonight, Peter?' said Joel.

'Yeah, cool - and Mum won't get to see my bruises!'

'Great!' Tamara sulked. 'Oh why did I have to be born a girl? Boys have all the fun! I have to go home and put up with Presten, while you two have a great time.'

'Yeah, it stinks, doesn't it?' Joel sympathised. 'If it was up to us you could stay too, but you know the rules.'

'Yeah, I know, it's in case we do bla de bla...' Tamara said with annoyance.

They both looked at her quizzically.

'You know, this - bla de bla sex thing.' Tamara raised her eyes in a rather bored gesture. 'I don't know what all the fuss is about. It's not fair.'

'Well there must be something to it, Tamara, or they wouldn't go on about it the way they do,' Joel teased, winking at Peter. 'Grown-ups seem to think it's pretty important.'

'Yeah, but we all know it's how you get babies,' Tamara went on flatly. 'None of us want babies right now, do we? So what's the big deal? I mean, come on,' she mocked. 'I bet neither of you know how to do it anyway - and I certainly don't!' she added quickly.

'I know how animals do it, I've seen them,' Peter said, in a matter-of-fact way.

'Eoow, you mean you've watched them?' Tamara screwed up her nose in disgust.

'I live on a farm, Tamara - my Dad breeds cows! Sometimes I have to help my Dad.'

MIRACLE IN A STORM

'So, what do they do then - the cows?' Tamara asked, casually twisting a lock of hair round her finger, trying to look as if she wasn't really bothered.

'Well,' Peter answered, 'you take the male bull into a big stable where the female cow is waiting...'

'And?' Tamara urged, leaning forward.

Peter leaned forward to whisper in her ear, 'The cow goes... MOO!'

'Oh - grow up!' Tamara huffed hotly. 'Anyway, people are very different from animals.'

'Hey, come on, if Peter says there's going to be a storm, then there's going to be a storm - let's get going.' Joel leapt from the den onto the rope and swung down to the ground.

'Oh bla de bla...' Tamara muttered, then catching hold of the swinging rope she pushed it to Peter. 'Here, Peter.'

By the time they reached Grandad's cottage, the weather had worsened considerably. Tamara was still in a bit of a sulk as they entered the kitchen. Joel poured out three tumblers of milk and put the biscuit tin on the kitchen table; the three friends sat round it munching.

'Oh look, Peter, Grandad has mended your jacket,' Joel said with a mouth full of biscuit, as he inspected the jacket.

Peter took the jacket from Joel and looked at it.

'Hey, that's great!' Peter beamed. 'He's cleaned it up too. Mum will never know!'

'The old man has his uses, doesn't he?' Joel said dryly.

'I still think it's not fair,' Tamara said miserably.

'Look,' Joel said, rather impatiently now. 'We know you don't think it's fair, neither do we, but do you have to keep saying it?'

'Actually, Joel,' Peter said, 'I think Tamara might just have to stay. The storm is going to be upon us very quickly now: it wouldn't be safe to let her ride home.'

'Oh great! That's brilliant!' Tamara exclaimed excitedly.

'Well, O.K. let's see what Grandad says - maybe he could phone your parents, Tamara, and tell them you'll be sleeping in the spare room.'

'I didn't think you had a spare room, Joel?' Peter asked.

'We don't really - this is Grandad's cottage, remember - designed for pygmies - you can't swing a cat in it. There's Grandad's bedroom and mine. My room *is* the spare room!'

'Bla de flipping bla...' Tamara drawled in amazement.

'Maybe Grandad will sleep on the couch, like he does when Mum stays, and let Tamara have his room,' Joel added.

'Aah but that won't be as much *fun*!' Tamara argued. 'I want a midnight *feast*! With *ghost* stories...'

Just then Grandad walked in from outside.

'I've bedded Cherokee down for the night, Tamara,' he said. 'It's not safe to ride home; there's a storm building up and it's going to be a corker. What do you say, Peter?'

'That's very sensible, Mr Jacob, it's going to be a corker all right. Oh and thanks for mending my coat.'

'Well we couldn't send you back to your Mum with it the way it was could we?' Grandad smiled. 'I think we'll batten down the hatches for the evening. You two had better stay over. I'm sure Joel can lend you something to wear for bed.'

They all tried hard to keep straight faces as Grandad went on.

'Peter, you'd better ring your parents and let them know you're staying. Tamara, you'd better let me speak to your parents first. I think it will be better coming from me, don't you?'

'Oh absolutely, Mr Jacob, thank you.' Tamara now found it impossible to keep the wide grin off her face, as Grandad headed for the phone in the hall.

'Is your Grandad psychic or what?' Tamara whispered under her breath.

+

They weren't wrong, the storm attacked them from all quarters. Lightning lit up the sky with blinding flashes, as the rain lashed, the wind thrashed, and thunder crashed all around. It was as if the might of God had unleashed His vengeance on all that was

Miracle in a Storm

wrong with the world, in one night. The roofs of the barn and outbuildings flapped and clattered as if some terrifying beast was trying to get out. They heard the sound of lambs bleating and Cherokee whinnying from the barn.

Grandad snuggled in his rocking chair by the open fire, a glass of his favourite tipple in his hand. Rodney whimpered in fear and padded round the lounge unable to settle, finally finding solace at Grandad's feet. Martha normally spent the night outside, hunting, and slept in the barn, but even she just wanted to curl up in Rodney's bed for the night.

Meanwhile, the three friends, who were not in the least bit tired, had organised their sleeping arrangements. They'd tossed a coin: Peter got the camp bed and Tamara got the Lilo, which they set up in Joel's room with mounds of pillows, blankets and quilts. Peter was quite comfortable in a pair of Joel's pyjamas, while they fell about laughing at Tamara, who, completely swamped by another pair, elected to wear one of Grandad's T-shirts. This also swamped her like a tent, but at least there were no trousers to try and keep up.

Grandad wasn't supposed to know about the feast they smuggled upstairs, but he'd enjoyed enough midnight feasts himself to guess the probability. He smiled to himself, pretending not to notice their padded nightclothes stuffed full of booty, when they said goodnight and slipped upstairs.

They settled down comfortably with a feast of peanuts, cake, chocolate and crisps. Joel switched off the light; it was much more exciting with just the lantern and the flashing lightning, which lit up the whole room as it struck. He closed the curtains.

'Oh leave the curtains, Joel...' Tamara cried. 'We'll be able to see the lightning flashing in the sky - it'll be more exciting!'

'I think we'd better shut them, Tamara.' Joel shivered, as he remembered his near-death experience and the spooky events of the previous evening.

'You're not scared of a bit of thunder and lightning, are you, Joel?' Tamara teased.

'Of course not!' Joel retorted quickly.

'I think we should leave them shut.' Peter said coming to Joel's defence. 'The lightning is so strong, we'll still see its effect through the curtains.'

'Yeah,' Joel teased. 'They'll stop it from coming right into the room and striking us! Unless frazzled hair and popping-out eyes is the look you're going for, Tamara?'

'Eoow...' Tamara pulled a face. 'Joel, sometimes you can be so, bla de bla...'

They stayed awake till after midnight, talking, feasting and playing games, as the storm raged on. Grandad boosted supplies, bringing up hot cocoa and (more) chocolate cake. They hastily hid all the sweet wrappers under the bedclothes when he entered the room. Then he sat and told them all a spooky story, while the lightning continued to light up the room with brilliant blue flashes. It was kind of scary and exciting, but cosy, all at the same time, because they were safely tucked up inside.

Finally they drifted off to sleep. Grandad switched off the lantern before tiptoeing off to bed himself.

+

The early-morning call from Cedric was right on time. He seemed to be demanding - 'Get out of your pit and feed me.' Tamara climbed out of her air-bed and ambled, half asleep, to the window.

'It's so eerily quiet after last night's storm,' Tamara said, pulling back the curtains and rubbing her eyes.

'I feel like I've had about three minutes' sleep,' Joel moaned, turning over, covering his head with a pillow.

Peter, immune to early-morning farm noises, slumbered on.

'Holy cockerel!' Tamara cried suddenly, as she looked out of the window.

'I know, Cedric is an absolute pain,' Joel said. 'Here, open the window and throw this boot at him.' He reached for a boot and flung it over to Tamara.

'I don't mean Cedric, Joel.' Tamara beckoned. 'Come and

Miracle in a Storm

look at this!'

'Don't tell me, the barn has disintegrated in the storm,' Joel said, lazily climbing out of bed and ambling over to the window. 'Wow...' he whistled. 'Hey! Peter, wake up!' Joel rushed over to Peter's camp bed and shook him. 'Peter, come on! You've got to see this!'

'What is it? Is there a fire?' Peter sat up and reached for his callipers.

'Leave those - there isn't time; come on, I'll help you to the window.' Joel helped him up.

'Yikes!' Peter exclaimed, staring out of the window. 'Looks like God is as sorry this morning as He was angry last night - I've never seen anything like it.'

For what they were looking at was the hugest and brightest, most colourful rainbow they had ever seen. It was so big it seemed to fill the whole sky, stretching right down to the land.

'Neither have I,' Tamara said excitedly. 'Look where it ends; it seems to vanish into the ground right at...'

'ZIONICA!' they all shouted together.

'Isn't there supposed to be a pot of gold at the end of a rainbow?' Tamara pointed out.

'What are we waiting for?' Joel shouted. 'Let's get a closer look.'

The boys hastily threw on their clothes, while Tamara ran into the bathroom to do the same. All three jumped and slid down the stairs, then ran out of the door. Tamara and Joel were half carrying, half dragging Peter, callipers clanging.

When they reached the brow of the small hill at the edge of Zionica, they stopped to stare at the rainbow's glory. It was still very early and the sun was only just up, but the rainbow filled everywhere with warmth and light. It was so real and so close, they felt bathed in its warm and brilliant glow.

'It's awesome,' Tamara murmured wistfully.

'Awesome,' Joel and Peter echoed.

'A rainbow is a sign from God, isn't it?' Tamara asked curiously.

'He must have something very important to say,' Peter replied. 'I wonder what He wants to say?'

'Yes - it could almost be Heaven itself...' Joel pondered. Then the rainbow dissolved, right before their eyes.

'Oh come back...' Tamara beckoned with disappointment. 'How can it just vanish?'

The warm glow had been so wonderful, they hadn't wanted it to end. Slowly they walked down the hill towards their tree, then Peter suddenly stopped.

'What's that?' He cocked his head to listen.

Then they all heard it, a sort of soft, laboured breathing and faint grunting.

'Where's it coming from?' Joel asked, as he continued down the dip. Then suddenly he knelt down. 'Over here!' he shouted.

The others rushed over to Joel.

'It's an injured animal, a hare or something; it's too big to be a rabbit; it's alive - only just.'

Peter and Tamara knelt down beside Joel and looked at the animal. Its colour was snow white and they could see its sides slowly moving up and down with weak breaths.

'Since when have you seen a hare with ears that small, Joel?' Peter said, lifting the animal's head. 'This isn't a hare! It's a foal.'

'A foal? But how has a foal got here?' Tamara said in astonishment. 'Where's his mother?'

'Dunno,' Peter said, mystified.

'What - did he just drop out of the sky or something?' Tamara said, expecting the boys to come up with some magical explanation.

'It looks like that, doesn't it?' Joel joked.

'The most likely explanation is that his stable must have been damaged in the storm last night and he got out,' Peter surmised. 'His owner will come looking for him when he discovers he's missing. We'd better take him to your Grandad's barn; he'll perish out here. Can you manage to carry him, Joel?'

'Yeah, no sweat.' Joel picked up the tiny creature. The foal was not much smaller than Rodney and Joel guessed, rightly, not as heavy. Too weak to struggle, the foal allowed himself to be carried.

When they got to the barn, Joel laid him down in some fresh straw.

'Isn't he beautiful?' Tamara whispered. 'He's positively titcharious, just like a miniature Cherokee. What shall we do with him now?'

'We'd better check him over, see if he's injured,' Peter said, taking charge.

Peter was used to caring for animals, particularly when they were injured or sick. At home he often tended to the sick-bay animals, while his Dad concentrated on the productive ones. He began to gently feel the foal all over, checking his legs, back and stomach.

'I can't see anything wrong with him, I think he's just exhausted,' Peter concluded, as he moved the little animal's head, checking his eyes and ears. Then suddenly, as he moved his hand between its ears, Peter froze like a statue.

It appeared to Joel and Tamara, as if a bolt of lightning had struck Peter - a very bright light seemed to shoot from the foal straight into him, surrounding him with a glowing aura. This alarming vision lasted for about three seconds. Then the light disappeared and he snapped out of suspended animation. He shook his head as though dazed. Joel and Tamara stared at him with their mouths wide open.

'Tell me I didn't see that, Tamara,' Joel said weakly.

'You - didn't - see - that - Joel - and neither did I...' Tamara stammered.

'Then what exactly *did* we see?' said Joel, puzzled.

'I er - what exactly?' Tamara pulled a confused face.

Peter stood up. He looked at them, a little scared.

'Something just happened, didn't it?'

'Er something...' Joel shrugged, trying to make light of it. '...I think it must have been the sun coming up at a strange angle through the window - it seemed to shine right on you, made you look a bit weird.'

Peter started to walk towards them, but tripped.

'Ouch!' He sat down on the floor and started to adjust his callipers. 'These callipers are pinching.' He looked up at his two friends, who were looking at him very strangely indeed.

'What's the matter with you two? You look like you've just seen a ghost.' Peter looked worried.

'Peter...' Tamara murmured incredulously. 'Your face...'

'What? What about my face? Oh right, my black eye, it looks ten times worse this morning?' Peter said with a forced laugh. 'It doesn't feel that bad though.'

'W - what black eye, P - Peter? Your face looks f - fine to me,' Tamara stammered.

'You're right, Peter,' said Joel, seriously. 'It did look ten times worse when you got up this morning, but now your bruises have gone - your face is back to normal.'

'It can't be!' Peter exclaimed. 'It was like my Mum's blueberry pie half an hour ago.'

'Well it's peaches and cream now,' Joel mused.

Peter stared at Joel in disbelief.

'You're serious, aren't you?' he said.

'I can't explain it, Peter - come on.' Joel leaned down and helped Peter up. 'Let's go in for breakfast - see what Grandad says about the foal.'

They cooked a breakfast feast in the kitchen, while Grandad was still out feeding his flock and attempting to repair the storm damage. They couldn't understand the mystery of Peter's missing bruises, although Peter certainly didn't miss them. By the time Grandad came back inside, they were sitting at the table tucking into bacon, egg, sausage, beans, and toast. The kitchen almost looked as if it had been hit by a nuclear blast, however, the food was delicious.

Grandad pulled up a chair and joined them. The friends marvelled at the rainbow and how they'd never seen one quite like it.

'Have you ever seen a rainbow like that before, Mr Jacob?'

Miracle in a Storm

Tamara inquired.

'I have.' Grandad surprised them. 'We do see some spectacular rainbows here, but I only remember once seeing one that brilliant.' he replied wistfully.

'When was that, Mr Jacob?' Tamara pressed.

They all looked at Grandad with eager anticipation.

'Many years ago - in fact I must have been about your age, Joel. There was something most extraordinary about that rainbow.'

'What was that, Mr Jacob?' asked Tamara, intrigued.

'Well we'd had an incredible storm the night before,' Grandad began enthusiastically, 'just like last night, only it was different...'

'Please go on,' Tamara urged.

'Well it was a snow storm. It was winter and the following morning there was snow everywhere. There were just a few clouds in the sky and this huge brilliant rainbow. It was in exactly the same place as this morning and just like you, I raced over to look at it. It was so big and bright, the light from it made the snow rainbow-coloured. It was the most incredible sight. The pond had frozen over and... well.' Grandad shrugged as though he had been going to say something else but suddenly changed his mind.

'What happened, Grandad?' Joel urged.

'Nothing... that's it.' Grandad said dismissively.

'Wow,' Peter whistled.

Tamara nudged Joel.

'Go on,' she whispered to Joel. 'Tell your Grandad about the foal we found, Joel.'

Grandad sat up with interest.

'Yeah, Grandad, do you know anyone local whose mare has recently had a white foal?'

'Pure white, Mr Jacob,' Tamara added eagerly.

Grandad looked at Joel with some concern.

'No, no one. What's this about finding a foal - white you say?'

'Yes, Mr Jacob,' Tamara said excitedly. 'It's beautiful, like snow...'

'It must have got out in the storm last night,' Joel explained. 'Only we found it, half dead, down in Zionica when we went to look at the rainbow.'

'I'm sure it's just exhausted, Mr Jacob. I couldn't find anything wrong with it when I examined it,' Peter said.

'But look at Peter's face, Mr Jacob!' Tamara added.

Grandad looked at Peter.

'Oh my hat! The last time I saw that face it was nearly the colour of a rainbow.' He leaned forward to scrutinise Peter's face. 'How radically curious,' Grandad said, astonished. 'You'd better tell me exactly what happened.'

They explained the earlier incident in the barn when, after they had found the little foal, the light seemed to have a climacteric effect on Peter. Grandad listened quietly, then sat back in his chair pondering. They wondered if he believed them, or if he thought they were making it all up, though Peter's face spoke for itself. The suspense ended with Grandad standing up.

'Is it still in the barn?' he asked anxiously.

'Yes, it's in the stall next to Cherokee,' said Joel.

'Well you can't leave it there, it might be in danger. Go and fetch it into the house - and bring some fresh straw.'

They looked at Grandad, then at each other, utterly confused.

+

'Has your Grandad gone batty, Joel?' Tamara said with exasperation, as the three friends hurried to the barn. 'Since when has a barn been dangerous to horses? Why are Cherokee and the other animals in there if it's dangerous?'.

'I just don't know, Tamara...' Joel shook his head. Then suddenly, he caught Tamara's arm and stopped her; she followed his bewildered gaze to Peter and her jaw dropped. He was striding out towards the barn as they'd never seen him before, callipers clanging as usual - but not a limp in sight.

CHAPTER TWO

Losers in the Lane

Ever since he could remember, Peter had always had a limp. He needed to wear callipers to support his crooked legs and feet, ravaged by polio and general malnutrition when he was a baby. But now, crazy as it seemed, Peter was walking with two perfectly normal, straight and strong legs. It was a miracle - pure and simple.

Inside the barn, Cherokee was leaning over the side of her stall, her nostrils blowing gently over the foal, as though comforting him. Peter and Joel gently lifted the little foal and carried him out of the barn. Cherokee gave a little whinny, almost as if she was calling after them not to take the baby.

They took him into the kitchen along with some straw. Grandad made a little bed with the straw in the alcove under the stairs and they laid him in it.

'Well now, aren't we a beauty?' Grandad smiled at the little animal.

The foal seemed to be recovering and raised his head, blinking his big eyes at Grandad, as if he was answering him, acknowledging the compliment. Grandad had warmed some fresh milk in a baby bottle.

'Here, Peter. I keep this bottle for the sickly lambs; you know what to do.' Grandad handed the bottle to Peter.

'Can we give him a name, Mr Jacob?' Tamara pleaded. 'I mean we've got to call him something till his owner comes for him.'

'Yes, Tamara, love, what do you suggest?'

'Well he arrived with the storm; how about we call him, Storm?'

'Fits him perfectly, love.'

Tamara knelt down by Peter and cradled Storm's head, while

Peter gave him the milk.

'Hello, Storm, my name is Tamara, and this is Peter, Joel and Mr Jacob - and we're going to look after you. Oh I wish we could keep him, he's so cute.'

'That's impossible, I'm afraid,' said Grandad. 'Make the most of him, Tamara, he won't be with us for long, he will have to go back, you know.'

Peter gave the bottle to Tamara and struggled to stand up in his callipers.

'Peter, you might as well take those callipers off, lad,' Grandad said. 'You won't be needing them any more; they're more of a hindrance now.' With that, Grandad headed for the door to the hall, calling back: 'You'd better get ready, it's Sunday. We'll have to leave for Church in half an hour.'

They looked down at Peter's legs, then up at each other, perplexed at Grandad's mysterious behavior.

+

Grandad always attended Church on Sundays, but it was only recently that the local Church had grown in popularity. The front-row pews were now full every Sunday morning. This was largely owing to the apparent sudden spiritual awareness of almost the entire female teenage population of the Parish, who were always early (first there get the best seats). This spate of Christian fervour amongst these blushing young girls was undoubtedly connected with G.R.J. - That was the girls' code for, Gorgeous Reverend John.

The young, enigmatic (and single) Reverend John Matthews was installed as the incumbent Vicar of St Mary's when the old Vicar retired the previous year. John Matthews brought a refreshingly modern approach to worship. The children loved him, he played the guitar and sang as he told stories. In fact if he hadn't been a Vicar, Matthews could have been a successful singer and musician. He was very popular with the ladies - unlike most Vicars they remembered, who had shiny heads, fringed by the friar's "ring of grey". Matthews on the contrary had a good head of hair.

+

Peter felt very self-conscious as he walked into Church minus his callipers. He felt as if every eye was staring at him, like little hot pinpricks in his back.

'Stay close behind me, Peter,' Grandad said protectively. 'Joel, you stay at the back behind Peter and Tamara.'

The three friends followed Grandad down the aisle of the Church. Joel thought the fact that Grandad took it all so calmly was evidence that he knew more than he was telling and he was determined to find out exactly what that was.

Peter's parents were thankfully right at the front of the Church. Although they turned round like everyone else, they didn't have a good view of Peter because he was hiding behind Grandad. The last thing Peter wanted was some sort of scene in front of everyone, where he would have to explain things - the absence of his callipers, for instance.

Tamara's parents were not so far up; Presten was with them, seated next to the aisle. As Grandad passed them, he suddenly stopped and immediately turned his head. He looked down at Presten, who had surreptitiously stuck his foot out ready to trip Peter as he followed. Presten's smirking face dissolved into an irritated scowl and slowly he pulled in his foot. Then Grandad gave Mr and Mrs Goodchild a friendly nod and continued on up the aisle.

Tamara glared at Presten disapprovingly as she passed, then smiled sweetly at her parents, who beamed and waved back. She was their pride and joy and generally made up for all the headaches Presten caused. Presten shrank back in his pew with a look of hatred on his face, as Joel walked past flashing him a piercing stare.

They reached an empty pew and filed in to take their seats. Grandad leaned forward to pray, while Tamara leaned to Joel.

'I told you your Grandad was psychic,' she whispered. 'How else could he have known about Presten's foot?'

'I could have guessed Presten would try something sneaky and unimaginative like that,' Joel whispered back. 'He's so predictable.'

Joel beckoned Peter to listen too. Peter leaned towards them.

'I'm convinced Grandad knows more than he's letting on,' Joel continued. 'There's something mysterious going on here and I'm going to get to the bottom of it. See if you two can get your parents to let you stay over again and we'll drag it out of him tonight.'

They both nodded. Matthews announced the opening hymn, the organ started to play and they stood up to sing.

> *There is a green hill far away*
> *without a city wall,*
> *where the dear Lord was crucified,*
> *who died to save us all.*
>
> *We may not know, we cannot tell*
> *what pains He had to bear;*
> *but we believe it was for us*
> *He hung and suffered there.*

When they came out of Church, Joel asked Grandad if Peter and Tamara could stay over again. Grandad said it was fine by him as long as it was O.K. with their parents. Tamara's parents were surprisingly accommodating, much to Tamara's glee and Presten's annoyance as he snarled behind their backs. They seemed more concerned that it might be putting Joel's Grandad out, but Joel explained that Grandad spent too much time on his own and loved having them to stay.

The dodgy bit was Peter's parents. When they saw him without his callipers, they were very shocked. They couldn't believe that he was suddenly healed. Reluctantly they agreed to let him stay but Peter had to promise to go to see the Doctor with his mother first thing Monday morning.

Tamara went home with her parents to pick up some clothes and her toothbrush. Joel accompanied Peter and his parents back to their farm to collect Peter's stuff.

Peter ran up the stairs to quickly pack a bag, while Joel waited in the farmhouse kitchen with a glass of fresh farm milk and a little piece of heaven on earth; that is a huge chunk of Mrs Jordan's famous chocolate cake. Peter's mum was a fantastic cook and she was always in the kitchen baking.

As Joel drank the milk and scoffed the cake, Mr and Mrs Jordan marvelled that never before in his whole life had Peter run up the stairs. They tried to get some information out of Joel about what had happened.

'It could be one of those unexplained phenomena you read about, Mrs Jordan,' Joel said a little cagily, then took a large bite of cake so he didn't have to speak. He breathed a sigh of relief as Peter came to the rescue carrying a small holdall.

'Here, Joel, take this for your Grandad.' Mrs Jordan presented Joel with an enormous chocolate cake, which almost completely covered the dinner plate it was sitting on.

'Thanks, Mrs Jordan, your chocolate cake is the best!' Joel grinned.

Joel and Peter set off down the lane to Grandad's place, Joel carefully carrying the chocolate cake. Suddenly, who should spring out from behind a large tree but Presten and two members of his delinquent posse, Will and Jud (short for George). Of course, Presten wouldn't have risked a confrontation on his own while Joel was about, he was too chicken.

Presten stood in the middle of the lane barring their way. Will and Jud stood behind him, goading him on. Presten carried a heavy baseball bat and slapped the palm of his hand with it intimidatingly.

'Where's your stilts, Tin Legs?' Presten sneered at Peter.

'Get lost, Presten,' Joel threatened.

'I obviously didn't do a good-enough job on you yesterday, Jordan. I thought you'd be looking like a pickled cabbage by now. We're gonna have to do something about that - aren't we lads?' He tipped his head to Will and Jud and they guffawed, nodding their heads stupidly.

'Yeah, that's right, we'll have t' do a better job this time, Pres',' Jud sneered.

'What's that you've got, Asher?' Presten looked at the cake Joel was carrying. Of all the things Joel needed in his mitts right now, a massive sticky chocolate cake was not one of them.

'None of your business, Presten. Get out of our way!' Joel shouted with a confidence he wished he was feeling. Presten was a walkover on his own, but three of them, one armed with a baseball bat, greatly reduced the odds.

'Give that to me and I'll let you go,' Presten lied.
Will and Jud smirked and Presten raised his baseball bat, snarling threateningly.

'Yeah, Asher, give us that cake!' Jud demanded.

'I'd just as soon give you a dose of the flu, Jud,' Joel spat.

'Get them, Pres'!' Will scowled sadistically.

'Shouldn't you be on a lead, will?' Joel sniped.

Presten started to walk slowly towards Peter and Joel.

'Your mate ain't gonna be able to help you now, Jordan,' he sneered, swinging his bat in an attempt to intimidate them.

'Presten, you're a joke!' Joel put the cake down on the road and rolled up his sleeves. 'Clear off and take Coco and Buttons with you.'

'Yeah, sling your hook, Porky!' Peter surprised himself at his own sudden fearlessness. He dropped his bag and quickly rolled up his sleeves.

'Getting brave all of a sudden, aren't you, Jordan?' Presten sniggered. 'Want another thrashing do you?'

'You heard, Presten!' Joel threatened. 'Back off!'

Presten took a quick backward glance, checking Will and Jud were right behind him. Reassured that they were, he got a surge of conceited confidence.

'Or what, Asher?' Presten challenged defiantly.

Joel suddenly saw red and, imagining himself on the rugby

pitch playing for the cup of the year, he lurched forward:

'OR THIS!' he shouted. Diving head first like a charging bull, his head landed smack in Presten's stomach. This knocked Presten backwards with such a force that he might have been catapulted right over the hedge had not Will and Jud been there to break his fall. This in turn sent Will and Jud flying like skittles in a bowling alley. All three of them lay winded and groaning on the muddy grass verge.

Peter and Joel slapped their right hands together in the air. 'Way to go!' they cried together.

'Get the cake, Peter!' Joel yelled, grabbing Peter's bag.

Peter picked up the cake and the pair of them scarpered, laughing their heads off, before Presten and his two minions had a chance to recover.

'I'll get you, Asher!' Presten shouted painfully.

Joel couldn't resist yelling back.

'Well we've still got the cake, loser!'

+

By the time they arrived back at Grandad's, Tamara was already there. Her parents had dropped her off in their posh car and Grandad had given them a basket of fresh eggs. Tamara had spent the time bottle-feeding Storm, until he dropped off to sleep just like a baby. He seemed quite at home in Grandad's kitchen (although some health inspectors might have had something to say about it!) Grandad had now made a baby stable under the stairs with some wood.

Rodney was skulking about, jealous of this cute new guest that was demanding everyone's attention. He'd collected all his belongings - Grandad's old slipper, a half-eaten dog chew and a squeaky toy that had lost its squeak and tried to lie on them all at once, guarding them. Occasionally he ventured up to sniff Storm.

It was lunchtime, so the three of them made a load of sandwiches and packed them with some very large chunks of Mrs Jordan's chocolate cake. Then they set off for Zionica to spend the afternoon there.

When they climbed up to the den, they were thrilled to find masses of tadpoles had hatched out in the jam jars. They decided by a vote that Peter had the largest tadpole, but Joel had the most tadpoles. However, Tamara claimed to have the cutest tadpole, a point the boys couldn't (or decided not to) argue against.

By this time they were ravenous and tucked into the nosh with relish. Tamara almost cried with laughter as they told her about their defeat of Presten and his two clownish cronies outside Peter's farm.

'Yeah, they went flying like skittles,' Peter chuckled. 'It's the funniest thing I've seen since - well - since the snowballing.'

All three of them roared with laughter.

'I'd love to have seen that!' Tamara giggled helplessly.

'Anyway, on a more serious note,' Joel said, 'I'm convinced there's something Grandad is not telling us - he knows something.'

'Yes, he was so matter-of-fact when we told him about the light affecting Peter in the barn,' Tamara said curiously. 'The way he told Peter he wouldn't need the callipers any more - how did he know?'

'And why did he think the foal would be in danger - in the barn?' Peter said, baffled.

'That's what I just don't understand,' Joel added. 'I mean, if it's dangerous for the foal, why are the other animals in there? What's in the barn that's only dangerous to foals?'

'Or is it this particular foal..?' Peter mused.

'And I hate to sound weird but...' Tamara shrugged. 'What about the light thing? We both saw it, Joel. Was it really the sun through the window? And how can bruises just simply disappear? What exactly was it that healed Peter?'

'I haven't got any answers, but I'm convinced Grandad has,' Joel said determinedly.

'So how are we going to get him to spill?' Tamara went on.

'Well that's one of the reasons I thought you two should stay over. It's Sunday. If we can't get him talking on Sunday evening we never will.' Joel frowned, thoughtfully.

They both looked quizzically at him.

'Grandad is a great one for traditions,' Joel explained. 'On Sundays, Grandma always did a big roast dinner, followed by a sticky pudding or juicy pie. She always started with a small sherry while she made the gravy, then a glass of wine with the meal, then she had a cherry brandy by the fire after the dishes were done. The only thing Grandad does differently is the drink after dinner - he has a brandy and benedictine! Do you get my drift now?' Joel spread his hands.

'Sure do, by the time he has his brandy and benedictine...' Peter began.

'He'll be singing like a parrot!' Tamara interrupted impetuously.

'Exactly,' Joel grinned smugly. 'And it's a canary, Tamara - singing like a canary; and *sick* as a parrot.'

'Oh bla de bla!' Tamara shrugged.

'But we'll have to be careful how we do it,' Joel warned. 'If he thinks he's being tricked, he'll just clam up and send us upstairs. Grandad loves talking once he gets going. We'll get him started on something safe, then engineer the subject round.' Joel gave a big sigh. 'We've *got* to get him to talk; I can't stand not knowing.'

CHAPTER THREE

Thieves in the Night

After the Sunday roast, which they had in the early evening, the three friends insisted Grandad went into the lounge while they cleared up the dishes. When there were just a few left to put away, Peter and Tamara followed Grandad, while Joel finished off.

Grandad was standing by the fireplace; he had his brandy cocktail in one hand and in the other he held a small framed picture. He gazed affectionately at it.

'Is that your wife in the photograph, Mr Jacob?' Tamara asked quietly.

'Yes, Tamara, love; she was a good lady, Mrs Jacob,' Grandad replied fondly.

'I bet you miss her,' Tamara said.

'More than I can say,' Grandad went on. 'It's a terrible thing, you know, cancer. She lived a good life, always thinking of others - and she never smoked.'

Just then, Joel joined them from the kitchen.

'Don't you wonder sometimes why God lets these things happen, Mr Jacob?' Tamara continued. 'I mean, why does He let a good, kind lady like Mrs Jacob get cancer?'

Grandad put the picture back on the mantelpiece and sat down in his rocking chair with a sigh.

'Come, sit down.' Grandad beckoned.

They got themselves comfortable on the rug by the fire, then looked up at Grandad, waiting for him to speak.

'This is a mistake that people tend to make: it's easy for them to blame God for things like cancer,' Grandad explained. 'But the reality is, God provides the great minds of eminent Doctors and Scientists, to fight against this evil disease. He gives them the tools and ingredients they need. The evil of cancer is a product of the devil and when human beings finally discover the cure for all cancer, the devil will most likely conjure up something else equally sinister. In fact: now that a lot of cancer is treatable, it just proves that good will ultimately triumph over evil.' Grandad paused to sip his drink, then went on. 'A lot of people think the devil is a myth, conjured up in the imagination of storytellers. A monstrous, two horned creature with burning coals for eyes and a pointed tail. That visual image may very well be a myth, but the devil himself is as real as you and me.'

The three friends stared up at Grandad, eager to hear more.

'The devil used to be an Angel in Heaven, but he rebelled against God's authority. He became greedy, selfish, downright evil and destructive. He wanted power for himself and tried to incite other Angels to join him. God threw him out of Heaven - cast out in disgrace - a fallen Angel. From that moment, the devil began to wage an evil war against God, taking as many poor souls as possible with him into the darkness with false promises and lies. God knew that the ultimate sacrifice was unavoidable, because only the ransom of His own Son's blood would defeat this festering evil which threatened to destroy all the love and beauty He had created. When Jesus became that *ultimate sacrifice*, knowing full well what was at stake, he did indeed defeat the devil. Of course, the devil is still out there, consumed with hate and burning with rage like a furnace, perpetrating evil wherever he can, constantly trying to entice people to follow him. But now, because of Jesus, the devil has lost the battle - he knows his time is limited and that his ultimate fate will be to burn in a fiery pit for eternity. Until then, the devil strives to manifest evil and havoc on earth: causing nasty diseases and disasters around the world is the devil's stock in trade. His main objective is to turn as many people as possible away from God. He knows this will hurt God the most. So he uses people.'

'Uses people?' Tamara asked intently. 'How, Mr Jacob?'

'Well, Tamara,' Grandad smiled, 'unfortunately, everyone isn't good like you. There are, sadly, some bad people in the world, who do bad things. That's why we have prisons and it's why *you* are always being drilled about not talking to strangers. But babies are not born bad. The devil seeks out people who will follow him and encourages them to be bad and, unfortunately, some listen. That's the sad thing; if everyone renounced the devil, he wouldn't have any power, he gets his power from those who listen and follow him.' Grandad paused.

'So evil people in history were..?' Peter frowned.

'Hitler, for instance,' Grandad nodded, 'was one of his prize conquests - so obedient to his master, he could have been the devil himself. But these people don't profit in the end. They're led down a dead-end street by their own greed and ill judgement and will eventually suffer the same fate as the devil. He knows all too well what is written down for him and it's his aim to take as many of us with him as possible.'

'Sounds like Presten is one of them,' Joel said, tersely.

'Well there's time for Presten yet, Joel; he's young, he may grow out of this...'

'Beastliness!' Tamara interjected.

'I was going to say phase,' Grandad continued with an amused smile. 'Presten could eventually see the light and turn into a very nice young man, who knows?'

'Oh yeah and I might turn into a singing peacock!' Joel said scathingly.

'Well anyway, Presten is someone to be wary of, as you already know. Curious, though - if you jumble up the letters in "Presten" what you might end up with,' Grandad said, thoughtfully.

Joel picked up a pen and paper from a nearby table and the three of them started trying to work out what Grandad meant.

'Serpent!' Peter shouted. 'The devil came down to earth as a serpent, didn't he, Mr Jacob?'

'Correct, Peter,' Grandad nodded.

'Well that explains a lot,' said Joel.

'Oh you mustn't read anything into that - we're only talking about a twelve-year-old boy here,' Grandad smiled.

'So, Grandad, what do you think about the young foal we

found? Where do you think he's from?' Joel was trying to engineer the subject round to what might have healed Peter.

'Storm is not an ordinary foal,' Grandad replied plainly.

'Oh?' Joel asked.

'Yes, I'm quite certain that what we have in our kitchen is...' They all leaned forward in eager anticipation.

'...is a young Unicorn,' Grandad said simply.

'A Unicorn?' they all sang in unison.

'But - I thought Unicorns were -' Tamara started.

'Just another mythical creature that doesn't really exist?' Grandad finished Tamara's sentence. 'Well technically speaking, that's what they are - now.'

'But, Grandad - I don't understand - how can they be mythical, non-existent creatures, if we've got one in our kitchen?' Joel insisted, more confused than ever.

Grandad gave a deep sigh.

'Well now, where shall I start?' He rubbed his chin. 'Unicorns were not always just mythical creatures. A few thousand years ago they roamed the earth just like other animals. But they were sadly mistreated by a few unscrupulous individuals, who hunted and killed them for their horns.'

'Oh how positively beastly!' Tamara cried. 'Why, Mr Jacob?'

'It was widely believed that the horn of a Unicorn had healing properties, therefore it became very valuable and people would pay a fortune to get hold of one. However, for all practical purposes, the horn had to be detached from the animal and ground up to make a potion. Consequently, Unicorns paid the price with their lives.' Grandad sighed.

'And this depleted their numbers and made them rare and consequently even more valuable?' Joel surmised.

'Precisely,' Grandad nodded. 'And so the vicious circle carried on. That is, until the great flood in Noah's day.'

The children frowned curiously at Grandad as he continued in a low voice. 'When God instructed Noah to put two of each animal in the ark to be saved, He apparently left out the Unicorn.'

'But why didn't He want them saved as well?' Tamara cried.

'Isn't it blindingly obvious?' Joel said. 'He was probably so upset at all the cruelty and killing for greed, He must have wanted to spare their suffering.'

'Correct, Joel, that is my interpretation,' Grandad said. 'So the Unicorn became extinct with the great flood. God wiped them out of very existence, totally.'

'But that still doesn't explain...' Joel frowned.

'The one in the kitchen.' Grandad pondered. 'Hmm.'

'Oh please go on, Mr Jacob,' Tamara urged. 'How do you *know* Storm is a Unicorn and not just a young pony? I thought Unicorns had a long horn on their forehead?'

Grandad suddenly put down his glass and stood up.

'Come with me,' he beckoned as he went into the kitchen.

Curious, the three friends followed him. He bent down and very carefully lifted up Storm's wispy forelock.

They all gasped as they looked on. For there, protruding from the tiny animal's forehead, was the burgeon of a very small horn, about half an inch long.

'Of course, it will get much bigger as he grows,' Grandad explained. 'The horns of young Unicorns are short, so they don't injure each other during play. By the time Storm is fully grown, this horn could be anything from twelve to eighteen inches long.'

'Wow!' Peter said, amazed.

'Are you saying then, Mr Jacob, that it was Storm's horn that healed Peter?' Tamara asked intelligently.

'I am, Tamara. That is precisely what I believe happened.'

'I thought the horn had to be ground up to make a potion?' Peter said with a confused frown.

'How did he get here, Grandad?' Joel persisted. 'Where did he come from - if Unicorns were wiped out of existence?'

'And why is he in the kitchen? What's so dangerous about the barn?' Peter asked.

'Do you think someone will try to kill him - for his horn?' Tamara went on. 'Is that why we can't leave him in the barn?'

'And how do you know all this Unicorn stuff, Grandad?'

'All right! All right!' Grandad shook his head. 'I'll try to

THIEVES IN THE NIGHT

explain, but first, get into your pyjamas, while I make some cocoa.'

'Oh!' They all wailed in frustration at the interruption. Three kids had never got ready for bed faster. They raced into their pyjamas and were back downstairs on the rug by the time Grandad came in with a tray of steaming cocoa. He shook his head and chuckled in amusement.

'So, you want to hear about Unicorns?' Grandad began.

'Please, Grandad, tell us what you know,' Joel pleaded.

Grandad returned to his rocking chair and looked down at the three faces, all looking up at him with eager anticipation. He smiled affectionately.

'O.K.' He continued. 'Some believe that Unicorns originated in India. They had always been peaceful, beautiful creatures and the healing properties of their horns made them special. There's lots of evidence that Unicorns existed, most notably in the Bible itself - where generally the horn both signifies, and is used to describe, strength. Unicorns have always been regarded as biblical creatures - even referred to in some services.' Grandad paused thoughtfully. 'But for some reason, the Unicorn was excised from the modern Bible.'

Grandad reached into a small drawer in the table by his chair and pulled out a worn book that looked very, very old. It was black with faded gold-leaf edging to the pages and gold lettering which read, 'Holy Bible'.

'This is a very old Bible,' Grandad said, as he opened it to the book of Deuteronomy, chapter 33. 'Here, Tamara, read the first sentence of verse 17.' Grandad pointed to it.

Tamara read it aloud, *"His glory is like the firstling of his bullock, and his horns are like the horns of unicorns."*

'Now,' Grandad said, picking up his regular Bible from the table top, 'look at the same verse in this modern version.'

Tamara read the verse out again from the new Bible.

"In majesty he is like a firstborn bull; his horns are the horns of a wild ox." Holy cow, Mr Jacob! You're right - they've changed the Unicorn to a wild Ox! But who would change it?'

'Yes, Unicorns must have been mentioned for a reason,' said Joel.

'Precisely, see what I mean? The Bible was written thousands of years ago - about events that happened thousands of years ago. Now who indeed changed what was originally written, under whose authority and why?' Grandad took a sip of his drink. 'Now that's just one example; there are several others.'

'But that's really sad, Mr Jacob. Unicorns are beautiful creatures,' Tamara exclaimed.

'Quite,' Grandad agreed. 'The name, Unicorn, is also significant. Derived from Latin, "uni" means "one" and "cornu" means "horn" thereby distinguishing a single horn, referred to in the old Bible, to be good. The devil who is bad, is generally depicted as having two horns.'

'Yes, the animal referred to in the original Bible had one horn,' Peter pointed out. 'The Ox in the new one has two horns!'

'That's right,' Grandad said. 'All very curious, don't you think?'

They all nodded, fascinated.

Grandad went on. 'There are some who believe that because of its healing powers and purity, the Unicorn was resurrected as a *heavenly body* two thousand years ago, to celebrate the resurrection of Christ.' Grandad took another sip of his drink, giving his mesmerised audience time to digest this information. 'There is a school of thought that views the Unicorn as a very symbol of - Christ Himself.'

'Wow, so how..?' Joel began.

'...did a heavenly body manifest itself here?' Grandad shrugged. 'I don't quite know, but I have an idea it's something to do with that unusual rainbow. I think that, somehow, the rainbow allowed Storm to literally - fall to earth.'

'So what you're saying, Grandad, is the rainbow must be a kind of gateway between Heaven and earth,' Joel said incredulously, 'and that somehow, Storm has come through it?'

'Well, crazy as it sounds, yes, but what I don't know is how - or why.'

'A rainbow is a sign from God, isn't it, Mr Jacob?' said Peter.

'Yes, that's true, Peter.'

'Do you think He's trying to tell us something?' Tamara suggested.

'I don't know.' Grandad frowned. 'But I do suspect that while Storm is here, he could be in grave danger.'

'Why, Grandad? What's in the barn that could harm him?'

'Maybe I'm being over-cautious,' Grandad said, 'but while he's here, he's mortal, which means he could be harmed or even killed.'

'But who would want to kill him?' Tamara asked, shocked.

'Remember what the devil did through Herod two thousand years ago, in a desperate attempt to destroy the infant Christ. He had all boys of two years and under slaughtered! Imagine if the devil were to find the resurrected symbol of Christ - here on earth - another helpless babe - what might he do? That's why we cannot leave Storm in the barn. A stable fooled the devil once before, when he expected God's Son to be born among royalty and riches.' Grandad leaned forward and looked at them earnestly. 'If anything was to happen to this symbol of purity and goodness - this symbol of Christ Himself - if the devil got his hands on him...' Grandad shook his head gravely, '...it could spell disaster for the whole of mankind.'

All three of them went suddenly pale and gulped, while Grandad carried on in earnest.

'He must be protected at all costs and returned from whence he came, as soon as possible. Now the devil is crafty, he's bound to know that something has slipped through. You can bet he will be searching everywhere, even as we speak, to find our little Storm; we must not let him succeed.'

'How come you know all this, Mr Jacob?' Tamara asked.

'Well, Tamara, love, I've done a lot of reading and research about Unicorns. I became fascinated and wanted to know all I could about them, ever since...' Grandad suddenly stopped. 'I'm talking too much now; perhaps I shouldn't have had that last brandy and benedictine.'

'Please go on, Grandad - ever since what?' Joel urged.
Joel, Peter and Tamara looked up anxious for Grandad to continue.

Then suddenly Rodney seemed to remember that he was actually a dog and not a couch potato; he started growling, then barking fiercely he leapt out of his basket and sped into the kitchen. There followed an almighty crashing sound, then Rodney could be heard yelping.

They all ran into the kitchen. The back door was swinging on its hinges and the baby stable Grandad had put up under the stairs had been demolished. Rodney lay panting by the broken pieces of wood, but there was no sign of Storm. Peter knelt down and looked through the straw, then looked up at the others.

'He's gone - Storm has gone!' he cried desperately.

'No! No!' Tamara burst into tears and turned to Joel. 'Joel, we've got to find him, we've got to get him back!'

Grandad peered outside and inspected the back door for damage, while Peter began to check over Rodney. After carefully examining the dog (who was lapping up the sympathy and attention) Peter stood up.

'Good old Rodney, he's obviously tried to protect Storm. I think he's O.K. just had a bit of a fright. But look at this,' Peter held up a small piece of cloth. 'Rodney had this in his teeth!'

Joel took the cloth from Peter and looked at it.

'What is it?' Tamara asked.

'It appears we have some forensic evidence,' Joel mused. 'Looks like the culprit didn't go unpunished. It's a piece of someone's pants, I think. There are tiny spots of blood on it, probably caused by Rodney's teeth sinking into the villain's backside.' Joel bent down and patted Rodney. 'Well done, Rodders.'

Tamara suddenly leapt forward and snatched the cloth from Joel. It was a particular grey jersey with a particular pattern.

'Presten!' she screamed. 'This is off Presten's jogging pants!'

Joel and Peter looked at her, stunned.

'Tamara is right!' Joel looked closer. 'I'd recognise that

material anywhere. Who else but Presten would wear something that uncool? How dare he sneak in here!'

'And what does he want with our Storm? Where's he taken him?' Tamara raised an eyebrow in fury, as she turned from being upset to being angry. 'That beastly, evil monster!' With that, Tamara fled from the house, down the yard to the gate.

'Joel! Stop her!' yelled Grandad.

They all ran outside into the dark night, chasing after Tamara to the gate. It had been raining and the ground was still wet.

'Tamara! Wait!' Joel shouted.

But she was determined to catch her wicked brother. She reached the gate and ran out into the lane. Joel saw her for a split second in the headlights of a passing car. Then there was a terrible screeching of tyres as the driver desperately tried to stop in the wet.

Joel felt as if his heart had stopped, as he reached Tamara first. She was lying face down on the wet road, the headlights shining on her. He threw himself down and turned her over. She was unconscious and there was blood coming from her nose and on her head, the bloodstained cloth still gripped in her hand. Peter and Grandad reached them and looked on in horror, as the driver got out of his car and rushed over to Joel and the seemingly lifeless Tamara.

'I - I couldn't stop in time...' the distraught stranger cried. 'She ran out so fast...'

CHAPTER FOUR

Storm's Passion

Little sobs as Mrs Goodchild wept into her handkerchief, punctuated by the annoyingly loud tick-tock of a wall clock and Grandad occasionally blowing his nose, were the only sounds that could be heard. Mr Goodchild, distraught himself, did his best to comfort his wife as they sat in the hospital waiting room.

Joel and Peter sat in silence, every tick of the clock a painful reminder that all they could do was wait. They were hardly able to believe that such a dreadful thing could have happened to Tamara. They felt responsible, that they should have taken better care of her.

Presten stood next to his parents. It must have been too painful for him to sit down. He was still wearing the jogging pants, (with a dog-bite-sized hole on the bottom) that he must have been wearing when he sneaked into Grandad's kitchen.

Eventually the Doctor entered the room and everyone stood up as he approached Mr and Mrs Goodchild.

'I'm afraid your daughter is still unconscious,' the Doctor began quietly. 'There's been some internal bleeding and we've had to put her on a life-support machine. We'll run some more tests in the morning. You can see her for a couple of minutes - I'm sorry, but just Mr and Mrs Goodchild at the moment, please.

The Doctor led Tamara's parents away, while Joel, Peter and Grandad were left, feeling empty.

'Well, lads, I'll go and call a taxi to take us home - there's nothing we can do here now,' Grandad muttered woefully, then walked off to find a phone.

Joel looked ferociously at Presten, who trembled in fear like a frightened rabbit.

'You - you can't touch me here -' Presten squeaked, looking as if he was about to wet himself. 'Not in the hospital. I'll shout for the Doctor.'

'We don't give a stuff about you, Presten! Where is our foal?' Joel spat. He hoped that Presten hadn't heard their conversation with Grandad earlier, about Storm being a Unicorn.

'It's quite safe - Will and Jud are taking care of it - and it'll be safe as long as I am.' Presten threatened.

'Safe? With Will and Jud? They couldn't take care of a cold sore!' Joel scowled. 'If anything happens to that foal, Presten, I'll come after you and thrash your fat, scaredy butt.'

'My Dad might have something to say about that, Asher,' Presten smirked pompously. He had a habit of abusing his Father's high standing in the local community.

Joel stepped closer to Presten and glared at him angrily.

'Your Dad is too concerned about your sister to bother about you, you little wimp. By the way, does he know it's your fault she's where she is?'

Fear suddenly gripped Presten's face, at the thought of his Father finding out what he'd done and he looked as if he was about to be sick.

'Hmm, I thought not,' Joel snarled with contempt.

'Don't you dare! Don't you dare say anything, or I'll - I'll beat your mate to pulp when you've gone, Asher!'

'You just bring that foal back tonight and don't *you* dare hurt a hair of his head!' Joel demanded coldly.

Just then Grandad returned.

'Taxi will be here in a few minutes, boys; we'll go outside and wait, shall we?'

Peter and Joel followed Grandad outside. As he was leaving, Joel threw Presten a warning glance, causing him to give an involuntary, cowardly whimper.

Later that evening Grandad lit a candle and said a few prayers for Tamara. Joel and Peter sat in Joel's bedroom, miserably mulling over how they could have avoided the accident. If only Joel had kept hold of Tamara and not let her run off. If only he could have run faster and stopped her. If only Peter hadn't shown her the material from Presten's pants. If only

Presten wasn't such a jerk.

Suddenly they heard a knock at the front door. Joel and Peter rushed downstairs, hoping it was good news about Tamara. Grandad was standing in the open doorway.

'Mr Goodchild!' Grandad was surprised to see Tamara's Father on the doorstep. 'Is Tamara..?'

'There's no change yet, I'm afraid, Mr Jacob. We've come to apologise,' Mr Goodchild announced.

'Apologise? But...'

'William and George came round to the house with their parents,' Mr Goodchild explained. 'It seems the boys got scared after Tamara was hurt.'

Joel and Peter looked at each other, then walked up behind Grandad as Mr Goodchild continued.

'They've come clean about their little prank, sneaking into your kitchen with Presten.' He stepped to the side. 'I believe Presten has something that belongs to you, Mr Jacob?' He pushed Presten forward.

Presten looked down sheepishly.

Joel and Peter gasped as they saw the baby Unicorn in Presten's arms. Rodney's lip lifted and he growled through his teeth, as he peered round at Presten from the safe position behind Grandad's legs. Joel took Storm and handed him to Peter, who immediately started checking the little foal over.

'Well?' Mr Goodchild said sternly. 'Haven't you got something to say to Mr Jacob, Presten?'

'I - I'm s - s orry, M - Mr Jacob,' Presten stammered nervously. 'We d - didn't mean to s - st - steal your foal. Will and Jud a - and me, we were j - just spying on Joel and Peter - it was just a game, when we saw the foal, we - we thought...'

'Go on, Presten,' Mr Goodchild urged crossly.

'We thought it would be fun to - to borrow it - we were going to bring it back. Your dog tried to stop us taking the foal. Before we knew it, all the wood came crashing down...' Presten looked down miserably. 'I hope your dog is all right.'

'Obviously I will pay for any damage and vet's bills Presten has caused,' Mr Goodchild added.

'That's not necessary, Mr Goodchild. It's very brave of Presten to come and own up,' Grandad said, turning to Presten with a kindly smile. 'Rodney seems O.K. and I'm sure the foal is all right too. We must pray for your sister's recovery, Presten, that's all that matters now.'

Presten studied his feet intently.

'I'll send Presten over in the morning - to collect Tamara's pony,' said Mr Goodchild.

Presten looked at his father with sudden alarm and gulped.

'Oh no - I - I don't want to go near that animal, Dad! It doesn't like me - it tries to bite me...'

If the situation hadn't been so serious, Joel and Peter would have found Presten's cowardly outburst amusing.

'The pony is all right here, Mr Goodchild, you can leave her as long as you want, till Tamara is well enough to collect Cherokee herself.'

'That's very generous, Mr Jacob.' Mr Goodchild turned to Presten. 'Go and get in the car now, Presten - and think yourself lucky Mr Jacob hasn't called the police!'

Without looking up, Presten shuffled off to the car.

'Thank you.' Mr Goodchild gripped Grandad's hand. Grandad nodded sorrowfully.

+

Next morning, Joel and Peter collected the eggs in relative silence, while Grandad fed the animals and let Cherokee into the paddock for some exercise. Rodney lay on guard in front of the baby stable, which Grandad had rebuilt under the stair alcove in the kitchen. Peter made up a bottle of warm milk to feed Storm. Rodney appeared to have become quite attached to Storm; either that or he was hoping some milk might get spilt so he could lick it up. Then shortly after breakfast, Peter's Mum collected him for the dreaded (and as far as Peter was concerned, pointless) visit to the Doctor's surgery.

As Peter expected, the Doctor hadn't got an explanation for his apparent *miracle recovery*; he used the stock reply Doctors tend to use when they don't have an answer: "It's just one of those things." He suggested that they donate the callipers to the hospital. There was no doubt that both Peter's legs and feet were now completely normal, just as if he'd never had polio at all.

The next couple of days were almost intolerable. Joel and Peter couldn't think about anything but Tamara, lying there unconscious in hospital, when she should have been hanging out with them. The results of the tests had not been very encouraging and she was still on the life-support machine. Everyone was worried about her.

To make things worse, Storm was deteriorating. He was now so weak that he could hardly lift his little head to drink from the bottle. A few feeble gulps were all he could manage at a time. Grandad was feeding him a couple of sips every fifteen minutes. They took it in turns to massage his little body and legs to keep his circulation going. The poor little soul just lay there looking pitiful, hardly opening his eyes.

In between feeding Storm and looking after the other animals, Grandad spent much time on his knees praying for Tamara. He also secretly enjoyed taking over Tamara's role of pampering the pony and was much amused by all the little tricks Tamara had taught her.

Then by Wednesday, at least they were allowed to see Tamara. She was still in a coma and the Doctors couldn't seem to give them any encouraging words about her recovery. She was in a private room and family and friends were allowed to visit any time within reason. So instead of spending the day up in Zionica, Joel and Peter packed a rucksack with loads of books, CDs, games and biscuits, crisps and sweets. They read stories to Tamara and played some of her favourite CDs, hoping that she would hear something and wake up. They talked to her and brought her up to date on Storm's condition.

Tamara's Mum and Dad popped in regularly, but Presten was warned to stay away. They thought that if she sensed he was there, it might distress her (which of course it would have done). He was in terrible disgrace, being held responsible for her running out onto the road in the first place.

Tamara's hospital room was full of flowers, cuddly toys and all manner of presents and cards from everybody in the village and from her school. She'd have been thrilled if she'd seen it all; it was as if three Christmases had come at once.

By Thursday, there was still no sign of Tamara waking up. The Doctors were shaking their heads in despair. Storm was still very weak. Doom had descended like a dark cloud over everyone. Then, when they were alone with Tamara, Joel pushed the door shut and whispered to Peter.

'Peter - we should bring Storm here, you know, to Tamara. If he healed you, he *must* be able to heal her too.'

'Yes, I agree, Joel, it's worth a try, but how do you think we would get him past the Doctors and Nurses? How would we explain bringing a pony into the hospital - and a sick pony at that? Storm is very weak. Then don't forget your Grandad; I don't think he would agree to it.'

'I know, it's not going to be easy, but I'm sure we can think of something - we can't just do nothing!'

'Maybe we could try tomorrow,' Peter said. 'It's Good Friday and there'll just be a skeleton staff here.'

'Hey, good thinking, Peter. Grandad will be going to Church after breakfast. It's this witness-procession thing he does every Good Friday. You know, when a man dresses up like Jesus and drags a cross round the village - they call it "acting out the Passion" - he'll be out all morning. We can sneak Storm out and bring him back again before Grandad returns.' Joel leaned over Tamara and took hold of her limp hand. 'Don't worry, Tamara, we'll have you back with us by lunchtime tomorrow - good as new.'

Usually during the holidays, Joel would spend the odd night at Peter's farm. Now, though, he didn't want to leave Grandad alone. Under the circumstances, Grandad and the two boys decided it would be a good idea if Peter moved into Grandad's cottage for a few days, then they could all take turns keeping a watch on Storm, in between visiting Tamara.

The following morning, Good Friday, Joel and Peter were up early, battling Cedric for the eggs. They didn't want to lose any time. They planned to set off for the hospital with Storm wrapped in a blanket, as soon as Grandad had left for Church. Joel started to make the breakfast, while Peter bent down to feed Storm. Suddenly Peter shouted.

'Joel - here - quick!'

Joel rushed over. Peter had blood on his hands.

'Peter! What have you done? Are you hurt?'

'No - it's not my blood. Joel - it's Storm, he's bleeding! Look, there's blood on the straw.'

'That weasel, Presten! What's he done?' Joel got up and ran to open the door, yelling outside. 'Grandad! Come quickly!'

Grandad raced into the kitchen looking anxious.

'What's happened?' Grandad puffed.

'It's Storm, Grandad, he's injured...'

After inspecting Storm, Grandad sat down at the kitchen table, shaking his head and looking very confused.

'What's wrong with him, Grandad? Is he badly hurt?'

'Sit down, lads.'

They sat at the kitchen table and looked anxiously at Grandad.

'This is more serious than I thought, boys,' Grandad said gravely. 'I just can't believe it, it's too incredible.'

'What, Grandad - what is it?'

'Amazing as this might sound, Storm appears to have what you would call, *stigmata*.'

'Stigmata? Isn't that something to do with the wounds on Jesus' hands and feet?' Peter asked, mystified.

'Yes, that's right, Peter.' Grandad nodded.

'Huh?' Joel said, confused.

'Oh it's happened before, Joel, but as far as I know only to people. The first recorded example was, I believe, in the thirteenth century - Saint Francis of Assisi, the Patron Saint of animals. It's when someone experiences an extreme spiritual

STORM'S PASSION

closeness to Jesus - their hands and feet bleed inexplicably, as though wounded by nails, like Jesus when He was nailed to the cross.' Grandad explained: 'Bizarre as it seems, it looks like our little Storm is acting out the, *passion of Jesus*. It's Good Friday - the anniversary of the crucifixion. What concerns me, is if Storm acts out the Passion to its conclusion...'

'You mean he might die?' Joel cried.

'The longer he stays here, the more he is in mortal danger. We've somehow got to get him back where he came from. If he dies...' Grandad looked very grave. 'The world and everyone in it may pay the price.'

Joel and Peter gulped, as they stared at Grandad in horror.

'What do you mean, Grandad?' Joel shuddered. 'The world and everyone in it may pay *what* price?'

'Remember, if we believe that the Unicorn is a symbol and the celebration of the resurrection of God's Son, what do you think might happen if that symbol is extinguished? God has almost washed His hands of man before. That's why He sent Jesus in the first place, to mediate on our behalf, because He was fed up with all the wickedness on earth. Maybe this could be the last straw! God created the world in six days; how long would it take Him to destroy it?'

'But we don't know where Storm is from - or how to send him back,' said Peter, anxiously.

'I think I might know a way,' Grandad said. 'But we need another storm, or at least a little rain.' He gazed pensively through the window. 'I suspect, boys, the only way we'll get him back, is the same way he arrived.'

Joel and Peter looked at each other in confusion and shrugged. Grandad went on.

'All this week you've seen me praying for Tamara. I've also been praying for a storm because - what usually follows a storm?'

'A rainbow,' both boys answered.

'Precisely - if a rainbow allowed him to come here, then presumably it can send him home too.'

Both boys stared at Grandad, suddenly speechless. With all this upset about Tamara, they'd forgotten about the fantastic circumstances surrounding Storm's arrival and Grandad's insistence that he be sent back as soon as possible.

'Trouble is, I think the energy that came out of him and went into Peter, left him very weak and vulnerable. I fear that if he stays with us much longer, he may be unable to return home at all. He could turn irreversibly mortal, in which case he will die with unspeakable consequences. You see, I don't think he's supposed to be here at all; I think he is here by some accident.'

'You mean - it's my fault he's dying?' Peter cried, deeply distressed. 'Because healing me drained his power?'

'Oh no, of course not, Peter. He would have got slowly weaker anyway. Because of where he's from, that power was a special magical energy. He's so young and tiny that he only has a very small amount of power in his horn. I suspect that the longer he stays earthbound, the weaker it will become and the higher the risk of his losing it altogether.'

'Does this mean that he hasn't got enough power to heal Tamara?' Joel asked hesitantly.

'I'm afraid so, Joel, I don't think he could heal a pimple at the moment.' Grandad shrugged.

'Oh if only he hadn't healed me!' Peter cried. 'I'd gladly have my callipers back, if only he had enough power to heal Tamara.'

'You weren't seriously thinking of taking him to the hospital, were you?' Grandad raised his eyebrows at the boys, who both looked down guiltily.

'Had you thought about how you were going to get him past the Doctors and Nurses?' Grandad shook his head. 'They wouldn't allow it. And I'm not sure it would be the right thing to do anyway.'

Joel and Peter looked at each other, mortified. They were banking on smuggling Storm into the hospital to Tamara. Now, their one hope of saving her had gone. Peter suddenly stood up with tears welling in his eyes.

'It's my fault! Tamara might die and it's my fault! If Storm hadn't healed me, he might have had enough power left to heal her - it should be me in that hospital! Why can't it be me?'

'Of course it's not your fault, Peter.' Grandad tried to explain. 'You mustn't blame yourself; it's nothing you did. Tamara had an accident. That's what it was - an accident.'

'I'll never forgive myself if she dies!' cried Peter running out of the house, distraught.

Joel got up from the kitchen table.

'I'd better go after him, Grandad, I've never seem him so upset,' he said sadly. 'I think I know where he'll be.'

Grandad nodded, too upset to speak.

CHAPTER FIVE

Fire and Brimstone

Leaning into the wind which was growing stronger by the minute, Joel shivered a little and pulled his coat round him as he walked over the field to Zionica. The sky was getting darker as the temperature dropped. He climbed up the tree to the den and sure enough Peter was sitting there, staring glumly at his feet. Joel sat down next to him.

'You O.K. Peter?' Joel muttered.

'Yeah, I guess,' Peter said awkwardly, without looking up. Then after a pause he went on. 'I've let all the tadpoles go - the wind was blowing the jars about.'

Joel nodded.

'Grandad is right, you know, Peter,' he said quietly. 'You can't blame yourself - any more than I could blame myself for not running fast enough to catch up with her. She'd tell you off big-style if she could see you now. What do you think she'd say?'

'Oh probably, *"Holy misery, Peter - pull yourself together, you're so bla de bla de bla."*'

'Hey, you've got that right, pal, that's exactly what she'd say.'

'What are we gonna do, Joel? We can't just sit here - while she's lying there.'

'There's nothing we can do, Peter. We're utterly powerless. We've no choice but to leave it to the Doctors. Well actually,' Joel went on thoughtfully, 'there is something we could do for her.'

Peter looked up with a glimmer of hope, as Joel continued.

'We could save Storm; that's what she would want us to do. She would want us to get him home so that he didn't die. That's one thing we could do that would make her happy.'

'You're right, Joel.' Peter suddenly cheered up. 'That would make her happy. In fact if she were here now, she'd be driving us batty, talking about nothing else but saving Storm - and you know what?'

'What?'

'If your Grandad's theory is right, we won't have long to wait; his prayers have been answered. There's a heck of a storm building up. Joel...' Peter looked up at the dark sky. 'The heavens are going to open any time now.'

'Well come on! What are we sitting here for?' Joel grabbed hold of the rope and, out of habit, held it still for Peter.

'No, after you. I can leap as well as anyone now, you know.' They exchanged grins, then Joel slid down the rope, Peter slid down after him and they set off at a fast pace.

'Race you!' Peter shouted.

They both felt so much better now they had a plan, something positive to do.

The heavens opened all right and the rain pelted down. By the time Joel and Peter arrived at Grandad's kitchen, they were completely soaked. Grandad seemed to have cheered up too.

'Well we've got our storm, lads,' he said cheerily.

'We know, Grandad, we're drenched. Just tell us what you want us to do.'

'First of all, get out of those wet things, then I'll tell you.'

Ten minutes later the boys were back in the kitchen, warm and dry again.

'Right,' Grandad started. 'Whatever you do today, lads, you must be back before nightfall. One of us has got to be with Storm all through the night until first light, then we take him to Zionica. He'll need feeding every half hour, just a few sips at a time. We need to keep a watch on his breathing, noting any change and keep up the gentle massage and stroking.' Grandad paused and smiled encouragingly. 'As long as we can keep him alive until morning, we should be able to send him back and once he's home - I reckon he'll be as good as new again. Tonight is going to be a test, boys - Good Friday. If Storm survives the night, I think he'll be O.K.'

The Kairos

They looked at Storm, all forlorn and breathing weakly, in his little stable under the stairs, little bandages on his feet. It was almost inconceivable that so much depended on such a tiny, fragile animal.

'O.K. Grandad, we just want to see Tamara for an hour or so and we'll come straight back.'

'All right, but you must eat something first.'

+

Joel and Peter picked at a light lunch, but they weren't really hungry. Joel's Mum telephoned. Grandad said not to worry her with all that was going on; he didn't want her to drive over in a panic. Joel found it a strain just chatting cheerily to her, when he really wanted to blurt everything out. However, he managed to keep the conversation light and cheerful.

When the boys got to the hospital, Tamara looked exactly the same, as if she was just sleeping. All the technology, tubes, pipes and drips were connected and working as before. They told her of their plan for Storm at first light. They talked as though she really could hear them, hoping that maybe, deep down in her subconscious mind, she could. Peter found a frog puppet with a yellow crown on its head amongst all the presents and he talked in a funny voice, pretending it was the puppet speaking.

'Hello, you look just like a sleeping princess, I wonder if a kiss from a prince will wake you up?' Peter put the puppet up to her face in a pretend kiss, but she didn't even stir. 'I guess it's not the same from a frog prince, is it, Tamara?' He said dejectedly.

Tamara's Mother and Father entered the room.

'You boys are such good friends to our Tamara,' Mrs Goodchild praised them. 'I'm sure she would appreciate all this - if she only knew,' she added glumly.

'Oh it's possible she does know, Mrs Goodchild,' said Joel, encouragingly. 'I've heard of people in comas coming round when they hear familiar voices and music. Maybe that'll work with Tamara too.'

'I hope so, dear,' Mrs Goodchild smiled.

Just then, they were interrupted by a Doctor coming into the room.

'Hello, Mr and Mrs Goodchild.'

'Hello, Doctor,' they replied.

'Would you step into my consulting room for a moment. I need to speak with you.'

'Of course,' Mr Goodchild answered, then he and his wife anxiously followed the Doctor.

'I wonder what that was all about?' Peter said curiously.

'They won't tell us anything, we're not family.' Joel shrugged despondently, glancing out of the window. 'We'd better get back now, Peter. What's the weather outlook?'

'Oh don't worry, it's going to bucket down all night; there'll be a fair wind too,' Peter answered, without even looking out of the window.

+

That evening, Joel, Peter and Grandad stayed in the kitchen, playing various board and card games, while the wind and rain raged outside. Grandad lit a fire in the kitchen grate and they took it in turns to tend to Storm.

As dusk descended, Grandad lit a paschal candle and produced a glass bottle of what looked like water. He took the top off and poured some of it into a small silver dish. Then he took a brand new, one-inch paint brush out of a packet.

What are you doing, Grandad? Surely you're not going to start decorating now?' Joel asked, puzzled.

'I got this from the Vicar this morning; it's Holy Water,' Grandad said earnestly. Then he unlatched the back door, stepped outside and painted a large cross on the outside of the door with the Holy Water. Stepping back inside, he locked and bolted the door. He refilled the dish, took it and some clean gauze over to Storm and unravelled the bandages from round

Storm's hooves.

Joel and Peter leaned over to watch Grandad as he delicately dabbed the Holy Water on the tiny wounds on the undersides of Storm's heels. At this point they began to wonder if Grandad was losing his marbles. But their bemused expressions changed to ones of amazement when; as the water touched the stigmata wounds, they instantly shrank.

'Wow! That's awesome! Did you see that, Joel?' Peter said, incredulously.

'Yeah - the holes are healing up!' Joel could hardly believe it either.

Grandad got a clean piece of gauze, dipped it into the water, then lightly sponged Storm round his horn, making the sign of the cross on his forehead.

'Gosh, Mr Jacob, you're really taking this seriously, aren't you?' said Peter.

'Yeah, come on, Grandad - isn't this is a bit over the top?' Joel said sceptically.

Grandad looked gravely at Peter and Joel.

'It is vital that we take these precautions. Do you realise that the future of the human race and indeed the whole world may just rest on our returning this little animal, alive, to where he belongs? Have you any idea of the responsibility that's been inadvertently thrust upon us?'

Both boys looked shocked, as Grandad continued in earnest.

'Peter... Joel...' Grandad went on emphatically. 'We're not just fighting for the life of this little animal. We're fighting for LIFE itself! The very essence - the spark - the spirit - the infinite and eternal energy that IS - all our very souls. This little creature is a symbol that represents Jesus Christ - *"The Light of the World"*- He who came into the world to defeat the one who rules the darkness and imprisons souls in hell. Now do you understand the seriousness of what we have stumbled upon and the task we *have* to do?'

'Yes... I - I think so,' Joel gulped and nodded.

Grandad looked at Peter.

'Yes...' Peter agreed.

'The devil will be out looking for Storm tonight; he will leave no stone unturned. He may or may not have discovered the whereabouts of Storm, through Presten. We don't know as yet whether Presten has been touched by the devil, or if he's just a mischievous lad. The devil works in darkness: he won't see the Holy Water cross on our door; neither will he be able to see past it, or enter through it. We're safe - as long as we don't let him in.'

'Well we wouldn't be that stupid, Grandad.'

'Don't underestimate the devil, Joel; he's a trickster. Don't expect him to come knocking at the door saying, *"please let me in, I'm the devil."* He is a master of deception. We could unknowingly let him in - he has powers and disguises you wouldn't even dream of. It's best to be vigilant and, whatever happens, that door *must* stay locked and bolted until sunrise.'

The two boys looked at Grandad, struggling to take it all in. They'd been bombarded with so much fantastic information and witnessed such strange events: that their minds were reeling dizzily, like ferris wheels.

Neither Grandad nor the boys wanted to go to sleep or even to bed. They were far too anxious and the old rule, safety in numbers, seemed the best strategy. So they all stayed up, keeping watchful eyes on Storm. They repeated the bathing with Holy water every so often, till the holes in Storm's heels were minuscule.

After some time, Peter looked up from the game they were playing and nodded towards Storm.

'You know, he definitely looks brighter. What do you think, Mr Jacob?'

Grandad glanced at Storm.

'Peter, you're right, his eyes look wider and brighter and his breathing seems easier. What time is it?'

'Quarter past eleven,' Peter replied, with a slight yawn.

'We must stay vigilant;' Grandad went on, 'there's time for mischief yet.' Before he had finished speaking, a chill swept over them, making them shiver, and the paschal candle flickered.

'Brr, that was a chilly draught. Joel shivered.

Grandad got up and poked the fire, putting more coal on it.

'What's that scratching?' Peter said, shuddering nervously.

They all listened and heard the scratching coming from the back door, then they heard a meow.

'Oh it's only Martha,' Joel laughed and stood up.

'Sit down, Joel,' Grandad ordered.

'What? - Surely we can let Martha in out of the rain?'

'We don't know that it is Martha. I said sit down. If it is she can find a sheltered spot in the barn to get out of the rain.'

'All right.' Joel shrugged and sat down.

They carried on with their game. The scratching stopped and the meow faded and went away.

'Great! The last station. I'll buy it!' Joel said, with a smug grin. 'Now I own all the stations. You'd better watch out if you land on my property - you'll pay a massive fine now.' Joel got his fake money ready to pay for the station and Grandad, who was acting as banker, got out the card. An eerie chill seemed to brush over them again and they all shuddered. Then they were suddenly startled by an unexpected knock at the door.

'Who could that be?' Joel looked at Grandad.

'Either of you two expecting anyone?' Grandad asked.

The two boys shook their heads.

'Then we just ignore it. Your throw, Peter.' Grandad calmly swapped the station card for Joel's money.

The knocking came again, then there was the sound of a familiar voice shouting.

'Hey, open the door, let me in.'

This made them all jump and they were suddenly ice-cold and felt little prickles starting to creep up the backs of their necks. The candle flickered again and this time it went out.

'It's Mum!' Joel gasped in astonishment. 'Grandad, Mum is here! She must have been driving all night!' Joel jumped up to answer the back door.

Grandad leapt from his chair and grabbed Joel's arm.

'Ignore it, Joel.'

'For goodness' sake, Grandad - you're going too far! That's Mum out there and I'm going to let her in!' Joel struggled.

'No!' Grandad shouted firmly.

'Hey, come on guys, it's cold and wet out here - open up!' the voice pleaded again.

'Grandad, please!' Joel begged. 'We've got to let her in.'

'Didn't you speak to Mum at lunchtime?' Grandad shouted.

'Yes, but...' Joel started.

'Didn't we tell her everything was all right?'

'Yes...'

'Joel - I can't explain what that is out there, but I know it's not your Mum,' Grandad said firmly. 'If you don't believe me, pick up the phone and ring her now.'

Joel's eyes filled slightly. 'Don't be daft, Grandad - she's outside. Please open the door!' he begged. He began to fear that Grandad really was losing his marbles.

'I said pick up the phone and call her - NOW!'

Joel went reluctantly to the hall, picked up the phone and dialled his home number; it rang three times.

'Grandad, what's the point in ringing her at home, when she's out there on the doorstep getting drenched? I don't care what you say. I'm letting her...' Joel suddenly froze as Mum's voice came sleepily down the telephone.

'Hello...'

Joel's patronising expression dissolved into one of sheer horror.

'Mum?' Joel gasped as he almost dropped the phone. 'Is that you?'

'Joel - it's almost midnight - is there a problem?' came Mum's concerned voice.

'N - no, Mum - I'm sorry I woke you - I just wanted to say goodnight - and I love you, Mum.'

'I love you too, Joel and I'm sorry I can't be with you over Easter. This project has me tied up all week. I'll see you next weekend - goodnight, love.'

'Goodnight, Mum.' Joel replaced the receiver. An icy feeling came over him, chilling him to his very soul.

'Joel, you've gone all white - like a ghost,' Peter said nervously.

'If that was Mum on the phone at home - then who..?'

'Whoever - whatever is gone,' Grandad said, calmly lighting the candle again. 'It was probably just the wind. Let's continue our game, shall we? Come and sit down, Joel.'

'Right...' Joel's wobbly legs somehow managed to get him back to the table and he shakily sat down again.

'Come on, Joel, it's your go,' Grandad urged, trying to take the boys' minds off the scariness of what had just happened.

They carried on with the game, but Joel's heart wasn't in it. After making an effort, he sat back in his chair.

'I'm sorry, Grandad, I can't get into this right now. Can we have a break?'

'O.K. I guess it's about time to do Storm again. You get the bottle of milk and I'll do his feet,' Grandad said.

Suddenly there was a loud BANG! as if a cannon-ball had been shot at the back door, and the whole door shook. The three of them jumped out of their chairs and nearly out of their skins. Rodney fled upstairs, yelping in fear.

'What the heck was that?' Peter cried.

'Well I don't think it was the wind,' Joel said shakily.

'Why didn't I send you two to Peter's? What was I thinking of, letting you stay here tonight?' Grandad cursed.

'We wouldn't have gone, that's why,' Joel answered bravely.

BANG! There it went again. Then whatever it was started hammering on the door, hammering and banging. The door started vibrating noisily like a hammer drill, as though it would fall off its hinges at any moment.

'Grandad - we're under attack! What are we going to do?'

'Don't panic, it can't get in unless we let it.'

'It?' Peter shrieked. 'What do you mean - it? What is it?'

The banging stopped and there was another eerie silence, like the calm before a storm when you know something is about to erupt, but this was something else - something creepy seemed

FIRE AND BRIMSTONE

to be hanging in the air - a menacing feeling of lurking evil. They waited, too scared to speak, then - WHOOSH! - the wind seemed to gust right down the chimney, making the fire flare. The candle went out again and despite the raging, roaring fire, a chill once again brushed over the three of them, making the hairs stand up on the backs of their necks. Then the fire died down again.

'Grandad, what's happening?' Joel shrieked.

Grandad struck a match and re-lit the candle.

'Come on, Joel,' he urged, trying to stay calm. 'Let's get on with Storm, shall we? Peter, sit down - and try to calm down, both of you. Everything is going to be all right.'

Peter hesitantly sat down at the table, while Joel and Grandad crouched down to tend to Storm. Peter was as white as a sheet and shaking all over; he sat staring into the fire. As he watched the glowing embers, the flames danced hypnotically before him; his tired eyes seemed to dance with the flames and his mind drifted into a daze. He felt light-headed, as the flames seemed to grow and dance more and more wildly, drawing him nearer.

The wind again started to gust fiercely down the chimney, making the fire flare and roar; it sounded like an angry wild beast, trying to break out of a cage. The cards and fake money were blown up into the air and scattered around the room and the candle went out yet again. Joel jumped up, panic stricken.

'Grandad, you've got to do something!' he cried in fear.

The flames of the fire were growing unnaturally long. They seemed to be reaching out into the room like hideous snakes, hissing, their forked tongues protruding further and further, spitting out burning-hot coals.

Peter stood up and started moving very slowly towards the fire, a trance-like expression on his face.

'Peter!' Grandad shouted.

Peter ignored Grandad, as though he didn't even hear him. He just carried on slowly walking towards the fire. Then the snake-like flames seemed to take on the appearance of a huge red dragon with two heads, gnashing its fierce jaws. It appeared to engulf half the room and the monstrous vision looked as if it was about to consume them.

'It's getting its power from Peter!' Grandad shouted.

'How?' Joel cried frantically.

'I - I don't know,' Grandad cursed in frustration.

'Peter!' Joel shouted. 'Peter - come away from the fire - turn away - Peter!'

Joel tried to get near Peter, but the flames wouldn't let him. They seemed to be separating them, drawing Peter nearer and nearer.

'Quick!' Grandad pulled Joel to the stair alcove where Storm was bedded down. 'Hold my hand and make a triangle with the alcove, in front of Storm. This represents the eternal trinity - the Father, Son and Holy Spirit, pointing towards Heaven. It will affirm our allegiance to God and further strengthen us.'

They stood firm in the triangle, clinging onto the stair rails, while it seemed that all the bowels of hell raged around them.

'PETER! PETER!' Joel screamed, hanging onto Grandad and the stair rails. 'Grandad - what are we going to do?'

'Peter, don't look into the fire - turn round!' Grandad yelled. 'Peter! For God's sake turn away!' He closed his eyes and started to pray loud and fast. 'O Lord Jesus Christ, Lamb of God, that takes away the sins of the world, have mercy on us. O Christ, with the Holy Spirit, who art most high in the glory of God the Father - help us!'

Suddenly Grandad opened his eyes like a light switch clicking on.

'CHIMNEY! How could I forget that?' he shouted. 'I put the Holy Water on the door, but forgot about the chimney! Joel, he's getting in through the chimney and he's feeding on the fire!'

Joel looked at the bottle of Holy Water, sitting out of reach on the draining board. Then all of a sudden he let go of Grandad's hand, leapt across the room and snatched up the bottle. He turned and hurled it at the fireplace as if he was scoring for the rugby world cup. The bottle exploded like a Molotov cocktail, smashing to smithereens in the fire grate; the Holy Water splashed up the chimney and everywhere. There was a horrible piercing screech, like that of an injured wild animal; it sounded so hideously evil, it chilled them to the depths of their souls. Instantly, the flames and coals were sucked back into the fireplace, as if drawn by a powerful vacuum. Then the fire died down to a small glow and everything miraculously returned to normal and was by contrast incredibly still.

Peter collapsed in a heap on the hearth rug. Joel and Grandad rushed over and knelt down beside him. Joel lifted Peter's shoulders and tried to rouse his unconscious friend.

'Peter, are you all right?' Joel cried.

Peter opened his eyes and looked up at Joel and Grandad.

'It was the weirdest thing. I was being drawn towards the fire. I knew it would be utter doom, but I - I couldn't stop myself - it was like I wasn't in control of my own actions,' Peter said, still a little dazed. 'How is Storm?'

'Storm!' Grandad cried.

They all looked towards the alcove under the stairs. Grandad rushed over to Storm and checked the little Unicorn.

'The holes have completely disappeared!'

Storm looked up with big bright-blue eyes and blinked.

'Well hello, little fella,' Grandad smiled.

Then, for the first time, Storm began to stir.

'Look - he's trying to stand up - Peter, I think he's going to be O.K.' Joel sighed with relief.

Then with one big heave the little Unicorn struggled up onto his feet, but he had grown to about twice the size he was before. His white coat seemed to have taken on a kind of iridescent sheen. Then, to the astonishment of the three of them, Storm's horn suddenly sprouted to about four inches long and began to sparkle like crystal shimmering in sunlight.

The candle suddenly flickered, then burst into a brightly burning flame. They all wiped their brows and sighed, relieved that the nightmare appeared to be over.

Then Grandad and the two exhausted boys heard Cedric crow. It was Saturday morning, the start of a new day. The three of them looked at each other with relieved smiles.

The Kairos

'Phew, I never thought I would be so happy to hear Cedric crowing at 6 a.m.' said Joel, whose legs felt like very wobbly jelly. 'This has been the longest night of my life!'

Grandad went to the window and peered outside. The first fingers of light were stretching up from the east, fanning out over the sky. The rain had stopped and the wind had dropped to a gentle breeze. Joel and Peter joined Grandad at the window and they all gratefully watched the miracle birth of a brand new day.

'Thank God for a new dawn,' said Grandad, putting a hand on each boy's shoulders. 'A new dawn and new hope - hey, lads?'

The two boys looked up at Grandad and smiled in agreement. Then they heard a weak little bark and looked round. Rodney was crouching halfway down the stairs, peering down at them, no doubt wondering if it was safe to come down.

'Some guard dog you are, Rodney!' Joel mocked.

'Yes, you can come down, now the action has finished,' Grandad chortled.

They all laughed as Rodney ran down wagging his tail.

CHAPTER SIX

Two Dispatched Heavenwards

Ludicrous as it seemed, compared with the previous night's adventures, sending a baby Unicorn back to Heaven ranked as "par for the course." So the two boys went along with Grandad's instructions without any notion of anything being odd at all. They wrapped up against the chilly weather, while Grandad wrapped a woollen blanket round Storm.

'We mustn't lose any time, boys,' Grandad urged. 'So much depends on the success of what we are about to do and the window of opportunity will be brief. One of us should carry Storm; he's obviously feeling better and we don't want him frisking off for a little play in the field. I suspect that's how he ended up here in the first place - scampering into places he shouldn't.'

'I'll carry him, Grandad,' Joel volunteered, picking up the baby Unicorn all snuggled up in the blanket.

Although he'd grown to nearly twice his previous size, Storm was still light enough for a fit and strong, twelve-year-old rugby captain to carry.

'I wish Tamara could be here to see him,' said Peter.

'Don't worry, Peter, we'll tell her exactly how cute he looked, won't we, Grandad?' Joel raised an eyebrow comically.

'We can show her,' Grandad grinned, pointing a camera at the two boys with Storm and taking a snapshot.

+

As the three of them reached the brow of the hill on the fringe of Zionica, the sun was shedding its new light over all the land. They stopped for a moment, then gasped as they watched the most fantastic rainbow materialise before their eyes. It spanned the whole sky in a huge arc, with Zionica at its centre. Just as before, the light was so bright and powerful it shone all the way down to the earth and encompassed them in the dome of its warm glow. It was the most wonderful experience ever. Then a second fantastic thing happened. As they watched, a beautiful, full-grown Unicorn appeared at the centre of the plateau. He stood there in the light, head and tail held majestically high. Although he was pure white, the rainbow seemed to reflect off him, shimmering like a prism from a crystal. With power and grace he reared up and then stood proud, the soft breeze ruffling his mane against his steely neck.

Grandad caught his breath, he was clearly shocked. Then pulling himself together, he shakily urged Joel with a whisper.

'Go on, Joel, he's waiting for Storm.'

Joel stepped forward and carried the baby Unicorn over to the plateau. He placed the baby within a few feet of the magnificent Unicorn, removed the blanket and stood back. The large Unicorn walked forward and bowed his head to nuzzle the baby, then Storm reached up to nuzzle him back. As the two muzzles met, a piercingly bright light shot upwards and the pair seemed to vanish up into it instantly. The rainbow glowed warmly for a few seconds, then it too vanished.

Grandad and Peter walked down to the plateau as Joel turned excitedly to them.

'You both saw that - didn't you? It wasn't a dream, you saw it too?' Joel cried.

'It was the most awesome sight ever!' Peter shrilled.

Dazed, Grandad turned and silently headed back to the cottage.

+

Over breakfast, the boys talked excitedly about what had just happened.

'No one must hear about any of this, boys,' Grandad warned. 'We should keep it a secret; you must both promise me.'

'Of course,' they both nodded.

'Heaven knows, we'd have all manner of reporters and TV crews, to say nothing of businessmen looking to exploit the area. Zionica would lose its magic and be spoilt for ever. You must never speak of it outside us three. You understand, don't you, boys?' Grandad implored.

'We certainly do, Grandad. We would become a circus act with Peter the centre of a freak-fest - after his *miracle healing*,' Joel said dryly.

'Yeah - for sure no one will hear it from my lips, Mr Jacob; you don't need to worry about that,' Peter said emphatically. 'Except perhaps - could we - I mean, would it be all right to..?'

'I think Peter means Tamara, Grandad. You know we've been talking to her while she's been in a coma. We've told her everything about Storm. Can we tell her he's home, safely?'

'I can't see a problem with that, lads. As long as you make sure nobody else is listening, you can tell her.' Grandad smiled.

'Hey, you know the adult Unicorn that came for Storm?' Joel said curiously. 'His horn was all jagged at the end. I'd expected it to be smooth, round and pointed, like you see in pictures of Unicorns.'

'It was probably a trick of the light, Joel,' Grandad said, mysteriously averting his eyes.

'No, Grandad, I was so close I could almost touch him. It looked like the end had broken off.'

'Maybe he broke it in a fierce battle for the herd,' Peter dramatised.

Grandad stood up.

'Oh my hat! Look at the time. I've not fed the animals yet. Why don't you two give me a hand to feed them and then you can get off to the hospital to see Tamara?'

'Sure thing, Mr Jacob.' Peter jumped up. 'Come on, Joel, I can't wait to tell Tamara about this morning.'

They rushed round the yard feeding Grandad's animals, which were all impatient and irritable at being kept waiting for breakfast. They were usually fed at first light, so there were a few protesting bleats and some impatient pushing and shoving as the animals dived greedily into the troughs. Joel had his foot stamped on by one particularly irate and rather heavy sheep. Cedric was even grumpier than usual - if that was possible. By the time the boys got to Cherokee in the barn, Grandad had already fed her. Then the boys moaned as he told them they could muck out her stable.

'I wonder if we ought to ride her,' Peter suggested. 'You know, keep the cogs oiled so she's not too wild when Tamara is better. We don't want Tamara to be thrown and end up back in hospital again, do we?'

'Have you gone completely mad, Peter?' Joel looked at him as though he had suddenly grown another head. 'You never learned to ride because of your callipers and there's no way I'm going to ride it - there's more chance of my entering a beauty contest! And there's less than zero chance of that!'

'How bad can she be? She's only a small pony.' Peter laughed. 'It might be fun.'

Joel gave Peter a tongue-in-cheek look.

'So - we'll let her into the paddock again then?' Peter conceded.

'Correction - YOU can let it into the paddock. Compare me to Presten if you must, but I ain't going near it. I'll muck out the stable.'

Peter led the pony outside, then returned to help Joel.

'The things we do for mates!' Joel cursed, heaping manure from Cherokee's stable onto a wheelbarrow.

'I'm sure Tamara would do the same for us,' Peter replied.

'Oh yes, what a picture, Tamara painstakingly rubbing linseed oil on my cricket bat - or cleaning mud off my rugby boots.' Joel raised an eyebrow at Peter, then picked up the full wheelbarrow and wheeled it outside to tip on the muck heap, while Peter followed with a grin.

'You know, Joel,' said Peter pulling a face as his feet squelched into the waterlogged mixture of mud and manure at the bottom of the midden, 'I think we should have made Presten do this.'

'Maybe, Peter, but personally I'd rather muck out fifty stables myself than have that goon around us.'

'Yeah, I guess you're right.' Peter said with a shrug. 'At least we're doing something for Tamara. I still feel terribly guilty that I took away all Storm's power.'

'You know what Grandad said about how Storm wouldn't have had enough power by now anyway. We've got to have faith in the Doctors, Peter. She'll come round.'

'Do you really think so?' Peter bit his lip anxiously.

'Yeah, I do, especially with all the prayers Grandad is saying. I bet in a few days the three of us will be sitting in the den in Zionica, stuffing ourselves with Easter eggs.'

'I hope so, Joel.'

'Hey, come on, cheer up. Let's go and get cleaned up; we can't visit Tamara reeking of manure. Then again - the smell might be enough to wake her up!' Joel chuckled.

+

Twenty minutes later the two boys were both spick and span and saying goodbye to Grandad. They walked the hundred yards down the lane to the bus stop, to wait for the next bus to take them to the hospital.

When Joel and Peter arrived at the hospital and entered Tamara's room, Mr and Mrs Goodchild were sitting at her bedside, looking more distraught than ever. Mrs Goodchild was sobbing; Mr Goodchild was holding her hand.

'What is it? What's wrong?' Joel asked, anxiously. Mrs Goodchild stood up and fled from the room in tears. Mr Goodchild glanced sorrowfully at the boys, then hurriedly followed his wife. Peter and Joel rushed over to Tamara.

'She's still breathing.' Peter inspected the equipment. 'Everything is still connected and working - what could be wrong?' He flopped down on a chair, frowning.

'I wish I knew, Peter,' Joel sighed with frustration. 'It's not fair; friends care about people as much as family. Why won't they tell us what's going on?'

Just then the Doctor entered the room.

'Hello - Joel and Peter, isn't it?'

'Yes, Doctor,' Joel replied. 'Why are Tamara's parents so upset? What's wrong, Doctor?'

'I'm afraid it's not good news, boys. All our tests are complete now and we cannot ascertain that there is sufficient brain activity to indicate that Tamara will recover.'

'What do you mean "sufficient brain activity"?' Joel asked, suddenly panicking. 'Surely, if there's any brain function at all - she's still alive, isn't she?'

'Yes, Doctor - she's still breathing - her heart is still beating.' Peter pleaded: 'She's just asleep, isn't she?'

'Yes, she is still alive and she's breathing because this equipment is doing it for her,' the Doctor explained solemnly. 'Her vital functions would not be sustained without the equipment. Soon her internal organs will start to shut down - before long they will cease to function completely. I'm afraid there's nothing more we can do.' The Doctor went on in a low voice. 'In this sort of situation, it's kinder to switch off the machine and let nature take its course. We've got to let her go, boys.'

'Let her go?' Peter cried desperately. 'No! We can't let her die - she's only ten, Doctor - it's her eleventh birthday in a few weeks. Please, there must be something you can do?'

While Peter pleaded with the Doctor, Joel just stared, too numb with shock to speak. Then the Doctor continued.

'Believe me, boys, we've done everything humanly possible: there's no other option open to us. Mr and Mrs Goodchild wanted me to tell you this because they're too distraught at the moment.'

The Doctor's words seemed to waft over Joel now; he became suddenly dizzy and wasn't really hearing him at all. In fact he didn't even feel as if he was still in the room, but as if he was somehow outside looking in - like in a dream.

'There's going to be a short service of blessing here

TWO DISPATCHED HEAVENWARDS

tomorrow,' the Doctor went on. 'As it's Easter Sunday and there's a Church service in the morning, Reverend Matthews will be coming in the afternoon. The blessing will take place at half past two - then the machine will be switched off.'

'Switched off?' Peter exclaimed in disbelief. 'But that's too sudden - we need more time, Doctor!'

'I'm really sorry, boys,' the Doctor said, sympathetically. 'You can stay as long as you want today. The Nurse will be around to answer any questions you may have.' With that, he turned and left them alone with Tamara.

'Switch the machine off? Joel - we can't let them switch it off - we just can't!' Peter turned to Tamara. 'Tamara - we've saved Storm.' Tears welled up in his eyes and trickled slowly down his cheeks as he spoke, willing her to wake-up, to sit up and listen. 'You should have seen it, Tamara. We took Storm to Zionica at dawn this morning and a wonderful rainbow appeared - like the one we saw the other day when Storm arrived, remember? Storm stood up on all four feet, fully recovered. Then the most magnificent adult Unicorn came, he stood tall and proud; the colours of the rainbow sparkled all around him, as if from a crystal. He bent down and as his muzzle touched the young baby Unicorn, a blinding light shot upwards to Heaven and they both disappeared up into the light. It was the most fantastic sight in the whole universe. I wish you could have seen it.'

'What a beautiful story, Peter.' Mrs Goodchild was standing quietly in the doorway, listening.

Peter looked up with a start. In his grief, he'd forgotten his promise to Joel's Grandad, to make sure no one overheard him talking about Storm.

'You know, I'm sure that's exactly what Tamara would imagine Heaven to be like,' Mrs Goodchild went on bravely. 'Thank you so much. You will both come to the blessing tomorrow, won't you - and bring Mr Jacob?'

'Yes, Mrs Goodchild, we'll be here.' Peter sniffed and wiped his cheek with the back of his hand.

Usually, Joel was the spokesperson and Peter the quiet one.

The Kairos

This time though, Joel was numb and speechless with shock. He stared at Tamara, unable to believe what he'd just been told. He felt as if he'd got chewing gum stuffed inside his head.

'Joel - ? Are you all right, Joel?' Mrs Goodchild asked.

Joel slowly looked up at Mrs Goodchild. He had no idea how much of the story she'd heard and right then he didn't care.

'How could God let this happen? After all our prayers?' Joel said weakly. Grandad has almost worn his knees out.'

Suddenly Mr Goodchild swept into the room, his face twisted with rage.

'You can't blame God for this!' his voice almost squeaked as he choked with a mixture of anger and grief. 'This terrible tragedy that has taken our beautiful daughter from us so prematurely was not the result of *divine* action or inaction!' He gave a sardonic half-laugh. 'It's all too easy, isn't it? Oh here we go: another disaster, let's blame God again!' Then his distraught expression became cold as he went on mournfully. 'There's no escaping the fact that this is the result of a naughty boy's prank - killed by her own brother! God gave us all free will: Presten chose to break into your Grandad's house and steal his foal. Had he not done so, Tamara would have been safe inside instead of running out onto the road after him. The culpability lies clearly with Presten.'

Joel gasped, he was speechless with shock. Much as he disliked Presten, he almost found himself feeling sorry for him. Mr Goodchild spoke of him with such cold contempt, as though he hated his own Son and would never forgive him. Joel had enjoyed a close and loving relationship with his own father, whom he missed so much at times it really hurt. The thought of how terrible it would be to have your own father turn against you made him shudder. Presten would be paying for this for the rest of his life; the resulting bitterness could turn him irreversibly more evil than ever. Without his parents' love and support, Presten was a lost cause - beyond salvation.

Suddenly Joel blinked. What was the *matter* with him? He couldn't believe he was standing there with all these thoughts

TWO DISPATCHED HEAVENWARDS

racing through his head - above all, of Presten! - when he'd just been told one of his best friends was going to die, and it was Presten's fault. Surely he should be cursing Presten?

The boys didn't stay at the hospital much longer. They felt it would be more sensitive to leave Tamara's parents alone with her. Tamara looked so peaceful lying there; she still looked as if she was just asleep and would wake up at any moment. It was hard to believe that they would never see her again after tomorrow. Never again would they see her curiously raised eyebrows over her china-blue eyes, or her fun-loving smile, or hear her stylish, cheeky banter.

+

The two boys sat in silence on the bus home. Three times now in his twelve short years, Joel had been forced to deal with the loss of someone close. First Grandma, then Dad, now Tamara. He sat wondering to himself, who would be next?

Peter was the first to break the silence.

'We should have kept Storm for a bit longer.'

'Hey?' Joel snapped out of his private thoughts.

'He was getting better - stronger. If we'd kept him for a few more days, he might have been strong enough to heal Tamara.'

'Sssh,' Joel whispered. 'Keep your voice down. Peter, you're wrong, you know what Grandad said: the longer he stayed, the more danger he was in. Don't you remember, he would have become mortal and died with unspeakable consequences? He wouldn't have been able to heal Tamara anyway. What healed you was his magical, heavenly power, which became depleted. Had he become mortal, his horn would just have had healing properties, as opposed to magical power. We would have had to kill him to grind it up and make it into some sort of potion for her to - *swallow*. For that she would have had to be - *awake*. And even if it had worked, which it probably wouldn't have, she would never have forgiven you for killing him.'

The bus pulled up at the stop before theirs, by the village

Church. Joel looked out of the window, then quickly stood up.

'Come on, we're getting off here.'

Peter followed him dejectedly off the bus.

'Why are we getting off here? Ours is the next stop.'

'Because, Peter, I have a question for the Vicar.'

Joel strode up to the huge, heavy wooden door of the old country Church. The door creaked spookily as he pushed it open. They were conscious of their footsteps, which echoed loudly as they entered and crossed the stone-flagged floor. Then slowly and silently they walked up the carpeted aisle. Matthews must have heard them come in, as he came straight out of the vestry to greet them.

'Hello, Joel; hello, Peter,' Matthews said cheerily. 'How nice to see you. What can I do for you?'

'I've got a question, Vicar,' said Joel quickly. 'I want to know why Tamara has to die. Why hasn't God answered any of our prayers - especially as Grandad's knees must be worn to the bone by now? Why did God let this happen, Reverend Matthews? What has Tamara done to deserve this?'

'Phew - cut straight to the quick don't you, Joel?' Matthews remarked with concern. 'Now then, you'd better come and sit down, boys, this may take a while.'

The three of them sat in the choir pews in the chancel and Matthews paused momentarily to collect his thoughts.

'It's a terribly sad thing - to lose someone, especially someone so young and vibrant, with everything to live for, like our lovely Tamara,' Matthews began. 'I'll try to give you some words of comfort.'

'We don't want words of comfort, Vicar,' Joel said, a little impatiently. 'We want answers!'

'Yes, I can see how upset you are, Joel, quite understandably. You three are very close, aren't you?'

The boys nodded.

'You know, before He sent His Son, Jesus, to redeem man for their sins, sending a goat out into the desert to dump guilt on was God's way for people to be absolved of their sins, and so be accepted back into the fold, hence the word "scapegoat." It was a kindness. In His mercy, God was saying, "Come on, don't worry, I'll tell you what: let's load this old goat with everything you've done wrong and pack it off into the desert where it will be buried and forgotten, then you can begin again with a brand new slate." Matthews sighed and shook his head. 'How many times has God Himself been used as that scapegoat? God gets blamed when people don't understand something. They can't come up with a rational explanation, therefore it must be God's fault - He *let* it happen. It's all so convenient to blame God, isn't it?'

Joel shrugged and Peter screwed up his face in a confused frown.

'Let me ask you,' Matthews carried on, 'when you ask your parents for something, how often is the answer a clear and immediate, "yes"? Or is sometimes the answer, "perhaps" or, "I'm busy now but maybe later, I'll think about it," or even sometimes the answer is, "no"? They don't always give you exactly what you want every time you ask, even though you know without a doubt they love you. Am I right?'

'Yes, of course, Vicar.' Joel frowned.

'Well it's the same with God, you see. God always answers our prayers, but it's not always the answer we want or expect. Sometimes it's, "not yet", or even for His own reasons it might be, "no". Or He may answer our prayers in a way we hadn't thought of, but it has the same result.'

'You mean if we asked God for a million pounds, for instance, He would probably say, "no", but He might give us the means or tools to earn it ourselves?' Peter suggested.

'Well I suppose that's one way of looking at it, Peter,' Matthews smiled. 'I guess that shows a fair understanding of the principle. Shall we say rather, if we were hungry and asked God for food, He probably wouldn't turn the nearest stone into a loaf of bread. He would provide the means to grow the grain and harvest it, to make the bread.'

'Are you saying then, Vicar, that because God has provided

the Doctors and equipment to make Tamara better - *but she's still going to die* - it means that God is saying, "no" to us?' asked Joel pointedly.

'No, I'm not saying that, however we should be prepared if that's God's decision... But she's not dead yet, is she?'

'Does that mean there's still time for God to send us a miracle and that Tamara will wake up?' Joel persisted.

'I don't want to give you hope that a miracle will happen because then you may be very bitter if it doesn't. But my own view is that where there's life, there's always hope. We must have faith and keep on praying. If we want God to listen to us, we must keep on speaking to Him and not give up. Do you understand, boys?'

'I think so, Vicar. You mean the more we keep on asking God, the more the chances are He will say, "yes"?' Joel said hesitantly.

'In a nutshell, yes. How many times has your persistent asking eventually turned your parents' initial, "maybe" into, "O.K."?' Matthews raised his eyebrows and tilted his head knowingly. 'I think that is the simplest way I can explain a very complex subject. The more we talk to God, the more He listens; He likes us to talk to Him - that's why we pray, but remember, boys, Jesus is the healer. God gave Him the power because He is His Son. That is why He was able to heal the sick and even bring Lazarus back to life.' Matthews paused. 'In order for our prayers to be answered, we need to be forgiven for our sins. Remember, Jesus didn't say to the lame man, "Get up, you can now walk" - He said, *"Get up, your sins are forgiven."* That's a clue Jesus left us. You see, here on earth we're on the reject pile; much as we don't like to hear it, we're all sinners in the sin bin. God sent Jesus down to earth to see if there was anyone that could be saved. He sacrificed Himself on the cross for the forgiveness of our sins. That means He speaks to God on our behalf and God has promised to forgive us, if we believe and trust in Jesus and follow the signposts He left us. So therefore we should ask God through Jesus when we pray.'

'But we've done that, Vicar. Why hasn't God answered our prayers?' Joel persisted.

'Well, Joel, if we do all this and still our prayers don't appear to be answered, then there is most likely only one cause,' said Matthews confidently.

The boys sat up.

'What's that, Vicar?' Joel begged. 'We'll do anything, if God will answer our prayers and make Tamara well again.'

'Yes, anything,' Peter echoed.

'Hmm, as well as saying sorry, we should also forgive others who have hurt us. I mean really forgive and that's more than just saying the words isn't it? The pain of being hurt is difficult to overcome. Some people harbour grudges for years, but that just prevents the healing process that forgiveness nurtures. If we refuse to forgive someone, why should God forgive us? To be forgiven ourselves we have to forgive others, even if we don't think they deserve or want it. This is what being a Christian is - it's the crux of Jesus' teaching. Refusing to forgive is very often the reason why prayer requests are not granted.' Matthews looked kindly at the boys. 'You usually find when you take that courageous step to forgive, that the last obstacle to a prayer being answered is removed.' He continued in a low and sensitive voice. 'Is - is there someone - anyone you know - that you have not forgiven, or are possibly holding some sort of grudge against?' Joel and Peter both looked down awkwardly.

'I see.' Matthews smiled kindly. 'For your prayers to have the best chance of being heard, you must forgive this person in your heart. Judgement is not ours, is it? Believe me, boys, God's judgement is infinitely more powerful and wise than anything on earth.'

'But Presten is a dickhe..!' Joel started to rant but stopped just in time.

Matthews raised an eyebrow at Joel's inappropriate outburst.

'Remember you're in God's house, Joel. You were going to say - he's a...' Matthews nodded encouragingly. 'He's a dickensian sort of person with old-fashioned values on civilised humanity?'

'That's right, Vicar.' Joel nodded slowly. 'That's exactly what I meant to say - near enough.'

'Good, now you need to answer this question, boys: which is the stronger feeling, your love and concern for Tamara, or your - shall we say - disapproval of this other person?'

Joel and Peter knew he was right on both counts. He was right that they did hold a grudge and he was right that it would be very hard to forgive Presten. But their concern for Tamara was stronger than whatever they felt for Presten and they desperately wanted a miracle.

'You know, boys,' Matthews went on, 'Jesus said that when two or more people pray together in His name, there He will be. Why don't we do that now - together?' Matthews smiled. The boys nodded and smiled up at him.

+

Matthews saw them out of the Church after the prayer.

'I'm proud of you two boys. Be assured your mail has been dispatched Heavenwards. Just don't expect instant results. The Boss has His own agenda; you need to give it time.'

'Time is the one thing we don't have, Vicar - as you know they switch the machine off tomorrow.' Joel said despondently.

'Yes, I'll be there. You'll both be coming to the blessing, won't you?'

They both nodded.

'Give my regards to your Grandad, Joel. I know he's terribly upset about this dreadful business and we mustn't let him blame himself.'

'Yes, Vicar.' Joel smiled up at Matthews.

CHAPTER SEVEN

A Holy Reunion

One of the hardest things Joel would ever have to do was to tell Grandad the grim news about Tamara. He wanted to put off this unpleasant task for as long as possible, so instead of going straight back to Grandad's cottage, he and Peter slipped past the gate and made their way up to Zionica. This would give them a chance to discuss everything on their own, which they both felt the need to do.

When they climbed up to the den it was quiet and still and relatively warm, in contrast to all the inclement weather they'd been having lately. There was plenty of food in the rucksack they'd taken to the hospital and even if that had run out, there was an abundance of nosh in the den's store. However, despite the adequate 'booty', they didn't feel much like eating at all and just picked at biscuits and crisps.

'I'm sorry about Tamara's Mum hearing me telling Tamara about, you know, Storm and everything,' Peter said, as he bit into a ginger nut, 'especially after I promised your Grandad no one would hear me. I wonder how much of it she heard.'

'Oh I shouldn't worry about that, Peter. I'm sure Mrs Goodchild thought you were making it all up for Tamara - I mean, she would, wouldn't she? Nobody else heard and even if they did, it sounded much too far-fetched for anyone to believe you were describing something that had actually happened.' Joel tipped the last crumbs from a crisp packet into his mouth, blew the empty bag up like a balloon and popped it loudly with a clap of his hands.

'Mr Goodchild gave you a right roasting, didn't he? Were you scared?' Peter asked.

'No, not really. He wasn't angry at me, he was just upset. Anyway what he said was right - people do blame God for things that go wrong.'

Peter nodded.

'Strangely enough, I felt myself feeling sorry for Presten,' Joel went on.

'Huh?' Peter pulled a disbelieving face.

'Oh I know he's a pain in the butt and we fantasise about throwing him into a vat of pig muck, but the way his Dad spoke about him...' Joel shook his head. 'I don't see my Father now, but I always feel he's with me - watching over me - cheering me on - lifting me up when I'm down. I can't imagine anything worse than being despised by your own Father. I think I'd rather die than lose the love and respect of my Father.'

Peter shuffled a little uncomfortably. He loved his Father too, but he was adopted and he didn't want to talk about it.

'What do you think about the Vicar's explanation?' he quickly changed the subject. 'You seem really cool about it all. Do you believe all that?'

'Well there are only two possibilities aren't there, Peter?' Joel said studiously. 'Either Matthews is a lunatic and it's all a load of codswallop, in which case millions of people have been hoodwinked for centuries. Or, Matthews is right and if that's the case, it's the most staggeringly important thing I've heard in the whole world. Matthews said we had to have faith, he said there was time yet - and don't forget *he's* the one doing the blessing tomorrow!' Joel went on earnestly, 'Peter, Matthews doesn't strike me as a lunatic. So if he still thinks there's a chance...'

Peter looked at Joel realising the seriousness of what he had just said. Joel continued.

'I've *got* to believe that he's right, because what's the alternative? If Matthews is wrong and it's all a load of codswallop, then all hope has gone, hasn't it? There's nothing to hang on to and Tamara will die. But if he's right - we've still got a chance! So I'm with Matthews. How about you? Did you forgive Presten in the prayer?'

'I did.' Peter pulled a woeful face. 'It was really hard, but as soon as I realised that caring for Tamara was infinitely more important than my dislike of Presten, I was able to do it. You?'

'Yeah, ditto.' Joel gave a little laugh. 'The things you do for mates! She'd be falling over laughing, watching us two wouldn't she?'

'Yeah, especially you on the muck heap this morning,' Peter chuckled. 'Joel...' Peter suddenly became serious. 'Do you think we should go and tell your Grandad about Tamara? He has a right to know.'

'Yeah.' Joel nodded with a heavy sigh. 'I must admit I've been trying to put it off - O.K. come on.'

+

With heavy hearts, the two of them crept into Grandad's cottage. Grandad was sitting in his rocking chair by the fire in the lounge; he was very upset indeed. Although it was only just after five o'clock, he already had a brandy and benedictine in his hand and he seemed a little woozy. Mr Goodchild had telephoned earlier and given him the bad news about Tamara.

Joel felt guilty about his feeling of relief; he hadn't wanted to tell Grandad at all. Now at least he had been spared the grim duty of breaking the devastating news to him.

'I've succumbed to my weakness, lads,' Grandad muttered, tilting his glass.

'It's O.K. to have a drink, Grandad, if it makes you feel better - it's not as if you do it all the time, is it?' Joel said sympathetically.

'I just want to have a quiet read of my Bible now, Joel.' Grandad sniffed and buried his head in his Bible - mainly so the boys wouldn't see that his eyes were a touch moist. 'Why don't you two go upstairs and clean up for tea?'

+

It was now Easter eve and the night dragged on interminably. Joel tossed and turned and hardly slept at all. He just wanted the night to be over so they could get back to the hospital. By morning, surely everything *must* be all right, after the Vicar's "Heavenwards dispatch", as Matthews had called it.

On Easter morning they were all up before dawn (or before Cedric). Grandad held a dawn vigil on the plateau in Zionica (this was normal Easter Sunday routine for Grandad). Joel and Peter fed all the animals, while Grandad cooked a breakfast, which they were all too upset to eat.

Easter Sunday meant a special service in Church, but they persuaded Grandad to take them to the hospital early, before the service. They all piled into Grandad's old Jeep and set off. It was sunny for a change. Joel thought that was a good sign and this seemed to boost their hopes and cheer them up.

On arriving at the hospital, Joel and Peter rushed inside, each with a large Easter egg for Tamara. Their faces dropped when they saw her. She looked exactly the same; all the life-support equipment was still going: nothing had changed at all. Mrs Goodchild, aided by a Nurse, was brushing Tamara's hair.

'Has she woken up at all yet?' Peter pressed, still hoping for a miracle.

Mrs Goodchild shook her head slowly as she replied.

'I'm afraid not, love; there's no change at all.'

'But how can that be?' Joel cried. 'I was certain she would have woken up by now!'

'We've all been praying for a miracle, boys, but I guess it's not to be,' Mrs Goodchild replied sadly, as Grandad walked into the room.

'I'm so sorry, Mrs Goodchild.' Grandad turned to the boys. 'Come on, boys, let's get to the Church. We'll come back after the service.'

With heavy hearts, they put down the Easter eggs among all the other presents and despondently followed Grandad outside.

There was a special Holy Communion for Easter and Joel and Peter went up to the altar rail with Grandad, to receive the bread and the wine.

'The Body of Christ... feed on Him and remember He died for

A HOLY REUNION

you,' said Reverend Matthews as he offered the bread.

+

They went back to the hospital after Church, in the desperate hope of a miracle - but still there was no change. Mrs Goodchild was trying to decide which dress to put on Tamara for the blessing. Peter and Joel knew Tamara would be horrified that her Mother was going to put her in a frilly dress for her last moments on earth, but they couldn't say anything. It was more than either of them could bear and it was still over two hours till the blessing, so they went back to Grandad's.

Grandad and the two boys felt frustrated and at a loose end. Now Storm had gone they didn't even have him to nurse. There was nothing to do but wait. At lunchtime they made a pretence of eating, pushing bits of food around their plates with their forks.

'I can't eat anything, Grandad - may I be excused?'

'And me, Mr Jacob?' said Peter.

Grandad nodded. He understood, pushing his own plate away too.

'It's nearly one o'clock. Don't go far. We should leave here by two o'clock, boys. We want to get there in good time.'

+

Joel and Peter wandered outside and made their way gloomily up to Zionica. Instead of climbing up to the den they went up to the plateau, where only the previous day they had said goodbye to Storm. It all seemed such a far-off dream now.

They sat on the grass and although the sun was shining through the patchy clouds, a faint sprinkle of rain began to fall.

'That's just great,' Joel muttered. 'Now we come out without our coats and get rained on.'

'It's only a light shower, Joel. Maybe there'll be another rainbow and Storm will come back,' Peter said, with a vague glimmer of hope. 'Do you think if we asked him to come back, he would hear us? I mean, he'll have his magical healing power back now, won't he?' Peter said desperately clutching at straws.

'I don't know. He may have got into trouble for coming here in the first place and who knows what goes on up there. He might even be grounded - in a heavenly way, so to speak.' Joel rubbed his chilly arms and stood up. 'Let's ask him!'

'What?' Peter stared at Joel as if he'd suddenly gone mad.

'Let's shout him, ask him to come back! What have we got to lose?'

'Joel - you're mental!'

'This is the last ditch, Peter - I'll try anything.'

Joel was getting quite wet now; the rain was running down his hair and face as he looked upwards and started shouting.

'Come back! Come back, Storm! We need you - please, please come back!'

Peter stood up and started shouting too.

'We're both mental!' He grinned, then yelled upwards 'Come back! Please, Storm - come back!'

The boys grinned at each other as they carried on shouting their heads off. The rain was soaking the pair of them while they demanded at the tops of their voices that Storm return.

Then all of a sudden, colour exploded from the sky and a bolt of light shot down to the plateau. As if they'd been struck by lightning and before they knew what was happening, everything suddenly went black and they felt they were being pulled at speed through a long tunnel. Then they saw an incredibly bright light. They were heading towards it and there was nothing they could do about it - but they didn't want to do anything. The light was so warm and bright, inviting and wonderful; they just had to reach it. As they got nearer, they could make out vague shapes - of people - then they both passed out.

+

'Joel...' a soft voice spoke.

Joel opened his eyes and looked up. Everywhere was bright,

A HOLY REUNION

warm, golden and glowing. Flashes of colour like crystals in the sunlight gently swept and swirled around, while sparkling lights twinkled like stars in a moonlit sky. He could hear the most beautiful music and soft angelic singing from the sweetest voices - like nothing on earth. He was looking at the face of what could only have been described as an Angel; he just knew that because her smile could have melted an iceberg. His eyes seemed drawn to hers, as if by a powerful magnet. She was completely surrounded by a glowing, sparkling aura of light, which moved with her every time she moved her head or a hand; the light glittered all round her like gold dust.

'You're with us now, are you, Joel?' She laughed. 'My name is Charis.'

Joel couldn't take his eyes off her; he was momentarily speechless, then he heard Peter.

'What's happened? Where are we?' Peter said, slowly.
Joel moved his head and saw that Peter too, had a beautiful angelic being standing over him, smiling.

'Everything is all right, Peter, don't worry,' Peter's Angel said softly. 'My name is Aleathia and I'm here to take care of you.'

Charis took hold of Joel's hand and he felt that he was floating on air as she helped him to stand up. He looked down, still holding the Angel's hand, and was shocked to see that he *was* floating on air. His head was a little above the Angel's.
He looked at Peter and he too had floated up. Joel returned his gaze to Charis and frowned; she laughed again and gently pulled him back down to her level.

'There's no gravity here, Joel; you'll get used to it.'

'Used to it? Are we dead?' Joel panicked.

'I'll take over here, Charis.' A man's voice spoke.

'Oh is there a problem, Nathan?' Charis asked.

'It's family business - and they're both Kairos.'

'Oh my wings!' Charis exclaimed. 'The second in only twenty-three years - and two at once! We'll be catching up with the Morisco zone's record at this rate.'

'That'll take some doing, Charis; they've held the record for five hundred years,' said Aleathia.

'Well we'll leave you to it then. Blessed is He.' Charis beamed a beautiful smile.

'Blessed is He,' Aleathia murmured sweetly.

'Blessed is He,' the man responded. Dressed all in white, he was surrounded by an aura of light like that which enveloped Charis and Aleathia. He bowed his head as the Angels floated away. Then he turned to Joel and Peter and smiled. 'Well now, what have you two got yourselves into?'

Joel's eyes almost popped out of his head as he stared at the man standing in front of him.

'DAD!' Joel exclaimed in utter shock.

The man before him was none other than Nathan Asher, deceased - Joel's Father.

CHAPTER EIGHT

Angelic Hosts

"Verbally challenged" would have been the polite way to describe Joel at that moment, as he stared, wide-eyed and disbelievingly, at his Father. He thought he must be dreaming; how could this be? Dad had died four years ago and yet there he was, large as life!

Nathan Asher smiled at the boys. A soft golden glow ebbed all around him and was so real it seemed tangible.

'Hello, Son.' Nathan beamed, spreading out his arms.

Joel sank softly into his Father's arms, melting in the fabulous glow. He felt he was totally immersed in pure love and an overwhelming feeling of peace suddenly came over him; it was like nothing he'd ever felt before. He felt so safe, he could have stayed there for ever. Nathan held out an arm to Peter.

'Peter, come,' he invited warmly.

Peter floated over to them and he too became immersed in the wonderful glow. Then Nathan stood back a little and looked at them.

'It's wonderful to see you two boys,' he said smiling.

'This - this is incredible...' Joel choked. 'I - I thought you were dead?'

'Only my earthly body died, Joel. I - my spirit didn't die.'

'But that - that means you're - you're in Heaven?' Joel stammered in amazement.

Nathan nodded.

'And we're here too - so that means - me and Peter are dead?'

'No - don't worry, I'll explain everything to you both. So much has happened to you two recently, your heads must be in a perpetual spin,' Nathan smiled at them. 'You've been very worried about your friend, Tamara?'

They both nodded.

'Well He has heard all your prayers and this morning at the altar rail, He heard you again. You both said exactly the same thing as you received the Eucharist sacrament. What was it you said when you received the communion bread, Peter?'

'T - t - take me instead...' Peter said, hesitantly.

Joel looked at Peter, shocked.

'What did you say, Joel?' Nathan looked at him.

'I - I said that too...' he murmured weakly.

'That was the point when His plan for you two boys was confirmed. Your prayers He had already decided how to answer well before then.' Nathan smiled again.

'So Tamara has woken up? She's all right? We've died in her place?' Joel said.

'Well - no...' Nathan began to explain.

'But I don't understand, Mr Asher...' Peter frowned in confusion. 'Surely she must have recovered - if we're here in her place?'

'Not exactly - if you'd just let me finish.' Nathan smiled. patiently. 'You haven't died in Tamara's place; in fact you haven't died at all.'

'But how can we be in Heaven, if we haven't died?' Joel was really confused now.

'Well you haven't arrived in the usual way, that's for sure. You've found the 'Kairos' gateway' - the Unicorns also discovered that a rainbow can be used as a bridge between the earthly and celestial elements. As you can see looking around here, this whole place exists through light and colour. God made light and you know colour is just different degrees of light - without light, there would be no colour. That's why a rainbow is a sign from God - it's a reflection of Heaven, the infinite source of light. The Unicorns are not supposed to use it, but sometimes they slip down, out of curiosity and to play. Grandad's place is ideal for them: it's very private. Unfortunately, last week the baby got left behind - when you went rushing out to see the rainbow. Thank you for all you did to protect and return him.'

'It was a pleasure.' Peter smiled. 'Does anyone else know

about this 'Kairos' gateway', Mr Asher?'

'Not this one at the moment, but don't worry, there's no danger of people falling into it by accident. Only a child, of good, pure and true heart can pass through it - and then only under invitation from He,' Nathan explained.

'Invitation from He?' Peter frowned curiously.

'Yes, you didn't fall into it by accident, boys; you were summoned.'

'Summoned?' Joel cried in astonishment.

'Yes, chosen, if you like,' Nathan said. 'In fact *you've* been destined for the Kairos since before you were born, Joel.'

'*Before* I was born?' Joel whistled.

'Yes - even before *I* was born. God really does have a plan and every one of us has a role to play.'

'Wait a minute,' said Peter. 'You said "not this one"? You mean there are other gateways?'

'Yes, there are other special places like your Zionica. In fact there's at least one in almost every country, but they're not in constant use. As you heard Charis say, there have been no Kairos' through this one in twenty-three earth years. Some of them haven't been used for centuries. Only children of a very special kind can enter this way; everyone else comes through the normal route - the way I did four years ago and Grandma did before that. So, when such a child is found, it's an occasion for much rejoicing; there's so much we can do.'

'What do you mean, Dad?' Joel asked curiously. 'What can we do? What have we been chosen for?'

'Well, Joel, we can see everything up here, but those of us who have come here in the normal way, are not allowed to communicate with people on earth. Interfering with human free will is also forbidden - everyone has to make their own choices - but there are things we can do with special children who are able to visit us in the way you two have.' Nathan continued in earnest. 'You see, boys - you can go back! We can tell - even show you, things that will enable you to be of great service in the fight against evil back in the world.'

'Wow,' Peter whistled.

'What kind of things, Dad?' Joel persisted.

'Although God sealed the evil one's fate with the ransom of His Son, the spiritual battle is still being fought. The devil is in effect, having a massive tantrum. There is no doubt that he has lost the fight, but the devil is still in the world and still, unfortunately, able to attract followers. That is why there is so much misery and strife on earth - it's the negative energy that comes from people who do not realise they are being manipulated by the devil. The Kairos are part of God's army fighting for good. The specific things you can do we'll go into later, but first...'

'Why are only children able to use this gateway, Dad?' Joel interrupted. 'What do you mean, how are we special?'

'Children have a special quality that, sadly, many adults lose.' Nathan explained. 'Jesus said that only if you become like little children can you get into Heaven. This doesn't mean that everyone has got to start behaving like children. We all know that children can be mischievous. However, children can be regarded as innocent and pure because generally speaking, they are incapable of premeditated wickedness. They're not in control of their own lives, decisions are made *for* them. What He really meant was, children have the special quality of loving unconditionally no matter what - it's not negotiable. They have an endless capacity to love and expect to be loved back regardless of circumstances, influences, behaviour or anything else. They're also dependent, needing their parents in the same way that God wants everyone to depend on Him.'

'Hey, that always confused me - about becoming like children to get into Heaven, but I understand it now - I think,' Peter said.

'But, Dad, what's happening about Tamara?' Joel said anxiously. 'You said He had decided *how* to answer our prayers. What did you mean? Please just tell us she's all right.'

'Well it depends on you, Joel. She hasn't woken up yet - you're the one who is to wake her.'

'Me?' Joel said in astonishment.

'I said He had made His decision on how to answer your prayers *and* about what to do with the two of you.'

'What to do with us?' Joel asked curiously. 'Is He here now? Is Jesus here?'

'Yes, He's always here,' Nathan answered.

'But shouldn't Jesus be with Tamara?' Peter asked.

'He *is* with Tamara also, Peter, just as He is with every lonely, sick, abused, hungry or frightened child. He doesn't have to be in just one place, you know that. He can be everywhere at once - He is *passim* - omnipresent and omniscient.'

'What about God?' Joel asked. 'Where's He?'

'Jesus *is* God, Joel.' Nathan smiled.

'I thought Jesus was God's Son,' Joel frowned.

'Yes - *He* is God in three Persons - God the Father, God the Son and God the Holy Spirit. This is what the Holy Trinity is; the three sides of God, complete and inseparable.'

Joel and Peter frowned, trying to understand it all.

'I'll let you into a secret,' Nathan said with a smile. 'No one up here fully understands it either; we're not meant to. To put it bluntly, we're none of us clever enough - despite the fact that up here we have immeasurably more intelligence than when we were mortal on earth.'

'How is that, Dad?' Joel frowned.

'People on earth only use a very small percentage of their brain capacity; that physiological restriction is removed up here. So even the most intelligent Scientist or Mathematician on earth - even Einstein - could never be that clever. If we understood it all, that would make us like God and we're not God. Only God understands everything.'

'Are we allowed to see Him?' Peter asked hesitantly.

'He doesn't want you to see Him yet; you will, but not now. He doesn't want you to be overawed any more than you already are. You will not see His full glory though; you only see that when you come here for real, as I have done. You will not be allowed to see much of the true beauty here. I'm very limited in how much I can actually show you. If I were to let you see what it was really like here, you would probably refuse to go back.' Nathan smiled. 'And we can't have that - you still have a lot to do on earth, boys. He has work for you.'

'Work? You mean He's going to give us a mission?' Joel said excitedly.

'Yes, I guess you could call it that, Joel,' Nathan answered. 'First though, there is someone here that He wants *you* to see, Peter.'

Nathan gestured to his side and a woman appeared beside him. She was very pretty, with blonde hair and blue eyes - she looked remarkably like Peter and was surrounded by an aura of light like those of Nathan and the Angels.

'Peter, this is Anna, your natural Mother.' Nathan went on. 'Contrary to what your parents were told and subsequently told you, your Mother did not abandon you at the orphanage, Peter. She did everything she could to keep you and feed you, often going hungry herself. She was only sixteen and unmarried when she gave birth to you. Your biological Father had taken her by force and abused her. She was forbidden to see him again by her family and ordered to give the baby - *you* - up. When she refused to give you up, she was ostracised by her family and the community. In short she became an outcast, forced to live on the streets with every down-and-out, drug addict, beggar and villain. She did very basic, menial jobs that no one else would do, for which she earned a pittance. Then through lack of proper food and necessities, she fell very ill and could not afford medical care. She struggled on, then when you were eighteen months old, she died. You were taken by the authorities and placed in the orphanage, where you were found six months later by the Jordans, your adoptive parents. It was of course He who led the Jordans to the orphanage in Hungary. It was He who, with the help of a child just like you, smoothed over all the obstacles that lay in their way to legally adopting you and taking you out of the country. So if it wasn't for children like you two, you might still be in that orphanage now, Peter.' Nathan turned to Anna. 'Anna, this is your Son, Peter.'

Anna beamed a beautiful smile and held out her golden arms.

'Peter, my Son.'

Peter nestled softly into the arms of his natural Mother for the first time in ten years. They embraced with all the love and affection of a Mother and Son.

'Before we discuss the mission that He has for you,' Nathan continued. 'I'm allowed to answer certain questions that you are bound to have.'

'I'm worried about Tamara, Dad. We haven't got a lot of time. The Doctors are switching the machine off this afternoon and we have to leave for the hospital at two o'clock.'

'I'm so proud you're my Son, Joel.' Nathan smiled affectionately. 'Here you are in Heaven, with the opportunity to ask the ultimate questions, but all you can think about is your sick friend. There's no need worry. God invented time for earth. Time as you know it doesn't exist up here. You could be here for a hundred years and hardly a minute would have passed on earth. A thousand years is like a day here. Jesus was born yesterday morning, crucified last night and resurrected this morning.'

Joel stared, awestruck, at his Father.

'Awesome...' Peter gulped.

'About Tamara,' Nathan continued. 'Your prayers will be granted and He has effected a way for you to wake her.'

An older woman, who was also surrounded in the wonderful light, suddenly appeared in front of them. She looked at them with a big, happy, beaming smile and Joel recognised her immediately.

'Yes, Joel, Grandad has the key.' She said.

A grin exploded on Joel's astonished face.

'Grandma!'

Grandma hugged Joel.

'Hello, boys,' she said delightedly. 'I'm here to give you a message for Grandad - it's regarding young Tamara. I want you to tell him "what wasn't right for a sixty-year-old woman *is* right for a ten-year-old girl" and that he is to give to you the secret he keeps and the mystery will be no more. Finally, Joel, I must stress to you, it can only be used once, for the purpose it has been granted. Then it must be returned to its rightful owner - it's long overdue.'

'Rightful owner? But what is it? And who is the rightful owner?' Joel said, more confused than ever.

'You'll know, Joel. God bless you both and Grandad.'

With that, Grandma disappeared.

'I'm sorry, Joel,' Nathan said. 'It's not permitted for anyone here to communicate with the world. Grandma was granted a special dispensation from He, to see you only in answer to your prayers on this one occasion. It's a great and special honour for you and for Grandma, as it is extremely rare for this to be sanctioned. Anna and I are acting as your Guardians.'

'But what's Grandad got to do with all this, Dad?'

'Grandad was once standing where you are now,' said Nathan.

'I knew there was something he wasn't telling us!' Joel cried. 'No wonder he knew all about Unicorns - why didn't he tell us?'

'Oh he doesn't remember any of it,' Nathan explained as he beckoned them to follow him.

The boys floated along after Nathan, looking inquisitively around. Anna followed behind them. They were being led through a large hall that didn't seem to have any boundaries: even as they looked upwards, it seemed to go on for ever.

Twinkling crystals cast prismatic effects everywhere the boys looked. There were gold archways on either side, but they couldn't see through them because each archway had a different coloured, misty light shining within it. A sparkling precious jewel shone from the pinnacle of every archway, corresponding to the colour within.

Nathan led them to an area with large pearl-and-gold chairs and beckoned them to sit. The cushions didn't indent at all as they settled on them like feathers. Joel thought it really did feel heavenly as he and Peter sat by his Father and Anna. He was beaming with so much happiness he felt that he would burst. Nathan smiled at the boys as they bounced lightly on the chairs, laughing at their sudden strange weightlessness.

'This must be what it's like walking on the moon,' Joel giggled.

'Not quite, Joel; the moon has a little gravity,' Nathan said smiling.

'Tell us about Grandad and the Unicorns, Dad. Why doesn't he remember?'

'Grandad was only about your age when he came here, Joel. He named the special place in the field where you have your den, "Zionica" after coming here. He doesn't remember that now of course; all he remembers is the name. He knows about Unicorns because he's studied the subject; he cannot remember the real reason why he has a fascination for them.' Nathan paused. 'You see, as I mentioned earlier, only pure-in-heart children are able to pass through the Kairos gateway. Once Grandad reached sixteen, everything about here was erased from his memory. The same will happen to you two on the eve of your sixteenth birthdays. Grandad was allowed to see Storm's Heavenly return yesterday; it was a gift, in honour of his lifetime of loyalty and faith - we knew he would keep it among the three of you.'

'But didn't Charis say we were the second in twenty-three years?' Peter asked.

'Yes, Dad, that would make Grandad about forty-two when he came here?' Joel frowned.

'No, Joel - that would make your mother eleven when she came here.' Nathan explained.

'Mum too?'

'Uh huh, you see, Zionica's special gateway is a third-generation secret in our family,' Nathan answered.

'But she doesn't remember either?' Joel surmised.

'Correct - neither can she remember why she wanted to call you *Joel*, but she made herself a note on the eve of her sixteenth birthday to call her first-born Son Joel.'

'Is that allowed - to make a note before you forget all this? Why *did* Mum want to call me Joel?'

'When you get back, have a look in Grandad's Bible. Turn to the book of Joel and see what the very last line of the very last chapter says; then you will understand. She knew she wouldn't remember why she wrote the note, but it was a comfort to her to write it before her memory of all this was erased.' Nathan smiled at the two boys who were struggling to take it all in. 'Obviously, boys, you mustn't tell anyone about any of this,' he continued, 'should you attempt to, it would be a dreadful betrayal of trust. I know neither of you would ever betray a trust of any kind, that's one of the reasons why you've been chosen. However, if you did attempt to, you would be struck dumb or something equally prohibitive and your memory instantly erased. Also remember, Joel, that Peter will reach sixteen a short while before you. Once Peter reaches sixteen, you will not be able to discuss it with him either; he wouldn't have a clue what you were talking about. Do you both understand?'

They nodded; although their minds were in something of a whirl.

'Good.' Nathan went on. 'About making yourself a note. You will each be permitted to make a note to yourself as a special memento before your sixteenth birthday. However, be warned, it must not give anything away. It's just so you know before you forget everything that you'll be keeping a little part of this to treasure for the rest of your lives on earth. Call it a consolation for having this part of your memory erased. Incidentally, you do get it back when you come here for real.'

'Did Grandad write himself a note?' Joel asked.

'Yes, and he was allowed to keep a memento too, but it's only on loan and is for a special purpose. That purpose is about to be fulfilled; you will find out how when you give Grandma's message to Grandad. That will also confirm to you that life on earth is not a pot-luck affair. God really does have a plan.'

'Wow - this is all so incredible,' Joel said, in amazement.

'Tell us about the Angels, Mr Asher?' Peter asked enthusiastically. 'Are they all that beautiful?'

'Yes, Peter, they're all just as beautiful, but they don't all look like Charis and Aleathia. There are lots of Angels, Peter, and they all have different jobs. Charis and Aleathia look the way they do because they're Reception Angels - that is, they receive new arrivals. Their role is to put people at ease as soon as they get here. When new arrivals see such beauty, they forget their fear very quickly. As you can imagine, many new arrivals have suffered one trauma or another, some require several Angels to care for them and settle them in - you understand? Some people were not prepared for death, but had their lives cut short unexpectedly. In such cases much sensitivity is required and the Regular Angels are well suited to this work.'

'Regular Angels?' Joel asked.

'Oh yes, there are several orders of Angels; you will meet some of them. The Seraphs, the Cherubim, the Archangels...'

'What happens to people when they arrive here, Dad?'

'Each individual is different, Joel; everyone is cared for according to their needs and these are dependent on many things. There are no set rules, simply because you cannot account for every potential situation. The whole system is dynamic. Some are severely traumatised and need time to recover - victims of crime, war, terror or severe accidents, for instance. On the other hand, some people who have suffered a long and painful illness, literally leap for joy to be suddenly free of pain. And of course they get to meet up again with old friends and family members. Everybody gets what they need, sometimes God might decide to send someone back.'

'You mean like us they haven't actually died?' Peter asked.

'Some people have a "near death" experience. This is when they nearly die but He sends them back. You see, some people go through the whole of their lives without learning the lesson they were supposed to learn. We've all got a purpose, boys; we all face opportunities, challenges and choices. The whole experience of our very short lives on earth is supposed to teach us something. It's like a journey through a complicated maze, with a set goal. Trouble is, no one knows what their goal is, but they're expected to discover it - like I said, God has a plan. He made the rules after all and He can make exceptions to any rule if He so wishes. If He feels someone deserves another chance

The Kairos

He may give them one. His mercy is endless - especially when it comes to children, sometimes they get a complete new life!'

'Wow - you mean some people on earth have been there before - as someone else?' Peter asked, astonished.

'Children have not had the time to discover their purpose or choose their path, have they? Usually they are reborn into the same family. Oh don't get me wrong, this is extremely rare and only happens if God thinks it is an exceptional and deserving situation.' Nathan explained. 'He made the rules for a reason and He doesn't change them unless He feels there is just cause.'

The boys listened intently as Nathan continued.

'Think of life on earth as being like a computer game, for instance. You start with so many lives and have targets to reach, with various goals and obstacles on the way. When you reach the first target, you get to another level and so the game continues with progressively more difficult targets, till you get the best score you can manage, in the seventy to a hundred or so years you're usually given.'

'What other jobs do Angels do, Dad?' Joel asked.

'Many and varied. Some elect to go down to earth to work among people. They make great sacrifices in His name. Their sole purpose is to bring comfort and relief where there is great suffering. In order to do so, they selflessly endure suffering themselves, refusing any personal reward - they're happy to do it. These Angels prefer to be, shall we say, not in the sphere of Charis' and Aleathia's looks - that would draw attention to them. They tend to look much plainer, to blend in with ordinary people. You would be amazed if I told you who some of these Angels were that live among people.'

'Oh please tell us, Dad. Who are they?' Joel asked.

'No,' Nathan shook his head and smiled in amusement. 'That is one of the questions I have to pass on, Joel. Who else though, but an Angel would choose to leave the relative comfort and safety of a convent, where she could spend her days worshipping God, to live and do His work instead in the blackest and most desperate hole on earth, in order to help those who need it most?

If you want to find an Angel - look among the poor, the sick and the suffering.' Nathan smiled. 'There are Angels living among people on earth every day and the people don't know it. It puts a new spin on "do unto others as you would have them do unto you," doesn't it, boys?'

'Awesome - how can you tell if there's an Angel about, Mr Asher?' Peter asked.

'Most people can't,' Nathan replied plainly. 'There are a few people who are able to sense them. Most people have the vision of an Angel being like the picture of Angel Gabriel, emerging from a cloud in his white robe, with large wings and a halo. Not so. Yes, there are some magnificent Angels, but you might find an Angel living rough, a down-and-out on the street, dressed in rags. This is so they can mingle among some of the most desperate people who need them most. Think twice before you curse the shabby, unshaven old man hanging about the street corner outside a pub. He might be an Angel, waiting for the hapless old drunk who will fall out of the pub and need him.'

'Do people become Angels when they die?' Joel asked.

'Angels have always been Angels, Joel and they always will be Angels, doing His will. Even the devil was once an Angel, but he's been cast out for - for devil mongering. Angels are completely different beings to us - they're as different from us as we are from, say, plants for instance.'

The boys nodded.

'I said God has a plan.' Nathan continued. 'He sends ambassadors down to the world on various missions. The most famous of all was of course His own Son. Jesus had a life up here before being sent to earth; He was God's Son here before becoming human on earth. There were many others - John the Baptist was another famous one, along with various prophets and Saints through the ages. They were all sent for a specific purpose which they knew about before becoming human - in much the same way as a soldier or a secret agent is briefed prior to an exercise or a mission. God places people where He wants them. Take the Queen of England, for instance; it is not an accident of birth that she sits on the throne; she's been placed where God wants her to be.'

'So, what do you do up here? What's it like in Heaven?' Peter pressed.

'Well we're not dead, we're very much alive and we're the same people we were down on earth. The spirit that is you is renascent - reborn here in Heaven - and lives on in eternal life. Only there's an element missing here that makes all the difference and that is fear - there is no fear here. No fear of crime or illness or accidents or loss and no fear of death. It's true, He wipes away every tear. We have love, peace and happiness. We get to meet people who've gone before us and we find out how perfect God's plan really is. He created man in His image and when our earthly bodies die, we live here with Him in paradise - and it is paradise. We all have our particular jobs, but because God's love is infinite, we live in the most perfect love. It's difficult to describe and probably even more difficult for you to understand because a mortal's capacity to love is different. Think of the person you love the most in the whole world, someone you would do anything for - your Mother, for example. This is the love everyone here feels for everyone else. It's like all being part of the same close family. It's not something that can be described, only experienced.'

The mesmerised boys listened in wonder as Nathan talked. Then with a smile, he rose from his chair.

'And you two will have to wait a long time for that because there are many earthly experiences in store for you first.' He beckoned the boys to follow him again.

Joel and Peter rose from their chairs and floated after him, Anna following behind as before. They were starting to get used to the floating thing and now found that being weightless was fun. Peter nudged Joel lightly in the back and grinned as he watched him float several feet. When he came to a stop, Joel did a roll in mid-air and giggled, as Peter spread out his arms and glided upwards like a bird in flight. They both laughed whimsically. Then Peter noticed an archway with a beautiful pale lilac light that seemed to impel him to go through it.

'What's through here, Mr Asher?' Peter asked curiously as he floated towards it. Then suddenly he froze and looked up, terrified. A huge man, at least ten or twelve feet tall, appeared at the entrance, blocking the way. The man, also dressed in white and with his arms folded, glowed radiantly and was shrouded in the misty lilac light of the archway. Although the sight in front of Peter was so mighty and he was initially frightened, the being's face was not threatening and he looked at Peter with a kind, even gentle expression which seemed to contradict the scary, guard-like stance.

Nathan suddenly appeared in a flash in front of Peter, coming between him and the mighty man, who vanished back inside the archway.

'No, no, no, not that one.' Nathan barred the way.

'Hey - how did you do that?' Peter cried.

'Never mind, there are things you must not see yet, Peter.'

'Who or what was that?' Joel asked, bewildered.

'That was one of the Gatekeepers. You must not attempt to enter any of these archways, either of you. I'm afraid you're restricted to this area till it's time for you to go back...'

'What is this area, Dad?' Joel interrupted.

'This is reception - I guess for you, a kind of hospitality area.'

'You mean like the arrival and departure lounges at airports?' Joel said.

'Yes,' Nathan said simply. 'That's basically what it is. Come, I want to show you something. This is one archway you can go through and you will use it quite frequently.'

They followed Nathan through a turquoise-blue archway. As he glided through it, the area opened up before him, as if a room was forming in his path. It reminded the boys of the story of Moses, when God parted the Red Sea for the Israelites.

The same warm glowing light was all around, the prismatic effect gently swirling and sparkling. It was as if the whole fabric of Heaven was a mass of rainbows, intermingled with twinkling crystal stars.

'Wow - this place is awesome!' Peter whistled.
Nathan came to a stop.

'We call this the Vista,' he announced. 'We can see anything we want here, boys. We can play back the past or watch the present in real time - what's happening right now. We can even glimpse the potential future, but it can only be potential because the future hasn't happened yet and it is dependent on people making choices.'

'Wow, that's cool, Dad,' Joel said excitedly.

'It's brilliant!' Peter enthused. 'Can I see me ten years from now?'

'I'm not sure that's a good idea, Peter. It will only show the potential you in ten years' time. It's not good to see your own future. I can tell you, Peter, that you have the potential to become a great Veterinary Surgeon, if you study hard, but remember, anything you see here you will forget on the eve of your sixteenth birthday,' Nathan warned.

'Show us Tamara, Dad,' Joel said, hesitantly.

The boys turned and followed Nathan's gaze - they didn't know what they were supposed to be looking at as everywhere looked just the same. As they watched, a vision of Tamara appeared, almost like a hologram. It was like watching a large screen, but there were no edges to it. Curiously, she wasn't lying in bed at the hospital as they had expected. The view was of Tamara stuck in some sort of vortex like tunnel. She appeared to be having a bit of a struggle, as if she was not sure whether to continue up the tunnel or turn back. She kept looking back, not seeming to know what to do; her lips were mouthing words but no sound came out.

'What's happening to her, Mr Asher?' Peter asked, distraught.

'It's the life support-machine,' Nathan explained. 'She's neither one thing nor the other at the moment. Technically she should have died and come through the tunnel and be here by now, but because the machine is keeping her alive, she cannot make that journey up the tunnel. She'll be in suspended animation until action is taken on earth which is beyond her control. Sadly this is all too common with people in comas on life-support; we see it a lot.'

'Poor Tamara,' Joel said weakly. 'She looks tormented. Isn't there anything you can do, Dad?'

'Oh don't worry, she doesn't know what's happening, she's asleep; this is her subconscious, like a dream. I'm afraid there's nothing we can do from up here for people in this situation. If the Doctors are certain a person will not come round, it really is kinder to switch off the machine so their spirit can move on. Keeping them trapped like this just delays their development, but people on earth can be very stubborn and refuse to let go of loved ones. A spirit can be trapped like this for years. I guess you can't blame people - they tend to see their own loss rather than the progression of their loved one's spirit to a higher plane.'

'But Tamara won't be stuck in the tunnel for much longer, will she, Dad? Didn't you and Grandma say God had answered our prayers?'

'Yes, Joel, when you get back, you will be able to free her one way or the other. You can let the Doctors switch off the machine and she will complete the journey through the tunnel, where you know she'll be in good hands. Or you can give Grandad the message from Grandma and see what he comes up with. There you go, see - another choice.'

'You said earlier that He had a mission for us, Dad? What does He want us to do?' Joel asked.

'Yes, I'm coming to that, it's why I've brought you to the Vista.' Nathan continued.

'What - does He want us to convert Presten into a good, caring person?' Joel said, with mock humour. 'There's more chance of Rodney becoming a star racing whippet!'

'It's much more serious than purging a young delinquent,' Nathan said gravely. 'And it's not without some considerable danger. You could choose to decline this responsibility, but if you did, your memory of all this would be wiped out instantly and you would be returned oblivious to it. Whatever you decide, Tamara will be all right.' Nathan paused to let this sink in.

The Kairos

'Go on, Dad,' Joel said with conviction. 'There's no way either of us would decline it, however dangerous.' Joel glanced at Peter for assurance.

'That's right, Mr Asher, whatever it is, we want to do it,' Peter said, steadfastly.

'As you wish.' Nathan said pensively, as he collected his thoughts. 'O.K. - Joel, do you remember anything about when I died, or were you too young?' Nathan asked hesitantly.

'I remember vaguely you were working on a very big case. It kept you in the office till late every night. I missed your coming in to say goodnight and reading my bedtime story. Mum missed you too; she blamed the accident on your working too hard - she said you must have been really tired from overwork and fallen asleep at the wheel.'

'I'm sorry I wasn't there for you, Joel. The case I was working on was very serious. I was collaborating with the police at Scotland Yard and we were nearing a critical point. We were about to unmask a dangerous criminal and expose the details of his evil operations. I had intended making it up to you: I was planning to take you and Mum on holiday - but Joel - I didn't fall asleep at the wheel...' Nathan looked at Joel in earnest. 'I was murdered - in cold blood...'

Joel and Peter looked aghast - Joel felt as if he had been suddenly stabbed in the heart with a red-hot knife.

'Murdered!' they both gasped together.

CHAPTER NINE

A Great C o - Mission

Every drop of blood seemed to drain from Joel's face; his mouth suddenly became very dry and he went weak at the knees. This couldn't be true, he told himself; how could it be? Why would anyone want to murder his Dad? Then as this grim discovery suddenly hit him, shock turned to rage, and he felt the anger rising in his chest as if it would burst. Someone had intentionally killed his Father, robbing him of a Dad. He didn't want to believe it; there must be some mistake.

'No! You mean someone deliberately took you away from us?' Joel cried angrily. 'But how come the police didn't know that?'

'They assumed, like everyone else, that I'd been working too hard and fell asleep while driving the car near the river. There was no evidence or motive to suggest otherwise'

'Who did it, Dad?'

'I understand you're upset, Joel,' Nathan said trying to comfort him.

'Upset? I'm furious! Who could possibly want to kill you?' Unable to contain his grief, Joel flopped down on a nearby chair, sinking his head into his hands, but because of his weightlessness he bounced straight up again, several feet in the air. There he hovered, still in the sitting position, head buried in his hands.

Peter made as if to follow him up, but Anna placed her hand on his arm.

'I should leave this to Nathan, Peter.' Anna whispered. 'Joel needs to overcome and deal with this shock in order to carry out Nathan's plan.'

'Can you see any clearer up there?' Nathan called, then floated up and put an arm round his Son. 'It's not a sin to be angry, Joel; it's how you deal with anger that is important. I know it's hard for you, bringing back all that pain and I'm sorry to be the one to do it. But, Son, I need you to get past your own private grief now; what's at stake is too important. You see, my murder was just the tip of the iceberg. Your mission is to expose the evil plethora of crime behind it. You must be strong and deal with your anger; only then can we do something about the situation. You know, I - I was offered a get-out clause - for someone else to tell you and work with you on this because I'm so personally involved - but I thought it would be better to tell you myself. It will give us a chance to work together for a while - you know, Father and Son, as we might have done in the world had this not happened.'

Joel looked up through tearful eyes, as Nathan went on.

'Sorry I cracked a joke about seeing clearer up here - but that did look quite funny.'

'It felt funny too,' Joel said with a laugh.

'That's better, let's put a brave face on, shall we?' Nathan urged.

The pair floated down again to Peter, who looked on sympathetically. Joel was his very best friend and he hated seeing the hurt he was going through.

'All right, mate?' Peter asked supportively.

'Yeah, sure, I'm cool.' Joel nodded with a strained smile.

'That's the spirit,' Nathan said smiling. 'I can tell you, Joel, that you have the potential to become a great lawyer and barrister and that you could put many really bad villains behind bars, and in doing so, save many lives. Just think of all those kids who could grow up, go to college, get married and have their own kids who might never otherwise have been born. All because *you* relentlessly pioneered to eradicate an evil that could have destroyed it all.'

Joel looked wistfully into his Father's eyes and swallowed weakly. He felt humbled by the wonderful, idealistic magnanimity of his Father and he decided there and then that he was going to be just like him.

Nathan looked anxiously at Joel. 'Are we in business then, Son?' he asked.

'Definitely,' came the positive reply.

'Are you with us, Peter?' Nathan asked.

'Ready and willing, Mr Asher. What do you want us to do?'

Nathan turned towards the Vista and images began to appear.

'I've had to scratch around for views that would not be too distressing for you, boys, but that would still give you an insight into the gravity of the situation,' Nathan said seriously.

First they saw kids - teenagers mostly, some younger, some older. Sleeping rough on the streets, hanging around street corners - all sitting-ducks, for any unscrupulous villain who had given control of his mind to the devil. The one thing they mostly had in common, was that they were out of their heads on drugs.

Unsavoury characters prowled the streets, preying on these poor kids' vulnerability, handing out more drugs. They took all the money these unfortunate souls had begged, borrowed or, in desperation stolen. The view changed and they saw young children and babies, unsupervised, dirty and hungry, while their mothers were stupefied by drugs.

'Shocking, isn't it?' Nathan said. 'The saddest thing is, that these were the mildest views I could find, to show you the weeping sore that is festered and spread by drug traffickers. The real result would be too upsetting to show you, but I'm sure you get the picture.'

'Who's responsible for all this, Dad?' Joel choked.

'This man.' Nathan nodded towards the Vista.

They saw a large black car and the Vista took them inside it. A stocky, middle-aged, dark-haired man dressed in a black suit was sitting in the back. He was shouting down a mobile phone and smoking a big cigar. He opened a black attaché case: it was full of huge wads of money.

'Blood money, boys.' Nathan went on, 'Money that has been procured by organised crime, causing pain, suffering, misery and death - and the ruination of the young and vulnerable. This is what I and others were fighting against and it's the reason I was killed.'

'Who is he, Dad?'

'The man I was about to put behind bars for a very long time, Joaquin Lilith, Mr Evil himself. An infectious ulcer permeating humanity; police code name "Hyena".'

'Hyena?' the boys both asked together.

'Yes, the police felt he was laughing at them - the Laughing Hyena - but also because of the way he operates - a cold, hard and cunning murderer, completely without mercy, careful not to risk himself or the discovery of his identity. The police have no idea who the Hyena really is. He runs the biggest organised crime racket in the country; he literally gets away with murder and he's laughing all the way to the bank.' Nathan frowned. 'Every time the police get close, Lilith vanishes like a rat down the sewers.'

'How does he get away with it, Dad?' Joel asked, horrified.

'Watch the Vista; it'll all become clear to you both,' Nathan said quietly.

The car pulled up. The chauffeur alighted and opened the door for Lilith. He got out and entered a building through a door held open for him by a policeman and they saw to their complete amazement, where it was.

Joel and Peter both gasped.

'Is that...?' Peter, began stunned.

'Yes, I'm afraid it is, Joel. I wonder what the Prime Minister would say, if he knew the Hyena - a kingpin of crime - was a Senior Officer in the Metropolitan Police Force? A major component in a network of organised crime, spreading destruction and misery; he is one of the very men entrusted with shaping the strategy for the whole country's fight against the festering sore he is himself perpetrating. Of course he's laughing at them, he even knows his own police code name! Being one of the top dogs at New Scotland Yard, he has access to top-secret files and the Gold Control room. Basically, if the law were on to him, he'd be one of the first people to know about it, and always able to stay one step ahead.'

A GREAT CO-MISSION

'So, where the law is concerned, he's invisible!' Joel cried in exasperation.

'Couple this with a massive network of villains and gangsters, also under his control and it's easy to see how he constantly eludes capture and manages to stay incognito.' Nathan nodded.

'Is he the man who killed you, Mr Asher?' Peter asked, a little awkwardly.

'Indirectly, Peter - that is, he gave the order. The grim act itself was carried out by someone you may recognise, Joel.'

The image changed to that of a tall man with mousy hair. He was sitting at a desk, typing on a laptop computer.

'That's your old office, isn't it, Dad?' Joel asked hesitantly.

'Yes, Son,' Nathan nodded.

The view moved to the man's face and Joel gasped.

'Dan Sadler?' Joel exclaimed in disbelief. 'That's Dan Sadler isn't it?'

'Uh huh,' Nathan said grimly.

'But he was your partner - one of your best friends!'

'A "faux ami" as it turned out, Joel.' Nathan sighed with a shrug.

'But - why would Dan Sadler want you dead? I don't understand.'

'To stop me. He's with Lilith; they're in cahoots,' Nathan continued. 'Lilith is *the* main man at the helm of the drug trafficking business in the UK and Sadler is in his pocket. Unfortunately, Sadler can be bought: he was paid a very large sum to keep Lilith protected from discovery and out of court - and ultimately prison. I had been working on this case with Detective John Smith; you may remember him - he came to the house a few times.'

'He still does, Mum likes him.' Joel said, then suddenly gasped. 'So did Sadler! Mum trusts him - she may be in danger!'

'No, she's not,' Nathan said calmly. 'Mum is not a threat to Sadler: he won't hurt her, I'm sure of that.'

'Phew, you had me worried for a minute then, Dad.'

'Getting back to Smith,' Nathan continued, 'he was

collaborating with those we called the *"squeakers"* or you may have heard them called, *"squealers"*.'

'Hey?' Peter frowned.

'Crims who tell on each other - isn't that right, Dad?' Joel volunteered.

'That's right, Son. They're generally criminals who are involved in crime themselves to a lesser extent. They give the police inside information to catch the bigger fish, in return for leniency for themselves. You must have heard the saying - "Set a thief to catch a thief"? Sometimes they demand payment and Smith has access to a slush fund for this purpose.

'The day before I died, Smith telephoned me at the office. He was really excited because he thought he was close to discovering the identity of the Hyena. He'd made a big breakthrough with a squeaker who was quite high up in Lilith's camp. The squeaker had provided him with critical and damning evidence - audio recordings, videotapes and, most importantly, a floppy-disk file, listing names, addresses, dealing venues, import routes, targets. In short, operational details sufficient to blast the rats right out of the sewers and cage the lot.'

'Lilith being the King Rat and Sadler the traitorous side-kick!' Joel added contemptuously.

'That's right.' Nathan continued, 'Caught with their snouts firmly in the trough. It was to be the coup of all time, flushing out those vermin with one yank of the chain. Of course neither Smith nor I knew of Sadler's or Lilith's involvement - and Smith still doesn't know.' Nathan sighed and shook his head. 'Sadler had listened in on my conversation with Smith and heard him arranging to come to my office the following evening. Then he hatched a plot to kill me before I discovered the truth.'

The view on the Vista changed to the past: it was Nathan, sitting at his desk in his office. The boys watched the image in shocked silence, as Nathan talked them through it.

'The night I died, Smith came to my office with a small briefcase full of all the evidence. He hadn't had a chance to look at everything; he just dropped off the case and left. He was on his way to some evening conference and couldn't stay. We planned to meet the following morning to go through all the evidence and consolidate the information, to put an ironclad case together. This would have given Smith the green-light to arrange a massive dawn swoop, catching the whole brood of vipers while they were napping in their pits. But we never got the chance.' Nathan shook his head in dismay. 'I'd started to make notes on my laptop computer, when Sadler came into my office on the pretence of a chat. He had stayed late in the office; he knew Smith had left me the briefcase with all the evidence and he knew his name and Lilith's would be in the file.'

The boys watched the Vista intently. They saw Sadler walk behind Nathan, pretending to look out of the window as he idly chatted.

'I was still typing on my laptop,' Nathan went on. 'I had my back to him and didn't see him take out a handkerchief soaked in chloroform. He stuck the handkerchief over my face and after a struggle I passed out. Sadler put a virus in my laptop which destroyed all my notes. He took my box of back-up disks and the briefcase with all the evidence. Then he dragged me to the lift, took me down to the basement car park and drove my car to the bend by the river. He belted me up in the driver's seat, locked me in the car and pushed it into the river - the rest is history.'

Distraught, Joel buried his head in his hands. He shuddered as he realised he had just witnessed his own Father's murder! Nathan put an arm round his Son for support.

'You're the last person in the world I wanted to see that, Joel,' Nathan said emotionally. 'But we need you - we need you to be strong - only with your help can we expose the culprits and end their reign of misery, death and destruction.'

'The two-faced rat!' Joel spat angrily, clenching his fists.

'It gets even more bizarre,' Nathan went on. 'Sadler was supposed to take the briefcase of evidence to Lilith, but he knew that, along with his own name, the names of all the squeakers were on the list. Giving the case to Lilith would have spelt certain death for the squeakers, once Lilith knew their identities.

Sadler kept the case - oh not out of any compassion for the squeakers. He told Lilith that he'd made copies of everything and that he'd also made certain arrangements. If anything happened to him, these copies would turn up in places that would make Lilith's hair stand on end. So Sadler now gets a big fat wodge of untraceable moolah from Lilith, as regular as clockwork.'

'The jammy git!' Joel hissed.

'Yes, but it's a double-edged sword.' Nathan grimaced. 'Now Lilith is petrified something might happen to Sadler. If someone else decided to do away with him, or if he simply had an accident, it would spell disaster for Lilith. So Lilith employs two of his heavies - vicious, murderous thugs - to watch Sadler round the clock, just to make sure no harm comes to him. His own personal bodyguards! Ha! Not to put too fine a point on it, boys, Sadler can't even go to the toilet without these two swamp brains standing guard. In short, they almost have to chew Sadler's food for him lest he chokes.'

The boys stared at Nathan in stunned silence.

'Yeah, and get this,' Nathan gave an ironic laugh. 'Tweedle-dum and Tweedle-dee have other orders. Lilith is so furious that Sadler has double-crossed him, that if anything happens to Lilith, then these two thickos have orders to kill Sadler - that's the double-edged sword, lads. Lilith and Sadler are both living on a knife-edge, scared to their bones of anything happening to either of them. They both know that if either one of them has an accident of any kind, it's curtains for the other. To top it all, boys, Sadler now has all the squeakers running scared *and* "in his pocket". Almost the entire criminal fraternity in England wants Sadler dead, but at the same time they're all terrified of what would happen to them on his demise. They all know he's the insider and has the file that could shop them to the law *and* to Lilith. It doesn't take Einstein to work out what Lilith would do to them, if he knew who the squeakers were, and Smith can do *nothing* because now, not one squeaker will go within spitting distance of him. It's a right mess, boys - blackmail and double blackmail, bluff and counter bluff. The end result is: Lilith is free to continue his iniquitous reign of crime, unhindered and the devil is laughing all the way to hell.'

'That's despicable!' Peter cried.

'O.K. Dad, how can we help?' Joel said determinedly.

'This is an extremely dangerous mission, as I warned you. We can offer very little protection when you are back in the world. We can tell you where someone or something is; we can predict with reasonable accuracy where people are going to be and what they might do. But we cannot *make* anyone do something, or *stop* them from doing anything. It's the "free will" thing. In short, if you get in trouble down there, we cannot intervene. By and large you're on your own - but not entirely...' Nathan paused .

'Go on,' Joel urged.

'I can tell you, though, that you can always trust the Ravens.'

Joel and Peter frowned curiously.

'Ravens?' They both echoed in unison.

'Yes.' Nathan explained: 'He commands the birds of the air. Ravens have a special bond with humans; they're ambassadors for good; they're brave, sensitive and intelligent. They'll look after you, warn you of imminent danger, go forth in reconnaissance and report important detail. They'll even bring you food, if you're hungry - although I must also warn you they can be extremely irritating at times - you'll see what I mean.'

'Are we going to wake up in a minute and find this has all been a confusing dream?' Peter asked incredulously.

'No, Peter; it's all true. People don't have the same dreams at the same time as other people. When you get back, you'll find that you both remember every detail and so you'll *know* that it wasn't a dream. That would not be the case with a mere dream.'

'Let's get down to it then, Dad. What are we to do?'

'Somehow you've got to locate the briefcase currently in Sadler's possession and ensure it gets to Smith, contents intact. Smith never got to scrutinise the file; he still doesn't know that Sadler is a duplicitous traitor. You have to get Smith to look at the file and discover the names of Sadler and Lilith and their involvement, otherwise he might just give the wretched case straight back to Sadler!' Nathan sighed. 'Yes, I'm afraid Sadler has been appointed the Barrister for the Prosecution - which basically means it would never get to court.'

'I thought you said Sadler made several copies?' Peter asked.

'Smart of you, Peter. I was just checking you were paying attention.' Nathan tilted his head and clicked his tongue. 'I said Sadler told Lilith he'd made several copies. But I can guarantee you, boys, that he never bothered to do it. It's just a sword of Damocles he's dangled over Lilith's head. As long as Lilith *thinks* he has several copies, Sadler is safe. These two villains need to be locked up for a very long time. That is why it has got to be done right. It's no good getting them on a lesser charge, they'd be out in a few years. These people are evil through and through. Oh a few years in prison might make them appear to reform - of course it would! But they've bought the devil's hype - he controls them. However, people are no good to the devil while they're locked up, so he doesn't waste time on them when they're in prison. That's why criminals seem rehabilitated, but many of them are not rehabilitated at all. They're just in a confused state, because they haven't got the devil talking to them and manipulating them all the time - they're suddenly on their own again. When this happens, some people fall into a deep depression, because they cannot believe or understand why they have done evil things. This is also why persistent criminals re-offend. As soon as they get out, the devil takes them over again. Trouble is, they don't know it's the devil working through them.' Nathan paused. 'Take the Barnes brothers, for instance - notoriously dangerous gangsters who, thank goodness, spent most of their lives in prison. Do you think they were the same in prison? No, they were like babies. That's why some people campaigned to have them released. But believe me, had they been released they would have taken up exactly where they left off - business as usual. They had the potential to be thoroughly evil, if they had been in a position to be useful to the devil. You could see it here - on the Vista.'

'They're here now anyway aren't they, Dad - the Barnes brothers?' Joel said innocently. 'They're both dead now.'

'Of course not!' Nathan raised his eyebrows. 'People like that don't come here, Joel - it would be grossly unfair to the people they swindled, terrorised and killed. Remember, when people come to Heaven, they have a right to live here in a loving and fear-free environment. No, the Barnes brothers have gone where they deserve to be - it was ultimately their own choice. You have the whole of your life on earth to make the choice. They came to the end of the line. Once you've made that choice and sided with the devil, there's no going back. You can't change your mind after you're dead. Anyway, getting back to Sadler and Lilith and their cronies, this brood of vipers must be locked up until they are too old to be a risk.' Nathan looked earnestly at the two boys. 'You don't have to accept this mission, boys; it would not be held against you at all. He will understand if you don't want to get involved; your memory of all this would be erased and you could return home as if nothing had happened. It's just that, well, it's quite rare that we find children who are able to visit us in this way. As you heard earlier, the last one was twenty-three years ago and it is impossible for *anyone* after the age of sixteen. If you two were to join the *Kairos*, we could achieve so much in the next four years.'

'The Kairos?' Joel and Peter echoed.

'You said that was a special gateway?' Joel said.

'Yes, it's also what we call the special group of children like yourselves. There are one hundred and fifty Kairos children in the world. There are always one hundred and fifty - no more, no less. As soon as a child reaches sixteen and has to leave, a new one has already been chosen. It just happens that way.'

'So two kids have just turned sixteen then?' Peter asked.

Nathan hesitated. 'I'm afraid only one...' His voice faltered.

'Oh... Does that mean only one of us can stay in the Kairos?' Joel frowned with disappointment.

'No, Joel, you're both in,' Anna said quietly, putting a golden hand of support on Nathan's arm. 'I'm afraid one has just been lost. Nathan is still concerned about it.'

'Lost?' Joel echoed.

Fortunately, it doesn't happen very often, but Kairos missions can be very dangerous, boys,' Anna explained.

'Thank you, Anna.' Nathan clutched her hand.

'What if we said no? You would only have a hundred and forty-eight.' Peter muttered.

'That never happens, Peter,' Nathan replied. 'The nature of the chosen children is such that none of them has ever turned down the chance to fight for good against evil - whatever the cost to themselves. But I suppose there's always the possibility that someone *could* say no.' He shrugged.

'Dad?' Joel said hesitantly.

'Yes, Joel?'

'Did Mum take on any missions?'

'Yes, you'll hear of some of Mum's brave exploits - and Grandad's too. They've both well and truly earned their little piece of Heaven.'

'I feel humbled that we've been chosen,' Peter muttered.

'You've been chosen for who you are - inside. Nothing can be hidden from Him: He can look straight into your heart.' Nathan smiled kindly.

'It's so awesome...' Peter marvelled.

'Joel - Peter - we can give you the information you need that might well lead to Lilith's being placed firmly where he belongs - behind bars for the rest of his life on earth. Think of the lives that could be saved, the misery that could be avoided and the triumph of good over evil,' Nathan said wistfully.

'We wouldn't dream of turning this opportunity down, Mr Asher,' Peter said determinedly.

'That's right, Dad. Anyway, if the worst comes to the worst, at least now we know where we're coming.' Joel gave a nervous laugh.

'I knew that's what your answer would be - both of you.' Nathan smiled proudly.

Suddenly Peter felt a soft nudge in his back and he floated

round. It was a beautiful Unicorn, about the size of Cherokee; Aleathia was sitting on him. He shimmered like fluorescent, silver satin; he almost looked as if he was made of glass. Beautiful rainbow colours reflected all around him and his horn seemed to sprinkle glitter magically like gold dust.

'Hello again,' said Aleathia beaming. 'I thought you might like to see your friend. This is Farga, or as you called him, Storm.'

'Storm!' Peter cried happily. 'You've grown so much!' He fussed over the little Unicorn.

'He's going to take you back to the Fugue when you're ready, in gratitude for your saving him.' Aleathia smiled.

'The Fugue?' Peter said, puzzled.

'The Fugue is the tunnel you travelled through to get here,' Nathan explained.

Another Unicorn glided up majestically behind Storm. He was almost twice as big as Storm and Charis was perched high on his back. It was the same Unicorn that had come to the plateau in Zionica to bring Storm home. Joel recognised his jagged horn.

'Cheyiea is going to take you, Joel.' Charis beamed.

Joel looked at Cheyiea with some reservations; he'd never ridden before. Sensing his nervousness, Charis smiled at him.

'There's nothing to be afraid of, Joel; he's quite safe, you know.'

Joel turned to his Father. 'So where is this briefcase then, Dad? How do you suggest we get it?' he asked. 'Sadler is miles away in the City.'

'We can talk about that when you come back. First though, don't you have a friend to save?'

'Tamara!' Joel cried. 'How long have we been here?'

'As I told you, time doesn't exist here. You haven't been here any time at all. Now you should go back and do what you have to do for your friend. Think carefully about the challenge you face - and the risks - and when you are absolutely positive about your decision, you must come back and we'll discuss the plan.'

'When shall we come back?' Joel asked.

'As soon as you're ready - the sooner the better. It would be good to get this mission accomplished before you go back to school. The Kairos do not operate during term-time. So you've got one week. However, if you do not return within three-earth days, your memory of all this will be automatically erased and you will live your lives as normal, oblivious to the Kairos.'

'You mean I'd forget about seeing you and the fact that you were murdered?'

'Yes - everything. Now off you go. Your rides are waiting.'

Aleathia helped Peter glide up onto Storm's back, where he perched lightly behind her.

'Joel...' Charis called softly and held out a golden hand. Joel gave Charis his hand and she cupped it gently in hers. Cheyiea bowed down, lowering his shoulder; Charis gave a gentle tug and Joel glided up onto Cheyiea's back behind her.

'I'll be seeing you real soon, Dad.'

'Yes, Son, I believe you will.'

'Goodbye for now, Mum,' Peter grinned.

'Goodbye, my Son,' Anna called back happily.

The Unicorns began to float up. Joel had expected the Unicorn to be bouncy, with hard, rippling muscles, but it actually felt as if he was sitting on a bed of feathers. He seemed to be floating round on a very soft carousel, round and round and round...

CHAPTER TEN

Arrival of the Magi

'You'll catch your death of cold, if you're not careful - Joel!' Grandad threw Joel's coat over his shoulders. 'Joel - Joel!'

Joel slowly opened his eyes and looked up at Grandad, who was leaning over him. Then he looked round with a start. He was sitting on the plateau in Zionica. Peter was sitting next to him, looking a little dazed. Grandad had wrapped their coats round them.

'I thought you might need these,' said Grandad. 'You forgot to take your coats and it's getting chilly. I think we're going to have showers all afternoon. Look at you - you're both half-soaked already. You'd better come back to the house and dry out. We don't want colds and chills on top of everything else!'

Joel and Peter stood up as Grandad headed back in the direction of home.

'Did you just..?' Peter whispered to Joel, but Joel cut him short before he could say any more.

'Yes - ssh - we'll talk about it later,' Joel whispered, then he shouted after Grandad: 'What time is it, Grandad?'

'It's only just after one o'clock, Joel. There's plenty of time,' he called back.

'But it was nearly one o'clock when we left the house,' Peter whispered to Joel, blinking as if trying to wake himself up. 'That means we've only been gone a few minutes...'

The boys put on their coats and followed Grandad back to the house.

'Grandad...' Joel said, running up behind him. 'Grandad, I've got a message for you.'

'A message? What kind of message?'

'Well it's probably nothing - it may not mean anything at all really. Grandad, what would you say if I said it's a message from Grandma?' Joel looked hesitantly at Grandad, expecting him to say, "Don't be so silly" but he just sighed.

'Did you hear me, Grandad?' Joel asked. 'I said I had a message from Grandma...'

Grandad stopped and turned to face Joel.

'Joel,' he smiled sympathetically. 'I know this thing with Tamara has got you really upset - and it's made me think more about Grandma too, but don't get things out of perspective, Son. You'll feel better after the blessing - then we can all move on.'

'Grandad, I mean it. Grandma said to tell you - she said: "What wasn't right for a sixty-year-old woman *is* right for a ten-year-old girl." She said you had what we needed to make Tamara better and that you would understand.'

Grandad stared at Joel, incredulously.

Joel looked up, pleading at Grandad.

'What did she mean, Grandad? What is it that you've got? Whatever it is, Grandma said you must give it to me - it's to do with making Tamara better...'

Grandad looked taken aback.

'Well I've heard many strange things in my time, Joel - nothing really surprises me now.' He said. 'People do have vivid dreams that appear very real. Why didn't you tell me about this vision when you woke up this morning?'

'Oh I just forgot,' Joel answered quickly, thinking on his feet. He couldn't say he'd just seen Grandma and Dad, in Heaven!

+

After Joel and Peter had dried out and changed, they sat in the kitchen with mugs of hot soup. Grandad had been sitting waiting for them. On the table in front of him was a carved wooden box, about four inches wide by six inches long and three inches deep. An old brass key lay next to it.

'So the riddle is finally going to be solved, although it still doesn't make much sense,' said Grandad.

'What riddle, Grandad?'

'This box has been on my dressing table for a long time. You must have seen it, Joel,' Grandad said.

'Yes, it's been there as long as I can remember. You always keep it locked, don't you?' Joel replied. 'Not that I've been snooping...' he quickly added.

Grandad nodded. 'That's because I've always known that it is important. The trouble is, I never knew why. The contents of the box are a complete mystery. There's a note that I've written to myself. The strange thing is, boys, I don't for the life of me remember writing the note, but it's definitely my handwriting.'

'What does it say, Grandad?' Joel asked, intrigued. Grandad picked up the key and unlocked the box. He pushed it over the table to Joel. Joel put his hand in the box and pulled out a small object which was wrapped in note paper. He opened the paper and a piece of what looked like dull, grey horn fell out into the box. He flattened out the note. Peter leaned over, eager to see what it said. There was a heading across the top which read, *"Genuine Unicorn Horn."*

Joel read the note out aloud.

'"Marcus, you won't remember writing this note, but you're writing it to yourself because it's important - very important. You must keep this safe and not let it leave your possession until a young messenger specifically asks for it. Then you must give it up and you'll know why. God bless."'

Joel looked up excitedly.

'It's signed, "Marcus Jacob" - you're right, Grandad: this is your handwriting - and it's your signature!'

'Wait a minute,' said Peter, looking inside the box. 'There's something else in here.' Peter put in his hand and pulled out another note folded round something small. He carefully unfolded the note and something fell out.

'It's a pin - a gold pin,' said Joel, picking it up and scrutinising it. 'Looks like it's in the shape of some letters - K -'

'No,' Peter said, taking the pin from Joel. 'One letter and a number - K 87. What does the note say, Joel?'

'It's Psalm 87...' Joel muttered slowly.

Suddenly Joel and Peter understood the significance of the pin. Peter exclaimed excitedly, 'Hey, that must be -' but a sharp nudge in the ankle from Joel shut him up quickly. 'Ouch! - Er, a very valuable pin...'

'Do you remember where you got these things, Grandad?' Joel asked quickly.

'Yes - well, the horn anyway, I think.' Grandad's brow furrowed in thought.

'You do?' Joel and Peter cried together, startled.

The boys looked at each other, slightly confused. They'd both expected Grandad to give a negative answer to that question.

'Hmm, it's all a bit of a blur. I have vague and very strange recollections of how it came into my possession - but why it's so important, why I wrote that note and what it all means is a complete mystery - except for Grandma's message; that makes sense.'

'How *did* you come by it, Grandad? Surely you didn't kill a Unicorn for it?'

'Of course not!' Grandad said with some indignation.

'Sorry, Grandad, that was a stupid question,' Joel said apologetically.

'All right, Son. Remember when we saw that big bright rainbow, the morning Storm arrived?'

They both nodded.

'I told you I'd seen one like it before, when I was about your age, Joel, but that one had been on a beautiful morning after a snowstorm - most unusual.'

'Yes, Grandad, I remember you saying that.'

'Like you, I rushed down to Zionica to look at it. When I got there, I noticed the pond was completely frozen over. Well, like most twelve-year-old boys, I couldn't resist the temptation of solid ice - it looked solid when I began skating on it. I remember I had such a wonderful time sliding across it. The sun was shining and there was pure white snow everywhere. Zionica looked like a Christmas card, with snow-covered trees.' Grandad smiled as he remembered. 'Then, I must have got too close to the edge of the pond, where the ice was thinner and had begun to melt a little in the sun. Before I knew it, the ice cracked under me and I slipped into the freezing-cold water. It was so cold it took my breath away. But then because the rest of the ice was solid and thick, I was trapped under it and I couldn't find a way to break out. I tried to punch a hole in it but it was like punching a brick wall in slow motion. I was getting very weak; everything was turning black and I thought I was going to die.'

'How terrifying!' Peter gasped. 'How did you get out?'

'Well the strangest thing happened. Just as I was about to sink into unconsciousness, what I thought was a sharp stick, or branch, was suddenly thrust through the ice right in front of me. There was an explosion of light and the ice all round the stick melted instantly and the water became warm. I reached up and grabbed hold of the stick and I felt myself being pulled up out of the water. Then I was laid down on the snow. I opened my eyes and saw what had pulled me out of the water and saved me from certain death.'

'What was it, Grandad?' Joel asked, although he thought he knew the answer already.

'Well I know this might sound like the crazy ranting of an old man, boys, but without a shadow of doubt, it was a Unicorn,' Grandad whispered. 'A big, white, powerful Unicorn, glistening like crystal in the sunshine. It was standing over me. It lowered its head and blew a breath into my mouth, which seemed to revive me. Then he galloped onto the plateau and as quickly as he had appeared, he vanished, like a shooting star, up into Heaven.'

'Wow...' Joel whistled.

'Awesome...' Peter murmured faintly.

'I might have thought I'd become delirious and was hallucinating,' Grandad went on, 'but when I came to properly, I opened my fingers and there it was - the evidence that I had not dreamt it at all. This small piece - the tip of his horn - must have broken off as he pulled me out of the water and I've kept it in this box all these years. That is why I have spent so much time reading and researching about Unicorns, trying to find out all I could about them. It's how I know they exist, though not necessarily in this world. As for the pin...' Grandad threw up his arms. 'I have absolutely no idea where that came from. It was on my bedside table with the Psalm, when I woke up on my sixteenth birthday.'

'So what did Grandma mean, when she said what wasn't right for a sixty-year-old woman *is* right for a ten-year-old girl?' Joel asked.

'Well, Joel, you may remember that your Grandma became very ill with the cancer and there was nothing more the Doctors could do. I suggested grinding the horn up and making some sort of potion with it for her to drink, in the hope that it still had some healing properties. She wouldn't hear of it, of course. She said that I should respect the message I had written to myself, that it must have meant something to me when I wrote it and that one day the riddle would be solved. She was always a very devout Christian, was your Grandma; she said it wouldn't be right for a sixty-year-old woman and that if God called her, she must go.'

'So that's what she meant...' Joel murmured thoughtfully.

'Yes, it always worried me about having to give it to a young messenger. How would I know when the right messenger came along? I'm so glad it's you, Joel. Now I realise its importance, but how I knew that all those years ago and subsequently wrote the note, is still a mystery.' Grandad shrugged. 'Whether there are any healing properties left after all this time remains to be seen, but it's worth a try - for a ten-year-old girl, although I don't know how we could administer it.' Grandad turned the box round and was going to pick up the piece of horn to examine it, but he suddenly froze and gasped.

'What? What is it, Grandad?' Joel frowned.

Grandad turned the box back towards Joel and Peter and their eyes almost popped out of their heads as they looked inside it. There, sitting on the soft velvet lining, was a brilliant, sparkling, jewel-like object. Light was streaming from it: it seemed to

ARRIVAL OF THE MAGI

radiate power.'

Joel and Peter stared, speechless.

'Well for sure, lads, it didn't look like *that* when I put it in the box. It was just a plain piece of dull horn...' Grandad said in amazement.

'Yeah,' Joel said. 'It was dull when it fell out of the note.'

'You must be careful not to touch it,' Grandad went on seriously. 'Whoever touches it now will probably absorb the power. Keep it very safe, Joel. I believe young Tamara is in need of this,' he said, unable to contain his excitement. He quickly locked the box and pushed it and the key across the table to Joel.

'It's almost quarter to two, boys,' Grandad said, standing up. 'We'd better set off for the hospital.'

'Wait a minute!' Joel said. 'We can't just waltz into the hospital and dump this on Tamara's head! Everyone will think we've gone loopy - how are we going to explain *this*?' He held up the box.

'Yes, you're right, Joel,' Grandad said. 'Let's think.'

'Well if it works in the same way as it did with me and Storm, there will be a blinding flash of light,' Peter said. 'I don't see how we can hide that.'

'Unless...' Joel said thoughtfully. 'Is there some way we can make it look like a short circuit? Make all the lights go out at the same time as the flash? You know what the hospital is like - they have just about every light on all day.'

'Yes, good idea, Joel,' Grandad said. 'I can stand near the door and create a diversion. As you lean over Tamara, I'll flip the light switch. This will divert everyone's attention for a second and give you a chance to slip the horn into Tamara's hand. That should do it. Everyone will just think it's some sort of power cut.'

'Brilliant, Grandad!' Joel beamed.

'Hey, you're so cool, Mr Jacob.' Peter grinned.

Grandad almost felt like a boy again himself as he contemplated the adventure.

'Obviously, boys, I wouldn't normally be advocating such a

trick - if I didn't firmly believe it was the right thing to do,' he said with a cough.

+

As Grandad drove to the hospital, Joel and Peter sat in silence, guarding the box with their lives. Their heads were filled with a whole range of emotions. They felt happy, special, apprehensive, confused and anxious for everything to go as planned. The responsibilities that now rested on their young shoulders were almost overpowering. Tamara's life lay in the balance, dependent on their getting the horn safely to her. Then there was the mission they must shortly undertake to bring Sadler and Lilith to justice. The incredible knowledge they now held which must be kept secret. But most of all for Joel, there had been the joy of seeing his Father again. He just wanted to bask in the memory of seeing him, knowing that he was not lost and that they would meet up again very soon.

Grandad pulled up in front of the hospital.

'You two get out here and go inside, boys. I'll just go and park,' he said.

Joel and Peter got out, Joel carrying their precious cargo. They started up the half-dozen steps to the entrance, while Grandad set off down the car park, looking for a space.

'How are we doing for time, Joel? I've left my watch in your bedroom,' Peter asked.

Joel took his left hand off the box and tilted his wrist to look at his watch.

'It's O.K. It's only -' Joel didn't get to finish his sentence. Just as he looked down at his watch, something in front of him tripped him up. He fell onto the steps and as he did so, let go of the all important box. It went flying up into the air, landing at the top of the steps by the entrance doors, as Joel landed flat on his face.

'Ha! Told you I'd get back at you, you righteous creep!' Presten laughed loudly, brandishing the stick he had thrust in front of Joel to trip him. 'What's this - the three wise men, bearing gifts? Three dozy donkeys, I say!' Presten jeered, then he leapt up the steps and snatched Grandad's box. 'Bit small for a casket, ain't it, Asher?'

'You miserable, ungodly animal!' Joel rushed at Presten with his fists clenched, but Peter jumped up and stopped him.

'That won't get us anywhere, Joel,' Peter said, then turned to Presten. 'Just give us the box back, Presten - you don't want to fight now, not with your sister in there.'

Presten shook the box and heard it rattle.

'Oh there's something inside,' he sneered as he tried to open it. 'What can it be - a parting gift, maybe?'

Joel mentally thanked God that Grandad had locked the box up again.

'Where's the key, Asher?' Presten demanded.

'We haven't got it, Presten. Grandad's got it,' Joel lied.

'Give it back, Presten!' Peter yelled, in desperation.

'You really want this, don't you?' Presten sniggered, then he snapped, 'What is it?'

'Look, Presten,' Joel urged, 'I forgive you for tripping me up. Just give us the box and we'll be on our way.'

'YOU *forgive* ME!' Presten shrieked angrily. 'Well I'm touched, but you see I don't need forgiving. I'm the one who's being persecuted here! I'm not allowed to see my own sister before she dies! My Father won't speak to me and my best friends have been ordered to keep away from me!'

'Presten, I'm really sorry about the way things are going for you,' Joel coaxed, 'but it's nothing to do with us and you can't say you didn't bring it on yourself. Just let us have our box so we can go in and see Tamara.'

'Sorry? You're sorry? Well we are charitable today,' Presten wailed scornfully. 'I get your forgiveness *and* your sympathy! Why should YOU see her, when I can't? You're not even family. Well let me tell you, you're never gonna see this precious box again. I'm gonna break it open and see for myself what's inside.' He glared at Joel, full of hate.

Presten already hated the two of them, but this had taken his enmity towards them to new depths. Suddenly, before they could stop him, Presten jumped down the steps in one leap. He turned and stared up at them with intense resentment and loathing.

'Hey, Asher - I still got the box - loser!'

With that, Presten ran off down the car park, right past Grandad who rushed up to the boys.

'What was that all about?' he asked, concernedly.

'Grandad - he's got the box!' Joel cried, panic-stricken. 'Presten has taken the box!'

'What are we gonna do, Mr Jacob?' Peter cried in anguish.

Grandad heaved a great sigh and shook his head.

'I should have expected something like this to happen. Why didn't I keep the box with me until we were safely inside?' he cursed, blaming himself, then checked his watch. 'It's twenty past two. The blessing starts in ten minutes; it'll probably take twenty minutes to half an hour. You two had better get after Presten and try to retrieve the box. I'll go inside and endeavour to stall them as long as I can, but if you're not back by three o'clock, I don't think we've got a chance of saving her.'

'Oh I could roast Presten on a spit for this!' Joel spat angrily. 'Come on, Peter, he can't have got very far - he's not exactly an athlete, is he?'

They set off in the direction which Presten had taken, while Grandad went into the hospital.

+

Joel and Peter ran like fury, searching everywhere for Presten, but he seemed to have vanished into thin air. After a while, they stopped to catch their breath. Joel, being a keen sportsman, was very fit and since his healing Peter too seemed to have boundless energy and strength. The pair of them stood there, scratching their heads. Presten was not fit at all, they couldn't understand how he could have disappeared so fast.

'This is crazy!' Joel exclaimed. 'There's no way Presten could

ARRIVAL OF THE MAGI

have got this far!'

'Well there's nowhere he could have turned off - it's a straight road,' Peter said, baffled.

'I wondered when you two slow coaches would twig that "Porky Pie" couldn't have run this far ahead of you,' a strange voice sounded.

'Who said that?' Joel looked round, startled.

'Over here,' the voice said.

They both turned in the direction of the voice, but there was no one there.

'Where are you?' Joel asked. 'Show yourself.'

'You're looking at me,' they heard the voice again.

'Where are you hiding? All we can see is a Raven on a gate,' Joel said, looking in the direction of a large Raven perched on a gate.

'Well it's not the gate you can hear,' the voice drawled with a hint of sarcasm.

'It's the bird!' Peter cried, in astonishment. 'It's you, isn't it?' he looked straight at the bird.

'Hallelujah!' The bird gazed upwards in mock wonder.

'You can talk?' Joel looked at the bird in amazement.

'No - I'm a Raven. Ravens weren't given the power of speech. But I can think. You can both hear the thoughts I transmit - and just so you know, that's all you can hear - only what I transmit, not everything I think.'

'Oh, well who are you - and how come we can hear you?' Joel asked.

'Name is Magee,' announced the Raven. 'I'm one of those that you have already seen.'

The boys frowned.

'Like Charis and Aleathia,' Magee added.

'Oh you mean you're an Angel? You welcome new arrivals too?' Peter asked.

'Don't be daft!' Another Raven landed on the gate next to Magee. 'They wouldn't put an Angel with an attitude problem in the arrivals job. He'd scare everyone to death, if they weren't already dead.'

'What do you mean - attitude problem? There's nothing wrong with my attitude!' Magee protested haughtily.

'Oh no? How about argumentative - sarcastic - pedantic - sorely lacking in tact..?' the second Raven ranted.

'Argumentative? Sarcastic? Lacking in tact? My feathers!' Magee said, dismissively.

'And grouchy.' the second Raven added.

'Huh!' Magee huffed, throwing the second Raven a particularly injured glance at that last remark. 'The only reason we haven't done Reception, is that we've been seconded on other important work.'

'Excuse me interrupting, you two,' Joel said, still unable to believe what was happening, 'but what is this all about?'

'Oh I do apologise for my friend. This is Maggi,' Magee explained. 'She can be a miserable old trout, but her heart's in the right place.'

'Miserable old trout?' Maggi cawed, indignantly. 'Well of all the...'

Magee turned back to Joel and Peter.

'She is Maggi, I am Magee; they call us jointly the Magi. We have been given the task -'

'Volunteered!' Maggi butted in.

'Yes, Maggi is quite right. We volunteered for the job.'

'Job? What job?' Peter frowned.

'Oh didn't I say? The job of protecting you two, of course.' Magee preened himself.

'Oh of course,' Peter said with a smile.

'Protecting us?' Joel laughed. 'Well I hope we don't need protecting when you two are having one of your arguments.'

'There's no need to make fun of us - we are here to help, you know,' Magee went on, 'and we've only been Ravens this time for a few days. We're still getting used to these bodies.'

'Yes, we've had to swap one set of wings for another, again,' Maggi cawed. 'It's like learning to fly all over again, but with gravity to contend with, you know.'

ARRIVAL OF THE MAGI

'Anyway you'll be glad of us when you're trapped in some dark dungeon and you need someone to bring you something to eat,' Magee said haughtily.

'Honestly, Magee,' Maggi cawed in amusement. 'Sometimes I'm sure you think you're still living in the fifteenth century. They don't have dungeons any more! As to whether these two young boys could end up in a dungeon - I ask you!'

'I'm only trying to illustrate the point, my dear, that they might be very glad of us one day,' Magee insisted.

'I'm sorry,' Joel said. 'I didn't mean to poke fun at you. Please continue.'

'Right, well as Angels assigned to protect you,' Magee continued, 'it is now our sole purpose -'

'And our duty,' Maggi broke in again.

'Will you stop interrupting?' Magee muttered. 'As I was saying, it is our purpose, yes and duty,' he gave Maggi a condescending look, 'to keep you two out of trouble and harm's way. You see, we're different from humans. We are programmed to do His will. Of course we could choose to refuse, but none of us ever does - we want to do His will.'

'Well there was one...' Maggi muttered.

'Oh yes, apart from him, that is - but we don't like to talk about him.' Magee shuddered.

'Or the ones who followed him...' Maggi added.

'That's right,' Magee agreed, then continued with an air of importance. 'Furthermore, we also have every Raven at our disposal.'

'Wow,' Peter said. 'Does that mean you could summon every Raven to come here?'

'Technically speaking, yes, but that would be a terrible waste of resources,' answered Magee.

'It would also spook the locals and they would start shooting at us,' Maggi added with a frown.

'Yes, while we're here, it's best for us to keep a low profile...'

'Magee, you're waffling again. Have you forgotten why we're here?' Maggi cut in.

'Why we're here? Oh yes, of course - well it's you who keeps interrupting!' Magee retorted, slightly irritated.

'ME? You're the one who's delayed it all! We could have told them ages ago where the fat boy was,' came Maggi's sulky reply.

'You mean we've been wasting time listening to you two arguing with each other, when all along you've known where Presten is?' Joel asked sternly.

'Yes. See, I told you!' Maggi cawed, smugly. 'Now come on, tell them.'

'There's no need to panic,' Magee said, dismissively.

'No need to panic! Don't you know our friend is about to have her life-support cut off?' Joel demanded: 'Tell us where he is - NOW!'

'Oh all right. If you'd taken a bit more time in your search, instead of hastily running off, you'd have found him anyway.' Magee went on apparently oblivious of Joel and Peter's anxiety.

'Magee!' Maggi chastised him.

'All right, all right, keep your feathers on,' Magee twittered. 'If you'd looked properly in the bus shelter outside the hospital, you could have saved yourself this silly marathon. The boy you seek was hiding under the seat, when you ran past with a cursory glance inside. Now he's sitting *on* the seat, busily trying to open your box with his penknife.'

'Oh you stupid pair of twits!' Joel shouted. 'Come on, Peter, let's get back before he succeeds.'

'Oh he won't do that,' Magee said with confidence.

'How can you say that? You don't know Presten,' Joel snapped, exasperated.

'Well we can't interfere with the free-will thing, so we can't stop the boy from trying to open the box. However...' Magee paused.

'Oh will you get on with it?' Maggi nudged Magee, almost knocking him off the gate.

'We can affect inanimate objects - like your box, for instance. He could try until doomsday and still never get that box open,' Magee announced proudly.

ARRIVAL OF THE MAGI

'Even with the key,' Maggi added enthusiastically.

'I should hurry back if I were you, or the blessing will be done and you'll be too late,' Magee said in an irritatingly smug manner.

Joel and Peter both looked at Magee in exasperation.

'And you two call yourselves Angels?' Joel muttered crossly.

The boys set off at a fast pace, while the two Ravens held up their heads haughtily.

'Do you suppose we'd better go and assist, Maggi?'

'I think we should, Magee.'

They flew after the boys.

+

When Joel and Peter arrived back at the bus shelter a little out of breath, Presten was still sitting on the bench inside, trying to prise open their box.

'What do you two nerds want?' Presten sneered.

'You know what we want, Presten. Give it to me now!' Joel demanded.

'Get lost,' Presten snapped rudely.

'Presten, You'd give that back now if you knew what was good for you!' Peter threatened.

'Or what, Jordan? What are you gonna do about it?' Presten replied insolently.

Maggi and Magee landed on the roof of the bus shelter.

'Magee - how about some of those resources you mentioned?' Joel shouted.

'Who are you talking to, you soft divvy?' Presten looked at Joel and curled one side of his lip in an ugly smirk.

'No one you know, Presten,' Joel replied.

'There's no one there.' Presten laughed. 'Surely you don't think I'm dumb enough to fall for that false back-up ploy we've all seen in a hundred cowboy and gangster films, Asher?'

Suddenly another Raven landed on the roof, followed by another and yet another. Soon there were scores of Ravens all over the bus shelter, on the ground in front of it, inside it, on the seat and round Peter and Joel. Before Presten knew what was happening, he was completely surrounded by Ravens.

'What's going on?' Presten panicked. 'Get these mangy vermin away from me!' He yelled, suddenly scared.

'Give us the box, Presten!' Peter shouted.

'Get out!' Presten screamed, cowering from the Ravens.

Joel started to walk into the bus shelter and the Ravens parted in front of him, making a pathway to Presten.

'What the heck?' Presten exclaimed. 'Get away - you freak!'

'Give, Presten.' Joel held out his hand for the box.

All of a sudden Magee flew with a loud squawk at Presten. The shock of that scared him witless. He threw the box at Joel and crouched on the ground, covering his head with his hands.

'Aagh! Get off me! Go away! Go away!' He cried wimpishly.

As soon as Joel had caught the box, the Ravens flew off in all directions, leaving just Maggi and Magee perched on the roof.

'Thanks, Magi!' Joel shouted up to the two Ravens.

'You're welcome,' came the twofold reply.

'Uh oh,' Maggi nudged Magee.

Magee followed Maggi's gaze and gulped, lowering his beak to his breast in a resigned shrug.

'You've done it now, Magee.' Maggi scolded him. 'How are we ever going to get promoted now? You're always getting us into trouble!'

'What is it?' Joel followed the birds' gaze.

'Look, Joel!' Peter cried, pointing at the sky. 'It - it's a shooting star - or a UFO...'

Joel and Peter watched the bright light, which seemed to be coming straight at them and judging by the Ravens' reaction, heralded impending doom.

'There's nothing there, you moron.' Presten sneered as he crawled out of the shelter and looked up.

'It's not a shooting star,' Magee shrugged despondently.

'And it's certainly no UFO.' Maggi explained. 'We know exactly what, or rather who, that is.'

ARRIVAL OF THE MAGI

Joel and Peter looked somewhat confused.

'It's Maguff,' Magee said gloomily.

'He's our Supervisor,' Maggi explained. 'The Angel in charge of all of us Earth Guardians. There's no need to worry, boys; he won't be mad at you two - and the other boy won't be able to see or hear anything.'

The star-like light arrived and hovered over them, then all of a sudden it flashed like a firework, bursting with hundreds of starry sparks, which then magically transformed into a very large and magnificent Golden Eagle. It was surrounded by a warm glowing light. The Eagle glared at Magee, tutted, shook its head, then turned to Joel and Peter.

'Maguff, at your service.' Maguff spoke with authority and gave a noble bow. 'I'm the Senior Angel in charge of the Magi, Kairos earthbound Guardians. Ordinarily I only get involved in matters requiring urgent management action - or as in this case,' Maguff said, turning a displeased eye on Magee, 'matters of a disciplinary nature!' He began to pace up and down with the air of a Major General addressing the troops.

Magee's neck seemed to stretch and he gulped weakly, as Maguff delivered his dressing down; while all Maggi could do was hide her head under a wing, occasionally peering out forlornly.

'What were you thinking of, Magee? Summoning every Raven within a twenty-mile radius! Of all the irresponsible, cockeyed, dumb stunts! What were you trying to achieve - mass target practice for the locals? Or were you simply showing off your power? Because I can have all that revoked, you know, Magee. How would the pair of you like to spend the next five hundred years as sewer rats?'

Maggi gasped, 'Maguff, I - I'm sure Magee sorely regrets...'

'It wasn't Magee's fault, Maguff.' Joel interrupted. 'It was me. I insisted on them being summoned - we were desperate - Magee had no choice...'

'Who are y' talking to now, Asher - your invisible friend?' Presten said, a little shakily, unable to hear the Bird Angels' side of the conversation. 'You've got what you wanted. Now clear off - you crazy crackpots! It's your fault my sister is going to die! She should have been at home instead of with you two weirdos!'

'Shut up, Presten!' Peter blurted out.

'Oh get lost, you nutter!' Presten pushed past Peter and ran off.

Maguff shook his head and sighed.

'One always has a choice, you know, Magee,' he coolly pointed out.

Magee hung his head dejectedly.

'Maguff...' Joel persisted. 'Don't be too hard on Magee. He was just trying to help - our friend is about to have her life-support cut off.'

'Oh, yes.' Maguff stopped pacing and looked compassionately at Joel, then turned back to Magee. 'Well all right, Magee; you're lucky that your charge has spoken up for you. I'll take his plea for mitigation into consideration. Please - be more sensible in future! One more dumb, risky incident and I'm afraid I'll have to have your wings.'

Maggi breathed such a heavy sigh of relief that she almost collapsed.

'Yes, thank you, Maguff.' Magee looked up and nodded gratefully.

'Well what are you two standing there for?' Maguff boomed at the boys. 'It's almost three o'clock! Get yourselves down to that hospital PDQ. You've got a life to save!'

'Let's hope we're in time. Come on, Peter!' Joel cried.

The two boys ran off in the direction of the hospital.

CHAPTER ELEVEN

A Blessing and the Gauntlet

One by one, Tamara's close friends and relatives had said their goodbyes with kisses and tears. Reverend Matthews had just finished the blessing service at her bedside and they were getting ready to switch off the life-support machine.

However, two very close friends were absent - Joel and Peter had failed to turn up for their last goodbye. Grandad had kept looking at his watch and then in a final attempt to stall the action, he had asked if he could say a prayer before the switch-off. He was kneeling by Tamara, praying privately for the boys to get there - with the box. The Doctor's hand was hovering over the switch that would send Tamara flying up the tunnel in which the Vista had shown her trapped, when suddenly...

'Wait!' Joel shouted, as he and Peter ran breathlessly into the room.

Everyone looked round in surprise.

'W - we haven't said goodbye...' Joel said awkwardly.

The Doctor lowered his hand.

'All right, boys - two minutes. I'm sorry, but I've got other patients waiting to see me. You should really have been here half an hour ago.'

'Thank you, Doctor. We're very sorry.' Joel breathed a sigh of relief, then exchanged glances with Grandad, who winked and moved swiftly to the door. Joel and Peter walked up to Tamara's bedside. Joel opened the box and glanced at Grandad again. Grandad gave a slight nod and put his hand on the light switch.

'Bright in here, isn't it?' he said, flicking the switch. 'Aagh!' Grandad clutched at his chest, as though he had suffered an electric shock.

The light went out and a blinding flash occurred as Joel tipped the horn out of the box into Tamara's hand and closed her fingers around it. The bright light pulsated for a second around Tamara, then it disappeared. Everyone saw the flash, but because they had turned in response to Grandad's cry, they did not see the extraordinary light that surrounded Tamara, bathing her from head to foot.

'Mr Jacob!' Mrs Goodchild shrieked. 'Doctor - quick!'

Everyone crowded round Grandad, except Joel and Peter, who were beaming the biggest smiles of their entire lives at Tamara, who was now sitting up in bed.

'Eoow! Mum, how could you put this vile dress on me? Where are my jeans?' Tamara cried.

With that, Grandad recovered instantly and everyone turned and stared at Tamara with open mouths, as though she'd just arrived from outer space. Mrs Goodchild rushed up to her and hugged her so tightly that Tamara had to beg for air. It was all very emotional.

'Well this truly *is* a blessing,' Matthews said with a wink at Joel and Peter.

'Yes, Vicar, thank you so much.' Mr Goodchild shook Matthews by the hand so vigorously, that he almost disjointed his whole arm.

Everyone started talking excitedly at once, with claims of the second miracle in one week. However, Joel, Peter and Grandad did what they could to discourage that idea. The last thing they wanted was any kind of reporter sniffing around, investigating claims of miracles.

Joel and Peter started showing Tamara all the cards and presents she'd been sent. She announced she was absolutely starving and begged for a plate of chips with tomato sauce, which the nurses were only too pleased to rustle up. Joel had surreptitiously retrieved the horn, which now looked dull and grey, as it had when it fell out of the note and he carefully put it back in the box under lock and key.

Tamara was horrified to find out how close she had been to "handing in her riding boots" and declared that she couldn't wait to get back on Cherokee for a good gallop.

'So, I bet I've missed loads of exciting stuff, while you two were enjoying yourselves. What's been happening then?' Tamara asked.

Joel and Peter looked at each other and then back at her.

'Nothing really,' Peter replied with a shrug. 'Been really quiet, hasn't it, Joel?'

'Yeah, that's right, there's been nothing happening. We've been nearly dying of boredom.' Joel nodded in agreement.

'Huh - yeah, I suppose that was a silly question,' Tamara said. 'I mean what could possibly happen in this sleepy old place?'

'Joel and Peter have spent most of their time here, Tamara, love,' Mrs Goodchild explained happily, 'trying to wake you up with wonderful stories about Unicorns.'

'Unicorns!' Tamara cried. 'Oh what's happened to Storm?'

Grandad looked at Peter and Joel reproachfully.

'Oh you know what Peter is like,' Joel said dismissively. 'He's always making up these stories...'

'The foal is perfectly well now, Tamara. He was collected yesterday and is now safe and well in his rightful home,' Grandad explained.

+

The Doctor wanted to keep Tamara in the hospital for a couple of days for some tests, but she refused point blank. She'd already missed most of the Easter holiday and wasn't going to be detained a minute longer than absolutely necessary.

'I was nearly dead - now I'm as alive as I ever was. You can't keep me a bla de bla prisoner in here. I want to get out and start living!' she insisted, in her typically cheeky but cute way.

'Well we can't argue with that, darling,' Mrs Goodchild said beaming.

'It's nice to have you back, Tamara,' Joel said with a grin. Everyone nodded in agreement.

The Doctor insisted on giving Grandad a full examination before he left the hospital and he called out the electricians to check for a fault. Grandad felt really guilty; it was such a shocking waste of the Doctor's time when there was absolutely nothing wrong with either him or the light switch. However, he reckoned it was a small price to pay to see Tamara well again.

+

That evening, after a good meal, Joel and Peter collapsed in exhaustion on the couch in Grandad's lounge. Grandad flopped into his rocking chair, feeling just the same. They'd all missed a lot of sleep over the last few days and as relief came over them, all they wanted to do was to crash out in their beds.

Joel picked up Grandad's Bible from the table by his chair and turned to the last page of the book of Joel. He smiled at Peter as they both read the last line, then he placed it back on the table.

'You were really cool today, Grandad,' Joel said proudly, unable to stifle a yawn.

'Yeah, you're the best, Mr Jacob,' Peter agreed, catching Joel's yawn.

'Thanks, boys.' Grandad smiled modestly. 'I guess we'll all sleep well tonight, eh?'

The boys finally crawled into their pyjamas and then into bed and were asleep by the time their heads hit the pillows.

+

At daybreak the familiar call from Cedric awoke them. They had a comfortable feeling that all was well. Tamara was better; Storm had been safely returned and life was back to relative normality - except that life would never be 'normal' again as far as Joel and Peter were concerned, until they were sixteen.

'Are you awake, Peter?' Joel whispered, propping up his pillows.

'Unfortunately, I am now.' Peter sat up and stretched.

'I was just slowly coming round to the belief that it was all over and then I realised - it's far from over, isn't it, Peter? It's only just beginning.'

'It really happened then - I mean, your Dad and everything?'

'Well if we'd any thoughts that maybe we'd dreamt the whole thing, I think they would have been well and truly bashed on the bonce by those quarrelling Magi yesterday. I mean, we couldn't possibly have dreamt them up as well!' Joel laughed.

'Hey, they were something, weren't they?' Peter chuckled. 'So what do you think we should do, Joel?'

'You mean, do we take on the mission - or forget the whole thing?'

'What do you want to do?'

'Well I'll put it this way, Peter. I'd not seen my Dad for four years. If I've got the chance of seeing him again over the next four years, I'm going to take it. I don't care how dangerous this mission is. I'm not a kid any more, I'm nearly thirteen. My Dad has work for me to do, he's counting on me. Peter, he's my Dad and I'm not going to let him down, whatever it takes. What do you say?'

'You don't think I'd let my best mate face all that danger and excitement without me, do you? Of course I'm going to do it! I'm right there with you, Joel, every step of the way.'

'So what do we tell Tamara? You know she's going to want to come up to Zionica with us. We can't make it look like we're leaving her out, can we? But there will be times when we'll need to go up to Zionica on our own, to discuss and plan things. How can we do that without hurting her feelings?'

'Especially after what she's been through.' Peter sighed. 'But remember what your Dad said about time up there. It felt like we'd been there for hours, didn't it? But when we got back, we found we'd only been gone a few minutes. I'm sure we can work something out, Joel.'

'Yes, you're probably right. We'll just have to play it by ear for a while till we know more about what we're doing. Come on, let's get up and wrestle that manic cockerel for some eggs. If my hunch is right, someone will be arriving any time now to collect Cherokee.'

'Your Grandad will miss the pony, he's fond of her.'
'Grandad gets fond of anything with four legs and a tail. You know what he's like - soft as mush.'

+

Before they'd finished breakfast, the feisty Tamara had arrived, full of beans and ready for anything. She joined them at the breakfast table and pinched their toast soldiers, dipping them into the boy's eggs.

'What are we going to do today? Have you made any plans?' Tamara inquired eagerly.

'No, er, we - thought you'd want to take Cherokee out for a ride. We didn't think you'd want to bother with us until you'd told her how much you'd missed her at least a hundred times,' Joel teased, trying to sound casual.

'Oh in that case we can spend the day in Zionica - after my ride, can't we?'

'Yes, that's a great idea, Tamara. You can spend the morning with Cherokee and we'll all hang around and do stuff this afternoon,' replied Joel.

'You're not trying to get rid of me, are you?' Tamara asked suspiciously.

'What do you mean? Of course not,' Joel said quickly.

'O.K. then this afternoon you can tell me all about what happened to Storm. See you later.' Tamara jumped up and went outside.

'Good, that will give us a chance to go back to Dad and find out exactly what his plan is,' Joel muttered to Peter.

+

Joel and Peter packed some food to leave in the tree den for lunch when they got back, then headed for Zionica.

'We can't delay this any longer, Peter,' Joel said seriously.

'I wonder if we have to wait for rain and a rainbow every time we go. That could be a little inconvenient,' Peter said.

'Well we can't wait for rain,' Joel said with some urgency. 'Dad said if we didn't return in three days, our memories would be erased. I'm not risking that happening now I've got my Dad back; the sooner we go the better.'

'I guess there's only one thing to do then, Joel.' Peter nodded a little nervously.

They left their things in the den, then made their way to the plateau. They stopped at the edge of the plateau and looked at each other hesitantly. Both of them trembled with excitement as they gripped hands and stepped onto the plateau together.

CHAPTER TWELVE

A Beautiful Spanish Mentor

Unexpectedly, they didn't have to wait at all, as the second their feet hit the plateau, Joel and Peter were scooped up by the light which carried them through the Fugue tunnel, just as before. They could see the bright light at the top and before they knew it, they were looking up at the beautiful smiles of Charis and Aleathia.

'Hello again, boys,' Charis said beaming. 'We were expecting you this time and so were Nathan and Anna. We're all so glad you've decided to join us.'

Charis and Aleathia held the boys' hands and helped them up.

'Thanks, Charis,' Joel said smiling. Turning round, he saw Nathan and Anna standing by. 'Dad!' He grinned at Nathan.

'Welcome back, boys,' Nathan said delightedly.

'We knew you'd come,' said Anna proudly.

'What *is* that?' Peter asked, looking around in amazement. 'I remember beautiful singing last time we were here, but it wasn't quite like this...'

There were lots of Angels floating all around; they seemed to be excited and were singing with sweet, hypnotic voices. They were beautiful, elegant beings, all between six and nine feet tall. They each had six white wings: one small pair covered their glowing faces; another small pair covered their feet and a larger pair were used for flying. They carried gold-and-crystal sceptres and soft light glowed all around them.

'Oh that's the Seraphs.' Nathan smiled. 'They're celebrating. Every time there's a new Kairos member confirmed, they rejoice and sing like that. It's such a miracle when one such child is found, but on this occasion we've two together. That's a first for us here and a reason for much joy.'

Nathan looked proudly at Joel and Peter.

'How have you been, boys?'

'Great, Dad. I can't tell you how happy I've been since I've found you.' Joel beamed.

'And your friend, Tamara, is as perky as ever, I believe?' Nathan smiled happily.

'Yes, everything fell into place and suddenly it all made perfect sense. It was touch-and-go when Presten stole the box but...'

'The Magi helped you, did they not?'

'The Magi?' Joel whistled. 'Those quarrelsome Ravens are a bit testing to say the least.'

'Oh I see, they were on top form as usual, were they?'

'Top form? You mean that's a regular double act?' Joel frowned.

'I'm afraid so, Joel.' Nathan laughed. 'They've been together for a very long time - thousands of years; they're never apart - joined at the wing you might say. Maybe they were a bit cranky because it's a long time since they were last Ravens. But you can trust them with your lives. They would protect you at all costs.'

'Yes, they did come through in the end, Joel, didn't they?' Peter said, defending the Magi.

'That they did, good-style, and you did warn us about them, didn't you, Dad?' Joel nodded. 'Oh and that reminds me, I've got something I need to return with grateful thanks.' He took the small piece of Unicorn horn from his pocket and opened his hand. The horn was glistening like crystal.

Cheyiea appeared instantly by Joel's side and nudging him gently, he lowered his head in a bow. Joel lifted the piece of horn and placed it on the end of Cheyiea's horn. Like a magic glass slipper it fitted perfectly, making the horn complete.

'There you go, Cheyiea, as good as new. You've had to wait a long time for that, haven't you? We're all very grateful to you - thanks a lot.' Joel smiled cheerfully.

Cheyiea blinked and shook his head, flicking his long mane, then he flew off.

'So what happens now?' Joel asked eagerly.

'Come, follow me.' Nathan beckoned. 'Blessed is He,' he smiled at the Reception Angels and led the boys and Anna away.

'Blessed is He. See you later, boys,' Charis and Aleathia called after them.

+

Joel and Peter followed Nathan and Anna up the aisle of archways to the area with the pearl-and-gold chairs. Here Nathan sat them down.

'Now for every job you first need some basic training,' Nathan began. 'We cannot set you a task, particularly such an immensely important and dangerous one as this, without first arming you with some skills of the trade, so to speak. The best way to acquire them is to ride pillion with someone who already has them. So to ease you into the roles you have been chosen for, who better to show you the ropes but an experienced old hand?' Nathan motioned to his right. 'Boys, meet Maria Teresa - or Maité, as she likes to be called.'

A Spanish girl floated up in front of them and smiled confidently, tossing her head back. At fifteen, Maité was blossoming into a beautiful young woman, with smooth, olive, sun-tanned skin and compassionate, dark, almond-shaped eyes, framed by sleek, short, black, shiny hair.

'Maité, this is Joel and this is Peter,' Nathan said introducing them. 'Maité is from the Spanish arm of the Kairos, based at Morisco, where they have several members. She has very kindly agreed to help us with your initiation, as there are currently no British Kairos children. She is very experienced and has accomplished many successful missions. She will help you adapt to being part of the Kairos - but you'll have to learn fast, it's her sixteenth birthday this Saturday, so she leaves the Kairos on Friday.'

Maité looked the boys up and down, then spoke in fluent English with an attractive Spanish accent.

'So you are the two whelps to be weaned from mother's

milk?' she teased, raising an eyebrow and smiling with a twinkle in her eyes. She spoke like a seasoned professional taking on a couple of clueless, wet-behind-the-ears apprentices.

'I'm looking forward to getting my teeth into something a little more solid,' Joel replied smartly.

'Hmm - touché, maestro.' Maité nodded and held out her hand.

Joel rose from his chair and glided forward. Slipping his hand round Maité's, he looked her straight in the eye in an attempt to look cool, but her expressive eyes were still making fun of him. There was something quite enigmatic about her - it made his heart skip a beat.

'Well, Joel, I think we'll get on just fine.' Maité turned to Peter. 'What do you say, Peter?'

'Cool.' Peter gulped. He was used to girls fussing over him, but he'd never met one as cool, confident and alluring as Maité.

Nathan winked knowingly at the boys.

'Now the first thing, boys, is to present you with your number-mark,' Nathan said.

'Number-mark?' Joel said, puzzled. 'What's that?'

'It's your unique number in the Kairos. All the Kairos children have an identification number between one and one hundred and fifty. There's no ceremonial swearing-in or declaration of oaths in the Kairos - simply because you wouldn't have been selected to join and your number-mark would not accept you, if your heart wasn't committed to the cause,' Nathan explained. 'Your number stays with you all the time you are in the Kairos, then when you leave, you pass it on to your successor.'

'Oh so we don't merely become a hundred and forty-nine and a hundred and fifty?' said Peter.

'Oh no, that's not how it works, Peter. You take on the number of the member you've replaced. I have your numbers here. Peter, this is yours.'

Nathan held out his hand and balanced between his fore-finger and thumb, was a small light, about the size of a thumbnail. The light was in the shape of "K 18". It was like the gold pin they'd seen in Grandad's box, except that this wasn't a gold pin; in fact there was no substance to it at all - it was just pure light. Nathan placed it on Peter's forehead and Joel watched, open-mouthed, as the light seemed to be absorbed.

'K 18.' Peter smiled proudly. 'I felt that, Mr Asher. It felt good.'

Nathan smiled and turned to Joel. Between his finger and thumb was another light: this one was K 119. Joel felt the light dissolve into his forehead.

'You're right, Peter. That did feel good,' Joel remarked. Then he looked at Maité and saw a small glow on her forehead that he hadn't noticed before. 'You're Kairos 121,' he said to Maité.

'That's right,' Nathan said. 'Now you're truly a Kairos, you will be able to recognise other Kairos children and they will also know you.'

'Cool! Hey, Dad, what number was Grandad?'

'Oh let me think - 87 - yes, Grandad was 87,' answered Nathan.

'Grandad has a gold pin of his number,' said Joel.

'Yes, all the Kairos children get presented with their number as a gold pin when they leave. Although they don't remember its significance, they do all treasure it always; they know in their hearts it's special,' Nathan explained.

'What was Mum's number, Dad?' Joel asked quietly.

'23.' Nathan answered without hesitation.

'Psalm 23?' Joel muttered.

'Yes, Son, Mum was Psalm 23.' Nathan blinked. 'You've taken me seriously; you are learning fast.'

'I'm my Father's Son,' Joel replied proudly.

'Yes, I can see you are.' Nathan smiled. 'Now I'm going to leave you for a while in Maité's capable hands. Anna will stay with you too. I believe they've organised a small exercise for you - just to get your feet wet...' Nathan exchanged grins with Maité.

'You will be back, Dad?' Joel asked anxiously.

'Of course; don't worry, we'll have plenty of time together -

we'll be working very closely for the next four years. But now you should pay attention to Maité; she can give you invaluable help.' Nathan put a hand on each boy's shoulder. 'Remember, boys, you have the best defence *in* you...

> *'The Belt of Truth,*
> *the Breastplate of Righteousness,*
> *the Shoes of Readiness,*
> *the Shield of Faith,*
> *the Helmet of Salvation,*
> *the Sword of the Spirit and*
> *the Love of God.'*

With that, Nathan vanished before their eyes. Joel and Peter looked at Maité and gulped nervously.

'O.K. soldiers, attention!' Maité made the two boys jump as she shouted.

They looked at her with wide open mouths. Then she fell about, laughing.

'You should see your two faces; they are a picture.' Maité giggled. Then recovering, she beckoned them with her fingers and a teasing smile. 'Come, come, come,' she said quickly and without waiting, glided off.

'I don't know which is worse, quarrelsome Ravens or the Sergeant Major here,' Joel muttered to Peter with a 'tut'.

'Well you've got to admit, she's the prettiest, Joel,' Peter whispered back. 'Actually she's quite fun. I think we're going to enjoy this.'

'What?' Joel exclaimed as though Peter had gone mad.

Peter grinned and pushed off to glide after Maité. Joel shook his head and followed.

+

Maité, accompanied by Anna, led them through the turquoise archway to the Vista, where she adopted a more serious attitude.

They soon discovered that despite her cheeky sense of humour and teasing, Maité was a true, dedicated professional when it came to her missions. One hundred per cent committed, always putting others' safety before her own. She was certainly a worthy mentor to emulate.

Having been a Kairos child for almost six years, Maité was the longest-serving member of the group. First of all she gave the boys a potted history of her own endeavours, ranging from leading searchers to lost children, to providing Spanish police with evidence as to the whereabouts of a dangerous killer. Many people who would have been his future victims, walked the earth unaware that they were living lives they would have lost and having children that would never have been conceived but for this brave young girl.

'I cannot stress to you strongly enough, my friends, how important is our work in the Kairos,' Maité said. 'We are battling against a very dangerous foe. Satan has armies of evil-doers at his command. But we cannot fight him as he fights us; that would make us like him and give him more ammunition. Our best defence against him is the Christian armour described by Nathan, against which Satan is powerless. The end is already planned for Satan: he will expire in a fiery pit of sulphur. Those who do his evil work will join him.' Maité paused to let this profound statement sink in. Then her face softened and she smiled at the boys with a teasing look in her eyes as she continued. 'Any questions before we go into specifics?'

The two boys stared at her mesmerised and speechless. Then Peter nudged Joel.

'No - no - um, we're with you so far, Maité, aren't we, Peter?' Joel said, desperate not to appear an idiot.
Peter nodded. He didn't have one sensible question in his head, just a lot of mixed-up ones.

'Let's go into specifics, Maité,' Joel went on, hoping the specifics would clear up the confusion in his head.

'Good, good, this is good, you understand everything, hmm?' Maité nodded and waved her arms around magnanimously.

'Then I have a question for you.'

Joel and Peter looked at her anxiously. Joel could feel the heat rising under his collar.

'Which of you two boys can explain to me how we get from here into - shall we say, Scotland Yard - without raising some kind of suspicion?'

'You should have told us you ask questions at the end, Maité. We'd have made notes.' Joel shrugged in an attempt to appear cool, when inside he was feeling more like a boiling kettle.

'Of course you cannot answer that question - I have not explained it to you yet,' Maité said, cocking her head to one side and smiling coolly.

'I would have thought the answer to that question was quite obvious, Maité,' Joel said with a forced confidence.

'Oh a smart guy - go on then, Joel, give it to me.'

'The answer is simple: we can't. None of us could appear in Scotland Yard without raising some suspicion,' Joel said assertively.

'Correct. How did you know that was a trick question?'

'I didn't, I just used the laws of common sense.'

'Pretty good, you'll do well,' Maité said agreeably. 'O.K. - now in order to do the very important work we are chosen for, it is necessary for us to travel with speed. In short, we need to appear and disappear at will. We cannot do this via the Fugue, because we will need to go to different places. The Fugue only takes us back to our home base. Now for a simple trial. Where would you like to go?'

'How about my Grandad's barn?' Joel suggested.

'Hmm, an odd choice. You are given a choice of anywhere in the world. Personally I would have chosen a beach in the Caribbean, but if you want to go to Grandfather's barn, so be it,' Maité said with a playful shrug.

Joel started a little indignantly, then realising that to backpedal would just make him look even less cool, he looked down, cursing himself for such a dumb and unimaginative choice of destination.

Peter gave him a sympathetic look.

'Now,' Maité went on, 'all travel other than between Heaven and home base is done via the Vista. Let me show you. First you face the Vista and think of your desired destination - in this case,' Maité said exaggerating a sigh to tease Joel even more, 'Grandfather's barn.' Her eyes sparkled as she raised an eyebrow.

They watched the Vista and Grandad's barn appeared. Then the inside of the barn came into view and they saw Grandad.

'Oh what a shame.' Maité grinned. 'This is the beauty of the Vista: you can see if the coast is clear. As Grandfather is in the barn, we'll have to take Choice B - the Caribbean beach. Oh no, wait...'

As they watched, Grandad picked up a bale of hay and went back outside.

'You're in luck, Joel - the coast is clear after all.' Maité held out her hands. 'Come. Anna, you will watch the Vista?'

'I'll be here, Maité.' Anna nodded.

Peter took Maité's outstretched hand; Joel glided forward and took her other hand.

'Just glide into the Vista, boys,' Maité directed them.

The three of them stepped into the Vista and before they knew what was happening, they were standing in the middle of Grandad's barn.

'Wow!' Peter exclaimed. 'How awesome is that? How did we get here?'

Suddenly they heard a horse's hooves outside and Tamara's voice calling.

'Hello, Mr Jacob, can I leave Cherokee in your barn for a while?'

'Yes, Tamara, put her in her usual stall,' came Grandad's reply.

'Thanks, Mr Jacob.'

'Quick, it's Tamara, she's coming in here!' Joel cried. 'How do we get back?'

They saw the handle on the barn door move as Tamara lifted

it. Maité raised her hand in front of her and a schism appeared in mid-air like an ethereal curtain, opening. They walked forward into the schism as the barn door opened and suddenly they were gliding out of the Vista into Heaven again.

'And it's as simple as that,' Maité said with a shrug.

'Cool,' Joel said with a feigned nonchalance.

'Phew - that was a close call. Tamara almost bumped into us.' Peter whistled.

'Yes, you must take care when travelling through the Vista. No one must ever see you arrive or leave. Now let me go over the rules,' Maité continued. 'First check thoroughly on the Vista that there is no one about before you travel. You cannot just suddenly appear before someone on earth, for obvious reasons.'

'What if someone does accidentally see you, Maité?' Peter asked.

'Well we might be in Heaven but we are still human. However careful we are, mistakes do occasionally happen. But people are very good at dismissing things as *just their imagination*. Have you never thought you'd seen someone, then looked again and found that they weren't there?' Maité shrugged.

Both boys looked a little stunned. Maité smiled at them.

'All I'm saying, boys, is be as careful as you can. Now using the Vista is simple. You think of the place where you want to go and it will appear before your eyes. Then you simply glide into it. As you go through the Vista you open up a schism. To get back, lift up your hand anywhere in the vicinity of your arrival place and think Vista. The schism you created will open for you and you just walk into it. If for any reason you cannot return to the arrival place, then you must still put up your hand and think Vista. When you travel through it there is always someone watching from up here. The watcher will get your message and will create a schism for you. 'You must *never* travel through the Vista without making sure someone is watching. In no circumstances are you to try bringing anyone up through the Vista who is not a Kairos; it would result in their certain death. Remember, this is a place where people normally come only when they die. You are able to come and go for a reason and only because He allows it. Any flouting of the rules would mean the instant erasure of your memory and a return to your pre-Kairos life.

'No objects - coins, for instance maybe transported in this way. Only you and the clothes you wear will be accepted, though a limited amount of paper money is allowed, as sometimes our missions require it.

'Now please remember this very important rule - you can go anywhere in the present, but in no circumstances must you ever attempt to go into the past or the future. Only God can change time because He created it. In the whole history of the world as far as we know, He has only ever changed time once. That was when He made time stand still for about a day for Joshua, to help him defeat the Amorites. This was a very long time ago, even before Jesus came down to earth.' Maité smiled at her mesmerised audience.

'This is how powerful our Creator is - aren't you glad you're on the winning team?' She carried on. 'Please remember the past cannot be changed; it has already happened and time cannot be turned back. The future is a dynamic, constantly changing arena which does not yet exist - it is merely an empty void. Such notions as time travel are strictly for science fiction. The consequences of attempting it would be disastrous for you. There would be no return - it would be a one-way ticket to the wrong side - and oblivion. The results would be so dire that I dare not utter them - *comprende*?'

'Crystal clear, Maité.' Peter nodded.

'Ditto.' Joel gave a cool shrug.

'Good. Now Joel, you take us somewhere,' said Maité.

'Me?'

'Anywhere you like - er, within reason of course. Just remember, there are inbuilt mechanisms to stop the Vista being abused - you will not be allowed into the girl's changing-rooms for instance.'

'Neither of us would attempt anything so unworthy,' Joel said indignantly.

'I know, just kidding.' Maité smiled apologetically.

Joel hesitantly moved forward and took both Peter and Maité by the hand. They all looked into the Vista and there appeared an idyllic view of a deserted beach. Suddenly they all felt the warm, soft, white sand under their feet and the warm sea breeze against their skin and in their hair - and they heard the sound of the gently lapping, clear, blue sea.

'So you do have some taste, Joel?' Maité said teasingly.
'Hmm - every job has its perks.' Kicking off her sandals, she threw back her head and ran towards the sea, laughing.

Joel and Peter grinned at each other, shrugged, kicked off their own shoes and ran after Maité. Soon they were all splashing about in the water. For Joel and Peter, it was the most fun they'd had in what seemed like ages. After all the upset with Tamara, it felt really good to let their hair down.

+

After a time of playful tomfoolery in the water, the three of them lay under some palm trees, drying out in the heat. Joel was just about to doze off when he was suddenly startled. At first he thought he was dreaming when he heard a familiar voice.

'So how long did you think you could hide this from me, hey?' Tamara's voice was all too clear.

Joel opened his eyes. To his utter amazement he realised that he wasn't dreaming at all. Tamara's face was leaning right over him, with her unmistakable cheeky grin.

'Tamara! What are you doing here?' Joel sat up quickly and grabbed his shirt.

Peter and Maité sat up too and stared at Tamara.

'You know this person?' Maité inquired.

'This is - our friend, Tamara,' Joel answered, baffled.

Tamara looked at Maité and straight away Maité saw the faint 'K 63' on her forehead.

'Oh hello,' Maité greeted Tamara, getting up and shaking the sand off her. 'I'm Maité.'

'I know,' said Tamara. 'Anna sent me to get you.'

'Oh she did...?' Maité shrugged and smiled a little humorously.

Peter and Joel jumped to their feet and both started talking at once, wanting to know exactly how Tamara came to be there.

'I came here exactly the same way you did - through the Vista. I got fed up with waiting for you two. I thought we were going to hang about after my ride. I waited ages in Zionica and there was no sign of you. It was like you vanished into thin air. Your Grandad didn't know where you were either.'

'But wait a minute,' Joel said, confused. 'I thought time stood still - that we could stay in Heaven as long as we wanted while hardly any time would pass on earth?'

'But you're not in Heaven now, are you, Joel?' Tamara said with an amused smile.

'What do you mean? We've come through the Vista - surely...' Joel's voice tailed off as it began to dawn on him.

'No, Joel,' Maité said. 'Much as this idyllic beach feels like Heaven - we're in the world now. The second you step through the Vista into the world, you are subject to earth time laws. That is also the case when you watch events in real earth-time through the Vista. I thought you'd have twigged that when Nathan told you to learn fast - you've only got me for four more days. We must have been here a couple of hours.'

'That's right,' Tamara said. 'I went for a ride on Cherokee, then I put her in your Grandad's barn and gave her some corn. Then I went up to Zionica as arranged and waited for about an hour. When you didn't show up, I wandered round the field and as I stepped onto the plateau, I called your names out in frustration. The next thing I knew, I was hurtling up a tunnel and well, you know the rest. I've spent ages with Nathan and Anna; they've explained everything to me. I probably know as much as you now - and guess what? I've seen Storm, he's grown a lot.'

'We know, we've seen him too,' Peter said, happily. 'This is fantastic, Tamara. I'm so glad we don't have to keep it all secret from you. We were really worried about how we could do all this without letting something slip and you finding out - weren't we, Joel?'

'Yeah, what a relief,' Joel said then he took hold of Tamara by the shoulders and looked down at her anxiously. 'Are you sure you want to do this, Tamara? There's a lot of danger involved and we don't want you getting hurt. Look what you've been through already.'

Maité looked away awkwardly at this sudden show of concern from Joel for Tamara.

'Joel, I think it's great that you care.' Tamara said, surprised and a little embarrassed by his sudden display of feelings. 'But I've never been more sure about anything in my whole life.' Then looking him up and down, she said. 'You know, you've got a problem, Joel.'

'Oh?' Joel was curious.

'Yes, have you thought how you're going to explain your suntan to your Grandad? You'll have white bits - and you, Peter.'

Joel and Peter both looked down at their bare chests; they'd discarded their shirts earlier. They'd not been on the beach very long but the sun was so strong that they'd started to tan.

'Ooh...' Joel muttered, pulling a face. 'Well Grandad is as blind as a bat without his glasses - he won't notice.'

They all tipped the sand out of their shoes and shook their clothes. Then Maité put up her hand and opened the schism for them all.

Instantly they glided out of the Vista into utter mayhem. Nathan, Anna and the two Reception Angels, Charis and Aleathia, were waiting for them like a sort of welcome committee. There seemed to be a bit of a celebration going on.

The Seraphs had gone batty: they were flying around in a furore, fluttering their massive wings and swooping down. They were singing even louder than before and calling to each other. They all carried their gold-and-crystal sceptres, which they were shaking and waving, spreading tiny sparkling droplets of light everywhere, like showers of glitter. Everyone had to keep ducking to avoid the excited Seraphs.

'What's going on?' Peter cried.

'The Seraphs are rejoicing,' Anna explained. 'Ever since Tamara received her number-mark, it's been chaos. It's such a joyous occasion when another Kairos child is recruited so soon. This is their way of celebrating.'

A Seraph flew right at them; stopped and hovered over them. They looked up and the Seraph allowed them to see his beautiful, radiant face. Tipping up his sceptre, he sprinkled a shower of light over them; it tickled their faces and filled them with a warm glow of happiness.

'Thanks,' Joel said to the smiling Seraph.

'Wow! That must be some sort of happy dust!' Peter exclaimed.

'They're showering you with love - literally - that's why it feels so good,' Anna said laughing.

'You mean you can bottle it? Double wow!' said Peter, amazed.

The Seraph smiled warmly, then flew off to join the others.

'You all had a wonderful time,' Anna said smiling happily. 'I watched you splashing around in the water.'

'Yes, it was great fun,' said Joel. 'Dad must have really meant it when he said we were going to get our feet wet.'

'It was just a little treat we planned for you before the really serious work starts.' Nathan smiled, putting an arm round Tamara. 'Isn't it wonderful that your friend Tamara is now a Kairos too?'

'Yeah, keeping it a secret from her would have been a nightmare,' Peter said.

Tamara looked up at Nathan and smiled. Everyone was making such a fuss of her, while Maité stood quietly watching.

'But we've not forgotten why we're here. We're ready for action,' Joel insisted. 'What's next, Maité?'

'I think that is enough for now,' said Maité. 'We will meet again here at your English earth-time-ten o'clock tomorrow morning. We will go on a training mission together - it will be kindergarten.'

'O.K. Maité.' Joel smiled. 'See you then.'

*'Hasta pronto,' Maité bowed her head, then glided off in the direction of the Fugue.

'What's up with Maité?' Joel said, surprised. 'She seems a little quiet all of a sudden.'

'I think it might have something to do with all this celebrating,' Nathan said compassionately. 'It must be a reminder to her that in only a few days she will no longer be a Kairos and will have no memory of all this. She's been such a dedicated worker - letting go is going to be hard for her.'

'At least it will be short-lived,' Peter said. 'When she wakes up on Saturday, she won't be upset any more, will she?'
Joel looked thoughtfully in the direction Maité had taken.

'You three had better be on your way now too,' Nathan said. 'Come on, I'll take you to the Fugue.'

---

* See you soon

CHAPTER THIRTEEN

The Garden of Lilies

Joel, Peter and Tamara arrived at the plateau to find another unexpected welcome committee, in the ravenous shapes of the Magi. All the food that they'd left in the den had been tantalising the Ravens and now had to be eaten. The Ravens, of course, were only too delighted to oblige and the three friends were left in no doubt about the origin of the word *ravenous*, because those Ravens certainly could eat.

They were all hungry, and the birds more than earned their share, as they delighted and entertained the young friends with amazing stories of their heroics in times (even centuries!) past. Tamara loved the Magi and thought they were hilariously funny - particularly when Magee, who had been perched on a branch over Joel's shoulder, surreptitiously leaned forward and snuck the ham out of his sandwich while he wasn't looking.

+

Now that everything was back to normal - as far as everyone else was concerned - Peter decided he'd better show his face at home, at least for a night. Tamara's parents were so delighted to have her back and terrified of losing her again, that she also decided she'd better go home. First though, they made their way down to Grandad's kitchen where they found him munching on a sandwich.

'We're back, Grandad,' Joel said cheerily as they walked into the kitchen.

'Oh hello, kids. You found the boys then, Tamara? I told you they wouldn't be far away.'

'They were in Zionica all along, Mr Jacob,' Tamara replied. 'Weren't you, boys?'

THE GARDEN OF LILIES

'Yeah, it's not like we've been halfway round the world, is it?' Joel said with a grin. Then he suddenly realised that, although it seemed as if they'd been gone all day because of all that had happened, they had in fact only been gone about three hours. It felt very strange not having to explain to anyone where they'd been all that time, but they hadn't even been missed.

So, exhausted and bewildered but very, very proud and happy, the three friends went their own separate ways for the evening.

+

That night, after Joel had climbed into bed, he picked up the framed picture that he always kept on his bedside table. It was a photo from the last holiday with his parents, before Dad died. He looked affectionately at the picture of the three of them, a happy family together. If only Mum knew that he was seeing Dad again. How hard it was going to be not to tell her, when he was longing to blurt it out - *Mum, I've seen Dad and he's all right*. But he knew that to mention it at all would be to lose him again, along with the memory. He knew that was going to happen anyway, but not for another four years - and he was determined that he wasn't going to lose his Dad one second before he had to.

Then he began to realise how Maité must be feeling, now her time in the Kairos was nearly over. No wonder she suddenly became sad, when everyone else was rejoicing. They'd had such fun on the beach that day. He was starting to like Maité more than he was willing to admit, despite her constant teasing. Then, with his family photo pressed to his chest, he let his heavy eyelids close and drifted off into a dream.

+

Next morning, everyone was refreshed and feeling full of energy after a good night's sleep. Grandad was out on the yard tending his flock and Joel was clearing away the breakfast dishes, when Tamara and Peter arrived.

'I wonder if they'll give us something easy for our first mission. I can't see them throwing us in at the deep end with this Sadler person. What do you two think?' Tamara asked.

'Yes, I expect we'll be given a small test mission before the big one - something simple, I should think,' Peter mused.

'Yes, I agree, Peter.' Joel nodded. 'I bet it's something equivalent to helping old ladies across the road,' he mused.

'Or maybe rescuing a cat from up a tree.' Peter chortled.

'Oh do be sensible you two,' Tamara said, grumbling. 'This is something to be taken very seriously.'

'We're only having a bit of fun, Tamara,' Joel protested. 'This isn't like you at all. Of course we're taking it seriously. Can we have the funny Tamara back now please?'

'Oh bla de bla...' Tamara shrugged.

'That's better.' Joel smiled at her. 'Right, let's go, shall we?'

As they skipped up the yard on their way to Zionica, Joel called over to Grandad.

'I've done the dishes, Grandad - er, do you want me to do anything else?'

'No, Son, you go and enjoy yourself with your friends - you've only got a few more days of the holiday left,' Grandad shouted back.

'Thanks, Grandad, see you later.'

'He's right, you know.' Peter sounded surprised. 'So much has happened that time has sped by. I'd forgotten it's Tuesday - your Mum is coming on Saturday to take you back, Joel.'

'Well at least you two have had an action-packed couple of weeks,' Tamara said with a hint of resentment. 'I've spent most of the holiday flat on my back in the hospital.'

'Tamara!' Joel cried in annoyance. 'Look, we're sorry you've missed out on a bit of action, but you've certainly made up for it now. Stop this self-pitying lark - don't you get it? This means we've only got four days to get that case off Sadler and deliver it to Smith - to prove my Dad was murdered!'

'Yeah and don't forget we've only got Maité to help us until Friday.' Peter added.

'Oh guys - I'm so sorry - I *was* wallowing in self-pity wasn't I? Now I feel so selfish,' Tamara said weakly.

'Hey,' Joel turned to Tamara. 'If there's anything you're not, Tamara, it's selfish. You're one of the most caring and unselfish people I know and *that* is why you're part of this.'

Tamara looked up at Joel, bit her lip and nodded.

'I'm sorry I shouted at you,' Joel said. 'O.K.?'

'O.K.' Tamara smiled.

'Shucks.' Peter remarked, 'This kind of dashes your theory about cutting our teeth helping old ladies over the road, Joel. I guess we're gonna get chucked in at the deep end after all.'

'Maybe that's the best thing, Peter. Isn't it exciting? Come on, let's go.' Joel suddenly started running towards Zionica, shouting 'We've got a world to save!'

Peter and Tamara grinned at each other, then chased after him.

+

Maité greeted the three friends at the top of the Fugue.

'Aah, I'm pleased to see you're keen.'

'Thanks, Maité,' Joel said grinning. 'Where are Charis and Aleathia?'

'What? Do you expect an Angel welcome committee every time you travel through the Fugue?' Maité replied in jest. 'They're having a break - even Angels get a break, you know, Joel.'

'Oh sorry, I didn't mean...' Joel began, a little embarrassed.

'I'm playing with you, Joel; have you no sense of humour?' Maité grinned. 'Come, amigos, we have much to do.' She glided off up the hall of archways.

Joel, Peter and Tamara took off and flew after her. Maité stopped at one of the archways. It had a diamond jewel at its pinnacle and a white light glowing from within. She turned to face them.

'This is the first stop for a new Kairos member.' Maité began seriously. 'All new Kairos members must visit here before they undertake any missions. You need to see this for your own good.'

'That sounds a bit serious, Maité,' Tamara said hesitantly. 'Should we be afraid?'

'No, there's nothing to fear, but you should be prepared,' Maité answered.

'Prepared for what, Maité?' asked Peter.

'For truth - for tears - for anything, amigo. Follow me.' Maité glided into the archway. The others looked at each other with trepidation, then followed. As they came out through the other end, it was like going out on a beautiful sunny day in the world. Their feet suddenly hit the ground and they were walking instead of gliding.

'Gravity!' Joel remarked, surprised. 'Is this another gateway back to the world?'

'No, we're still in Heaven, Joel,' Maité replied. 'This is the only chamber up here that appears to have permanent gravity. It's not actual gravity - it's a kind of *virtual gravity* - simulated for a special purpose.'

'What is that heavenly smell?' Tamara asked, breathing in the delicious scent. 'It's the most wonderful fragrance ever.'

'Our Lady has been here, Tamara; it is the sweet scent of the white Lily of the Valley. Everywhere our Lady goes, she leaves the beautiful fragrance, so you always know where she's been - or if she's about.'

'Our Lady?' Tamara gasped. 'You mean..?'

'Yes, I mean Our Gracious Lady. She visits here often and devotes much of her time to this place. It is a passion of hers, naturally.'

'Oh why is that, Maité? Where are we?' Tamara asked.

'The Garden of Lilies. It is the Nursery, of course.'

'Oh I see, she likes flowers then?' Tamara said quite innocently.

Maité threw back her head and laughed.

'No! The babes, it is the children.' She giggled, 'The children are Our Lady's Lilies; she nurtures and cares for the children.

THE GARDEN OF LILIES

Where else would the most gracious Mother of all be found?'

'Oh forgive me for being so stupid.' Tamara could have kicked herself.

'It's an easy mistake to make, Tamara, and you would not be here if you were even slightly stupid,' Maité said reassuringly.

'Tell us what She looks like, Maité? Will we recognise Her?'

'You would know Her instantly. You will have never seen beauty or felt love like it. She radiates beauty and a love so powerful it stops you in your tracks. I've only seen her once in all the time I've been in the Kairos. She is very careful not to be seen more than once by - forgive me - people who are not dead. You see, She is so perfect, you fall in love with Her instantly and if you saw Her more than once you simply wouldn't want to leave - you would want to die for Her. It's hardly surprising really, I mean God did choose her to have His Son after all. Now, you need to know about this place because when a child is lost, this is where they come.'

'When you say "lost," Maité you mean..?' Tamara began to voice what they were all thinking.

'When they die, Tamara. This is Heaven's Nursery,' Maité went on to explain. 'Where all children without exception come when they die. While we're on that subject,' she continued somberly. 'I must point out that what you are undertaking in the Kairos is not without risk. Sadly we do occasionally lose Kairos children, though thankfully not many. That is one of the reasons why it is not practical to borrow Kairos children from other countries. For instance, if anything happened to me while in England, how would it be explained to my family? How did I get there? How so fast? This is why we generally have to work in our own countries. While I am in England with you, there is significant risk - it's why I can only stay for short periods.'

Joel, Tamara and Peter listened intently as Maité continued.

'The mission Nathan has for you is long overdue. Those villains have been targets of the Kairos for a long time, but remember, you are the only Kairos children in England. This is why everyone is so excited to have you join us. There have been no English Kairos children to take on the mission - until now.'

The three newcomers nodded and looked around; the Garden of Lilies was a beautiful place. It was like a sunny meadow or a park, with grass, trees and lots of flowers. There were birds and tame animals; streams, fountains, waterfalls and rocks. They saw children playing. An African girl, about thirteen years old, noticed them and ran up to Maité.

'Maité!' she said hugging her. 'How nice to see you.'

'Hello, Jean.' Maité greeted her warmly. 'Say hello to our new Kairos members; Joel, Peter and Tamara.'

'Welcome.' Jean smiled.

'Thanks,' all three said together.

'How are you finding everything, Jean?' Maité asked.

'Fine, I'm O.K.' Jean smiled. 'Well I won't keep you, Maité. Good luck.' With that, she ran back to the other children.

*'Adios, mi amiga,' Maité called after her, then turned back to Joel, Peter and Tamara. 'Jean hasn't been here very long. She was Kairos 18. But now you have taken her place, Peter.'

'Oh, why, Maité! What happened to her?' Peter asked concerned.

'She was working on a mission involving a mother and three young children. The mother was suffering severe mental depression, brought on by years of drug and alcohol abuse. Jean was assigned to comfort the children, who were being neglected. She was trying to talk the mother round - to help her. The mother decided she couldn't cope with the children any longer. She strapped them into her car and placed a hose from the exhaust into the vehicle, leaving the engine running.'

Joel, Peter and Tamara gasped in horror.

'We knew what the mother was most likely going to do - we'd all seen it on the Vista,' Maité explained. 'But you see, unlike the past, the future can be changed. If you see your own probable future and you don't like what you see, you have a chance to do something about it. You can make any decision you like about yourself, however, you are not supposed to interfere with other people's futures - the free will thing, you know? Jean spent

---

*Goodbye (go with God) my friend

weeks patiently talking to the mother, trying to help her through the fog of confusion in her mind. When the time came - when the mother put the little ones in the car - Jean begged and pleaded tearfully for mercy for the children, but the woman could not be persuaded and it is absolutely forbidden to interfere. He is adamant that people shall have free will to make their own decisions. That is how He made us - with intelligence - to decide for ourselves what is right and what is wrong. If He interfered with our decisions, then we would be no different from other animals. Ultimately we all have to choose for ourselves: it is our responsibility to find the way - or perish.'

'The way?' Tamara asked.

'Yes, Tamara. You would not be here if you did not already know the way.'

'Jesus is the way.' Tamara said.

'Correct. Now as I was saying, of course the children were distressed and crying. We watched helplessly through the Vista...' Maité's voice faltered as a trace of a tear moistened her eyes. 'I'm sorry. My eyes always seem to water when I come in here - it's the Lilies - some say the Lilies are Our Lady's tears.' Maité sniffed, then took a deep breath and went on. 'Jean carried out her mission with complete dedication and did the only thing she felt she could - leapt into the car to comfort the children causing her to perish with them.'

The three friends gasped as Maité continued.

'As Jean could not stop the woman, so in turn we could not stop Jean. Her mission was to comfort the children in their time of need, not to die with them. It was her own decision to carry her mission to the very end and she gave her life for it.'

'What a tragedy!' Tamara said shocked.

'Yes, those children sadly were still going to die, but think of all the children that Jean might have saved, had she lived and stayed in the Kairos for the next three years till she was sixteen.'

They all nodded sympathetically.

'This is a very difficult part of our work in the Kairos; respecting the law of free will. If you don't think you can handle that, you must leave the Kairos now,' Maité warned. 'See those children playing over there.'

They all looked at the three children with Jean; their ages were about three, five and seven. They were having such a wonderful time, laughing and playing.

'They're the ones who perished in the car with her.' Maité explained.

Tamara suddenly felt a slight tug at her blouse and turned round. She almost fell over backwards in surprise, because standing there was a large cartoon-like duck, as alive as she was. The duck gave a friendly smile. He was about four feet tall, was white all over but for a bright orange beak and had a cute tuft of feathers on top of his head. He looked at her with big doleful, but intelligent, eyes. He was leading a little boy, guiding him with one of his wings. The boy was about five years old and looked very shy.

'Hewo,' said the duck. 'I'm Twevor. Will you say hewo to my fwiend Wobert. He's new here and he wants to make some new fwiends.'

'Well I'd love to,' Tamara said with a big smile, crouching down so her face was level with young Robert's. 'Hello, Robert, my name is Tamara - and this is Joel, Peter and Maité. So now you've got four new friends already. What's that your hiding in your jacket, Robert?'

'I've got a kitten,' said Robert, shyly. 'Do you want to see him?'

'Oh yes, please. I love kittens, Robert,' Tamara replied.

'His name is Peepoh,' said Robert. 'He's shy - look.' Robert opened his jacket a little and peeping out was a tiny baby kitten.

'Oh hello, Peepoh.' Tamara stroked the kitten's head gently. 'He's so cute. Where did you find him, Robert?'

'The beautiful Lady gave him to me. He still smells of her. Can you smell it?'

Tamara put her face close to the fluffy kitten and the lovely scent of the white Lily of the Valley wafted up her nose.

'Yes I can, Robert - isn't it lovely?'

'She's coming back,' Robert said. 'The Lady promised she would come and see me again.'

'Ooh, I've just seen my fwiend Tugs the Teddy,' Trevor said, tugging at Robert's sleeve. 'Come on, Wobert, I bet Tugs has got some sweets. Tugs has a very sweet toof, only one, 'cos he eats so many sweets, but his sweetie pocket nevew empties. Let's go and see if he has your favouwite. Tugs has evewyone's favouwite.'

Trevor and Robert waved goodbye and headed across the grass towards Tugs, who by then was surrounded by children shouting out their choice of sweets. Whatever they shouted always seemed to be in Tugs's sweetie pocket.

'Bye, Trevor - bye, Robert,' Tamara called.

'Ice cream?' Maité asked unexpectedly.

'Ice cream?' Joel echoed.

Maité walked up to a small booth about two feet square, and three feet high, then turned to face them.

'What flavours do you want?'

'What is there?' Joel asked.

'Anything your imagination can conjure up,' Maité replied.

'O.K. how about toffee and nuts with chocolate sauce?' Joel suggested.

Maité put her hand inside the seemingly empty booth, pulled out a perfect toffee-nut ice cream with oodles of chocolate sauce and handed it to Joel.

'Wow,' said Joel, taking a lick. 'This is good.'

'Tamara?' Maité asked.

'Oh um, let me see, how about maraschino cherry and mocha with a chocolate flake?'

Maité produced the ice cream exactly to order.

'Peter, what's your choice?'

'Can I have a strawberry ice, please?'

Maité put in her hand for the third time and pulled out Peter's order, then produced a huge Neapolitan ice cream for herself. They sat on the grass eating their ice creams and watching the children as they came and went about the place. All the children seemed so happy, full of laughter and fun.

When the four friends had finished their ice creams, Maité stood up.

'Now it's time to continue our journey.'

They all got up and followed Maité to a low-roofed building of soothing pastel colours with cute cherubim around.

'You must be careful in here - what you do and say.' Maité whispered in a low voice. 'If you must speak, please speak quietly and do not make any sudden movements. These are the new arrivals. You should not alarm already traumatised children, you understand? These children have no idea what has happened to them, or why they're here. Some were ill for a long time; some were wrenched from the world by accident, or crime. They were taken from the security of their parents and home. Some of them arrive in a very poor state. There are lots of Angels in here and you must not get in their way. You are here simply to observe. I must warn you, however, that you may be asked to help in the Baby Unit - it is the busiest place here.'

'Yes, Maité, we understand,' Joel said seriously.

'This is the reason for the permanent gravity,' Maité added. 'The children and the Angels have enough to contend with, and weightlessness would only add to their problems. It's not real gravity, of course; there are no laws of physics here. Our Creator can make anything happen just by it being His will.'

They followed Maité inside. It was pretty much as she'd described it. The place was teaming with Angels, all beautiful like Charis and Aleathia. Soft Angelic singing was just audible in the background and colourful crystals twinkled everywhere, just like in the Adults' Reception area. They slowly followed Maité through the building, ending up at the Baby Unit. Here the smell of the white Lily of the Valley was particularly strong.

'These are the babes,' Maité whispered, as they stood at the entrance. 'Our Lady has been here quite recently - you can tell by the fresh fragrance.'

The three friends looked inside and had to stifle gasps. There were rows and rows of tiny cots which seemed to go on forever and there were many Angels in attendance.

'How come there are so many?' Peter asked in disbelief.

'Yes, it's tragic, isn't it?' Maité said sadly. 'Babies die for lots of different reasons, many of them drug-related I'm afraid. Also of course the pregnancy terminated cases come here. You see, people think that life begins at birth or at some time near birth, but actually life is allocated at conception - the moment the seed enters the egg. Many of these babies arrived here before they could be born into the world.'

'Oh!' Tamara gasped, trying to keep her voice to a low whisper. 'How dreadful!'

'Yes, it's fortunate that, whatever their physical state when they leave the world, He makes them perfect when they arrive here,' Maité explained.

An Angel saw them at the entrance and approached them. She had a tiny baby in her arms.

'Hello, Maité, I'm so glad to see you - we could really do with a hand. You three must be the new Kairos members?' The Angel smiled at them. 'I'm Arianna, I run the Baby Unit. We can use all the help we can get here. You're welcome any time you like; just turn up and there'll be plenty for you to do.'

Maité introduced the new recruits to Arianna.

'Welcome aboard.' Arianna smiled, then placed the little baby in Tamara's arms. 'Here, Tamara. We've called her Rachel. Her Mother was a heroin addict, so Rachel was born addicted to the drug also, two months premature. She only lived for one hour.'

'What shall I do?' Tamara asked, taking the baby from Arianna.

'Just hold her, cuddle her and speak to her softly. Obviously she's not in pain any more - she's quite comfortable - but she's been through a very painful and traumatic time. She just needs to feel loved for a while. She won't be here long, a few days maybe - earth time that is - then she'll be born again. Here, Joel, you take this one.' Arianna picked up another baby. 'This is Stephen; he was a cot death. It's sad, but it happens. He'll find his family again soon though, he'll probably be sent back to the same parents...'

'Wait a minute...' Joel interrupted. 'What do you mean - "born again" - "sent back" I don't understand?'

'Oh that often happens with cot deaths and miscarriages - the baby is destined to be born into that particular family - sometimes it can take two or three goes! When a woman on earth has two or three miscarriages, she hasn't lost two or three children - it's the same child trying to get through - they usually succeed eventually.' Arianna explained. 'You see, He made all the rules in the first place, He can change anything at any time. He knows all of us individually, you know, and He makes decisions about us all individually. His mercy is endless. Babies haven't had the opportunity to make a choice have they? It's only fair they get another chance, don't you think?'

'I - I see.' Joel said with a mixture of amazement and hesitation. 'But, I've never held a baby, Arianna...' he added nervously.

'There's nothing to it; you'll manage.' Arianna smiled and turned to a young woman who was gazing down at a baby she was cuddling. 'Are you coping all right, Catherine?'
The young woman smiled and nodded without taking her eyes off the baby.

'Catherine arrived yesterday at the same time as her baby,' Arianna explained. 'Her husband was using a mobile phone while driving the car. He lost control on a bend and hit a tree. The whole of the left side of the car was demolished. The Father survived, but Catherine and the baby died instantly. In situations like that, the parent is not separated from the child - they both come through the Nursery Fugue together. Peter, why don't you take Andrew?' Arianna picked up another baby and placed it in Peter's arms. 'Andrew was six weeks old; he was killed by his Father when he wouldn't stop crying. His Mother hadn't fed him - he was just hungry and needed changing. His mother and father had been on a drink and drugs binge; they were so out of their heads they didn't know what they were doing.'

Suddenly an Angel called over to Arianna. 'Arianna, we have

new twins over here!'

'Sorry. Do you mind if I leave you? I'm needed.'

Arianna vanished and reappeared instantly next to the Angel who had called her. Maité picked up a little baby and rocked it gently.

After they had been in the Nursery for some time, Tamara felt that if she stayed a minute longer she would not be able to control her tears. She wanted to run outside as fast as her legs would carry her. But with a supreme effort to stay calm and not alarm the children, she turned and walked quietly outside. The others followed.

Once they were all outside, Maité put an arm around Tamara, who was sitting on a small bench with her head in her hands.

'You can only stay in there for so long before it gets too upsetting - then it's time to leave,' Maité said sympathetically. 'I make no apology for showing you these things, in particular the devastating results of the abuse of drugs. Because as you know, in your first mission, you will be directly involved in the battle against this evil. If you cannot handle it, then you would be unable to carry on in the Kairos and Nathan would arrange for you to leave and this part of your memory would be erased.'

'Are you all right, Tamara?' Joel asked, concerned.

'Do you think we'd better take her home, Joel?' Peter said in a worried tone.

'NO!' Tamara suddenly exclaimed, lifting her head, tears falling down her cheeks. 'Don't you see - now it's even more important than ever that we do this? I want to do everything I possibly can to stop this evil drug thing. Children like these don't stand a chance with villains like Lilith about. I don't care what happens to me.' Tamara stood up and wiped her face. 'Maité...' Though her voice trembled, she was determined. 'I want to start right now - I want to stop that disgusting varmint, Lilith, from destroying any more mothers and children with his evil drugs.'

Suddenly there was a flash of light and Nathan appeared in front of them.

'Dad!' Joel exclaimed.

'Hey, you guys.' Nathan smiled at them. 'I'm sorry you had to witness that, but we had to know that you're strong enough to stand it. And you had to know why we need you so much, the challenges you'd face, the risks you'd be taking and just what you'd be fighting for.'

'We're with you, Dad, whatever it takes,' Joel said with conviction.

'I'm so proud of all of you,' Nathan said. 'Let's formulate our plan to blast this brood of vipers out of their stinking pit.' He wrapped his golden arms around them all and instantly they were transported to the Vista Chamber.

CHAPTER FOURTEEN

A Snake in the Grass

Everywhere was cloaked in the turquoise-blue hue of the Chamber. Joel, Peter, Tamara and Maité faced the Vista, Nathan turned to face them. They listened intently as he began to speak.

'I've been watching Sadler for quite some time now through the Vista, studying his every move,' Nathan said. 'He's such a creature of habit that I could follow his routine blindfolded. I know where he goes, whom he sees, where he buys his socks - and how often he changes them.'

'That's great attention to detail, Dad but unless he keeps the case in his sock drawer, I couldn't give a stuff about his socks...'

'Yes of course, sorry, Son.'

'Where *does* he keep the case, Mr Asher?' Peter asked.

Nathan gave a wry smile.

'If you had something that was almost as important for keeping you alive as the air that you breath, where do you think you might keep it?' Nathan looked at the thoughtful faces in front of him.

'In a safe deposit box - securely locked away in a large reputable bank?' Joel proposed.

'Good, Joel,' Nathan said. 'That is probably where an intelligent and discerning person with any common sense would keep something that important. However, Sadler is in no way discerning and seems bereft of any common sense - on the contrary we believe he is seriously unhinged. Which is why this sad and misguided villain, keeps the case in a drawer under his bed.'

'What?' Joel exclaimed in disbelief.

'Yes, Son. Our deluded Sadler keeps it in his town house. You know those large beds that come with drawers underneath? I guess they're supposed to be for putting clean laundry in, but

Sadler thinks they're the ideal hiding place for critical, damning evidence - and dirty moolah!'

'Dirty moolah?' Tamara said looking puzzled.

'Ill-gotten gains he extorts from Lilith.' Nathan explained. 'Fairly obviously he cannot put this in a bank without raising suspicion. He's got the case in one drawer and the money - his intended retirement fund - stuffed in another.' Nathan grimaced.

'People used to hide their money under the mattress in the old days,' Tamara said, bewildered.

'It seems that Sadler is still living in the past.' Joel said with a wry smile.

'At least that makes it easier to swipe, Nathan,' Maité remarked. 'It would be a lot harder to get if it were in a safe deposit box.'

'Good point, Maité,' Nathan said. 'It just shows what a careless amateur we're dealing with and that makes it all the more dangerous for you,' he warned. 'When someone is that irrational, you need to be prepared for anything. Now the next thing is - Uz and Buz.'

'Uz and Buz?' Peter said with a frown. 'Who on earth are Uz and Buz?'

'I never said this would be easy,' Nathan replied with a sigh. 'Uz and Buz are the pair of extremely large and terrifyingly ferocious Rottweilers, Sadler lets loose in his town house.'

'Holy mutts!' Tamara exclaimed.

'So much for helping old ladies across the road...' Peter muttered.

'Now you might say,' Nathan continued, 'well that's just fine; we'll wait till Sadler takes these beasts out for a walk. Only trouble is, Sadler never takes them for a walk - that's what Jethro is for.'

'Jethro?' Joel queried.

'Hmm. It's not enough that Sadler has two full-time bodyguards paid for by Lilith. He also employs his own thicko, his private little stooge, to follow him around for protection and be at his beck and call.'

'Great!' Joel cried sarcastically. 'So we've now got Uz, Buz and Jethro to dodge!'

'Correct. Not forgetting, of course, Simms and Levi, the two henchmen provided by Lilith. Don't underestimate these two; they're out of the same mould as Lilith. They're mean and dangerous men. The only lives that have any value to them are their own - and Lilith's - but only because he pays them well.'

'This is sounding more like a picnic by the minute,' Joel said, astonished.

'What do you suggest we do, Mr Asher?' Peter asked earnestly. 'How can we get this case?'

'Glad you asked that, Peter. So you're not ready to throw in the towel yet?' Nathan smiled.

'Absolutely not. We're with you all the way.' Joel replied confidently.

Everyone nodded in agreement.

'I think the best way to approach this,' Nathan continued, 'is the Trojan Horse method. You get invited into the enemy's lair.'

'Oh yeah, sure. Sadler is going to invite us to tea so we can steal his retirement fund!' Joel retorted.

'Joel - Joel - why the scepticism? Sadler *is* going to invite you in for tea, as you put it,' Nathan went on. 'Don't forget, he doesn't know what you know, he thinks he's in the clear. Sadler is wallowing like a hippo in a mud bath right now. He couldn't see a light bulb flash in front of his face. Let's look at the facts. One - he was one of your Father's closest friends and still is friendly with your Mother. Two - he was your Father's business partner, that makes him the most qualified person for you to consult about your deceased Father. You were only eight when I died, Joel, too young to ask searching questions. Now you're twelve, it's quite conceivable that you could be going through a phase when you want to find out more about your Father. Who better to consult than your Father's trusted friend and business partner? See where I'm coming from?'

'Trusted friend and business partner? Duplicitous, slimy, murdering snake, you mean!' Joel spat.

'Joel, you've got to get past your resentment if this mission is to have any chance of success,' Nathan said seriously.' If Sadler has one shred of decency, he will be a little sympathetic to your plight and possibly even feel a tiny bit guilty. This is his chance to offload some of that guilt. Joel - you are to pay Sadler a visit.'

Joel stared at his Father in horror.

'You mean - you really expect me to go to the house of the man who murdered you in cold blood and sit and have tea with him?' Joel cried, trembling.

Nathan placed his hands on Joel's shoulders and looked him squarely in the eyes.

'Not only must you do this, Joel, but you will behave as if you believe that Sadler was my best friend and trusted business partner. That is how Sadler will expect you to behave. Should you raise his suspicions, your life and this mission will be in jeopardy. You must be absolutely clear on that - the end will justify the means.'

Joel looked up at his Father.

'Can you do it - for the sake of the mission?' Nathan asked.

Breathing a heavy sigh, Joel nodded bravely. 'It's going to be very hard, Dad, but, yes, I can do it, I know I can.' Joel bit his lip.

'That's the Spirit, Son,' Nathan said with an encouraging smile. 'You can take Peter with you. It will be quite understandable for you to take a friend. Maité, Anna and I will keep watch via the Vista throughout.'

'What about me?' Tamara asked.

'I'm coming to you, Tamara,' Nathan said. 'Now today is Tuesday and every Tuesday evening is law night at Wiggies. That's a Bar in the City where members of the legal profession gather. Solicitors, Barristers, Judges, they all meet for a drink - it's part of the old boy network, you know. Sadler goes straight to the Bar from the office and will not be home until late. So we'll have to wait until tomorrow to put our plan into action. This is a benefit though as Lilith is off tomorrow, which means that if anything leaks out at Scotland Yard, Lilith won't hear about it until the following morning. By which time however, if all goes according to plan, he will have been exposed - and arrested.'

'What exactly is the plan, Dad?'

'We wait till we see Sadler arriving home from work tomorrow evening - it's usually about six o'clock, after he's been to the gym. Then you two boys will go through the Vista and knock on his front door.' Nathan showed Sadler's town house on the Vista. 'I'm sure he'll invite you in when he realises who you are, Joel. I believe it will be Simms's shift for keeping watch, he'll be in his car, parked in the street at the front. He'll be listening to sport on the radio - if he's not asleep. I don't think Simms will pay any attention to two young boys visiting Sadler. While you're there, Peter, you must excuse yourself to go to the bathroom and then find Sadler's bedroom.'

The Vista took them inside the three-storey house and up the stairs. Sadler's bedroom was over the hall next to the bathroom.

'Joel,' Nathan continued, 'you'll keep Sadler talking - about me or him or anything, to give Peter time to manoeuvre. Remember, Peter, you've got three moving targets to dodge - Uz, Buz and Jethro. I suggest you wait until Jethro takes Uz and Buz to the park before excusing yourself. When you've got the case, Peter, slip outside into the back yard. Tamara, you'll be watching through the Vista. As soon as you see Peter open the back door, you step through the Vista *into* the back yard and take the case from him. You'll then have to wait in the alley at the back. Peter then returns to Joel and Sadler. Peter, you must give Joel a signal as to whether you've succeeded or not. If you've succeeded in getting the case out to Tamara, you will say as you enter the room - "Do you think we should be going, Joel? We want to get back before dark." As soon as you hear that, Joel, the pair of you must get out as quickly as possible without arousing suspicion. You must not leave Tamara outside with the case any longer than is absolutely necessary. She will not be able to bring the case up through the Vista and she will be in grave danger if she is found with it. Peter, if you fail to locate the case and pass it on as planned, you will instead say - "Am I interrupting something?" If you hear that, Joel, you must make out you're upset and ask Peter to accompany you to the bathroom. There you can talk in private and you'll need to think on your feet according to Peter's information - maybe even abort the operation and we'll have to come up with another plan. Now, assuming everything goes according to plan, you say goodbye to Sadler and leave the way you came in, via the front door. Then make your way round to the back - without alerting Simms. Get Tamara and the case, hail a taxi and take the case to Scotland Yard. Once inside Scotland Yard, you will ask to see Detective John Smith. As soon as Smith sees the case he will recognise it and usher you directly into his office. Remember, Smith thinks the case is at the bottom of the Thames! You must get Smith to open the case and look at the list detailing Sadler and Lilith's involvement. Then your mission is accomplished. You will go to a quiet location and Maité will come through the Vista and bring you all back. Oh and you'll have the Magi at hand.' Nathan added, 'While you're inside Sadler's house, Maggi and Magee will be keeping watch. Any questions?'

'Sounds like taking candy from a baby, Dad,' Joel grinned. 'It's lucky for us Sadler is such a beanhead.'

'Yeah, it looks like you've thought of everything, Mr Asher.' Peter smiled confidently.

'Well, don't let that make you complacent. You know what is said of the best-laid plans? No one who passes the exams Sadler has passed can be a complete beanhead. It's imperative that you remain vigilant at all times - you never know what might be lurking round the corner ready to trip you up,' Nathan warned.

They all nodded.

'Now there's nothing more we can do today,' Nathan said finally. 'So we'll meet here tomorrow, six p.m. G.M.T.'

+

Peter went back home to the farm for the afternoon to help his

A SNAKE IN THE GRASS

Dad and it was a good job he did. One of the cows gave birth to twin calves and help was needed to pull them out and to get them breathing. This was a task Peter was well able to deal with. He knew just what to do, having watched his Father many times before. So both calves were saved.

Joel was feeling a little guilty that he'd not spent much time with Grandad this holiday. So that afternoon he helped him to repair a fence and paint it with creosote. This gave them a chance to have a really good Grandfather - Grandson talk. Joel actually quite enjoyed the afternoon. Grandad had always been a good talker and he never ran out of interesting stories.

However the whole afternoon was periodically interrupted by Magee, who kept fluttering past, now and then settling nearby, throwing in the odd humorous comment. This infuriated Joel, as he couldn't reply to any of it and just had to let the old Raven rave on regardless. Every time Joel and Grandad moved further down the fence, so did the Raven.

'Well this has scotched any plans you might have had of becoming a carpenter when you grow up, Joel, judging by the state of that fence,' Magee remarked dryly, from over Joel's shoulder.

Joel bit his lip to stop himself from talking back, throwing Magee a warning glance instead.

'Don't worry, Pops can't hear me; only you can,' Magee went on. 'Does he know what a straight line is? My feathers! And this is before his evening tipple!'

Magee was quite a witty old bird really and, irritating as he could be at times, Joel appreciated his dry sense of humour, which was not dissimilar to his own. He couldn't help letting out the odd chortle, which he tried to disguise with a cough in case Grandad thought he'd gone mad or something. But, he frequently felt like throwing something at Magee and almost did.

'That Raven seems very interested in what we're doing, Joel,' Grandad remarked in amusement, standing up to rest his back.

'Oh really, Grandad, er, I hadn't noticed,' Joel muttered.

'Beautiful bird, isn't he?' Grandad commented.

'At least someone round here has good taste,' Magee said, preening himself.

'You know, Joel,' Grandad went on, 'Ravens have a special affinity with humans.'

Magee nodded proudly.

'Sometimes you could swear that they understand what you're saying,' Grandad added.

'Not as daft as he's pudding-faced is he?' Magee observed.

'Mind you, sometimes they can be quarrelsome birds with absolutely no common sense.' Grandad chuckled.

'Huh! Indeed!' Magee said haughtily.

'Yes, Grandad, they can be quite annoying at times,' Joel said, glaring at Magee.

'You can go off people, you know!' Magee huffed indignantly then spreading his wings he flew off.

'I think that's just about it for now - I don't think my back could stand much more of this today. What do you think, Joel?' Grandad stood up and admired their handiwork.

'Well it's not exactly straight, is it, Grandad? But as fences go, it's functional...' Joel said. As he surveyed the fence, he had to agree with Magee. It was a good job he was going to be a Barrister like his Dad.

+

Whilst Joel had been helping Grandad, Tamara had decided that Cherokee needed her mane, tail and feet washing. She got a bucket of soapy water and spent the afternoon pampering and fussing over the little pony. She plaited her mane, putting little ribbons in it, and polished her saddle and bridle. She had a lovely chat with Maggi. Being just outside the barn, they were out of earshot of Grandad and Joel. So Tamara and Maggi chatted away all afternoon.

Maggi told Tamara she and Magee had been Angels for seven thousand years and were quite inseparable. She regaled Tamara with wonderful tales of assignments they'd had over the years.

This wasn't the first time they'd been Ravens. In fact Maggi and Magee had been Ravens forty-eight times. Once they had kept five people, who were trapped in a cave, alive for two weeks. They ferried parcels of food - anything they could purloin until a Kairos member led rescuers to where they were.

'I know we seem to argue a lot,' Maggi mused. 'But who wouldn't, when they'd been together as long as we have?'

+

As there were only a few days of the holiday left, Peter's parents let him go back again to Joel's Grandad's place for the night. Tamara was concerned that her Mum would worry about her, so she decided to go home early and set off on her shining brown and white pony, complete with coloured ribbons.

That night, when Joel and Peter were fast asleep in bed, they were both suddenly woken up.

'Joel - Peter,' a voice whispered.

The two boys sat bolt upright. Joel snatched his lantern from the bedside table and quickly switched it on, shining it around the room.

'Who's there?' Joel whispered.

Then they saw at the end of Joel's bed, a faint, glowing figure. Joel blinked several times before he realised that it was his Father.

'Dad, is that you? What is it?' he whispered. 'You look so - different...'

'Get up, Joel, and you, Peter,' Nathan whispered urgently. 'Throw on some clothes; there's an emergency. I need you both to come with me now. I'll open a schism to the Vista for you.'

Joel glanced at the clock on his bedside table. It was five to eleven. Both boys leapt out of bed and started to dress quickly.

'Quiet. You don't want to wake Grandad,' Nathan whispered. 'Put some padding in your beds, just in case he puts his head round the door.'

They put their dressing gowns under their bedcovers. Nathan

put up a wispy, golden arm to open a schism and the three of them were suddenly gliding out of the Vista into Heaven. Then, Nathan's appearance returned to a more solid radiance.

'A young boy is in trouble,' Nathan began. 'He's a runaway who thinks no one loves him or cares about him. His parents had been punishing him for something he'd done, but now it's gone too far and they're worried sick. The police are out looking for him, but they won't find him. He was hiding out in a derelict mine shaft and has fallen through some rotting timber. He'll never get out on his own and no one will look for him there - at least not until they've tried all the bus and train routes. They think he's run off to the City, you see. By then it will be too late. He's on a narrow ledge about two feet wide, above a sheer drop of a hundred feet. The ledge is not stable - it could collapse at any minute. Your mission, boys, is to get him out.'

'Of course we'll get him out, Dad,' said Joel.

They all turned to face the Vista and Nathan showed them the view of a disused mine. Although it was late at night, thankfully there was a clear moonlit sky. The view took them inside the mine itself; it was dark, wet and scary.

'Poor kid, he must be petrified, it's so creepy.' Peter shuddered.

The view went further inside the mine. - down a dark and dingy tunnel, through the rotting timber that had caved in and caused the boy to slip onto the ledge, about ten feet down the shaft. The view gave a close-up of the boy; he was sitting on a rucksack balanced on the ledge, shivering and whimpering like a frightened animal. Joel and Peter caught their breath - it was Presten!

'Yes, lads,' Nathan said wearily, 'I'm afraid it's Tamara's brother. You've got to get him out quickly. One slip and he's gone - and that ledge isn't going to hold out much longer.'

'Poor Mrs Goodchild,' said Peter sympathetically. 'She's just recovering from the shock of almost losing Tamara and now she faces losing Presten - she must be at her wits end.'

'I'm sure you're right, Peter.' Nathan continued, 'It's very dark in there, boys; there's not much moonlight filtering through. Do you think you can manage between you to get him out?'

'Sure thing, Dad.' Joel nodded bravely.

'Good. Now, the Magi are already there, waiting for you.' Nathan put a hand on each boy's shoulder. 'Be careful, boys; it's as dangerous as dangerous can be. The whole thing could cave in at any minute and bury you all with rubble. The chances of any of you getting out alive then, would be negligible.'

'We'll be all right, Mr Asher,' Peter assured him.

'Joel...' Nathan said gravely, 'Don't do anything foolish - you know what I mean? Without you the Sadler - Lilith mission is a dead duck.'

'We'll be careful, Dad. Promise.' Joel smiled, bravely trying to conceal his nerves.

Without losing any more time, Joel and Peter glided through the Vista, landing in the grass near the entrance to the mine shaft. They looked at each other in trepidation.

'Our first mission, Joel,' Peter said with nervous excitement.

'Yeah.' Joel tutted. 'Wouldn't you just know it had to be saving Presten? Come on then, let's get the weasel out.'

Joel poked his head inside the entrance to the mine.

'It's pretty dark in here, Peter. Damp and musty too.' Joel's voice trembled.

Then, they both nearly jumped out of their skins as something flew out of the mine.

'About time!' A haughty voice echoed. It was Magee; he landed on a beam at the entrance.

'Magee!' Joel cried. 'Are you trying to give me a heart attack or something?'

'Oh sorree...' Magee said, disgruntled. 'I thought Nathan would have told you to expect us.'

'He did,' Joel replied. 'He said you would be waiting for us, not springing out, frightening us to death!'

'There you are, see!' Maggi said in her usual uppity style as she flew out and joined Magee on the beam. 'I told you we should have waited outside.'

'How was I to know they'd get all startled?' Magee went on, ruffled, 'I thought we should keep our eyes on the boy what's about to plunge down a one-hundred-foot ravine!'

'*Who*, Magee - the boy *who* is about to plunge down the ravine,' Maggi said correcting him.

'Oh whatever...' Magee wittered.

'TIME-OUT!' Joel thundered.

It was the Ravens' turn to jump. In fact they very nearly fell off the beam. They both stared at Joel in shocked silence.

'That's better,' Joel said calmly. 'This is not the time for another of your arguments. Now let's formulate a plan to rescue the boy, shall we?'

'Hmm,' Magee said with a haughty but injured air. In fact if Ravens had a bottom lip, Magee's would probably have been wobbling at that moment. 'Well, what do you suggest?'

'We need some light. Magee. How long would it take you to fly to my Grandad's house and back? And how strong is your beak?'

'Well.' Magee coughed. 'I can transport myself there instantly and you should know that Angels are super-strong. The fact that I now happen to be in a Raven's body does not detract from that. However, if you wish me to carry something I will have to fly back - on the wing so to speak, I cannot otherwise transport objects in an instant, only myself.'

'How far are we from Grandad's?' Joel asked.

'Oh it's not far at all, Joel,' said Peter, butting in. 'This old mine shaft is no more than three miles as the Crow...'

Maggi looked at Peter and coughed.

'I mean as the Raven flies,' Peter said smiling at Maggi.

'O.K. that's not bad.' Joel continued, 'Magee, I want you to fly in through my bedroom window, which I'm sure is open. There's a large lantern on my bedside table. It's quite heavy but it's got a ring on the top. Do you think you could carry it in your beak and bring it here?'

'Affirmative,' said Magee, trying hard not to appear upset at being shouted at - although he clearly was.

'Give me an ETA?'
'10 minutes.'
'Make it 5.'
Magee instantly vanished into thin air.

'I knew there must have been a reason why I had to fit that lantern into my bulging travel bag,' Joel muttered.

They stood waiting, then Maggi broke the silence.

'You know, you really got to him, Joel,' she said quietly. 'No one has ever shouted at him before, except Maguff - and me of course. I - I could tell he was upset.'

'I know.' Joel nodded. 'So could I.'

'Look!' Peter yelled and pointed at the sky.

They followed Peter's gaze and saw a light like a shooting star moving swiftly across the dark sky. A closer inspection revealed a black dot with wings above the bright light.

'Is that Maguff again, Maggi?' Joel said, as they watched it coming towards them.

'No, that's not Maguff. It's Magee - he's here already!' Peter yelled.

Magee flew up and dropped the lantern into Joel's hands, then perched next to Maggi at the entrance to the mine.

'Thanks, Magee,' Joel said. 'Hey, I'm sorry I shouted at you, mate.'

'Apology accepted.' Magee cocked his head on one side proudly, then looking up at Joel he added coyly, 'I never thanked you for sticking up for me with Maguff the other day. It was good of you, especially after the way I behaved - I - I'm sorry, Joel.'

'Well I couldn't let you sentence poor old Maggi to five hundred years as a sewer rat, could I?' Joel smiled at Magee.
Maggi threw Magee a cross look, while Magee looked down sheepishly.

'Right, come on then - let's get that weasel out.' Joel said, leading the way with his lantern.

The party of rescuers ventured into the mine shaft. The boys felt their way along the wall as they slowly shifted their feet.

'Presten!' Joel called out.

'Asher!' Presten screamed. 'Is that you?'

'Yeah, where are you?' Joel shouted back.

'About fifteen feet from the entrance. Just keep going straight ahead. There's a kind of wooden platform, but it's rotten - I've fallen through it. Get me out of here!'

Joel and Peter edged their way along the tunnel into the shaft in the direction of Presten's voice. Then suddenly they saw the platform, with a jagged edge where half the floor had caved in. They stopped and Joel shone the lantern over the side. They saw Presten huddled on the ledge.

'We can see you!' Joel called down. 'How are you doing?'

'How do you think, dummy? I'm stuck down a disgusting, filthy pit on a tiny ledge that's about to crash!' Presten screamed rudely. 'How the devil did you find me anyway?'

'Not through him, that's for sure,' Joel muttered.

'So what's the plan, Asher? How's the big hero going to rescue me now?' Presten called up.

'What's the state of the ledge you're standing on, Presten?' Joel called.

'It's just a few rotting wooden planks and joists held up by rusty scaffolding. Looks like it's going to fall apart at any minute. I feel like I'm standing on the skin of a rice pudding. I'm scared, Asher - get me out of here!' Presten whimpered.

Joel and Peter looked around, sizing the place up.

'Presten is pretty heavy,' Joel said. 'I don't think the two of us could pull him up from that far down. You're taller and lighter than me, Peter. Presten and I could pull you up. If I lower you down and Presten stands on your shoulders, I think I can pull him up over the top. Then Presten can help me pull you up, if you stand on his rucksack. What do you say?'

'Well I guess it's a plan, Joel.' Peter shrugged bravely. 'I can't think of a better one.'

'What are you two divvies hatching?' Presten shouted. 'Can't you see this whole ledge is about to fall apart? Hurry up!'

'Presten, I'm going to lower Peter down to you. You'll have to grab his legs and help him down. Then climb onto Peter's shoulders - I can pull you up from there. Then we'll pull Peter up between us.'

'Come on then, Jordan, get down here! This place gives me the creeps!' Presten yelled.

'I don't think you can trust that boy, Joel.' Maggi muttered with concern.

'You're right, Maggi,' Joel said. 'We can trust him about as much as a starving dog in a butcher's shop - but we ain't got a choice. Come on, Peter, I'll help you down.'

'I've got a bad feeling about this, Magee,' Maggi muttered.

'Yes, I too, Maggi dearest,' Magee responded, nudging Maggi gently with his head.

Joel found the strongest part of the platform edge. He broke out into little beads of sweat, as with trembling arms he helped to steady Peter while he slowly climbed down over the ledge.

'Have you got him, Presten?' Joel said straining.

'Yeah, yeah, let go,' Presten yelled back.

Presten guided Peter's legs down to the ledge, but didn't take much of his weight. Joel let go and Peter dropped the last six inches or so; his feet slipped as they touched the ledge and he fell on one of his knees, grazing it. The ledge shifted precariously.

'You stupid moron!' Presten screamed, clinging to Peter. 'Don't bother getting up, Jordan. Let me get on your back.'

Peter stooped on the tiny ledge, holding on to the wall and a rusty metal pipe. Presten stamped a foot hard on Peter's shoulder. Peter winced with pain as Presten jumped up and placed his other foot heavily on Peter's other shoulder.

'Right, get up, dweeb!' Presten barked. 'I can't reach Asher's hands from this far down.'

Peter grimaced with strain as he slowly and carefully straightened up, keeping his body flat against the wall. Presten reached up with both hands.

'Careful - careful, Jordan!' Presten shrieked in a terrified, squeaky voice. Then slowly he reached up with his hands again.

'Right, pull me up, Asher - quick!'

Joel reached down and grabbed hold of Presten's arms. Now Presten liked his food and he ate a lot. He ate as much of all the wrong food as he could lay his sticky, podgy fingers on. He must have weighed around eleven stone. That was a mighty weight for a twelve-year-old boy who was only five feet three inches tall. Peter was five feet four inches tall. Standing on Peter's shoulders, Presten reached up. His head was about one foot below the top of the hole. Joel scrambled to the edge and was able to haul him up to relative safety. As soon as he was up on *terra firma*, Presten pushed Joel away and yelled down to Peter.

'Hand me up my rucksack, Jordan!'

'No! Peter needs to stand on it!' Joel shouted. 'It will be easier for us to lift him up. It's only a rucksack, Presten.'

'Only a rucksack!' Presten screamed with rage. 'My most valuable possessions are in that rucksack, you moron.'

'Don't be a fool, Presten. We can come back in daylight with proper equipment to get your rucksack,' Joel argued. 'Help me lift Peter up - that ledge could go at any minute!'

'Lift him yourself!' Presten snarled and as he did so he pushed Joel violently. Joel lost his balance and tried to grab hold of Presten, but he jumped out of the way. Then in a flash, Joel realised he was falling over the edge of the chasm.

'Aah!' Joel screamed as he plunged headfirst, down, down, down, towards certain death. His last thought before he passed out was about his Dad and the mission that had now been thwarted.

'Joel!' Peter cried in horror as he saw Joel plunge down the shaft. 'Presten! What have you done?'

Presten looked suddenly very afraid; he turned and ran out of the mine shaft.

'Magee!' Peter shouted in sheer panic.

Magee took off at speed, headlong down the shaft. Suddenly Joel stopped in mid-air and a strange light seemed to glow around him. Magee crash-landed onto Joel's back as Joel started floating slowly upwards, almost as if he was flying. Peter thought that

Joel was dead, that this must be his spirit floating up to Heaven and that he, Peter, was able to see him because he was a Kairos. Then as Joel floated up past Peter to the safety of higher ground, Peter saw what was lifting Joel up. He could hardly believe what he saw. Maguff was flying underneath Joel, cradling him on his back. The strange glow was coming from Maguff!

Maguff set the unconscious Joel down on the floor of the tunnel. The glowing light which emanated from Maguff lit up the whole cavern, casting peculiar shadows around the place.

'Maguff!' Peter cried. 'You're a blessed Angel - how is he?'

'Joel's passed out!' Maggi shouted down to Peter. '- and so has Magee - they're both out cold.'

'Oh, I didn't realise Angels could pass out,' Peter called back surprised.

'Well I'll admit it's a rarity but Magee is getting on a bit now, you know,' Maggi replied.

She dipped one of her wings in a nearby pool of water and shook it over Magee. He opened his eyes and groaned, then got up and shook himself all over.

'Thank you, dear.' Magee teetered a little as though punch-drunk. 'How's our have-a-go hero?'

'He'll come round,' Maggi replied, dipping her wing in the water again and shaking it over Joel's face. Joel opened his eyes and blinked.

'Where am I?' Joel muttered in confusion. 'Magee - you saved me...' He clambered to his feet.

'Er - it wasn't me...' Magee nodded towards Maguff, who was standing behind Joel.

Joel turned round.

'Maguff!' he exclaimed.

'Yes, I'm not supposed to intervene in the Guardians' missions, but you are an important asset, Joel - a special case. I was ordered to save you.' Maguff looked apologetically at Magee. 'Good as your intentions were, Magee, I think you might have struggled to lift forty times your body weight. I'm sorry I knocked you out, but there wasn't exactly time to warn you and I couldn't take the risk of losing the asset - you understand.'

'N - no - I - I - er - was just trying to do my job...' Magee shrugged. 'But you saved the day, Maguff, er, it was lucky you were in the neighbourhood.'

'Yeah, thanks, Maguff,' Joel said.

'Like I said, it was an order. Anyway, I'll have to leave you now; I'm in the middle of an urgent call-out.' Maguff said.

'Peter!' Joel cried, jumping to his feet. 'What about Peter - you can save him now, Maguff.'

'I'm sorry, Joel I'm not allowed to intervene in the Kairos missions, unless by specific divine instruction. I'm in much demand by our Angels. This is your call.'

'I'm O.K. Joel!' Peter called up.

Maguff vanished.

'Peter, stay exactly where you are,' Joel shouted down.

'Well I don't think I could go anywhere if I wanted to, Joel,' Peter nervously replied.

'No, I mean you mustn't move a muscle. I need to know exactly where you are. I'm going to get you through the Vista and I don't want either of us to fall off the ledge - there's not much landing space - if you get my drift!'

'Joel, are you sure? You could miss the ledge and fall!' Peter cried. 'The ledge is creaking like billy-o already, Joel. I don't think it's going to hold me for much longer anyway - let alone you jumping onto it!'

'It'll be all right - as long as you don't move - just be ready to leap back with me through the Vista!' Joel turned to Magee. 'Thanks for trying to save me, Magee. I promise I'll never shout at you again.'

'Just don't go diving off too many cliffs,' Magee said earnestly. 'Joel... what you're about to attempt is very dangerous. I've never seen or heard of anyone trying to land on such a precise target from the Vista. I don't think you can be that accurate.'

'I've no choice, Magee,' Joel said. 'Peter is too far down for me to reach on my own. The Vista is our only chance.'

A SNAKE IN THE GRASS

Magee nodded reluctantly.

'Good luck, Joel,' Maggi said, shaking her head.

'Yes, now go on before the whole caboodle caves in. We'll wait here.' Magee insisted.

'Thanks.' Joel smiled then hurried outside to the spot where they'd arrived and put up his hand. A schism opened up and he found himself gliding out of the Vista. Nathan caught him.

'Thank God,' Nathan said with much relief. 'Those quarrelsome Magi do have their uses.' He smiled, then became very serious. 'Joel, Magee is right. What you're about to attempt is to say the least, extremely difficult, even for someone who is well used to the Vista. Landing on a precise spot is almost on a par with a multi-pocket shot in trickiness, I've never seen it done - and you're not exactly a seasoned expert in using the Vista. How good is your snooker?'

'No one has ever needed to do it before, Dad. There's always a first time.' Joel said bravely.

'You've only got one shot, Son - if you misjudge this, it could be fatal for you and Peter.'

'I know, Dad, but that ledge is going to go - if I didn't try and Peter fell, I wouldn't be able to forgive myself. I've got to try.'

'O.K. Son, but please be careful. I don't know if Magee has the strength to repeat Maguff's stunt - and if you both fall together...' Nathan shook his head. 'Magee will be so confused as to which of you to try to save, he'll be completely dysfunctional.'

Joel nodded knowingly then turned back to the Vista. The narrow ledge was in clear view; the moonlight seemed somehow to be stronger. Peter was standing so still he was hardly breathing. The rotting wood was creaking and bits of the ledge were falling down the crevice.

With deep concentration, Joel looked at the ledge and put his hand out in front of him, ready to grab Peter. Nathan stood by with Anna, they both looked very tense. Then Joel glided into the Vista. Instantly he was on the ledge, right beside Peter and he grabbed hold of him. The ledge shifted and slumped a little; bits of rotting wood fell off it. Without delay Joel turned and opened up a schism. As they both made a leap for it, the entire ledge came away from the wall, creaking and crashing down into the depths of the shaft. Joel and Peter glided back through the Vista into Nathan's waiting arms. As he caught them he hugged them both tightly.

'Well done, both of you!' he said with heartfelt relief. 'You've done the Kairos proud.'

Anna wiped away her tears of relief and hugged them both.

'You'd better go back to your bedroom quickly,' Anna said urgently. 'Both of you, before Grandad discovers you're missing.'

Nathan showed Joel's bedroom on the Vista.

'There's just one thing I need to do first,' Joel said. 'Peter, you go back now and I'll see you in a few minutes.'
Peter looked curious.

'Go on, Peter.' Nathan nodded. 'It'll be all right.'
Peter shrugged. He was really exhausted and so didn't protest as he glided straight through the Vista. Then Joel showed a view of Tamara's house. Mrs Goodchild was distraught; Mr Goodchild was doing his best to comfort her. Then the view changed to Tamara's room. Tamara was sitting on her bed looking upset. Joel glided through the Vista.

'Joel -'Tamara whispered in surprise. 'What..?'

'Ssh.' Joel put his finger to his lips. 'I can't stay - it's about Presten.'

'I can't believe he's done this to Mum, after all she's been through...' Tamara said bitterly.

'Don't worry, Tamara. Presten is on the road by the old mine shaft. Go and tell your Dad you've just remembered he's always been fascinated by the old mine and goes there when he's fed up. If your Dad acts quickly, he'll find him near there now.'

'Thanks, Joel.' Tamara smiled up at him. 'You really are the best friend anyone could ever have.'

'Go on - I'll see you tomorrow.' Joel grinned, then raised his hand and went back through the schism. As Joel emerged from the Vista, Nathan took him by the hand.

'You are a true Kairos, Joel,' he said proudly. 'Despite the fact that Presten almost killed you and certainly left you for dead, you still put your duty to the Kairos first. That was a truly good thing you did, letting his family know where to find him. Thank you for not letting me down. I'll see you at 6 p.m. tomorrow, Son - now will you go back to bed!'

'Sure, Dad, I'm on my way.' Joel grinned happily. When he got back to his bedroom it was just as they had left it, complete with the lantern on the bedside table. 'Thanks, Magi,' he muttered, thinking they'd be long gone.

'You're welcome,' said two voices from the window ledge. Joel went over to the window.

'What are you two still doing here?' he said fondly.

'It's not - that we - wanted to see you were back safe and sound,' Magee murmured with a shrug. 'We were just - having a rest on the window ledge - that's all.'

'Yes, that's all,' Maggi said yawning.

'Goodnight, Angels.' Joel stroked them both on their necks.

+

Joel and Peter fell asleep, exhausted but relieved that the evening's episode in the mine shaft was over. They must have been asleep for about half an hour, when they were both woken again. Grandad had rushed into the room and put on the light.

'Grandad - what's the matter?' Joel asked sleepily.

'Oh thank God.' Grandad let out a huge sigh of relief.

'What is it, Mr Jacob?' Peter asked yawning.

Grandad sat down on Joel's bed and shook his head. 'Fancy me falling for that!' He chuckled. 'You know, boys, I think Tamara's brother is seriously deranged.'

'You mean you've only just realised that, Grandad?' Joel said teasingly. 'What's he done now?'

Of course Joel and Peter knew exactly what Presten had done, but they couldn't let Grandad know that.

The Kairos

'I've just had Presten's Father on the phone. Presten ran away from home this evening; he left a note saying that he knew they didn't care about him, so they'd never see him again. Naturally Mr and Mrs Goodchild were beside themselves and the police have been searching for him. Well, it turns out that Presten was hiding in the disused mine shaft about three miles from here. Mr Goodchild picked him up on the road near the mine. Now get this for delusion: Presten swears blind that the two of you were in the mine shaft at the same time as him!' He chortled. 'Not only that, but he also swears he saw you, Joel, plunge one hundred feet down the shaft to your death and that Peter was trapped on a two-foot ledge, ten feet down the shaft. Now how crazy is that?' Grandad scratched his head.

'Well I have to agree, Grandad - the words *deranged* and *deluded* do spring to mind, but as you can see for yourself, Peter and I are in our beds where you said goodnight to us at ten o'clock this evening. What do you think, Peter?'

'Yep, it looks like Presten has been telling porky pies - again.' Peter shrugged.

'I'm really sorry I woke you, guys,' Grandad apologised. 'Well, I'll go and ring Mr Goodchild and let him know you're safe and sound in your beds.'

'Don't be sorry, Grandad; you did the right thing, checking - and it was worth being woken up for the laugh,' Joel said with a grin, highly amused.

After Grandad had left the room, they could contain their amusement no longer and had to stifle their fit of giggles with their quilts.

CHAPTER FIFTEEN

A Bitter Appointment

Sympathy was in short supply the next day, when Tamara told the boys the outcome of Presten's eventual return home. The three of them had gone up to the tree den in Zionica to discuss the incredible recent events that had taken over their lives.

'Things look pretty grim for Presten,' said Tamara, seriously. 'Dad is still very angry about the accident and Mum is taking Presten to see a child psychologist. The silly little twit won't stop wittering on about you two being in the mine - despite your Grandad insisting that you were in bed at the time!'

'Yes, I dare say people will think Presten has definitely lost the plot,' Joel remarked with a hint of gleeful satisfaction.

'Do you think he deliberately pushed you over the edge, Joel? I mean, what are the chances that it was simply an accident?' Peter asked.

'It's difficult to say, Peter. It all happened so fast and there wasn't much light.' Joel paused thoughtfully. 'But whatever we think of Presten, I can't believe he's a cold-blooded killer - he's just a kid; but then again, he could have made some attempt to pull me back and didn't - in fact he jumped out of the way - probably in case I pulled him over the edge too.'

'He didn't go for help either,' Tamara added. 'Which makes him guilty of leaving you to die too, Peter - remember, Presten thought you were trapped on a two-foot ledge which was about to crash down the mineshaft.'

'Yes, but he did eventually tell your parents we were in the mine...' Peter said, unable to believe anyone could be that evil.

'So he did, but would he have reported your plight to the police, if my Dad hadn't picked him up? I think not,' said Tamara. 'And just remember this,' she added. 'Every notorious, convicted murderer rotting in prisons around the world, was once just a kid.'

'You've got a point, Tamara,' Peter said. 'He did swear revenge this holiday. A psychologist might be just what he needs.'

'A psychiatrist, you mean - to sort out the half-baked scrambled egg he's got instead of a brain,' Joel said dryly.

'You're taking all this very well, Joel,' Tamara remarked. 'I mean my brother did almost kill you.'

'Well he didn't succeed, so what's the point in dwelling on it?' Joel shrugged. 'Quite frankly I've got much more important things on my mind right now - let's go over our plan for this evening again - I don't want anything to go wrong.'

+

At five minutes to six that evening the three friends were at the edge of the plateau in Zionica. Peter and Tamara had told their parents they would again be staying the night at Joel's, so they wouldn't be expected back. The chances were it would be quite late by the time they'd chased half way across London with Sadler's case.

'Have you got some paper money for the taxi, Joel?' Tamara reminded him, 'You know you can't take coins up through the Fugue or the Vista.'

'Yeah,' Joel patted his shirt pocket. 'I always bring money on holiday to Grandad's - I don't know why; there's never much to spend it on. But it's a good job I did - it might have been difficult explaining to Grandad why I needed to borrow some.' Joel held out both his hands. 'Come on then, let's go.'

Tamara and Peter took Joel's hands and they stepped onto the plateau together. Maité, Anna and Nathan were waiting for them as they came up out of the Fugue and after the usual greetings, they all made their way through the hall of archways to the Vista.

After a quick recap of the plan to double-check everyone knew what they were doing, they were ready.

'Now, on a Wednesday,' said Nathan, 'Sadler always leaves

the office early. He goes to the gym for an hour, then gets fish and chips for supper and slumps in front of the television with several cans of beer. By now he should have just finished his supper and be opening his second or third can.

'Detective Smith is on the late shift; he finishes at 10 p.m. That should give you plenty of time to purloin the case and get to Scotland Yard before he clocks off.'

Nathan showed the view of Sadler's lounge on the Vista. Sadler was sprawled on an easy chair with one of his legs draped over the arm. He snapped the ring-pull off a can of beer. Another can lay empty on the table beside him, along with his screwed-up fish-and-chip paper.

'Such a creature of habit.' Nathan tutted.

'Such a sloth,' Joel muttered.

The view changed to the street outside, then focused on a small deserted alleyway down the side of Sadler's home.

'Ready?' Nathan asked.

Joel and Peter nodded.

'Good luck and God be with you,' Nathan said.

'Adios, friends,' Maité echoed. 'That means "Go with God" in Spanish, you know,' she said, attempting to help them forget their nerves.

They both smiled at Maité, then together Joel and Peter glided through the Vista. There was a chill wind as they arrived in the alleyway; a combination of this and their nerves caused them both to shiver a little as they stepped out onto the street. Sure enough there was Simms, sitting in his car outside Sadler's house. He gave them a dismissive glance as they walked gingerly up the steps to Sadler's front door and rang the bell. They both jumped and looked at each other nervously as they heard the two dogs barking ferociously.

'That's enough!' came Sadler's sharp command from within. The dogs stopped barking and the door opened. Sadler stood there with a can of beer in his hand. He was still wearing the tracksuit from his workout at the gym. Joel was used to seeing Sadler in a suit and hardly recognised the unshaven figure in front of him.

'Yeah?' Sadler said. He hadn't recognised Joel.

'Mr Sadler?' Joel asked hesitantly.

'Who wants him?' Sadler asked suspiciously.

'It's Joel, Mr Sadler - Joel Asher, Nathan Asher's Son - and this is my friend Peter Jordan.'

Sadler's jaw dropped and he almost dropped his beer too.

'Joel?' Sadler echoed. 'I didn't recognise you, you've grown. W - What are you doing here?'

Joel clenched his fists at his sides, fighting the urge to punch the duplicitous killer on the nose. But he had to get inside that house, so he took a deep breath.

'I wondered if you could spare me some time for a chat, Mr Sadler. You knew my Dad better than anyone and he always thought so highly of you. I was young when he died... I don't remember much...' Joel said, pleading respectfully.

'Of course, lad.' Sadler's attitude softened. 'Come in.'
He led the boys into the house. The two dogs emitted low threatening growls through their bared teeth.

'Shut up, you two!' Sadler shouted at the dogs. 'I'll put them out in the back yard.' He grabbed them by their collars.

'NO!' Joel shouted suddenly, thinking quickly. Putting the dogs in the yard would put the mockers on the whole plan! That's where Tamara was to collect the case from Peter.

Sadler stopped, a little taken aback by the loud protest.

'Er, we love dogs, Mr Sadler. Peter especially has an affinity with dogs, don't you, Peter? Please can they stay with us? What are their names?' Joel forced himself to bend down and stroke one of the dogs, despite the fact that it looked as if it wanted to take his arm off.

As he bent to stroke it, the vicious beast snarled, curling back its lips to reveal a set of razor-sharp fangs, which made Joel feel very uneasy to say the least.

'Peter...' Joel gave Peter a look that was really a desperate cry for help.

Peter bent down and touched both the dogs on their heads. They instantly calmed down as he spoke to them.

'Hello, fellas,' he said kindly but firmly. Both dogs instantly calmed down and nuzzled Peter affectionately.

'Well I'll be doggone!' Sadler said in amazement. 'I've never seen these two take to anybody like that. They'd kill you as soon as look at you, normally.' Sadler let go of the dogs' collars and stood up. 'All right, they can come with us. This one is called Uz and the larger one is Buz. Here, take them into the lounge and I'll get you something to drink. Lemonade all right?'

'Yes, that's fine, Mr Sadler, thanks,' Joel said, feeling relieved. The last place he wanted those terrifying beasts was out in the back yard.

Sadler showed them into the lounge, then went off to the kitchen for the lemonade. While he was gone, Joel and Peter sat on a sofa. The dogs nuzzled Peter but still half snarled at Joel.

'Just keep those vicious brutes under control, Peter,' Joel whispered, squirming. 'They give me the creeps.'

Sadler came back with two tumblers of lemonade and sat on his easy chair.

'How's your Mum, Joel? She managing all right?' he inquired.

'She's fine, thank you, Mr Sadler; she misses Dad of course.' Joel just had to get that one in.

'Yes, I'm sure it must be hard for her.' Sadler squirmed uncomfortably, running a finger round inside his collar.

'Mr Sadler - I'd rather you didn't say anything to my Mum about this. She might get a bit upset - you know, being reminded about Dad - and she might wonder why I didn't talk to her about it, but well...'

'I understand, Joel. Sometimes a man has to ask a man about things,' Sadler said knowingly. 'How old are you now, Joel?'

'Twelve.'

'So you're in high school then? Are you doing well?'

'Yes, thank you. I'm Captain of the junior rugby team.'

'Captain already - at twelve?' Sadler grinned.

'I've always been mad keen on rugby, Mr Sadler.'

'That's the stuff!' Sadler beamed. 'Your Dad would have

been proud of you. What career are you going for, Joel. Any ideas?'

'Yes, absolutely, I want to be a Barrister, like my Dad.'

There was an awkward silence, then Sadler spoke again.

'So what can I tell you, Joel?'

'Well like I said before, Mr Sadler, I don't remember too much about my Dad. I was only eight when... ' Joel wanted to scream at Sadler, *WHEN YOU MURDERED HIM!* But he grimaced and bit his lip.

'When he had the accident.' Sadler finished Joel's sentence. 'So you want me to tell you what he was like, is that it?'

Joel felt a lump in his throat and nodded.

'I knew your Dad for many years, Joel. We were at University together; we studied - and partied - together. Then we ended up in the same Legal Practice as business partners. He was energetic, funny, witty. In fact he could be quite wild at times when he was young and carefree at Uni. But he never neglected his work, or his duty. The main thing that sticks in my mind about your Father, Joel, is that he had integrity. You could always count on him to do what he said and he couldn't be bought. He was one of the best Barristers I've known. Sometimes I wish I could be more like him...' Sadler drifted just for a moment. Maybe he was regretting the way things had turned out. Then he snapped out of it. 'His death was a great loss to the legal profession. I miss him too; he was a good and loyal friend.'

Joel gritted his teeth as he thought to himself, *Yeah, something you know absolutely nothing about. I bet you mean you miss him doing half your work for you, you two-faced snake.*

After an uneasy pause, Peter spoke.

'May I go to the bathroom, Mr Sadler,' he asked. 'I think I've drunk too much lemonade.'

'Of course, lad. Top of the stairs on the left. If you go too far you'll end up in my pit - not a pleasant experience, I have to warn you.' Sadler laughed.

'I'll steer well clear of that then, Mr Sadler,' Peter said, knowing full well as he left the room, that was exactly where he intended to go.

Great, thought Joel to himself, his brain racing on overdrive, *he's even saved Peter some time by giving him directions to his room, the schmuck. Fitting that he called it a pit - that's where snakes live. Go on, Peter, get that case and let's get out of here.*

Joel heard footsteps and a man entered the room holding two dog leads. Seeing the leads, the dogs jumped up excitedly.

'Hi, Boss, do you want me to take the dogs out now?' The man asked.

'Good idea, Jethro,' Sadler said. 'This is my late business partner's Son, Joel Asher.'

'Hello, Joel,' Jethro nodded awkwardly.

Joel forced a polite smile.

'You don't mind if Jethro takes the dogs for their exercise now, Joel? They've been stuck in the house all day.'

'Of course not.' Joel nodded

'Are you sure, Joel? I know you wanted them to stay - I suppose Jethro could take them later...'

'No, please - I - I don't want them to miss out on their walk because of me.' He was delighted that the slobbering monsters were finally leaving the room.

Jethro attached the leads to the excited dogs and to Joel's delight, they towed him away.

+

'Are you all right, Joel?' Sadler said.

Joel snapped out of his private thoughts and glanced at the clock on the mantelpiece. It was 6.45 p.m. - his mind had been drifting for nearly ten minutes. Where was Peter? He'd been gone for nearly fifteen minutes - what was keeping him?

'Yes, I'm fine, just a bit sad really - sad that I've missed so much of my Dad.'

'Well you've got your Mum to think about, haven't you? You're the man of the house now.'

Thanks to you, Joel thought, trying hard not to pull a contemptuous face. He wrung his hands together anxiously.

'Your friend has been gone for quite a while; do you think he's all right?' Sadler said without much real concern.

'I'm sure he's fine - he always spends ages in the bathroom - weak bladder - you know.' Joel answered, attempting to play down Peter's absence.

'I tell you what, Joel,' Sadler said. 'Why don't you go and check on your friend and make sure he hasn't washed himself down the plug hole, while I go and get myself another beer.'

Joel's mind raced again. The beer would be in the fridge - which would be in the kitchen - where the door to the back yard was located - where Peter could be right at that moment with the case. Joel jumped to his feet.

'Let me get your beer, Mr Sadler. I'm quite sure Peter is O.K.'

'No, don't trouble yourself, Joel.' Sadler leaned forward to get up.

'No!' Joel put up his hand and insisted, 'Stay where you are. If I can't get a beer for my Dad's best friend...' Those words almost choked him, but he had to keep Sadler out of the kitchen to protect Peter.

'Oh well, if you put it like that...' Sadler sat down again. 'It's in the fridge, go left out of here, down the hall past the bottom of the stairs and the kitchen is straight ahead of you - the way Jethro has just gone with the dogs.'

Oh no, Joel thought. *The dogs... in the kitchen! Why didn't Peter wait till the dogs had gone out for their walk before going to the bathroom - he went too soon.*

'I'll find it.' Joel ambled coolly out of the room, then scurried down the hall to the kitchen. There was no one there. Suddenly he gasped as a hand touched his shoulder. He spun round in fright.

'Oh it's you, Peter.' Joel let out a sigh of relief. 'What's happening? Why have you taken so long? Where's the case?' he whispered frantically.

'I've been in here for ages. I couldn't find the key to the back door,' Peter whispered back. 'Then that guy came in with the dogs - I assume it was Jethro. I hid behind this door.' Peter moved the door to expose the case hidden behind it. 'I thought I was done for, that the dogs would lead Jethro right to me, but fortunately the dogs like me, so the guard dog instinct didn't kick in. They were too excited about going out for a walk to bother with me anyway... at least I saw where the key is kept - although it doesn't really matter now; Jethro has left the door unlocked. I was just about to go outside when I heard you coming... I thought it might be Sadler.'

'Tops, mate you did good. Hurry up now - I've had just about as much as I can stand of play-acting to that creep,' Joel whispered.

'Have you found that beer, Joel?' Sadler called from the lounge.

'Yes, coming, Mr Sadler!' Joel called back, grabbing a can of beer from the fridge, then quietly to Peter. 'I'd better get back, Peter, before he comes looking for me.' He gave Peter the thumbs up and hurried back to the lounge.

'About time. What kept you?' asked Sadler.

'Sorry,' Joel said. 'I was a bit upset - about my Dad, you know - I just needed a few minutes.'

'Oh of course, lad. Sorry, I didn't think,' Sadler muttered. 'Your mate isn't back from the bathroom yet - shall we send out a search party?' Sadler attempted to cheer Joel up with a lame joke.

'Oh, he won't be long now.' Joel said with a forced smile. He sat down again, wondering how to drag out the conversation.

'Have you never married, Mr Sadler?' Joel asked, thinking this was really scraping the barrel.

'No, I've never met anyone I've wanted to give half my money to,' Sadler said, laughing.

Yeah, you would see it like that, wouldn't you? Joel thought to himself. Then he praised the Lord as Peter came back into the room.

'Do you think we should be going, Joel? We want to get back

before dark,' Peter said.

That was it! The signal! Joel jumped to his feet.

'Yes, Peter, I think we should. Well thanks, Mr Sadler, I appreciate your time. We won't take up any more of it.'

'You're welcome, Joel, any time. Give my best to your Mum - oh I forgot, your Mum is not supposed to know. It'll be our secret.'

'Thanks again, Mr Sadler.'

'I mean it, Joel; any time you want to come round is fine by me. If you ever need anything, well I hope I'll be the one you come to - there's nothing I wouldn't do for Nathan Asher's boy.'

Sure, Joel thought grimly. *That's the guilt talking - well you're going to have plenty of time to think about that, Mr Dan Sadler, when you've been nicked and locked up.* Joel smiled to himself.

Sadler showed Joel and Peter out at the front. As soon as they were past Simms's car, they rushed round the corner into the alleyway, then opened the gate to Sadler's back yard. There was Tamara all right, holding the case - petrified because she was hemmed in a corner by the viciously growling Uz and Buz!

Suddenly the back gate slammed shut behind them. Joel and Peter wheeled round. It was Jethro and he had a gun pointing right at them.

'Is that it now, or are there any more of you little blighters running around?' Jethro snapped. 'I don't know what you three are up to, but I'd guess it was no good. We'll see what Mr Sadler has to say about this, shall we?' Jethro opened the back door and pushed them all inside.

+

Sadler sat open-mouthed in his chair, still clutching a can of beer. He was staring at the case in Tamara's hand as Jethro pushed the three dejected friends into the room.

'I caught this one lurking outside in the yard with that case, Boss,' Jethro explained. 'The blonde boy was hiding in the kitchen with it when I took the dogs out. I pretended I hadn't seen him. I waited outside the gate and heard the blonde boy and the girl talking. I guess she must have been hiding in the kitchen too. The boy went back inside and shut the door, then the girl opened the gate to come out into the alley. I pushed her back inside. I figured the boys would come round the back for her, so I waited - then bingo - in they came.'

Sadler put down his beer can and slowly stood up, his eyes glued to the case. He was speechless, paralysed for a moment with shock. Then his senses seemed to return and he snatched the case from Tamara. He wrenched it open and breathed a sigh of relief that the contents were still intact. Then he snapped it shut.

'Well done, Jethro,' Sadler said, putting the case down and glaring at Joel. 'You really had me fooled, kid,' he said coldly. 'Who sent you and who else knows about this?'

'Detective John Smith of Scotland Yard knows about it, you murderer!' Joel spat.

'So the police have resorted to using kid detectives now have they? What is this - Scotland Yard's version of cutbacks? Down sizing? Give me a break! No one knows you're here, do they? But how did you know about the case?'

'Smith told us; he knows we're here,' Joel lied.

'If Smith knew about this he'd be here himself with a posse of cops - he certainly wouldn't send three kids.' Sadler laughed coldly. 'There's one way to find out for sure.' He picked up the phone and dialled Scotland Yard. 'Give me Detective John Smith. Tell him it's Dan Sadler.' He smirked as he was put through to Smith. 'I'm very well thanks, John. How's yourself? Uh huh - yeah - Oh I was just wondering if there was any news - anything coming up I should know about? - Yes, well you don't get to be a senior partner without being keen, John, you know that - No, O.K. sorry I bothered you - Yes, we must do that, call me.' Sadler replaced the phone and walked up to Joel with an evil grin on his face. 'Smith knows then, does he? I knew there was something not quite kosher about you.' Sadler poked Joel in the shoulder. 'Jethro, take our "amateur sleuth" and his friends down to the basement and lock them in. I'll deal with them later.'

'A pleasure, Boss,' Jethro said smirking.

'Give yourself up, Mr Sadler!' Tamara shouted bravely, 'while you've still got a chance - you'll get caught - you're being watched, you know!'

'Who's watching me - the rest of your school?' Sadler gave a cold, hard laugh.

'Move it!' Jethro snapped, ordering them out of the room. They were herded along the hall and down the stone steps, into the musty cellar. Pushing them onto wooden chairs he tied their hands firmly behind their backs with rope.

'There's no point in screaming; no one is going to hear you down here and if you do make a noise, I'll just come back and shut you up,' Jethro sneered menacingly. Then he slammed the solid wooden door shut behind him and turned the key, locking them in.

'Nice one,' Joel quipped. 'So what shall we do for an encore?'

'It's not as bad as it looks,' Maité said as she stepped through the Vista in front of them. Quickly she untied Tamara. 'We haven't much time. Sadler will not let you go; he intends to kill you all. You must come back with me now through my schism - the mission is aborted.'

Joel stamped his foot in frustration.

'I'm so sorry, I've blown it - let everyone down.' He hung his head sorrowfully.

'It's not your fault, amigo. These things happen all the time,' Maité said graciously.

Once free, Tamara untied Peter while Maité untied Joel.

'Come, we must leave,' Maité said urgently.

'I'm not leaving without that case.' Joel insisted. 'Who knows what Sadler might do with it now? What if he destroys it? The evidence would be gone for ever!'

'How are you going to get out of this room, Joel, except in a body bag? Think, man!' Maité cried. 'You've no choice!'

'Yeah, come on, mate,' Peter encouraged him. 'There's always tomorrow.'

'I said no noise!' They heard Jethro bellow, followed by the sound of his footsteps returning down the stone steps.

'Joel! Quick, now!' Maité grabbed hold of Joel's arm and opened the schism.

Before Joel knew it, they had all dived through the schism, just one second before Jethro opened the door.

Once through the Vista, they turned round to look through it and saw Jethro in the cellar, scratching his head, stunned by their disappearing act.

'Quick, show me Sadler?' Joel cried, desperately. 'What's he done with the case?'

A view of the lounge appeared on the Vista. Sadler was pacing up and down; the case was still there. Then Jethro came running in to tell Sadler about the baffling mystery of the vanishing children.

'They're gone, Boss!' Jethro cried 'The kids - they've escaped!'

'What? You buffoon, Jethro! How could you be such an imbecile?' Sadler began to curse angrily.

'I'm going back,' Joel declared.

'Don't be a fool, Joel,' Maité cried. 'Can't you see what you're up against here? These people are professional killers! They have no scruples.'

'Maité is right, Joel,' Nathan said sadly. 'The mission stands aborted.'

'No,' Joel said, quietly determined. 'What's at stake is too important - more important than me. Tonight might be the last chance we have to get that case. If Sadler decides to burn it, it's all over. Tamara and Peter can stay here but I'm going back.'

'You can't go on your own, Joel,' Peter protested. 'What if you run into the dogs? They'll eat you alive. I'll come with you... at least I can control Uz and Buz.'

'O.K. that makes sense. Peter comes, but Tamara stays,' Joel conceded.

'Ah, but...' Tamara started.

'That's the deal,' Joel interrupted. 'I'm not taking any

chances with you, Tamara. Besides we may need you later on, you're more useful up here on standby.'

'O.K.' Tamara nodded. 'Just, please don't do anything crazy.'

'Mama mia!' Maité exclaimed throwing her arms up in exasperation.

They all watched Sadler and Jethro on the Vista.

'They must have got outside - somehow, Boss,' Jethro whined.

Sadler looked at Jethro with contempt.

'Three kids, escape from a *locked* cellar - where they were *tied* to chairs - they get up the stairs, past the two of us - *and the dogs*, then just slip outside?' Sadler snarled sarcastically. 'Are you going soft on me, Jethro? What did you tie them up with, liquourice shoelaces? Maybe you forgot to lock the door - or maybe you *deliberately* let them go?' Sadler glared at him accusingly. 'Maybe you're losing it?'

'I'm really sorry, Boss,' Jethro muttered pathetically. 'I was sure I'd locked them in... honest.'

'You ignoramus, Jethro! Go and take the dogs out! It's about all you seem to be capable of,' Sadler spat.

Jethro skulked out of the room.

Sadler slumped into the easy chair and snapped open yet another can of beer. He looked at the case by the side of his chair and tapped his fingers impatiently on the table.

'Now is our chance, while Jethro is out with those two brutes,' Joel said, determinedly.

'What are we going to do?' Peter said. 'He's going to keep that case next to him all night.'

'And look at Sadler's clock; it's a quarter past seven. We've got to get to Smith before ten!' Tamara added anxiously.

'Then there's Grandad - he'll be looking for us soon, especially as we've got Tamara staying with us tonight,' Joel added.

'Believe me, boys, at the rate Sadler is drinking, he's surely going to have to go to the bathroom soon,' Nathan said. 'And he's sure to be falling asleep before too long. That's the time to act. Oh and don't worry about Grandad. I had one of our Angels visit him with a present.'

A view of Grandad flashed onto the Vista. He was sitting in his rocking chair with a bottle of malt whisky on the table next to him. He was out for the count and snoring loudly.

'Good old Marcus,' Nathan said with a grin. 'He never could resist a bit of best malt whisky - and he sure deserves it after all that fencing today, doesn't he, Joel?'

'Yes, Dad, I guess he does. Thanks,' Joel grinned.

The Vista returned to Sadler's lounge. Soon enough, Sadler staggered to his feet. There were eight empty beer cans lying on the table and on the floor by his chair. He lurched out of the room, grabbing hold of the stair bannisters.

'There he goes,' Nathan said.

'Good,' said Joel. 'We can steal in now while he's in the bathroom - if he makes it that far without collapsing. Come on, Peter... a toddler could snatch that case, the state Sadler is in.'

Without further thought, Joel leapt impetuously through the Vista and landed with a thud, falling over and twisting his ankle. In his haste, he'd forgotten to glide through the Vista and had taken off like an arrow from a bow. Quickly he scrambled to his feet, just as Peter landed more sedately next to him.

'Are you all right, Joel? You jumped through so fast... I thought you were going to go right through the wall on the other side of the room.' Peter whispered earnestly.

'Yeah, just twisted my ankle a bit, that's all. I forgot I was jumping out of zero gravity into earth's gravity. I won't do that again.' Joel said, feeling rather foolish. 'Right, I guess it's an open and shut case,' he grinned as he picked up the case. 'Come on, let's get out of here.' He hobbled to the lounge doorway, stepped into the hall and started making his way towards the front door.

'Peter, come on!' Joel whispered urgently.

'I think you'd better stop right there, Joel.' Sadler's voice was all too clear and sounded surprisingly sober.

Joel's heart sank, he turned around. Sadler was holding Peter by the arm with a gun trained at his head.

'Sorry, Joel.' Peter said despondently.

'It's not your fault, mate,' Joel shrugged.

Sadler gave a high pitched laugh.

'You two couldn't have made more noise if you'd arrived on stampeding bulls,' his face twisted into an evil scowl. 'I knew you were still in the house somewhere. Get in the lounge!'

Joel hobbled into the lounge and Sadler snatched the case off him.

'Where's Miss Snoop then?' Sadler demanded.

Both boys shrugged.

'Oh well, she won't get far.' Then he shouted, 'Jethro! Where is that idiot when you want him?'

They heard the back door slam.

'Jethro!' Sadler screamed again.

Jethro came running into the room like a well trained dog.

'What's going on, Boss?' He asked breathlessly. 'You!' he cried as he saw the boys. 'Where the devil did you two come from again?'

'It appears, Jethro, that these two amateur detectives think they must be late for their appointment with death!' Sadler hissed in evil humour. Then he turned to the boys. 'How do you know about the case? Tell me who sent you?'

'The Easter bunny,' Joel spat with contempt.

'Right!' Sadler held his gun to the side of Peter's head. 'You've got precisely three seconds to give me a straight answer or blondie gets it... One...'

'All right!' Joel shouted, his brain racing like an express train. He had to come up with something plausible and quickly. 'Lilith, he sent us.'

Sadler lowered the gun in stunned silence. Fear gripped his face at the mere mention of Lilith's name.

'Lilith? - No - Lilith isn't crazy enough to pull a stunt like this... using kids...'

'Tell me then, how would we know about Lilith, if he hadn't sent us? And doesn't he make his fortune, *exploiting kids*?

A BITTER APPOINTMENT

What's so different about us?' Joel pressed the point.

'What's he playing at?' Sadler looked uncertain. He picked up a can of beer, poured its contents down his throat, then crushed the can like an eggshell, chucking it onto the floor. He seemed to be swaying a bit and his hair was dishevelled. He looked a far cry from the smart Barrister he posed as during office hours. 'Jethro, tie these clowns up - and do it properly this time! I need to think.' Sadler flopped down on the easy chair and sank his fuzzy head into his hands.

'Right, Boss, you got it.' Jethro ran off to the kitchen and was back in seconds with a roll of wide, brown sticky tape. He proceeded to wrap the tape round Joel and Peter's wrists, with their hands behind their backs.

Sadler had broken out into little beads of sweat. The mere mention of Lilith's name had made him quiver like a big bowl of jelly. Joel decided to milk the situation while Sadler was all confused.

'And what's more,' Joel went on bravely, 'if we don't report back to Lilith by ten o'clock - *with* the case - he's coming here personally to get you.'

'Mother of God! What am I going to do?' Sadler stood up and started to wring his hands in anguish. 'What does he want? TELL ME WHAT HE WANTS!' Sadler screamed. He'd really lost it.

'Steady on, Boss,' Jethro entreated him. 'It ain't that bad.'

'Not that bad?' Sadler screeched hysterically. 'It couldn't possibly be worse, you dingbat! Here, watch these two - and don't let them get away this time.'

Sadler was just about to run upstairs - probably to get his passport, throw all the dirty money into a bag and do a runner - when the doorbell rang. He froze.

'NO! Oh no! He's here already - what am I going to do?' Sadler whimpered pathetically.

'You don't know it's him,' said Jethro. 'The kid said by ten o'clock. It won't be Lilith yet... I'll take this pair into the dining room. Open the door, Boss. Ignoring it will just raise suspicion.'

'Yes, I think you might be right for once, Jethro. O.K. keep those boys quiet. Where are the dogs?' Sadler spoke quickly, smoothing his dishevelled hair and attempting to pull himself together.

'They're shut in the back yard, Boss.'

'Right, O.K. get these two in the dining room and gag them.' Sadler put his gun in his pocket then went to open the front door.

Jethro grabbed the roll of tape and herded Joel and Peter through a set of double doors that led from Sadler's lounge into the dining room. He shut the doors, pushed the boys down onto two chairs facing the doors and taped their mouths up. He sat on the edge of the dining table, keeping his gun trained on the boys.

'One sound from either of you and you're both toast,' Jethro hissed.

They heard voices as Sadler was obviously bringing whoever it was into the lounge. They could just make out what Sadler and his visitor were saying.

'I just wanted to check everything was all right, Dan, after your rather rushed telephone call half an hour ago. I was worried that all was not quite as it should be.'

Joel and Peter quickly glanced at each other; they were both thinking the same thing. It must be Smith - and the case was still in the lounge; he was bound to see it and no doubt recognise it. They suddenly felt a glimmer of hope: maybe Smith would be able to rescue them *and* get the case after all.

'No, John, really, everything is fine,' Sadler said shakily and not at all convincingly. 'I just thought it was a while since we spoke, you know how it is?'

Sadler was digging a deeper hole for himself by the second. The sweat was dripping off him now. Then they heard a thud.

'What's this?' said Smith.

'Er, I can explain, John...' Sadler began to plead weakly.

Smith must have tripped over the case. *Good,* thought Joel, *now arrest him*! There was silence for a few seconds. Then suddenly and unexpectedly the double doors burst open and Smith stood there, gun levelled.

'FREEZE!' Smith yelled, then almost dropped his gun in shock as he clearly recognised Joel - the last person he expected to see!

Jethro threw down his gun and put his hands up in the air.

'You're O.K. now, kids, I'm the police,' Smith said, ripping the tape from their mouths, while keeping his gun and an eye trained on Jethro. He called back to Sadler. 'I knew something was wrong, Dan, I thought you were being held hostage - lucky I followed through my hunch and came o...'

Smith didn't finish his sentence. They heard a click and suddenly Sadler had his gun at the back of Smith's head.

'Not so fast, Smith,' Sadler drawled smugly. 'Drop it!'

Smith dropped his gun onto the floor and Jethro picked it up along with his own gun.

'Nice one, Boss,' Jethro said with a smirk.

'Tie him up, Jethro,' Sadler sneered.

Jethro handed Smith's gun to Sadler and began to tape the Detective's wrists behind his back.

'For goodness' sake, Jethro,' Sadler said bickering, while frisking Smith. 'This is the kind of thing I pay you for and I end up having to do everything myself. Now get down to the cellar and find out where these kids got out last time - and block it up! We'll put them all down there while we decide what to do. Drat - now we'll have three bodies to get rid of!' Sadler pushed Smith down onto a chair.

'Four with the girl - when we find her,' Jethro said.

'Yeah, we'll use these as bait; we don't want her running round, shooting her mouth off.' Sadler smirked.

Jethro scurried out of the room to check the cellar.

Joel felt the blood drain from his face. He and Peter stared at each other in shock, then they both stared at Smith as the painful truth dawned on them. They were going to die - Tamara and Maité would not be able to rescue them through the Vista, because *Smith* would be with them and that would be against the rules - using the Vista in public.

CHAPTER SIXTEEN

Lambs to the Slaughter

Unfortunately, the two boys now found themselves in the unhappy situation whereby the very man they hoped would rescue them, would now actually prevent them being rescued via the Vista. Joel continued to stare at Smith, he gulped nervously and his tongue stuck to the roof of his dry mouth, as he and Peter sat dejectedly contemplating their fate.

Sadler paced anxiously up and down in a sweat, waiting for Jethro.

'You won't get away with this, Sadler,' Smith barked.

'Just watch me,' Sadler spat.

'Anyway, what are you doing with a couple of kids? They're harmless; at least let the kids go. Where are your scruples, man?' Smith went on.

'He hasn't got any scruples, Detective Smith,' Joel muttered accusingly. 'He murdered my Dad.'

'Shut up!' Sadler hissed.

'What are you doing here, Joel?' Smith continued, ignoring Sadler.

'I said no talking!' Sadler screeched like a demon.

Suddenly Joel, who was sitting nearest to a door on his left that must have led to the kitchen, heard a slight creaking sound, as if someone was slowly opening it. He tried to look covertly with as little head movement as possible, in case it was one of his friends and he put them in danger. Someone was definitely there; the door had opened by about two inches. He couldn't tell who it was but hoped it wasn't one of his friends, as they'd surely be killed too. He leaned over to Peter and whispered.

'Bogey at nine o'clock.'

Peter looked in the direction of the door and his eyes nearly popped out of his head. Then Joel and Smith looked too and saw the cause of Peter's consternation - there was a gun barrel poking through the gap in the doorway. This definitely wasn't a friend.

'DUCK!' Joel screamed.

All three of them dived off their chairs and Sadler froze, as the door swung open and a huge man burst into the room toting the gun. It was Simms - all twenty stone of him.

'What the devil is going on, Sadler?' Simms bellowed.

'Simms!' Sadler screamed in terror, expecting that any moment now, Lilith would be coming in after him.

'There's been something going on here tonight, Sadler. I've just rung Lilith and he's instructed me to find out what it is. Why is Detective Smith here? Are you making a deal with the law?'

'LILITH?' Smith echoed incredulously, picking himself up. 'What's Lilith got to do with all this?'

'Lilith is the Hyena, Detective Smith - he and Sadler feed from the same trough,' Joel said grimly, as he and Peter also picked themselves up off the floor.

'But Lilith is a top crust at Scotland Yard!' Smith said in sheer amazement.

'Which makes him ideally placed, don't you think, Smith?' Sadler screeched with a high-pitched, hysterical laugh.

'Enough!' Simms thundered. 'Sadler, explain to me what's going on and be quick - I'm running out of patience.'

'Simms...' Sadler pleaded weakly. 'You've got it all wrong... I'd never make a deal with the law... Lilith knows that... What would I stand to gain..?'

As Sadler was talking, unbeknown to any of them, Jethro, having heard voices, had sneaked into the kitchen and seen Simms with the gun pointing in Sadler's direction. In his usual act first, think later style, he suddenly leapt into the room.

'And you just ran out of time, moron.' Jethro smirked as he coshed Simms on the head with his gun.

The burly Simms crashed to the floor like one of Dibnah's chimney stacks. He was out cold.

'Lord Almighty, Jethro!' Sadler wailed. 'What have you done?'

'What d - do y - you mean...?' Jethro stammered. 'That - g - guy had a gun on you, Boss...'

'That guy, Jethro, is Simms!' Sadler wrung his hands in anguish.

Jethro gasped as he realised his bungling gaffe.

'Yes, you idiot, Jethro!' Sadler went on mournfully. 'Lilith's psychotic butcher! If Simms doesn't report back to Lilith soon - I - *WE* are dead men!'

The colour drained from Jethro's face; he looked positively ghostly.

'I - I'm sorry, Boss. I didn't r - recognise him,' he stuttered pathetically.

'Jethro, how many times have you seen Simms? How could you make such a mistake?' Sadler lamented.

Jethro cut a pathetic figure as he looked down at the floor, like a schoolboy being ticked off by the Headmaster.

'Well?' Sadler demanded 'Did you find out how these meddlesome kids escaped last time?'

'Yeah, Boss. There's a narrow window, high up at the back of the cellar. I'm amazed they got through it, especially the big lad, but there's no other way out, so they must have managed some how. Anyway, I've blocked it up now so they won't get through it again.'

'Good, at least that's something,' Sadler sneered scornfully.

'I suppose we'll have to dispose of this lot in convoy,' Jethro remarked with reservation. 'We'll never get this many bodies in one car, especially Simms. He'll be a ton weight.'

'Jethro, how stupid are you?' Sadler wailed and slapped his own forehead in frustration. 'We can't kill Simms! He's one of Lilith's best men! Lilith would hunt us down like wild animals! Didn't you just hear me? Simms has got to report back to Lilith - tell him everything is all right. We'll just have to hope we can bring him round and make him believe that.'

'If the poor goon isn't dead already,' Smith chipped in humorously.

'Shut up, Smith!' Sadler snapped. 'Who asked you?' Then

he frowned suspiciously. 'You're remarkably blasé for a man who is about to die!'

Joel had to agree, he too thought Smith was surprisingly cheerful for a man about to be murdered - in cold blood - almost as if he was enjoying the show. Joel felt dazed, like a member of an audience watching a play that would very soon be over, and they'd all be clapping then going home. If only that was true.

'Jethro, get these idiots out of my face!' Sadler spat impatiently. 'Lock 'em all in the cellar - I'll try to revive Simms and apologise for the mistake.'

Once again Joel and Peter were unceremoniously herded - this time with Smith - down to the cellar.

'Home, sweet home,' Joel said dryly, as Jethro pushed them down the stone steps.

'Well don't get too comfortable - you ain't staying here long,' Jethro said with a bloodthirsty grin. 'If you know any prayers, kids, say 'em now.' Then he banged the door shut on them and turned the key, locking them in their tomb.

Smith turned round and presented his back to Joel.

'Here, Joel, see if you can jiggle this damned tape off my wrists.'

Joel edged his back to Smith and began tugging at the tape with his own taped-up hands. While he was doing this, he and Peter told Smith about Sadler and Lilith's nefarious collaboration. They told him everything - what had happened to the case and about Nathan's murder, the double-dealings, double-bluffs, Sadler blackmailing Lilith and the squeakers, the dirty money in the drawers under Sadler's bed. Smith listened quietly in amazement.

'How did you get involved in all this, Joel? What does your Mother think about it?' Smith asked.

Joel finally managed to yank the tape off Smith's wrists and swiftly turned to face him.

'My Mother doesn't know I'm here - and you're not to tell her,' Joel demanded with a sudden sharpness. 'If we ever get out of here, I mean. I need your word on that, Detective Smith.'

'O.K. Son.' Smith nodded and smiled. 'You have my word.' Joel breathed a sigh of relief.

'Thanks, Detective Smith.' He returned the smile.

Smith began ripping the tape off Joel. Then he did the same for Peter.

'How in Heaven do you know all this anyway, Joel?' Smith persisted.

Joel was suddenly lost for words. In his anxiousness to give Smith the low-down on Sadler and Lilith, he'd quite forgotten that he couldn't very well tell Smith the truth about how he'd come by the information. Certainly he couldn't say his Father told him - that would mean a one-way ticket to Nuttersville!

'Sadler...' Peter suddenly came to the rescue, 'Sadler told us himself... when he caught us earlier... uh - he - uh - was gloating... in fact ... wasn't he, Joel?'

'That's right, Detective Smith.' Joel nodded. 'He especially gloated about how stupid the police were and how easy it was to fool you.' Joel hoped throwing in that remark would galvanise Smith and take his attention off their all-too-thin explanation - especially how they came to be there in the first place!

'Oh he did, did he?' Smith said as he finished ripping the tape off Peter. 'Well, that didn't take long,' he added with satisfaction. 'Thank Heavens we're dealing with amateurs. Now how *did* you two get out of here last time?' Smith raised his eyebrows - almost as if he expected them to make something up.

Joel and Peter looked at each other, then followed Smith's gaze up to the tiny window at the back of the cellar that Jethro had just nailed up. As they looked at it, they realised that Smith wouldn't swallow their explanation. They'd have a job getting a scrawny cat through there, let alone the two of them.

Then suddenly the boys heard a familiar and very welcome voice.

'Room service!'

They recognised it immediately: it was unmistakably Magee.

'Up here...' called Magee, 'the ventilation hole.'

They looked up and saw a small hole in the wall about one brick wide and three bricks high. Joel rushed to the wall, dragged up a chair and stood on it. He was face to face with Magee, who was perched in the hole and in his beak, was a very pleasing sight indeed - a key!

'I'm not one to say I told you so but... Said Magee. 'Make out you found it here in the hole.'

'What would we do without you? Bless you.' Joel grinned.

'All part of the service,' Magee said preening himself.

'Without who?' Smith queried.

Joel jumped off the chair and held up the key.

'Without the key of course... like you said, Detective Smith, we're lucky we're dealing with amateurs - who happen to leave a spare key in here, in case any prisoners want to let themselves out.' Joel beamed and handed the key to Smith.

'I don't believe it!' Smith took the key, shaking his head in amusement. 'What a classic! Come on then, let's get out of here.'

'You won't leave without the case, will you, Detective Smith?' Joel said with some concern.

Smith turned and looked at Joel curiously.

'Why are you so concerned about the case, Joel?'

'Because there's something in it that will prove Sadler murdered my Dad,' Joel said solemnly.

'Oh?'

'The chloroform-soaked handkerchief - Sadler stuffed it into the case with everything else the night he killed my Dad.'

Smith pulled a silver pen out of his breast pocket and put an arm round Joel's shoulders.

'Do you know what this is, Joel?'

'Looks like a pen, Detective Smith.'

'Looks like a pen, Joel, and writes just like a pen - but do you know what else this is?

Joel shrugged, wondering where all this was leading.

'This, Son, is a bug - not the crawling type, mind, but a very sophisticated hi-tech recording device and it's connected by satellite to Scotland Yard.'

Joel and Peter gasped and stared open-mouthed at Smith as he continued.

'Everything that has been said tonight by you, Sadler, Jethro and Simms has gone directly back to the Yard - including what you've said just now about the handkerchief.' Smith sat down on the steps by the door and went on. 'I've had my suspicions about Sadler for quite some time. I've been watching him and the amateur lamb chumps who follow him everywhere he goes. Only these lambs aren't as white as snow. It doesn't take a boffin to know that a perfectly innocent Barrister, with nothing to hide doesn't have three full-time bodyguards. What's he got to guard?' Smith shrugged.

'I thought you were a bit too jovial for a man sentenced to death,' Joel said.

'Also, Sadler seems to have far too much money to throw around.' Smith continued. 'When he telephoned me this evening, I had a nasty feeling that something was about to go pop. Then I had a very strange visitor.'

'Oh? Who was that, Detective Smith?' Joel asked curiously.

'I don't exactly know, Joel. A young girl - she can't have been more than about ten or eleven. She walked straight into my office unannounced. She didn't go past the front desk, how she got into Scotland Yard with all its security, is baffling to say the least.'

'What did she say?' Joel asked nervously, knowing full well it could only have been Tamara.

'She said that I couldn't trust Dan Sadler, that I must go to his house straight away and take some back-up with me. If I didn't... she said innocent people were going to die. Now how she knew to send me here, and who I'd been on the phone to, is a mystery. Then she left the room as quickly as she came. I jumped up and started to follow her out, but my attention was suddenly diverted by a fierce tapping on the window... I looked round. There was a stupid Raven, knocking like fury with its beak on the window pane - I couldn't believe it - I thought the glass would break! It was almost as if the bird was - was trying to divert my attention!'

'Ahem! Is that all the thanks we get, for saving your butt, mate?' Magee cawed, still perched in the wall vent. 'Such a thankless job,' he said, shaking his head slowly from side to side.

'Well!' Maggi landed next to Magee. 'I don't know what you're so uppity about, Magee - it's me he's just called stupid!'

'Whatever...' Magee replied nonchalantly.

'I shooed the Raven away,' Smith continued, 'but by the time I got outside my office door, my mystery visitor had vanished - seemingly into thin air! I queried the front desk... but they just looked at me like I'd gone crazy... no one saw her come and no one saw her leave. You know what, boys,' Smith heaved a sigh, 'it might sound crazy, but I think I was visited by an Angel. She was beautiful... just how I would imagine an Angel to look.'

'Aah - what a nice man,' Maggi swooned. 'All right he's forgiven.'

'I think he was talking about Tamara, Maggi, not you...' Magee said in his typically tactless way. 'Anyway, as an Angel, your forgiveness should be automatic.'

'You know, Magee,' Maggi retorted, 'Sometimes you're a miserable, tactless - OLD - GERBIL! I apologise to all gerbils.' With that Maggi flew off in a huff.

Peter looked up at the air vent.

'You've done it now, mate,' he whispered.

'What? - What have I done now?' Magee hung his head. 'Me and my big beak... It seems every time I open it, I put my great clodhopping claw in it - now I suppose I'll have to go and eat worms as a penance,' he mused with a tut.

Joel and Peter looked at each other and couldn't help laughing at Magee's amusing banter.

'Oh go on then, call me a nutter, just like everyone else at the Yard this evening,' Smith protested. He was under the illusion that the boys were laughing at him, as he was oblivious to the Ravens.

This made the boys giggle even more.

'O.K. laugh if you must - but the fact remains,' Smith continued, 'that my suspicions were sufficiently aroused for me to bring forward, "Operation Shepherd."'

The boys snapped out of their mirth and looked at Smith in

puzzlement.

'Operation Shepherd?' The two boys queried in unison.

'That's right,' Smith said, smugly. 'I knew Sadler was into something big - something involving the underworld. I just didn't know what and I didn't have any evidence. I only knew that if I watched him closely, sooner or later he'd make a mistake and I'd have him. So I set up a surveillance strategy to find out exactly what our Mr Sadler was into - that, is Operation Shepherd. By now, boys, this place will be surrounded by police, ready to round up this little flock of villains.' Smith spoke into his pen, 'The Shepherd is safe, the sheep are ready to be rounded up; come and get them! Oh and by the way - these boys were never here - just as my Angel visit never happened...' Smith grinned at the boys and stood up, holding the key. 'Let's go, shall we, boys?'

'Any time you like, Detective Smith. I'll certainly be glad to leave this place,' Joel grinned back at him.

'Ditto to that!' Peter echoed.

As Smith unlocked the cellar door, they heard an almighty crash as the front door collapsed, followed by the sounds of running feet and shouting. By the time Joel, Peter and Smith had reached the lounge, Sadler and Jethro were handcuffed and under arrest, together with the dazed and groaning Simms. A uniformed Sergeant approached Smith.

'A job well done, Sir; all sheep present and counted. Congratulations!' the Sergeant said with a grin.

'What about Lilith?' Smith asked quickly.

'We picked him up, Sir, he's in custody, he's going to be sent down all right.' The Sergeant turned to Joel and Peter.

'Well done, you two,' he said congratulating them. 'The Commissioner asked me to say thank you to the brave boys who helped bring down this evil empire and its ruler.'

Joel and Peter beamed with delight.

'May I know both your names?' the Sergeant asked.

Before the boys could answer, Sadler, Jethro and Simms snarled as they were marched out by a squad of policemen. Smith picked up the case and rushed out after them.

'Don't forget this, officer; it's important evidence,' came Smith's voice from the hall.

'Tell them not to forget to look in the drawers under Sadler's bed,' Peter said hurriedly to the Sergeant. 'They're full of Sadler's dirty money.'

The Sergeant dashed out to tell them.

When there was no one else in the room, Joel returned to the spot where, only a short time ago, he had landed and twisted his ankle. He put up his hand and opened a schism.

'Quick, Peter, before the Sergeant returns and we have to answer that very awkward question.'

They both slipped through the schism and were instantly gliding out of the Vista to receive the most tumultuous applause. Nathan, Anna, Maité and Tamara had been watching the Vista and it was still running. Joel and Peter turned around to watch it too. They saw the Sergeant come back into the room with Smith.

'Where did those two go?' the Sergeant asked, baffled.

Smith rubbed his chin. 'Which two, Sergeant?'

'The boys, Sir; where did the boys go?'

'What boys? There were no boys here, Sergeant - were there?' The Sergeant looked at Smith, most perplexed.

'No, Sir, none at all.'

'There are a few unanswered questions, Sergeant, but I guess there are just some things we're not meant to know. Well done, Sergeant - a good, clean arrest. Well, I think I'll go to my favourite lady now and celebrate. Goodnight, Sergeant.' Smith made for the door.

'Goodnight, Sir.' The Sergeant shrugged, confused.

'Oh, Sergeant,' Smith said on his way out. 'Don't forget that moolah in the bed drawers, will you? I suspect that really is there.'

+

Nathan closed the Vista and turned to face the young heroes.

'Congratulations on a successful mission, all of you; I couldn't be prouder of you. What you've achieved here will benefit so many people in many ways for many years to come.'

The children were a little overwhelmed by it all, but still felt a sense of relief that Sadler and Lilith were exposed and caught, their reign of misery and crime over.

'Now you must go home before Grandad wakes up,' Nathan continued. 'First though, I have something for you.'

Nathan put a cube of light, no bigger than a large marble, into each one's right hand. As he gave Maité hers, he squeezed her hand affectionately.

'Maité, thank you so much for helping us get the new recruits started. You know what this is, don't you?'

Maité closed her fingers round the cube of light and nodded sadly.

'We'll see you on Friday, Maité,' Nathan said smiling.

*'Adios, compadre,' Maité murmured. Then, with moist eyes, she set off for the Fugue.

*'Mi amiga!' Joel flew after Maité, landing by her side. He held out his right hand and smiled. *'Muchas gracias.'

'You've been taking Spanish lessons, Joel?' Maité took his hand and returned the smile, wiping her moist cheek with her other hand.

'I've learned a little Spanish - but I've learned a lot of other things, thanks to you, Maité.'

'You do your Father proud. *Adios amigo.' Maité smiled.

*'Hasta pronto,' Joel muttered, watching her float away.

'Thanks for everything, Maité!' Tamara called.

'Yeah, thanks for saving us - and for everything,' Peter added.

'What is this?' Tamara turned back to Nathan, scrutinising the light cube.

'It's your invitation, Tamara,' Nathan explained. 'An invitation to the party.'

'A party?' Tamara and Peter cried in unison.

'Yes, Friday evening at 7 p.m. your time. You're to come here. It is your initiation celebration into the Kairos and it's

---

* Goodbye (go with God) good friend   * My friend!   * Thank you very much
* Goodbye (go with God) friend   * See you soon

Maité's passing-out.'

On hearing that, Joel flew back over to the others.

'So, we'll see Maité again, Dad?'

'Yes, she'll be here. It will all be hosted here and you will meet the rest of the Kairos. When you get home you will be able to read your invitations, but as soon as they've been read, they will automatically dissolve back into the light. Come, you must go back now. God be with you.'

'And also with you,' they all replied happily.

+

Soon enough Joel, Peter and Tamara found themselves standing once again on the plateau in Zionica, their first major mission having been a complete success. Travelling the Fugue now seemed almost as familiar a mode of transport as catching a bus.

The weary friends could hardly believe that after all that had happened, it was still only just after eight o'clock. Being early April, the sun had already set. They looked around and the dark, cloudless sky was speckled with stars. Although the air was a little chilly, they didn't feel a bit cold; they just felt a warm glow, the kind you get after something really special and exciting has happened.

The darkness meant they would easily be able to read their invitations, which they could hardly wait to do. The excited friends held up the light cubes and as they opened their fingers, they watched incredulously. The glowing cubes appeared to unroll themselves into flat squares that measured about four inches long and high. Then, droplets of light fell away from them like fireflies which dissolved into the air, these were the spaces in between the letters. All that remained were letters of light suspended in the air, forming easily readable words. The invitations read thus:

Welcome to the Kairos!
You are cordially invited to the:
Easter Kairos Celebration & Banquet
to be held at the
Andance Regis Ballroom
in Heaven
Friday 7.00 p.m. GMT
p.s. come hungry!
p.p.s. gowns will be provided!

'Wow - how amazing is that?' Tamara cried, beside herself with excitement. As she spoke, the glowing, golden letters vanished from sight, just as the spaces had done.

'Awesome!' Peter said blinking.

'I wonder what we'll have to do...' Joel said, a little apprehensively. 'What form our initiation will take?'

'I wonder what the gowns will be like?' Tamara sang gleefully. 'I just can't wait!'

'I don't like the idea of having to wear a poncey gown,' Joel muttered.

'I guess we'll just have to wait till Friday to find out,' said Peter.

'Oh come on, you two,' Tamara said. 'Aren't you a little bit excited? Maité will be there, Joel...' she added teasingly.

'It's getting chilly. Let's get back before we're missed.' Joel deliberately ignored Tamara's comment, pulled his jacket round him and set off for the house.

'Yeah, come on, Tamara. I'm really quite hungry now,' said Peter.

They all ran back to the old cottage, where they found that

Grandad was still asleep in his rocking chair. The bottle of whisky was on the table, almost untouched. Grandad was nursing a small glass in his lap.

'Your Grandad isn't joking when he says one glass of malt sends him to sleep, is he?' Peter remarked with a chuckle.

Joel gently lifted the glass from Grandad's fingers and as he did so, Grandad stirred.

'Oh hello - I must have dozed off.' Grandad yawned sleepily. 'An old friend came for a visit and brought me this lovely bottle of old malt whisky, but you know my trouble with malt. What time is it, Joel?'

'Nearly half past eight, Grandad. Who was your old friend?'

'Old Scobie. He's a man of the road really, Joel - you know, no fixed abode, travels from village to village, taking sustenance where he can. He's been coming here for years on and off; we always have a good chat. I usually sit him at the kitchen table and give him a meal. Sometimes he sleeps in the barn, then comes in for breakfast. He didn't stay tonight though - had some errand to do. Someone gave him this whisky but he doesn't drink, so he thought I might like it.'

'That was nice of him, Mr Jacob,' said Tamara.

'Yes, Tamara, he's a nice man. So what have you three been up to?'

'Oh not much, Grandad, just messing around in Zionica, that's all,' Joel answered casually. 'I'm starving - shall we make some sandwiches for supper?'

'Oh yes, good idea, Joel. I'm a bit peckish myself,' Grandad said. 'There's some of that lamb in the fridge and some roast beef and a few chicken legs. Oh and Peter's Mum came round earlier with another chocolate cake too.'

'Fantastic!' Joel said, rushing into the kitchen. 'Come on, Tamara, you can butter the bread; Peter, you can get the meat and I will slice the chocolate cake.'

'I bought some fresh doughnuts from the baker today as well,' Grandad called, 'in case you're still hungry after all that...'

A short while later they were all sitting at the kitchen table munching a veritable feast, when they heard a gentle tapping on the window. They looked up and saw the Magi sitting on the ledge outside.

'Look, Joel,' Grandad said in amusement. 'There's that old Raven that was watching us doing the fence earlier.'

'So it is, Grandad.' Joel got up and opened the window. 'Looks like he's brought his Mrs with him.'

'Did someone mention a feast, perchance?' Magee inquired nonchalantly.

'Oh they must be hungry. Grandad. Can we give them something to eat?'

'Of course. I wouldn't want any of God's creatures to go hungry, especially Ravens,' Grandad replied.

'Oh you know, I like this old duffel bag more every time I see him,' Magee cawed.

'Magee!' Maggi chastised him, 'Remember your manners. You shouldn't talk about Joel's Grandad like that.'

'Don't be silly, Maggi - I only meant that as a term of endearment, I didn't mean any harm by it - I mean, it's not as if he can hear us, is it?' Magee hung his head guiltily. 'Oh all right - I'm sorry, Joel, I didn't mean to call your Grandad an old duffel bag. There! Now I fancy some of that beef. How about you, Maggi?'

'Well yes, it would go down a treat,' Maggi agreed.

'Beef it is then,' Joel whispered with a grin.

'Um... you couldn't cut it into shreds for us, my dear, Joel, could you?' Maggi said sweetly. 'We've only got beaks you know.'

'And no teeth!' Magee added quickly.

'Well then, Magee,' Joel whispered playfully, 'perhaps you'd like me to chew yours for you as well?'

'Hmm.' Magee huffed, with mock indignation.

Joel put some shreds of beef on a saucer with some pieces of fresh bread and placed it on the window ledge.

'Room service!' Joel grinned. 'Enjoy your meal, friends.'

'Thank you, kind Sir,' Maggi said preening herself.

'You're welcome,' Grandad said smiling.

'Huh?' Magee exclaimed.

Joel, Peter and Tamara gasped, dropping their food and staring at Grandad open-mouthed, while the two Ravens almost fell off the window ledge.

'W - what did y - you say, Grandad?' Joel stuttered incredulously, because Grandad wasn't supposed to be able to hear the Magi.

'Oh...' Grandad looked up and laughed. 'I assumed the birds would be grateful for a tit bit and if they could talk they would have said thank you, so I said, "You're welcome." Sorry if I startled you, guys. I'm not going mad really; it was just me being jovial, that's all.' Grandad gave a little shrug.

They all laughed and a jolly good feast was had by all.

CHAPTER SEVENTEEN

I'll Lead You All in the Dance, Said He

So much had happened over the last couple of weeks, it suddenly hit Joel with a shock, when he woke up the next morning, that it was Thursday. In only two days time, the Easter holiday would be over and Mum would come to take him home. He contemplated glumly the prospect of returning to the routine of school again. He wasn't ready for that, things had only just begun, he had many questions. He wanted to spend time with his Father and to find out what his next mission would be. How could he concentrate on school work? How could he look Mum in the eye, knowing what he knew? He was sure that he would feel awkward. Would she suspect anything? Would he ever see Maité again?

Peter and Tamara came over after breakfast and the three of them spent the day hanging around Zionica, doing the kind of things they used to do before Tamara's accident - and the Kairos. The pond was teeming with life, the tadpoles were no doubt happy to be free of their jam jar prisons. However, by the time they became baby frogs, Joel would be back in the city, with Mum, Naomi and school.

The three friends attempted to amuse themselves in the den, but the fact was that they were too excited to concentrate on anything for long. They talked about the previous evening, analysing everything, not wanting to let the excitement go - it was like coming to the end of a really good book.

They marvelled at the ingenuity behind Smith's hi-tech pen. Joel and Peter praised Tamara's quick thinking in paying Smith a visit. They fell about laughing at the idea that Smith thought he'd been visited by an Angel - although Tamara was quite flattered by the description. They giggled helplessly at the ridiculous notion that Grandad might have heard the Ravens speaking. Then of course they couldn't stop talking about the forthcoming

Party. This also brought them to the upsetting subject of Maité leaving the Kairos. They knew she was devastated at having to leave. They'd got fond of Maité and they were all going to miss her - especially Joel, who to his embarrassment hadn't been able to keep secret the fact that he had a bit of a crush on her, although he was still denying it.

'It's perfectly beastly that poor Maité has to leave when she so wants to carry on being a part of the Kairos,' Tamara said sympathetically. 'It must be like having to leave your family.'

'She's so good too - what a waste,' Peter said in agreement.

'One day the three of us will be in the same boat,' Joel reminded them gloomily. 'Just imagine what it'll be like when we leave.'

'It really will be leaving family for you, Joel, when you have to say goodbye to your Dad,' Peter pointed out.

'Yeah, I don't want to think about it,' Joel said. 'Tamara will be the last to leave. She's going to have to keep it secret from us, Peter.'

'For two years!' Tamara cried. 'That I'm not looking forward to at all. It isn't easy keeping anything secret from you two, let alone something this big.'

'Well we don't have to think about it for a long time yet thankfully,' Joel said. 'I wonder what Maité will write in her note,' he added thoughtfully.

'She might tell you, Joel, if you ask her tomorrow evening,' Tamara said grinning teasingly at Joel. 'You've got a crush on her haven't you? You're in lurve!'

'Of course not!' Joel could feel his face turning the colour of beetroot and looked away quickly.

'There's no point denying it, Joel. It's as obvious as a Belisha beacon flashing on top of your head!' Tamara giggled.

'I'm not, I tell you - I like her just as you do,' Joel said in protest.

'Well what's this then?' Tamara pulled out a book from Joel's pile. '*Learn Spanish*! Got a sudden desire to learn Spanish, have you, Joel? Going on holiday - wouldn't be to Spain by any chance or more specifically, *Morisco*, would it?'

'Oh I - I don't know what that's doing there.' Joel snatched the book from Tamara.

'Yes, you do. I've seen you reading it,' she said laughing.

'So?' Joel said defensively.

'Oh bla de bla.' Tamara giggled mischievously. 'Anyway I happen to know she likes you too.'

'You do!' Joel took Tamara's bait. 'I mean - do you?' He added coolly.

'Yes, girls know these things,' Tamara went on amusingly. 'And that girl definitely has a twinkle in her eye for you, Joel - just as you have for her.'

'Oh bla de bla, Tamara!' Joel mimicked her irritably and grabbed the rope swing. 'I'm going back to the house to help Grandad.' He swung down to the ground, then shouted back up. 'Well are you two coming or not?'

Peter and Tamara smiled at each other knowingly.

'Sure, we'll be right down,' Peter called. Then he said quietly to Tamara, 'You shouldn't tease him like that, Tamara. It's not as if he's going to go on seeing her, is it? I mean he may never see her again - ever, after tomorrow night. Think how you'd feel if that was say, Cherokee.'

'Oh...' Tamara said ashamed. 'I didn't think. I feel really beastly now.'

'And so you should, but I bet you don't feel half as bad as he does right now,' Peter said. 'Just wait till you have the hots for some boy - then you'll know what it feels like. Come on, let's go.' Peter handed her the rope.

+

Eventually, after what seemed an eternity, Friday evening arrived. Joel told Grandad that they were going to take a feast to the tree den and have supper there by lantern light. This would excuse them from having to eat a big meal in front of him and they would be able to just leave the food in the den. There would be no problem with time, as they would not be going anywhere through the Vista. So they would be able to stay as long as they wanted at the party without much time passing on earth. They just wore jeans and casual tops; anything else would have aroused Grandad's suspicion. Anyway gowns were to be provided, so it didn't seem to be important what they wore.

As they lit the lanterns in the den, the Magi turned up.

'Having a little picnic again, are we?' Magee chirruped.

'You have a food-seeking antenna for a beak, don't you, Magee?' Joel said with a grin. 'Well it's your lucky day - all this food needs to be eaten and we can't eat any of it. We are going to a party.'

'Oh of course. It's the Kairos end-of-holiday bash, in Heaven. You'll enjoy that, especially the scrumptious food.' Magee said, drooling.

'And the lovely gowns,' Maggi chipped in dreamily. 'Oh what a pity we're stuck here as Ravens.'

'Well enjoy this little picnic then,' Tamara said smiling. 'You can have a nice little romantic dinner, just the two of you, by lantern light.'

Maggi bowed her head bashfully, while Magee stargazed aloofly, pretending he wasn't bothered.

'I'm sure the lighting will be adequate,' Magee muttered casually. 'Now off you go. You must get there in good time; it wouldn't do to arrive at the last minute.'

The three friends made their way to the plateau, while Magee held up a wing.

'Come here, Petal,' he said softly to Maggi.
Maggi sidled up under Magee's wing.

It was a clear night and the sky was peppered with stars. Joel, Peter and Tamara were already very excited, but the fresh breeze swirling around Zionica seemed to exhilarate them even more. They turned and waved to the huddled Magi, silhouetted by the lantern light. Then, holding hands, the three of them stepped excitedly onto the plateau and immediately the Fugue swept them upwards, magically to the stars.

The Kairos

At the top of the Fugue, they were met by beautiful, soft, angelic singing but instead of Charis and Aleathia, they were welcomed by two glowing Seraphs. The Seraphs didn't speak but hovered over the top of the Fugue, smiling tenderly and shaking their sceptres over all the Kairos arrivals.

'Ooh that's lovely!' Tamara positively glowed, as the droplets of love fell on her face.

'They're showering us with love again,' Peter said as a warm flush came all over him.

A cheeky glint came into Tamara's eyes as she looked up at the Seraphs.

'Better use that sparingly on Joel I think,' she said mischievously.

Joel looked around a little embarrassed and Peter threw Tamara a warning frown, as a steady stream of excited Kairos members began to arrive.

'I'm sorry...' Tamara winced. 'It just slipped out - I didn't mean it...'

A regular Angel greeted them in the way the Angels usually greeted each other.

'Blessed is He,' the Angel said beaming at them. 'Just keep going to your right.'

They joined the line of children gliding off to the right down the hall of archways. They came to an archway that seemed to be flashing all round with every colour of the rainbow. Outside this archway were two Cherubim Angels, one on either side. Unlike the tall, elegant and beautiful six-winged Seraphs, the Cherubim were cute, cuddly and between three and four feet tall with just one pair of small wings.

The Cherubim grinned happily at the children as they ushered them politely through the brightly flashing archway.

'Thank you.' Tamara leaned down and smiled at the Cherub on her right.

The little Cherub beamed a lovely smile and held up a hand to her, in it he held a blue rose.

'He means for you to take it,' a Chinese boy said from behind.

'Why, thank you again,' Tamara said delightedly, taking the rose. She put it to her face and smelt the beautiful, delicate fragrance, which was like nothing she'd ever smelt before. The Cherub smiled bashfully.

They glided through to the other side of the archway and their feet hit the ground with a jolt as the artificial gravity was activated. Two more regular Angels giggled as they welcomed them.

'The gravity in here takes everyone by surprise the first time,' one of the Angels said with amusement. 'Boys to the left and girls to the right, please: you'll see your changing-rooms just in front of you.'

The Angels handed out garments to everyone as they arrived. Soon the children emerged from the changing-rooms in their perfectly fitting attire. Tamara was wearing a beautiful scarlet velvet gown with gold insignia on the fitted bodice - K 63, her Kairos number. A floor-length, silver silk cloak with gold and purple tassels was attached to the shoulders of her gown by gold epaulettes. On her feet she wore dainty, glittery slippers.

'I feel like a Princess in this!' Tamara exclaimed preening herself.

'Well step this way, your majesty.' Joel laughed as he bowed to Tamara. He wore an almost knee-length blue tunic of fine linen over white linen trousers. The tunic had gold and purple tassels, a wide gold belt and gold insignia on the chest, displaying K 119. A short purple satin cloak was fastened by gold epaulettes to the shoulders. He wore soft white leather boots. Peter's garments were the same as Joel's. All the boys' were dressed the same; as were all the girls and everyone had their Kairos number on their chest.

The three of them looked around excitedly as the room filled up with children. It seemed that there were children of just about every nationality and colour, from Aborigines to Eskimos, Africans to European.

They were in an enormous banqueting hall, which was glowing with all manner of crystals and colours - not just all the colours of the rainbow, but all the colours under the sun.

There were small archways at intervals along the two long sides of the room; a mist within each archway obscured their passages. Fifteen large oval tables were dotted around the hall. Each table had ten chairs and ten silver-and-crystal place settings. There were five small gold taps with no handles spaced along the centre of each of the tables. At the top of the room there was one oblong table with seven chairs and seven settings, all of which were facing down the rest of the room.

There were regular Angels moving around, chatting to the children. Cherubim were flitting about, they seemed to be on duty, making sure everything was as it should be.

Charis and Aleathia came up to talk to them and congratulated them on their successful mission.

'Everyone is talking about it,' Charis said beaming. 'Nathan has been after those villains for quite some time, he's so proud of you all.'

'Yes, it's very exciting,' Aleathia added. 'You must be so thrilled at the outcome.'

Which was exactly what they were, but Aleathia pointing it out so forthrightly made the three of them blush a little. Joel felt a slight tap on his back. He turned round and saw Maité. He swallowed nervously as he noticed how beautiful she was, with her olive skin and dark hair, set off by her rich scarlet gown, she positively glowed with excitement. Then for some inexplicable reason which he couldn't at all fathom, Joel felt himself blushing yet again, so that his head felt like a giant tomato. At the same time, his heart seemed to give a bit of a hoppity leap and his tummy kind of fluttered. It was all very strange. He just hoped Maité would think his flush was only a reflection of her gown from all the bright crystals.

'What do you think so far, Joel?' Maité asked.
For a moment Joel felt all tongue tied.

'Um - um - it - it's - it's all so awesome, Maité,' he replied, pulling himself together. 'But I guess you must be used to all this by now.'

I'LL LEAD YOU ALL IN THE DANCE SAID HE

'You never get used to something this wonderful, Joel,' Maité replied wistfully. 'It's a precious experience and a wonderful opportunity to meet other Kairos children. It's good to be able to talk freely about our work. Also there are usually two or three Saints invited.'

'Saints?' Joel looked surprised.

'Oh yes - Patron Saints - related to children, you know - like the Patron Saint for Abandoned Children, that kind of thing.'

Joel nodded, hanging on her every word as she continued.

'We're all one big community, Joel. All the company of Heaven and earth - all the Saints, the Angels and Archangels, everyone who has ever gone before us and everyone still on earth - one world, one community, separated only by the Fugue.'

'Awesome,' Joel murmured, mesmerised.

'Yes, it is,' Maité agreed with a smile.

Tamara leaned forward to Joel.

'Maybe Saint Valentine will be here, Joel; that would be convenient, wouldn't it?' Tamara grinned cheekily.

Then to Joel's absolute mortification, Tamara raised an eyebrow and her lips began to twitch, as they did when some mischief was about to come out of her mouth. He already felt his own mouth going dry in anticipation; his face felt even more embarrassingly flushed, if that was possible and he felt little prickly things on the back of his neck. He wasn't wrong and it all seemed to happen in painful slow motion, while Joel could only open and shut his mouth in a fish like way.

'Holy Rudolf, Joel!' she said teasingly. 'Your face is almost the colour of our gowns!'

Joel didn't know whether he wanted to throttle Tamara or flee from the room - or both. However, sensing his acute embarrassment, Maité came to the rescue.

'Funny how the light plays tricks up here, isn't it?' She smiled down at Tamara. 'Tamara, your face is the colour of Joel's cloak!'

'What... Purple?' Tamara cried in horror.

Joel and Peter started to laugh, while Maité went on casually.

'The Saints sit at the top table with Nathan and Anna.'

'Just Nathan and Anna?' Joel inquired. 'What about everyone else's Guardians?'

'Everyone doesn't have their Guardian here with them, Joel,' Maité said with amusement. 'Oh - you don't know, do you?'

'Know what?' Joel looked confused.

'I just assumed you knew - Nathan is head of the Kairos. He is in charge of the whole group worldwide and Anna is his second in command.'

The three of them stared at Maité in surprise. They had all assumed Nathan and Anna had been there through everything because they were Joel and Peter's Guardians.

'My Dad? In charge of the Kairos?' Joel said slowly.

'It's purely a coincidence that Nathan is your Father and Guardian too. It's the same with Peter and Anna - just a coincidence. You were very privileged to see your Grandma, it's not normally allowed to see your dead relatives. You only see Nathan and Anna because they head up the Kairos.' Maité gave an amused chuckle. 'What - did you think everyone was given their missions by their own Guardians? If you thought that was the case, did you not wonder where Tamara's Guardian was?'

'Yes, I did wonder,' Tamara said.

'My Dad - in charge of the Kairos?' Joel repeated incredulously.

'Uh-huh, he's a vet too,' Maité went on.

Joel looked completely baffled now and he felt the perishing fish impersonation coming back.

'You know...' Maité explained, 'a Veteran - of the Kairos. He was the bravest and most successful Kairos child ever; his exploits are famous! That's why he took over a couple of years ago, when the old guy who had run it for many years went on to something else. Your Dad's a hero, Joel! All eyes will be watching you, once it gets round the Kairos that you're Nathan's Son.' Maité carried on seriously. 'I'm afraid you've much to live up to. Everyone is already talking about your death-defying leap in the mine shaft, comparing you to Nathan. You've set the precedent now, my friend: expectations will have been aroused and they don't even know yet that you're his Son. Just think what they'll say when they find that out!'

'Well let's hope we can keep it quiet then,' Joel muttered.

'You're giving me too glowing a report, Maité.' Nathan appeared by their sides seemingly from nowhere.

'Not at all, Señor; it is not glowing enough. I've heard about you, remember?'

'What was your Kairos number, Dad?' Joel asked.

'One hundred and nineteen, the same as you. Now that is not a coincidence, but an ordained sign. The issuing of Kairos numbers is not a lottery. Every child's number is specifically chosen for that child. It is his or her destiny - for you, Son, an inheritance.'

'Along with the legacy of Nathan's reputation, which you, I'm sure, will have no trouble living up to, Joel,' Anna added as she appeared by Nathan's side.

'Oh look - there's Saint Nicholas!' Maité grabbed Joel's hand. 'He's everyone's favourite. Come on, Joel. If there's something you especially want for Christmas, now is the time to mention it, but don't ask for anything material - this Saint Nicholas only bestows gifts money cannot buy.' Maité pulled Joel along towards a white-haired man dressed in a white linen robe.

'Saints alive!' Tamara exclaimed.
At this several people within earshot turned round and stared at her.

'Oops - sorry...' Tamara said with an embarrassed laugh.

+

After some time in which everyone generally moved around the room, meeting each other, a trumpet sounded. The room was suddenly silent and everyone stood still, looking towards the top table. Nathan was standing at the table with Anna and the five guest Saints.

'Welcome and thank you for coming to the end-of-Easter

The Kairos

Kairos ecumenical celebration and banquet in this beautiful Andance Regis Ballroom,' Nathan said, beginning his address. 'Blessed is He who comes in the name of the Lord.'

'Blessed is He,' the whole room echoed.

'Now you'll notice that you've all been allocated a seat.' Nathan waved an arm and one hundred and fifty brightly coloured balloons materialised, suspended over all the chairs. Each balloon had a number on it, in gold, between one and one hundred and fifty.

'This is merely a formality; you don't have to sit down at all. If you prefer, you can continue to mill about the room while you eat, or swap seats and meet each other and our revered Saints, who have kindly honoured us by accepting our invitations.' Nathan waved an arm to introduce the guests, who all graciously bowed their heads as he announced their names, while everyone clapped.

'Maria Goretti - Patroness of Youth and Women Victims of Violence.

'Jerome Emiliani - Patron of Abandoned Children.

'Charles Lwanga - Patron of African Youth.

'Nicholas of Tolentino - Patron of Animals and Babies.

'And last but not least, Nicholas of Bari - commonly associated with Christmas time.'

There was a loud cheer as St Nicholas was announced. Nathan waved his arm again and the mist that had obscured the entrances to all the archways down the long sides of the room, cleared.

'Tonight this party is to thank you for the very important work that you do and it's for you to enjoy. It's all self-service and you'll find a different culinary delight within each archway. Every taste is catered for. Just enter any of the archways leading off from the ballroom and there will be a feast for your eyes and taste buds. From The Chinese Lantern to The American Diner to The Ice-cream Parlour, Bella Pasta, The Sombrero, The Soda Fountain, The French Confection, The Indian Curry Tent, The Chocolate Factory and many more. If you fancy it, you'll find it. I particularly recommend the hot chocolate sauce in The

Ice-cream Parlour - it is truly Heaven. Enjoy!' Nathan grinned.

Everyone immediately began to migrate through the archways, emerging with platefuls of delicious food.

'How are we supposed to get to know all these people?' Tamara asked as they were coming out of The Spanish Flamenco archway, each with a plateful of the most scrumptious paella ever seen or tasted. 'Most of them are foreign. Or does everyone speak English up here?'

'Mr Asher gave his introduction in English,' Peter pointed out. 'Everyone must understand English I suppose.'

'No, he didn't.' Maité laughed. 'You've still a lot to learn, haven't you?'

Tamara, Joel and Peter looked a little confused.

'You *heard* Nathan speak in English.' Maité explained: 'He actually spoke in 'tongue'. You will speak in 'tongue' here too; there are no language barriers here. Regardless of who is speaking, everyone hears in their native vernacular. Look - take Ashok for instance; he's Indian - can't speak a word of English... Ashok!' Maité called to the young Indian boy.

Ashok, a handsome, dark skinned boy, turned and flashed a huge white smile as he walked up to greet Maité.

'Hello, Maité,' Ashok said cheerily.

'These are the new recruits from Zionica, England, Ashok.' She introduced them. 'Tamara, Peter and Joel.'

'Hi, welcome aboard,' Ashok said in perfect English as he shook their hands. When he shook Joel's hand he suddenly became excited. 'Hey - Joel - from Zionica? You're the one who leapt through the Vista into the mine!'

'Well... I guess...' Joel shrugged modestly.

'Everyone is talking about it,' Ashok went on. 'It's never been attempted before; we didn't know it was possible - well done!'

'Oh by the way, Peter,' Maité added, 'you must learn to call Nathan by his Christian name and not "Mr Asher." Everybody uses Christian names in the Kairos.'

Joel looked around at the sea of different coloured faces.

'I've never seen such a varied mix of nationalities before.'

He exclaimed. 'Is everyone here a Christian?'

'Of course,' Ashok smiled. 'You know no one can go to the Father unless through the Son, Joel - He is the *only* way.'

'Yes, there are kids from all over the world up here, but despite their religion at birth, one way or another they've all come to know Jesus.' Maité explained and waved her arm. 'Take a look around you. There's Alon, he was born a Jew. Oh and Mia, she was born a Buddhist; Hammed and Amad, they were born Muslims and Nita was born a Hindu. Like everybody else, they had no choice where they were born or what religion they were born into.' She added. 'Everyone here has one thing in common, they've all accepted Jesus as their Lord and Saviour, it's why they're chosen. When they're sixteen and they forget about the Kairos, they will still accept him because He is in their hearts. Once Jesus is in your heart He is there forever. Fighting and war in the name of religion is all so pointless because there's only one Heaven. It doesn't matter where they live - when they die, everyone comes up through the same Fugue! It's not man's place to judge people because of their faith - or lack of it. That is for God alone to judge, He knows us all, He knows what's in our hearts, our innermost thoughts and desires, He knows the truth.'

'Holy Christmas!' Tamara exclaimed. 'You mean if someone died in Colombia or China for instance, they would come up through our Fugue, here?'

'There are many entry points to the Fugue, all over the world and they all lead to here - Heaven,' Maité continued. 'Remember though, you can only ever enter the Fugue through faith in Jesus Christ. Everyone has an earthly body and a Heavenly body. Most people have to wait till they've finished with their earthly bodies before they can travel the Fugue - and then it's a one-way trip. We have the privilege of using it freely for two-way traffic until we're sixteen. However, the entry points that we use, like your Zionica for instance, are different from the general public entries - only the Kairos can use these special gateways.'

'And the Unicorns...' Tamara added.

'Yes, them too - but they're not supposed to.' Maité said.

'Hey - come on, eat up, I want to take you to the Ice-cream Parlour; it's the best.'

The Ice-cream Parlour proved to be the most popular archway of the evening. There was every flavour and variety of ice cream on earth and, Joel was sure, some that hadn't been invented yet. There were all manner of extras like; marshmallow chunks, different types of biscuit, sweets, chocolates, sauces, things to sprinkle over and decorate the ice-cream.

After they'd all gorged themselves so that they couldn't possibly eat any more, everybody began to find their seats, unanimously claiming they'd never tasted food that good before. Joel was seated between Maité and Tamara; Peter was seated next to Tamara; then there were another six children at their table. The plates all magically vanished the instant the food was eaten.

'Oh good, I'm glad we've all been put on the same table,' Joel said with delight, smiling at Maité. 'I thought for a moment they might put you with other Spanish people, Maité.'

'No, you three have been put on the Spanish table, Joel. As there are only three of you, that's not enough English for you to have a table of your own, but in any case you're welcome to sit where you like, as Nathan said in his introduction.'

'Hey, I could do with another drink,' Peter said looking around.

'That's what these are for, Peter.' Maité picked up Joel's crystal glass and held it under one of the gold taps in the middle of the table. 'Hold your glass under the tap and think of the drink you want. How about you, Joel; what do you fancy? Something fizzy perhaps?'

Tamara leaned forward.

'What about a passion fruit crush, Joel?' she said, grinning with a cheeky glint in her eye.

Joel glared at Tamara.

'I think maybe bitter lemon with an olive for you, Tamara,' Maité said and handed the drink to her.

'Tomato juice I think.' Peter said, with a warning glance at

Tamara and held his glass under the gold tap.

When everyone was sitting down, there was another trumpet blast and the room became silent again.

'I trust everyone has had their fill?' Nathan inquired from his position at the top table.

There was a general cheer around the room, indicating the positive consensus of opinion.

'Good.' Nathan continued, 'Now I'm not going to make you sit through a long speech. Many of you know me well enough by now. I've sat through too many boring speeches myself to want to subject you to one. I merely want to quickly review our successes, introduce our new members and say farewell to loved and trusted members who are leaving us.

'New members, please stand as I call your names.

'Mwafu from Masaka, Uganda.

'Kizito from Masaka, Uganda.

'Monika from Cochabamba, Bolivia.

'Raj from Vasai, India.

'Joel from Zionica, England.

'Peter from Zionica, England.

'Tamara from Zionica, England.'

The seven new recruits stood smiling nervously as everyone cheered and clapped.

'Thank you and good luck in your missions. You've got an exciting few years ahead.'

The seven sat down again.

'And now, those who will be leaving us, please stand as I call your names.

'Li from Hung Ham, Hong Kong.

'Phillipe from Taize, France.

'Jean from Somerville, USA.

'Jody from Plainville, USA.

'Maité from Morisco, Spain.

'Miku from Osaka, Japan.

'Nicolau from San Luis, Brazil.'

The six fifteen-year-olds and thirteen-year-old Jean stood up and Nathan continued.

'Thank you for the wonderful years you've given us and the incredible sacrifices you've all made for the cause. Your dedication has been beyond question and an inspiration to others. We will miss you all. Good luck and God bless you in your future ventures.'

Everyone clapped again as the seven took a bow and sat down.

'I know you've all been worried about Jean, who is leaving us prematurely.' Nathan went on. 'I can now put your minds at rest and tell you that *He* has given special consideration to Jean's case in the light of her heroic action recently. Remember, He makes the rules, He can change them. This is one of those exceptions and I'm delighted to tell you that in Jean's case, He has made the decision that she will return to earth and have a second chance. In fact she will be returning to the same family; her mother is about to conceive a new baby and that is you, Jean. You will have the same parents - your younger sister, Leanne, will now become your older sister. So who knows, maybe we'll be seeing you here in the Kairos again in another eleven years. Good luck, Jean. You'll be leaving the Garden of Lilies in, ooh - following this party!'

There was another uproarious cheer at this good news and everyone turned to congratulate Jean, who positively beamed with joy as the trace of tears moistened her eyes and cheeks.

'Now for a review of recent Kairos missions,' Nathan announced proudly, turning to face a huge Vista behind him at the top of the room. All eyes focused intently on the Vista.

There followed a montage showing glimpses of Kairos missions over the Easter holidays. There was Maité descending a narrow and very deep pothole, down which a small child had fallen and been trapped for several hours. No adult could get down the hole as it was too narrow and it would have been far too dangerous to try digging, as the child could have fallen further or even been buried alive. However Maité triumphantly rescued the child, both of them emerging from the hole, completely covered in black, slimy mud. Another mission concerned a woman in the Third World who had been walking with six children for days without food or clean water. She had become quite delirious and hadn't realised she was within a few hundred yards of a missionary camp with fresh water and food. A young African Kairos called Wolisso led them to the camp and the woman cried as she was greeted by the missionaries. There was another round of applause, then Nathan continued.

'Finally, before we finish, I'd like to mention the successful first major mission of the English, Zionica, new recruits. These three pulled off a very dangerous mission at very short notice and with only a little training. Their brave efforts have ensnared a group of evil and dangerous kingpins of crime, ending their nefarious organisation. Well done, the Zionica team - Joel, Peter and Tamara and also again Maité from Morisco, who has been their mentor. This was a tremendous achievement.'

Everyone clapped again, while Joel, Peter, Tamara and Maité smiled proudly.

'Remember, though, that these villains are just one branch of an evil perennial weed. Unless we take action, another shoot will sprout and another and another. We are still battling against the deadly root. Now, I'd like to leave you with a groundbreaking *fait accompli* from this new team - a jump through the Vista with the precision landing of a jump jet on an aircraft carrier. This life-or-death, decisive action by Joel, one of our new recruits from Zionica, was all the more amazing because his experience of using the Vista was very limited. Peter was stranded on a rapidly disintegrating ledge - the only thing between him and certain death down a one-hundred-foot shaft. There was no time to lose. Joel glided through the Vista and landed with pinpoint accuracy next to Peter, he grabbed him and both of them jumped straight back into the Vista. As you can see, the moment Joel snatched Peter, the whole thing collapsed, hurtling down the shaft and could so easily have taken them both to oblivion. A brilliant manoeuvre - you've earned your wings.' Nathan said proudly as he continued. 'Everyone - I'd like to introduce my

I'LL LEAD YOU ALL IN THE DANCE SAID HE

Son - Joel.'

Everyone clapped and turned to look at Joel with admiration and there was a general buzz of excitement at this revelation.

'There you go again, Joel,' Peter muttered. 'Whatever you do, you always seem to be the hero.'

'No one is a hero on their own, Peter - you were the one who went down to the ledge to save Presten.' Joel gave a wry smile.

'Yeah and I've got the bruises on my shoulders to prove it,' Peter replied.

Maité leaned towards Joel and whispered.

'What were you saying about keeping it quiet? I'm afraid there's no hiding place for you now, Señor. You're, as they say, "in the public domain" now.'

'O.K. we have a treat for you,' Nathan went on. 'I'm sure you'll be delighted to hear that once again, the Melanesian Boys have agreed to give us a bit of a show. I've rattled on for long enough, so please give a warm welcome to the *spectacular Melanesian Boys!*'

Everyone cheered and applauded as the boys appeared on a raised platform to the right of the main table. They were all huddled in a sort of rugby-scrum type of circle.

'Who are they?' Joel asked Maité, struggling to be heard above the noise.

'They are from a community of Christian Brothers in Melanesia. These are former members of the Brothers who have passed away - obviously,' Maité replied as she clapped.

The Melanesian Boys were an African-style band; there were five of them. They wore grass skirts and strings of feathers and shells round their arms, ankles and necks. They played various instruments - bongo drums, maracas and pipes. They chanted, sang and danced a very lively performance. It was a splendid display; everyone enjoyed it and clapped and cheered as the Boys took a bow at the end.

After the Melanesian Boys' performance, Nathan stood up again.

'Magnificent, Boys. Now it is time for the final, girls'

choice dance, when the young ladies present chose a partner for the final dance - I have to warn you, boys, this is not optional, it is forbidden in the Kairos to refuse the final dance!'

Joel sank into his chair, in the hope that this would make him invisible to all the girls but Maité. But then, she had been in the Kairos for six years, there were bound to be other boys she would want to dance with.

All the girls stood up and several seemed to be heading for Joel. However, Tamara being on the same table, was first there, having leapt up. She tapped him on the shoulder. He turned round with a look of desperation - this could be the last time he would ever see Maité! As Tamara was about to claim him for the dance, he consoled himself with the thought that he couldn't dance anyway. At least if he had to make a fool of himself stepping on someone's toes, it didn't matter as much if it was Tamara's. He was just about to take her hand, when Peter stood up and took it instead.

'I'd be delighted, Tamara,' Peter said with a knowing look.

'But... Oh bla de bla, Peter.' She shrugged resignedly and allowed Peter to lead her away.

Joel began to panic, as he saw the queue of girls swarming towards him and suddenly wished for the artificial gravity to be switched off, so he could leap out of the way. Then, feeling a tap on his other shoulder, he turned back round. Maité held out her hand.

'Dance with me, Señor?' she smiled.

A feeling of overwhelming relief swept over him and he accepted her hand with a bashful smile. Upon this the other girls making their way over, sighed with disappointment and picked other partners, as the music began to play.

+

A trumpet sounded again and they all returned to their seats.

'Those who are leaving us.' Nathan announced, 'I'm told that it's time for your exit meeting.'

Suddenly a new archway appeared at the top of the room to the right of the main table. There were three brightly shining seven-point stars on either side of the archway and one at its pinnacle. A cloud formed within the archway and a soft breeze seemed to come from it which began to swirl gently around the room. Then two magnificent pearl-white Archangels, emitting a glowing aura of light, appeared from within the archway and hovered on either side of it. They were tall and slender like the Seraphs; the brilliant light radiated from the tips of their wings to the tips of their toes.

Then first one, then the other Archangel spread their wings and floated elegantly, one behind the other, around the banquet hall. Each must have had a wing span of about six meters. Everyone gasped as they watched the awesome sight. Then the Archangels settled on either side of the archway again. The cloud had gone and in its place, in between the two Archangels, a seven-tongued flame burned steadily.

'Wow!' Peter gasped.

'Holy hurricane...' Tamara whispered.

Joel, Peter and Tamara stared open-mouthed, as seven Doves emerged from the flame and flew into the room. Each of the seven Doves hovered over one of the leavers, ready to guide them through the archway.

The leavers started to make their way towards it.

'Maité!' Joel, without thinking, caught hold of her arm.

'Don't worry, Joel, I'm not leaving yet; I'll see you before I go. The flame is the signal for our private meeting with He - our Saviour. We are each to receive the seven gifts of the Holy Spirit, the gifts that will stay with us for all time. The greatest gift of all, of course, is Love.' She smiled.

Joel blushed slightly.

'We're given this honour when we leave the Kairos,' Maité continued. 'This is what I've looked forward to; the thought of it has been all I required to spur me on in the face of adversity and it will inspire you in the same way. You don't know how important you are, Joel. There are great things planned for you.'

She smiled affectionately, then nodding at the Dove hovering over her, she followed it through the archway of the flame. The archway closed up behind the last leaver.

'The rest of you may mingle until the leavers come back, then we'll close for the term.' Nathan sat down again, while everybody else got up and started talking.

Suddenly a man appeared in front of Tamara. Joel and Peter couldn't see His face because He had His back to them; they assumed He was another Saint or an Angel. They heard Him speak to Tamara.

'Tamara, isn't it?' He said.

'Y - y - y - yes...' she replied in a soft, almost star struck, hypnotic voice, as though overcome by the magnitude of someone, or something.

'My Mother asked me to thank you for all the extra help you've given in the Nursery, particularly the Baby Unit. Arianna is always grateful for extra help and my Mother takes a very keen interest in the Nursery, as you know.'

'It - it's a pleasure,' Tamara replied, obviously overcome with awe. 'I want to do everything I can.'

'You will, Tamara. It's good to see such dedication in one so young. Bless you.' The man vanished.

'Who was that?' Joel asked curiously.

'I, er... He was - He was - He - He had the most beautiful eyes I've ever seen. So beautiful I'll never forget them as long as I live,' Tamara said wistfully.

'Who did you say it was?' asked Peter.

'He s - s - s - said His Mother wanted Him to - th - th - th - thank me,' Tamara stammered.

'Yes, I heard,' Peter said. 'Well who's His Mother then?'

'Isn't it blindingly obvious?' Joel said pointedly 'Who takes a special interest in the Nursery?'
Peter gasped.

'But - He is having private meetings with the leavers...'
Nathan suddenly appeared next to them.

'Yes, boys, He is. Individual private meetings with all seven of them. He is also still with all those people on earth who need Him and call upon His name.' Nathan smiled affectionately. 'Have you not understood yet? He can be everywhere at once.'

'You mean we've just seen..?' Peter gulped.

'He turns up when you least expect Him to,' Nathan said. 'That is why you should always try to be prepared, because you never know *when* He will turn up, you just know that He will. So it's best to always be ready.'

The three of them stared at Nathan open-mouthed.

'You do not need to understand *how* this is, just that it *is*. There are things we are not meant to know or expected to understand; that is where faith comes in,' Nathan explained. 'He is all-powerful: He created Heaven, earth, time, light, life - how could we possibly understand all that? The answer is that we can't - no one can.'

Joel turned to Tamara.

'Anyway - when have you had time to go to the Nursery? You're always with us.'

'No, not always, Joel. I can be up here for a few hours and only be gone from earth for a few minutes. You don't need me to tell you that,' Tamara said simply.

'So you *can* keep secrets from us then?' Joel muttered.

'Tamara didn't want you to feel obliged to go too, Joel,' Nathan answered for her. 'Babies aren't quite your thing, are they?'

'I didn't think they were Tamara's thing either,' Joel said with a shrug. 'They don't have four hooves and a tail!'

Eventually, Maité and the other leavers returned. Joel looked at her in amazement. Light seemed to radiate from her face like the sun.

'Oh, Joel - Joel, I'm so happy,' Maité was glowing. 'I'm ready to go now.'

'But...' Joel said with a hint of urgency, 'How will I find you?'

'You will forget me, Joel.' Maité sighed. 'You're very young, there are too many years between us. You must go back to school, work hard and be that great Barrister you're meant to be.'

'So what's a few years?' Joel protested.

'Tomorrow I will no longer be in your head,' Maité said brushing his protests aside. 'If you came to Spain, I would not know you - and when you leave the Kairos, you will not remember me at all.'

'We got to know each other once - we can do it again...' Joel insisted, 'in the world - for real.'

'Joel, let's see what life has in store for us. Follow your destiny; what will be will be. Now I must say goodbye.'

'Sorry to interrupt you, guys,' Nathan said as he suddenly appeared again. 'It's time - everyone is starting to leave.'

'Adios, amigo.' Maité held out her hand to Joel.

'Adios.' Joel gripped her hand.

Maité said her goodbyes to Nathan, Peter and Tamara. Then, as she was going to say goodbye to other friends in the Kairos, Joel called after her.

'Maité! Hasta pronto!' he said smiling.

'See you - maybe, Joel.' Maité returned his smile.

'Dad,' Joel said, turning to Nathan. 'When you left the Kairos, what did you write on your note?'

'To find and marry Elizabeth Jacob - your Mother, Joel,' Nathan said without hesitation.

'What's our next mission, Dad?' Joel asked.

'You're not to concern yourself with that now, Son. It's important to concentrate on your school work. The Kairos is non operational during school term time.'

'I can't believe I will not see you all term. Can't I visit you?'

'I'm afraid not, Son. The Fugue is not for personal use, that would incur disciplinary action which could jeopardise your future with the Kairos. We must not let that happen. I cannot tell you yet, Son, but you're to play a very important role - one that requires a very special kind of person. You really are special, Joel, you don't know how special. Next holiday you will learn much more, be patient. Come on, I'll take you to the Fugue.'

Joel, Peter and Tamara returned the gowns and put on their

own clothes. As they passed through the archway to the main hall of archways, they became weightless again. They thanked the cute little Cherubim on their way out. Then to Tamara's delight, a surprise was awaiting them - Storm and Cheyiea.

'Storm!' Tamara cried with joy.

'They're inviting you to take a ride to the Fugue,' Nathan said. 'Storm, as you call him, has decided to change his name permanently to Storm from Farga, in honour of the victory of your mission.'

'Oh, Storm, what a wonderful tribute!' Tamara threw her arms around his neck and he nuzzled her affectionately.

'Well I'll say goodbye here,' Nathan said, a little emotionally. 'It's been wonderful having you three join the Kairos. You're going to be very important to our mission. But for now, you must forget about the Kairos and concentrate on your school studies. We'll meet again in the next holidays. God go with you.'

'Goodbye, Dad. I'm so glad I've found you and that we're going to be spending time together again.' He hugged Nathan.

Tamara floated up onto Storm. Peter floated up onto Cheyiea, then held out his hand to help Joel up behind him.

'No, you go on, Peter - no offence, Cheyiea, but I'll go under my own steam.' Joel waved them off.

Peter and Tamara set off for the Fugue on the Unicorns. Then Nathan gave Joel a kiss on his forehead.

'Will you pass that kiss on to Mum, Son,' Nathan said.

'I will, Dad.'

'She needs looking after; she's too young to be on her own. I approve of her choice.'

'What do you mean, Dad? What choice?'

'You'll find out when she's ready, Son - it's Mum's place to tell you, not mine.'

+

When their feet touched the ground in Zionica, it was only just after seven. It was unbelievable; they felt that it should have been midnight. They climbed up to the tree den and sat talking with the Magi about all that had happened.

Maggi and Magee had made a good job of demolishing the food in the den, but their evening had only just begun and as they weren't in the least bit tired, they wanted to hear every detail of the party in Heaven. Maggi was dying to be reminded of the beautiful gowns, while Magee was anxious for a description of the Kairos action montage. After about an hour, Tamara was yawning her head off.

'I'm so exhausted with all the excitement,' she yawned.

'Look!' Maggi suddenly exclaimed and flew onto a higher branch for a better view of the plateau.

'What is it?' Joel called.

Magee joined Maggi on the look-out branch.

'A visitor,' Magee called down.

Joel, Peter and Tamara leaned over the edge of the den to see who it was. They saw a small figure on the plateau, walking towards their tree.

'It's your Spanish friend,' Magee called. 'Boy, is she in trouble - using the Fugue like a personal taxi service!'

As the figure got closer, they saw her.

'Maité! Joel, Magee's right! It's Maité!' Peter said with some surprise.

'Maité?' Joel echoed. He grabbed the rope swing and leapt down to the ground. Then just in time, he stopped himself from running like a totally uncool idiot and attempted to pose in a rather more laid-back manner at the foot of the tree.

'What are you doing here?' Joel asked as Maité approached.

'I know... it's crazy... and totally not allowed... but I just wanted to see you, one more time... to say goodbye. My memory of the Kairos will not be erased until midnight,' she replied hesitantly. 'I'm sorry - I - I shouldn't have come...'

'N - no, no, please - come up,' Joel motioned to the tree ladder. He was taken aback at this apparent chink in her normally super-cool armour. Maybe she did like him after all.

They both climbed up to the den.

I'LL LEAD YOU ALL IN THE DANCE SAID HE

'Hello, Maité dear,' Maggi greeted her warmly.

*'Buenas tardes, mi amiga,' Maité said, climbing into the den.

'What a surprise,' Tamara said, trying to hide a touch of jealousy. 'I hope you're not going to get into trouble - I mean, how did you sneak into the Vista Chamber at this late hour?'

'Yeah, Maité we're not supposed to use the Vista without someone in Heaven watching.' Peter added.

'She Fugue hopped.' Magee said informatively.

'Fugue hopped?' Joel asked with a frown.

'Maité simply jumped from her Fugue in Morisco direct to this one.' Magee explained, 'It can be done if you know where the Kairos Fugue entry points are - but it's dodgy, very dodgy. You're in deep trouble if you get caught.' He added.

'Yes, it's a bit risky.' Maité admitted.

'What if you lose your memory while you're here, or if you can't get back through the Fugue?' Joel said with concern.

'I'll be O.K. as long as I'm back before midnight - that's when I turn into a pumpkin...' Maité grimaced.

They all looked sympathetically sorrowful.

'Hey, it's great to see you - isn't it, Joel?' Peter said, trying to sound cheery.

'Yeah, cool,' Joel attempted to sound casual, although inside he was thrilled.

'Well, Maggi, my little gooseberry, it's time for us to leave these youngsters for now,' Magee said. 'If we're not here we cannot report the misuse of the Fugue can we?'

'Yes, of course - well goodnight, friends, we'll be seeing you soon,' Maggi cawed.

They all called goodbye to the birds as they flew off into the night.

Peter stood up.

'Shall we go back to the house to ring your Dad and ask him to pick you up, Tamara?' he said.

'Sure.' Tamara stood up and stretched. 'Do you want a lift home, Peter?'

'That would be great, thanks. Er, we'll see you tomorrow

---

* Good evening, my friend

before you go, Joel?'

'Yeah. Oh Tamara...' Joel opened a small box he had placed in the den earlier and handed something to Tamara. 'Have a good birthday.'

'Aah, you remembered,' Tamara said with a grin.

'Yes, you'll be a whole year older next time I see you - let's hope you actually grow up a year.'

'Huh - oh bla de bla...' Tamara huffed. Then as she looked at the small gift, her expression changed to one of sheer delight. 'Joel... This is just fantastic - thank you.'

Joel, Peter and Maité grinned as Tamara stared at the photograph that Grandad had taken of the boys with Storm, on the day they sent him back home when she was in hospital.

'Hope all goes well, Maité,' Peter said.

'Ditto, Peter,' she replied.

Peter grabbed the rope; then giving Joel a sneaky wink, he slipped down.

'Maité - thanks - take care, O.K.' Tamara called.

'Adios, Tamara,' Maité replied.

Tamara followed Peter.

When the others had gone, Joel was able to relax a bit, not having to be on his guard for fear of being ridiculed yet again by Tamara. However, he did feel rather nervous being alone with Maité for the very first time. They sat and talked as they'd never talked before. The lanterns were still burning, but as it got later and darker, they became a little chilly. Maité shivered slightly.

'Here,' Joel said, opening a small chest and taking out a blanket. 'Wrap this round you.'

'Thanks.' Maité pulled the woollen blanket round her shoulders. 'I'll have to go soon - I can only use the Fugue until midnight and Spain is an hour ahead of here.'

Joel nodded and looked as if he wanted to say something.

'What?' Maité prompted.

'No, nothing - really,' Joel said hesitantly.

'Go on - you were going to say something?'

'I just wondered - er, what you wrote in your note,' Joel said.

'You don't have to tell me if you don't want to...' he added.
Maité smiled and took a piece of paper from her pocket.

'Here, I made a copy, read it.' She pushed it towards him.

Joel nervously took the paper, it was a piece of lined writing paper that looked as if it had been ripped from the bottom of a larger page. He unfolded it and read - *If you find a rugby-playing barrister, don't dismiss him out of court - he may be worth a try.*

A bubble seemed to rise from the pit of Joel's stomach, up to his mouth and he had to stifle a gasp - she did like him!

'That's going to bug you to death tomorrow, trying to work out what it means,' he said with a grin.

'I know.' Maité smiled, then she suddenly became serious. 'Maybe one day it will make sense...'

They looked at each other and their eyes met. They seemed to lean towards each other a little; then Maité turned away and snuggled down, resting her head on Joel's chest. He carefully put his arm round her shoulders.

+

Joel wriggled uncomfortably - he couldn't feel his arm. He had that dreadful sensation - his arm had gone to sleep and he had no control over it, as if it was suddenly not attached to his body.

Then he opened his eyes and realised with horror that his arm wasn't the only thing that had gone to sleep. For there, snuggled under his left armpit, fast asleep on his chest, was Maité. He lifted his right wrist and glanced at his watch.

'No!' he gasped with shock. The time was ten-past twelve - they'd been asleep for a couple of hours!

Maité suddenly woke up at Joel's loud gasp. She looked at Joel with fear in her eyes.

*'Qué es esto..? Hay algún problema... Tenemos que llamar a la policía!' She began to rant.

'Maité - please - calm down -' Joel grabbed at his limp arm.

'Who in Holy Heaven are you?' she screamed, sitting up quickly.

*What is this..? There is something wrong... We must call the police!

Joel's arm now tingled with pins and needles. He started rubbing it to get the circulation going again.

'How do you know my name?' Maité shrieked. 'What am I doing here? Where are we? Have I been kidnapped?'

'We fell asleep...' Joel tried to explain.

'I would not fall asleep - with a strange boy I've never even met - and - and - in a tree!' Maité looked around in a state of panic.

'You stupid boy!' Joel heard a stern voice from above. He looked up and saw Maguff perched on a branch looking extremely cross.

'Maguff! Thank Heaven. Can you help us?' Joel pleaded.

'Who are you talking to now - you nutter?' Maité cried. 'You've drugged me, haven't you? Let me go - let me go, you crazy psycho!' In sheer panic she backed away from Joel, not looking where she was going. Then suddenly she slipped and fell out of the den. 'Aaaagh!'

There was a thud as Maité landed on the ground at the foot of the tree. Then silence.

'Maité!' Joel screamed and leapt onto the rope swing, dropping like a stone to the ground. He leaned over her as Maguff landed beside them.

'She's only unconscious - luckily for you.' Maguff said. 'She hit her head in the fall.'

Joel lifted Maité's head and shoulders onto his lap.

'Maité... Maité...' Joel murmured in despair. He had a terrible feeling of déjà vu, remembering how he felt when he found Tamara under the wheels of a car, just two weeks before. 'Oh Maguff - what have I done?'

'Where are those wittering Magi?' Maguff asked crossly.

'Oh you can't blame them for this, Maguff! Give them a break will you! They left early. They wanted to give us some privacy. This is entirely my fault - no one else's - I should have stayed awake.'

'They are supposed to watch over you and keep you out of trouble!' Maguff boomed.

'Kicking off is not going to help, Maguff,' Joel said. 'What are we going to do?'

Maguff shook his head. 'What are *we* going to do? This is your mess, boy. If you keep flouting the rules you have to face the consequences. I suppose she'll have to stay here tonight; she'll be concussed. Then in the morning - if she's O.K. to travel - you'll have to put her on a plane back to Spain.'

'But you saw what she was like - she'll throw a fit when she comes round - she thinks she's been kidnapped! What if Grandad is arrested for kidnapping? How am I going to explain to her how she got to be in England?'

'I'm sorry, my dear boy but my hands are tied... The rules you see...'

'Oh stuff the rules!' Joel said with annoyance. 'Surely you can make exceptions. There must be something you can do? Can't you do anything off your own bat - or is your head just one big, silly old rule book? You know what they say - people can get promoted to their level of incompetence - maybe this applies to some Angels too. Maybe you've reached your limit, Maguff?'

'Well!' Maguff huffed. 'I certainly don't have to stay here to be insulted!'

Maité started groaning.

'Oh please, Maguff, she's coming round,' Joel pleaded. 'I didn't mean to insult you. I'll take all the blame and any punishment necessary, if you'll just help me get her home.'

Suddenly Maguff started to glow with that warm light that enveloped the Angels up in Heaven. He glowed for a few seconds, then returned to normal.

'You must carry some clout, boy.' Maguff said with a tut, shaking his head. 'Talk about having friends in high places. There must be something very big planned for you. I've just been given instructions about this matter - instructions that can only come from The Most High. I have to warn you that this will not be done for you again. Everyone is allowed one mistake and this is yours - remember that, Joel - no more mistakes.'

With that, Maguff vanished and Joel felt suddenly very dizzy.

THE KAIROS

Then he opened his eyes with a start. As if by magic, Joel was back in the den; the cramp in his arm had just woken him up. Maité was asleep on his chest. He looked at his watch and let out a huge sigh of relief: it was five minutes past ten. Joel looked up at the sky, overcome with awe - time had been changed - the clock had been turned back! It was at that moment it suddenly dawned on him - the importance of what lay ahead - as he wondered what on earth it was they had planned for him, that was so important to sanction the changing of time itself!

'Thanks.' He smiled. Then he gently shook Maité. 'Maité - wake up, it's time to go.'

Maité stirred and opened her eyes. She smiled up at him, then suddenly sat up in fright. For one scary second, Joel thought she'd still had her memory of the Kairos erased.

*'Estoy mareada,' she murmured. 'What time is it, Joel?'

'It's all right, everything is O.K. Maité. It's only just after ten. We just dozed off for a while.' Joel reassured her, breathing yet another sigh of relief.

'Phew,' Maité murmured. 'I should say goodbye... it wouldn't do to be an alien with amnesia in England.'

'I know. How would we explain that to my Grandad and your parents?'

They both laughed and stood up, then slipped quietly down the rope swing. They walked in silence to the edge of the plateau, then turned towards each other.

'I guess this is i...' Joel began but wasn't able to finish what he was saying - because his lips were otherwise engaged. Maité had leaned forward and before he knew what was happening, she had planted a kiss on his lips.

'I wish I could say I will never forget you, Joel, but I know this time tomorrow I won't even remember your name. Adios, my friend,' Maité said, her eyes showing a hint of moisture.

*'Hasta la vista, Maité,' Joel replied.

She stepped onto the plateau and vanished. Joel stood there for a minute, staring at the empty plateau. Then he felt the small piece of paper which he still had folded in his hand; he flattened

---

*I feel dizzy   *See you around

it out and read it again. His face broke into a huge grin. Not only did he still have Maité's note in his hand, but he suddenly realised, she'd come specially to leave it with him. No doubt she'd wake up the next morning and find its utterly confusing duplicate beside her bed.

+

Joel almost skipped into Grandad's lounge. He now understood the expression, "walking on air." He felt as if he was literally floating in Heaven. However, he was brought back to earth with a bump when he found Grandad, who appeared to be in a state of anxiety.

'Are you all right, Grandad?' Joel asked. 'You seem a bit edgy.'

'Your Mother is coming tomorrow, Son,' Grandad said seriously.

'It's all gone so quickly again, hasn't it, Grandad?'

'Yes, tempus fugit - time waits for no man, as they say.' he replied.

Joel chuckled to himself. If only Grandad knew that this very thing, reversal of time, had actually just occurred!

'I've been thinking, Joel,' Grandad continued hesitantly. 'There's no need to tell Mum about any of this Unicorn business, or miracle healing, is there, Son?'

'Not if you don't want to, Grandad.' Joel shrugged, inwardly relieved. He certainly didn't want to open that can of worms with Mum either.

'I mean, it's not that we want to keep anything from her, Son.' But we don't want her thinking we've gone soft in the head or anything, do we? And all this about Peter's healing and Tamara's miraculous recovery from death's door... It might all be a bit much for Mum - you know what I mean, don't you, Son?'

'Yes, Grandad, I know exactly what you mean.' Joel nodded in agreement.

'So we'll just keep it between the two of us.' Grandad gave a relieved smile.

'That's fine by me,' Joel said yawning, somewhat bemused by Grandad's state of anxiety. 'I'm tired now, I think I'll go to bed.'

'Yes, Son, and I'll not be far behind you - I'm just going to have a little nightcap - helps me sleep, you see.'

'You do that, Grandad. Goodnight.'

'Goodnight, Joel.' Grandad smiled and picked up his bottle of brandy.

Joel was happy to be climbing the crooked stairs to bed, although he was a little apprehensive about Mum's arrival the next day. Would he be able to behave normally, as though nothing had happened? Would Mum see through him - that he was hiding something? Would he feel deceitful, knowing he was in touch with Dad and yet not able to tell her?

With all these thoughts whizzing round in his head, together with the excitement of the evening, he was too exhausted to think clearly. Climbing into bed, he placed Maité's note under his pillow and smiled proudly to himself. Now he really did feel special. Time itself had been changed for him! Also, now he was different - no longer just a boy - he'd had his first kiss. With the memory of that, he switched off the lantern and fell into a deep sleep.

+

Next day, Peter arrived just in time for lunch, which on Saturdays at Grandad's was always bacon-and-sausage butties. Crispy bacon and little fat sausages in delicious freshly baked bread. This was followed by Mrs Jordan's chocolate cake. She had given Peter a huge chocolate cake for Joel to take home and a large angel cake for Grandad, which was one of his favourites. After they had eaten as much as they could possibly manage, they relaxed in the lounge, still waiting for Mum to arrive.

Eventually, at the end of the day, Peter said goodbye and set off down the yard to walk home.

'Hey,' Joel called after him. 'Don't take any nonsense from

that weazle Presten!'

'No worries, Joel,' Peter replied. 'Presten's rule of tyranny is history now, mate.'

'Let's hope so,' Joel nodded and waved.

+

Grandad made the evening meal, then Mum finally turned up - but not in her car.

'Oh no - what's happened now? Mum is in a strange car,' Joel said peeking through the window. 'I hope she's not broken down.' He opened the back door and ran outside.

Mum got out of the passenger side of the car and threw open her arms, as she usually did when they'd been separated for a while (much to Joel's embarrassment).

'I've missed you so much,' Mum cooed. 'I really need a hug right now.'

Then the driver's door opened. Joel looked over Mum's shoulder and caught his breath - Detective Smith stepped out of the vehicle. Joel gulped and started to panic; he thought the cat was out of the bag - that Smith had gone back on his word and told Mum everything. How on earth was he going to dig himself out of that hole?

'Oh, darling, you remember Detective John Smith - don't you, Joel?' Mum said, smiling at the Detective.

'Of course he remembers me, don't you, Joel?' Smith held out his hand.

'Er - er - yes - you used to work with my Dad,' Joel stammered, taking Smith's hand and wondering what on earth he had told Mum. 'What are you doing here, Detective Smith?'

'Just call me John.'

'Come inside, darling, and we'll explain everything,' said Mum ushering them into the house.

Once inside, with mugs of tea in their hands, they all went into the lounge. Joel was desperately trying not to look as panic stricken as he was feeling.

'Joel...' Mum said hesitantly. 'I need to talk to you love. I'm afraid it's going to be upsetting for you.'

Joel sat next to Mum on the settee. He was feeling more than a little strained. Was she going to tell him the recent news about his Father's death being murder, or was she going to ask what he had been doing in London - and how he had got there!

'Joel, you won't have heard yet, not having a television here,' Mum began, 'but it's in all the papers and all your school friends will know. I've spoken to Grandad about it and I asked him not to say anything to you until I got here. Joel - it's about your Father, love.'

Joel heaved a mental sigh of relief and thanked God that Smith had obviously kept his word and not mentioned seeing him to Mum. This also explained Grandad's state of anxiety the previous evening.

'Some evidence has come to light about his - his - death,' Mum continued rather emotionally. 'It seems that Dad didn't fall asleep at the wheel at all.' She took a deep breath and squeezed Joel's hand. 'I'm afraid he was - Joel - your Dad was murdered.'

Joel didn't have to worry about trying to look alarmed. One look at Mum's drained face and brimming eyes was so heart-wrenching - he couldn't bear to see her so upset and he took hold of her hand.

'They've caught the man who did it, Joel,' Mum went on shakily. 'You'll never believe it, but do you remember that man Dad used to bring to the house - his partner at the firm, Dan Sadler?'

'Yes, I never liked him,' Joel said scathingly.

'Apparently Sadler was involved in drugs and blackmail. He was part of some network of criminals, but they've all been caught, the whole lot of them, a cartel of organised crime. They'll all be going to prison for a very long time, Joel.' Mum paused. 'John was the man responsible for leading the investigation. Dad had been working with him when he died. Joel - John's been a tremendous support throughout all this - in fact I don't know what I'd have done without him - and well -

I'LL LEAD YOU ALL IN THE DANCE SAID HE

the truth is, darling, we've been seeing each other for a while. I didn't want to spring it on you, but with this latest development, he was worried about my driving all this way alone - that's why he's here. The thing is, Joel - John has asked me to marry him and - well, I've said yes.'

Joel was quite speechless at this sudden revelation. He had been having kittens, because he thought Smith had come to question him and that he was going to have to tell a pack of lies. He couldn't very well tell the truth about what had happened. Now he realised that Smith was just there as Mum's boyfriend! So that was what Dad had meant. He apparently approved of Smith as Mum's choice of marriage partner!

'Oh you're shocked, Joel; of course you are. I'm so sorry I had to tell you all this about Dad, but you do need to know. People will say things - ask questions - you need to be prepared.' Mum smiled. 'Let's hope that Dad can rest in peace now that Sadler has been caught and the truth has come to light.'
This reminded Joel about the kiss Dad gave him to pass to Mum.

'I'm sure he can now, Mum, and if he were here he would want to give you a kiss, so I'll give you one for him.' Joel kissed Mum on the forehead as Dad had done to him. 'That's from Dad.'

'Thank you, Joel.' Mum smiled and seemed to instantly cheer up. The drained look vanished from her face and she suddenly appeared more radiant, as if she'd been touched by an Angel. 'It's great to see you; I've missed you. Tell me about your holiday with Grandad. What exciting things have you been doing?'

'Oh there's not much to tell really, Mum.' Joel shrugged. 'Is there, Grandad?'

'No, been very quiet down here in the country, nothing out of the ordinary,' Grandad said casually, picking up the teapot from the hearth. 'More tea, anyone? I'd give you something stronger to celebrate, but with you driving straight back...'

Grandad gave Joel a wink and Joel noticed Smith's eyebrows raise in a slight frown, as he looked at them suspiciously.

The Kairos

'So, John, did you have a good drive down from the City?' Joel inquired, before Smith could ask any awkward questions.

'Yes, thank you, Joel, not too bad really. Er - heck of a long way though, isn't it? I mean it's a full day's journey - that is unless you have...' Smith leaned forward and rubbed his chin thoughtfully, 'wings - or something.' He handed his cup to Grandad. 'Tea is fine, Marcus. Just half a cup for me.'

+

As Joel settled in the back of Smith's car he wondered with trepidation what on earth they were all going to talk about on the way home. Would Smith let him off the hook, or would he continually refer to a certain subject? The last thing Joel felt like doing was making polite conversation. He decided the best thing was to pretend to fall asleep on the journey back. Then he would have the whole journey to bask in the luxury of the magnificent memories - the precious moments with Dad; the excitement of the successful mission; the cantankerous yet affectionate Magee and his Angel partner; the fabulous party in Heaven - and that all important first kiss. Also he could contemplate at his leisure the: "something *big* planned for him," Maguff had referred to - something big enough to justify changing time! Now that was an awe-inspiring thought and he couldn't wait for the next school holidays, to find out what it was. At the same time he was nervous and apprehensive. If so much depended on it, what if he was unable to accomplish it? What if he let Dad and all the Kairos down? Would he really have what it takes to pull it off? After the daring mine shaft exploit, he sensed that he would be under tremendous pressure, now "expectations had been set." For sure though, he was determined above all else, to succeed in his missions.

Joel waved to Grandad and also to Peter and Tamara, who had turned up to wave goodbye, as Smith drove them out of the yard. He nodded at the two Ravens who were perched nearby. Then leaning back, he closed his eyes.

Competition

Whilst writing this book, Lesley Cashin encoded a secret message in the text, to add to the mystery and fun! The secret message encapsulates the spirit of Bethelonia the Company and that of "The Kairos."

To enter the competition, you need to decipher the secret message. A tiebreaker will decide the winner from all the correct entries. The tiebreaker is; Who is your favourite character in the book "The Kairos" and why? One or two sentences would be adequate.

The competition is open to all children up to the age of sixteen years. Proof of age will be required from the winners. Entry will only be accepted by postal mail and must be accompanied by your purchase receipt for the book. Send your answer in a sealed envelope include your name, age, address, telephone number, where you bought the book from and your purchase receipt to:
The Kairos Competition, Bethelonia Publishing, B3, The Verdin Exchange, Winsford, Cheshire, CW7 2AN.

The first prize will be a 'state of the art' computer. There will be fifty runner up prizes of ten pound book tokens. There will also be a special bonus prize for the first person to E-Mail the web site: **www.bethelonia.com** with the decoded secret message! However E – Mailing will **not** count as your entry into the **main competition** – you can only do that by conventional mail. The closing date for the competition will be announced on the Website.

The winners and the prizes will be chosen personally by the author and will not be negotiable or transferable, neither will there be any cash alternative.
Good luck!